TAKEN IN

ALSO BY SG BRYANT

Boss

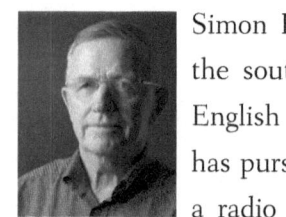 Simon Bryant grew up on a farm, a soldier settler block in the south-east of South Australia. After graduating with an English literature degree from the University of Adelaide, he has pursued a number of paths, including farming, managing a radio station, working in tourism, and, most recently, an extended spell in the public service in Canberra.

Now retired, he is dedicating his time to a lifelong interest in creative writing, and, in particular, to writing Australian historical fiction.

S G BRYANT

TAKEN IN

BORDER BOOKS

First published in 2019 by Border Books

Canberra ACT 2611

© Simon Bryant 2019

Cover and text design by Sandy Cull, www.sandycull.com
Cover images by Arcangel (photographer Valentino Sani),
Shutterstock, and Images of Yesteryear
Typeset in 12/17.25 Fairflied Light, by J&M Typesetting.

Printed and bound in Australia by IngramSpark and
Lightning Source Australia

ISBN 978-0-6480375-2-1

A catalogue record for this
book is available from the
National Library of Australia

For Nicola Tyndale-Biscoe,
with thanks for her generous support and encouragement.

CHAPTER ONE

AS IT ALWAYS DID, the green cable tram ground to a complaining halt, just outside Merton Hall in Domain Road. As she always did, Effie Davis emerged from the small shelter set up outside the school's wrought-iron gates, and stepped up into the dummy car. She smiled politely at the gripman and took her usual seat on the front bench. As the gripper was tightened and the tram squealed into reluctant forward motion, Effie felt her usual slight thrill of excitement, a pleasant anticipation of the journey ahead. Then, as the gripper took tight hold of the cable and the tram quickened to its full speed, she leaned forward, surreptitiously and as far as decorum would allow, the better to peer over the cast iron railing in front of her and watch the road ahead disappearing under her feet.

Even in the colder winter months, Effie chose this seat if it was available, preferring the thrill of the open-air dummy to the altogether more mundane, confined comfort of the attached saloon car trailing in its wake. Even at a sedate fifteen miles per hour, the smooth progress of the cable tram over the road surface seemed to her effortless and magical, almost like flying, or as someone had once suggested, just like a swan gliding over the water.

Although the start of winter was only days away, today required no stoic resolve against the cold. The late May sun shone brightly in a cloudless sky, pleasantly balmy and warming. Sufficiently warming in fact to make her soon appreciate the shade of the canvas canopy that served as their roof. Altogether a perfect Melbourne autumn afternoon, she thought, as they sailed gracefully along. It could not have been better weather for the rally.

Effie was wakened from her thoughts by the gripman's call, 'Mind the curve now!' as the tram made its sharp turn into St Kilda Road and headed towards the city. As she watched the botanic gardens looming on their right, and the larger city buildings fast approaching, Effie's thoughts began to focus more sharply on what lay ahead. Up until now, the Lady Teachers' resolution to take their cause for women's suffrage to the steps of Parliament House had seemed to Effie a bold and exciting idea, a necessary strategy to bring their just concerns to the attention of the Melbourne public.

But the imminent reality of the event was now beginning to stimulate other more disturbing possibilities in her mind. She found herself wondering about the likelihood of troublemakers – hooligans and larrikins who would have no appreciation of, or sympathy for, the worthiness of universal suffrage. She worried too about the police, who were meant to be protecting them, but who she suspected would also be unlikely to show much sympathy if things got out of hand.

The more these possibilities took hold, the more anxious she found herself becoming, and the more the planned rally began to assume an aura of foolhardiness rather than fun, danger rather than daring. Perhaps they had been reckless and silly to think that such a rally could take place without trouble arising. Perhaps she should have paid more attention to her colleague, Michael Standish, who had suggested there could be a spot of bother, and who had offered to come along to keep an eye on things.

Another squeal of the gripper announced their arrival at the terminus in Swanston Street, marked by its large engine house and towering brick chimney. The tram juddered to a halt and Effie stepped down onto the kerb and into the mingling crowd. Before she had a chance to even get her bearings, she felt her arm seized firmly from behind. Spinning around in alarm, she found herself staring into the smiling eyes of Lydia Smith.

'Oh my goodness, dear, you gave me a fright!' Effie gasped, as a wave of relief swept over her. She laughed at her own foolishness, and her nervousness melted away. Her friend Lydia always had this effect on Effie, her unremitting cheerfulness always an antidote for cold feet.

Beaming hugely, Lydia welcomed Effie with a warm hug and a kiss on each cheek.

'Hello, darling, I thought you'd be on this tram. Isn't this fun? I hear we're expecting quite a crowd. We'll show those old fogeys in parliament that we mean business. Come on, let's hurry, I don't want to miss a single moment.' And taking Effie's arm, she set off purposefully, with not the faintest hint of apprehension evident in her confident stride. This was Lydia, the most unlikely of suffragettes – beautiful, elegant and full of fun – but there was no one more committed to the women's cause. Perhaps this will be a lark after all, thought Effie, as she quickened her step to keep pace.

They made their way up Spring Street towards Parliament House, surrounded by chatter and bustle, a surge of people all heading in the same direction. By the time they arrived at the steps of parliament, this throng had coalesced into a large crowd, milling about in anticipation of the impending rally. The Lady Teachers were obviously out in force – Effie recognised many of her friends in the association, as well as a number of other women she knew from the Suffrage Society. Lydia of course seemed to know everyone, and was constantly darting away to greet a friend or colleague, before returning to Effie's side.

The event also seemed to have attracted a fair crowd of casual onlookers, by the look of them mainly clerks and city chaps, enjoying a sunny afternoon tea break. They too were in good humour, and seemed to Effie to be cheerfully disposed to the gathering, even if in a rather mocking way. All in all, the atmosphere was rather festive.

A sudden loud blast on a klaxon horn quelled the crowd's chatter and signalled the beginning of the rally. One by one, and to great acclaim, each speaker mounted the top step, stood at the small podium placed there and spoke their piece to the crowd below. Mrs Kenny from the Lady Teachers, then Vida Goldstein and several others, before it was the turn of the final speaker, the grand dame of women's suffrage in Victoria, Mrs Dugdale. That lady strode formidably to the dais and faced the crowd. Despite her advancing years, she carried herself as straight as ever, and her voice, when she addressed the crowd, had lost none of its stentorian vigour.

'My dear friends,' she boomed. 'Here we are yet again, gathered before this place.' And with a dramatic sweep of her arm she indicated the grand building behind them. 'Again we stand here, seeking to be granted the simple right of equal recognition with the other half of the species. And again, sadly, we must expect to be rejected by the ignorant buffoons who reside here.'

At this, loud boos from the women present and raucous cheers from the onlooking clerks.

'And we face this rejection, my friends, despite that this place has been presented with a petition signed by thirty thousand of the women of this state, asking for nothing more than that women should vote on equal terms with men. A petition so large, my friends, that unfurled, it extends over three hundred yards. Signatories that include the wife of the premier of this state. And what has been the result of that historic document? I'll tell you what – exactly nothing!'

Loud jeers, boos and cries of 'shame' from the women, more cheers from the clerks.

'What a travesty of democracy to ignore such an overwhelming and just demand from the women of Victoria! Why is it that the men of this institution' – with another sweep of her hand to the building behind her – 'why do they continue to ignore what should be as plain as the nose on their face?'

The boos and jeers grew even louder. Effie found herself joining in enthusiastically, all restraint now evaporated.

'New Zealand women have the vote! South Australian women have the vote! But here in Victoria we continue to suffer the injustice of disenfranchisement. And why? Because of the ignorance and moral weakness of the fools who inhabit this building. And might I remind you that they are men, every last one of them.'

Effie clapped and cheered along with the crowd, filled with admiration at the passion of this great woman, and fired with outrage at those who so spuriously resisted their just cause.

'My friends,' Mrs Dugdale went on, 'what is it about the male character that allows them such self-delusion, and makes them resistant to such transparently just arguments? I'll tell you what it is: it is the true evil of our times, the devil incarnate in our midst. It is the curse of male ignorance, ignorance that is holding our country and our people back, and preventing us from achieving our true potential.'

Further uproar greeted this pronouncement, but a distinct change in the tone of the male chorus of onlookers could now be detected. The good-humoured cheers were now less in evidence, replaced by a ground swell of jeers at this affront to the male of the species. Effie could detect among the lounging clerks a growing number of more roughly dressed men, clearly with a less benign view on women's suffrage.

But Mrs Dugdale was off and running and in no mood to moderate her stance. 'Why is it that the women of this country are always the ones that can see the path to enlightenment and reform? Why must we be the ones to fix the mess made by the foolishness and ignorance of men?'

'Why don't you shut your trap, you old bag?' came a shout from the back of the crowd. Cries of support and cheers greeted this witticism.

'I see we have a gentleman amongst us prepared to engage in rational debate,' retorted Mrs Dugdale, completely unabashed. 'That's about what I would expect from you, sir. You illustrate my point very well.'

Hearty cheers and laughter from the women in the crowd, more jeers and interjections from the troublemakers. 'Shut your cakehole, or we'll shut it for you!' 'Get back to the kitchen, you silly old tart!' And such like.

Effie's unrestrained enthusiasm was beginning to wane: she glanced behind her nervously. She was beginning to wish that Mrs Dugdale was not quite so provocative in her language. Behind her the crowd was continuing to grow and the jeers were now deafening, drowning out Mrs Dugdale's defiant ripostes. Effie began to feel the weight of the surging crowd pushing her forward, inexorably, towards the steps.

Cries and screams rang out as the women at the back of the crowd were shoved forward, and those in the ensuing crush at the front and middle were jammed together. Effie was amongst these, caught in the middle and squeezed so that she could scarcely breathe. The noise was overwhelming, women shouting and screaming, trying to push their way clear, but to no avail. Lydia was nowhere to be seen. Effie pushed desperately against the relentless press of bodies, struggling to catch her breath. She saw a couple of ruffians looming towards her, their faces angry and contorted, but she could not move to escape them. Dimly she heard whistles and shouts in the distance, then the weight of the crush began to force her off her feet, and she felt herself going down. She tried to scream, but it seemed that she could make no sound.

Then she felt large hands seize her around the waist and drag her roughly along the ground. She no longer felt the unbearable weight of the crowd as she was hauled into the clear. But her relief at being free from imminent suffocation was quickly replaced by alarm, as she caught a glimpse of her rescuer. He was a big gangly fellow, very tall, roughly dressed and unshaven. Was he one of the louts who had been pushing towards her? Effie wasn't sure, but she didn't much like the look of him. And he still had his arm around her shoulder as she sat there on the ground, recovering her breath and her composure.

'I'll thank you to take your hands off me, Sir,' she said, as soon as she had regained her breath and could muster sufficient gravitas. 'I'm sure you and your friends have done enough damage for the day. I hope you're satisfied.'

The lout seemed to find her comments amusing, a broad smile creasing his long angular face, but at least he released her and stepped back. 'Sorry, Madam,' he responded, in what seemed to her a very flippant manner. 'My humble apologies for saving your bacon. I should be ashamed of myself.' And he continued to grin.

Around them she saw that the police had arrived in force. The crowd was now dispersing and order was rapidly being restored.

Effie's relief at escaping the crush was now replaced by anger and indignation at this fellow's cavalier attitude. She climbed, somewhat unsteadily, to her feet, adjusting herself and doing her best to assume a haughty demeanour.

'Don't think you're so smart, just because you gave me some assistance. You and your friends are the cause of all this, you know, so you can take that smug grin off your face. You're lucky I don't report you to the law.'

To Effie's fury, the smug grin grew even broader. 'Madam, what a good idea. You can make your report to me, if you like. You see, I am the law.'

Effie stared at him. 'I don't believe you!' she replied, mustering her iciest tone. 'Prove it.'

Still smiling, Effie's rescuer reached into his rather threadbare jacket and produced a metal badge. 'Detective Sergeant Henry Holloway, at your service, Madam,' he grinned, waving the badge in front of her. 'Henry Holloway, of the Criminal Investigation Branch. But Harry to most people. To just about everyone, actually.'

Effie endeavoured to maintain strident outrage, but began to realise that this might seem rather foolish in the circumstances. So she settled on simmering indignation instead. 'Well, all right, I accept you are the law,' she said. 'In a manner of speaking. I know you're permitted to be in plain clothes, but I would have thought you could at least have dressed professionally. How can you expect the public to have any confidence in you, dressed like that?'

Detective Sergeant Holloway grinned again and, to her further annoyance, winked conspiratorially at her.

'I apologise for my get-up, Madam, but I'm undercover. We were expecting a spot of trouble today, so we thought we'd better turn up and mingle. You ladies have a habit of causing a bit of a fuss, it seems.'

Effie's hunt for a suitably cutting rejoinder to this comment was interrupted by the arrival of Lydia, who appeared out of the now dispersing crowd as breezy and cheerful as ever and, perplexingly, with still not a hair out of place.

'My goodness, that was a bit of a rum go,' she said with a laugh. 'Henrietta was up to her usual tricks, I'm afraid. She certainly doesn't believe in the art of gentle persuasion. But Effie, darling, what's happened to you? You're rather rumpled. And I see you've got a new friend.' And she smiled winningly at Harry Holloway.

'He's not my friend, he's a policeman, and I'm not quite sure what he's doing here. Making a nuisance of himself, mainly. Sergeant Holloway, this is my friend Lydia.'

'Call me Harry, everyone else does,' the sergeant said, shaking Lydia's extended hand enthusiastically. 'Now that I've met you, Lydia, perhaps you might take the trouble to introduce me to this young lady. She hasn't yet seen the need to do so herself.'

Effie reddened, and responded indignantly. 'I haven't had the chance to introduce myself, you mean, Sergeant. My name is Effie Davis, if you must know.'

Sergeant's Holloway's cheery grin grew even wider, and he extended a large paw in Effie's direction. She took it reluctantly and, as she had taught herself to do, looked him directly in the eye. She would not be intimidated by this buffoon. The sergeant shook her hand enthusiastically, and for longer than seemed strictly necessary.

'There, that's not so bad, is it?' he said. 'Now we're all good friends.'

Effie thought this rather presumptuous, and improper for a policeman to be so casual. But she said nothing and conjured up a thin smile.

'I'm so sorry,' Lydia exclaimed suddenly. 'I haven't introduced my friend, Moira.' And she ushered forward a small, slight woman who had been hovering at some distance in the background. Effie had not even really registered her presence. This, said Lydia, was her old friend, Miss Williamson.

Like Lydia, Moira was expensively dressed, but there the similarities ended. Where Lydia positively vibrated with colour, energy and sheer good spirits, Moira, as if in counterpoint, was demurely and conservatively clothed, to the point of drabness, and had a diffident and withdrawn air. She greeted them with a murmured hello, then lapsed into silence.

Not that she had the opportunity to say much anyway. Lydia was doing a very good job of monopolising the conversation, extolling Moira as a committed suffragette, well known in Melbourne for her dedication to the cause. Somehow, Effie could not see the demure and vaguely nervous woman standing before them as a suffragette firebrand. Any radical streak was certainly well concealed beneath her sober, brown gabardine coat and plaid skirt. She must have only been in her early forties, but somehow seemed older.

The annoying policeman continued to stand there, listening to Lydia's chatter, all the while wearing that infuriating smile. He seemed in no hurry to get back to business, doubtless Lydia was proving a more than attractive diversion. Finally he seemed to remember the call of duty, rousing himself and tipping his tatty old hat to them. 'Well, ladies, delightful as it has been, I must bid you farewell. Try to stay out of trouble, at least for the rest of the day, if you possibly can.' And he made his departure, irritatingly flippant to the end.

As soon as he had left them, Effie turned to her friend. 'Lydia, dear, would you say that I am a nasty sort of person? Someone who can't see the good in others?'

'Certainly not, darling. You're a perfect angel.'

'Then why does that fellow annoy me? I find him extremely condescending. Don't you think so?'

Lydia smiled sweetly. 'Well, I couldn't really say. I haven't known him quite as long as you. He's not terribly well-dressed, but apart from that, nothing much to complain about, I'd say.'

'Hmm,' Effie said, lips pursed.

'Perhaps it's because he's so tall,' Lydia added helpfully. 'Perhaps you find his height rather overwhelming.'

'Underwhelming, more likely,' Effie said. 'But enough of him. Come on, dear, I'm exhausted. Shall we go into town and have tea?'

'Good idea,' Lydia said. 'Let's. Will you join us, Moira?'

'No, no, I'm sorry, but I can't. I'm meeting Sir Anthony, and I can't keep him waiting.'

'Certainly not, that would be unforgivable,' Lydia said, and Effie thought she detected a wink in her direction.

Still wearing an anxious air, Moira hurried off. Effie raised her eyebrows. 'Sir Anthony indeed? She moves in exalted circles.'

For the first time, Lydia's serene expression clouded, and the faintest hint of a frown creased her brow. 'I must say she fusses too much over that man. Always at his beck and call.'

Effie's interest was now piqued. 'Just who is Sir Anthony? Is he some sort of relation to Miss Williamson?'

Lydia's expression assumed an air of conspiratorial intrigue. 'No darling, I think one could officially describe Moira as Sir Anthony Hartford's companion. He's a widower, you know. They've been courting now for a number of months.'

'Really?' Effie had heard of Sir Anthony Hartford, wealthy pastoralist and member of the Legislative Assembly. And rather older than Miss Williamson, she imagined. So this woman was his companion, whatever that might mean. Effie, despite her liberal aspirations, still felt a vague sense of scandal as she imagined the exact nature of the relationship between Moira Williamson and her wealthy elderly beau. But only a vague sense – it was difficult to visualise the timid woman she had just met as the mistress of a prominent Melbourne identity.

'It's rather the talk of Melbourne society at the moment,' Lydia said. 'He's very rich, you know. Moira has done very well for herself – from struggling seamstress to kept woman of the landed gentry.'

'It's a bit strange,' Effie mused. 'Such a relationship doesn't seem to fit with being a suffragette, somehow.'

'I suppose Moira can be a bit of an odd fish,' Lydia said. 'She doesn't give much away. I sometimes don't know what to make of her. Oh, well, it takes all types, I suppose.'

Taking Effie's arm, she shepherded her friend in the direction of Collins Street, and the beckoning comforts of the Hopetoun Tea Rooms.

CHAPTER TWO

EFFIE LEANED BACK IN HER CHAIR at the breakfast table, closed her eyes, and allowed herself to luxuriate in the sheer pleasure of the morning. It was the first day of school holidays and before her stretched three glorious weeks of freedom. Not even the prospect of Melbourne's fickle winter vagaries could dim her sunny mood. Nor could the unpleasant incident at yesterday's rally – the panic she had felt in the crush and her annoying policeman rescuer were already rapidly fading memories.

Nor did the presence of the rather odious Mr Harris across the table cloud her good spirits. She just knew that he would be eyeing her up and down surreptitiously, as he leaned over his porridge. Though she was only in her third week at Mrs Wilson's establishment, Effie had already developed a strong dislike for her fellow lodger. On several occasions recently, she had sensed his sideways leering inspection as they passed in the corridor, or in the street outside the boarding house. Not that there was ever anything that she could definitely say was improper about his behaviour. He was always more or less civil in his language, even if he was noticeably oily. Not quite openly lecherous, but certainly oily.

So Effie had resolved to be civil to Mr Harris in return, though she was at pains not to encourage him. And whenever possible, she tried to avoid being caught on her own with him.

But on this Monday morning, it was just she and Mr Harris at Mrs Wilson's breakfast table. And such was her carefree mood that Effie decided she didn't give a hoot whether Mr Harris was ogling her or not. Instead she allowed herself to reflect on the delightful prospect of her visit to the National Gallery that afternoon with Mr Standish. No, no, not Mr Standish … Michael. After all, he had invited her to call him so, with that lovely intimate smile he seemed to reserve just for her. Now that they were friends, he had said. So she had resolved not to be so bourgeois and conservative. Michael it would be from now on.

She tried to conjure up in her mind's eye a vision of Michael, sitting there in the teachers' room at school, leaning slightly towards her, as if taking her into his confidence. Fair hair pushed back off his face and falling long over his collar, square, strong, yet somehow refined and elegant features, piercing grey-blue eyes, a half-smile on his face as he chatted on about the theatre or music or art, a world of culture in which he seemed so immersed.

Effie felt enthralled by his presence. Here was a man who epitomised everything she had ever dreamed of in the male of the species. And not only was he handsome, charming and sophisticated, but Michael Standish was also that most rare creature, a progressive-thinking man. A man who did not smile patronisingly when she espoused her views on women's issues, but instead agreed with almost everything she said. And showed by his insightful comments that he was not just agreeing with her to be nice. Altogether, a wonderful man. And those eyes! Effie would love to spend her entire life looking into those eyes.

A piercing wail abruptly ended Effie's pleasant reverie; she started and sat bolt upright, staring disconcertedly about. Across the table,

Mr Harris was indeed leering at her, or sneering, she couldn't be sure which. She quickly realised that the sustained cries were those of a baby, and were coming from the open door of the guests' lounge behind her. She felt herself flushing at her panicky reaction.

'That woke you up quick smart,' Mr Harris ventured. 'Not used to the noise of the little ones, obviously.'

'Well, not here at any rate,' Effie retorted. Despite her resolve to be civil, she couldn't help but be peeved at the man's scornful manner. 'Whose baby is that?'

The crying was continuing at full strength.

'Just another of the old girl's brats. She takes them in every now and then.'

From upstairs came the voice of the old girl herself. 'You there, Miss Davis?' Mrs Wilson shouted. 'Would you mind, dearie? I'll be down in a second.'

Effie glanced about uncertainly. Mr Harris gestured to the other room. 'Go on, my girl, let's see what you're made of.' And he continued to smirk.

Infuriated by the man's condescending smugness, for a moment Effie considered remaining at her seat in stony silence. But Mrs Wilson was clearly not coming downstairs, and the baby was still crying for all it was worth, so she rose and walked as casually as she could into the lounge. She had no idea how she would calm the baby's now frenetic wailing.

A rickety cot sat on a small table by the hearth, where a coal fire burned. In the cot, wrapped in a none-too-clean blue sheet, lay the source of the commotion. Effie approached with some trepidation, leaned over and with difficulty extracted the baby from its cot. She remembered, from her limited experience with a cousin's child, to support its head as she lifted it clear. She held the tiny bundle to her breast and patted its back, gingerly at first, then with a little more force. She remembered that this was meant to be beneficial in some way.

Within seconds, and to her great surprise, the baby gave a loud belch, and almost immediately its cries died away. Effie continued to rub its back and soon felt through the sheet its body relaxing back toward sleep. And she could also feel, and smell, a wetness seeping into the shoulder of her shirt.

Effie was not sure whether to place the baby back in its cot, and for a moment or two stood in the centre of the room, uncertain as to how to proceed. She was saved by the burly figure of Mrs Wilson hurrying into the room from the direction of the lobby. She seized the child from Effie's arms and deposited it back in the cot, none too gently, it seemed to Effie. But the child did not object, and Effie could see that the pain that had upset it was now gone and it had fallen asleep. Its little face, peeping out from the swaddling sheet, was no longer scarlet and wrinkled, and it lay there at peace.

'Thanks for that, duckie,' Mrs Wilson said. 'Poor tyke had a touch of the wind. But you've settled him, no problem at all. But oh dear, he's left a bit of a mess on you. Let me fix that.' And taking an old rag from her apron pocket, she tried to wipe the yellow stain from Effie's shoulder.

'That's perfectly all right, Mrs Wilson, this shirt needed washing anyway,' Effie lied, resisting Mrs Wilson's efforts. She glanced again at the baby boy, asleep in the cot. 'He's so lovely,' she murmured, leaning over to touch his cheek. 'What's his name?'

'Alfred is his proper name, but I calls him Alfie. He looks like an Alfie to me.'

'He does, doesn't he? How long has he been with you? I haven't seen him here before.'

'Oh, a while,' Mrs Wilson seemed vague about the detail. 'A month or two, I reckon. I likes to keep him out of the way of my lodgers though. Which accounts for why you haven't come across him before. But I just had him down here for a while, to keep him warm while I was doing my cleaning.'

'Are you minding him for someone?'

'You could say that, dearie. I've taken him in. Out of the goodness of me heart. Doing a favour for a lady what's gone up bush. But now the baggage has done the dirty on me. Meant to pick him up weeks ago, but no sign of her. Flown the coop, I should think.'

'Oh dear,' Effie said. 'How sad. Poor little fellow.' And she reached over and gently stroked the baby's cheek once more with her forefinger. As she did so, he awoke and, reaching out, grasped her finger in his tiny hand. As he pulled her finger towards his mouth, Effie gave a low exclamation.

'Oh, look at that, Mrs Wilson. There, on his arm. A tiny heart!' She pointed to the inside of the baby's outstretched right arm, just below the elbow. There, emblazoned against the milk-white skin, was a bright red blotch, a birthmark, almost perfectly in the shape of a heart.

'Well, I never,' Mrs Wilson exclaimed. 'I never noticed that before. I reckon that's a sign, that is.' And she too reached over the cot, peering short-sightedly at the birthmark. Mrs Wilson's close proximity interrupted Effie's delight in the baby – a sharply rancid mix of sweat, mutton fat and alcohol emanated from her, forcing Effie to stand back and catch her breath. Seemingly oblivious to Effie's discomfort, Mrs Wilson rewrapped the baby in the cloth, hauled it from its cot, and held it to her ample bosom with one fat arm. Despite this rather rough approach, Effie had a sense that Mrs Wilson was a well-practised nurse. Certainly Alfie did not seem to object to the treatment. He promptly laid his head against the soft swell of her breast and went back to sleep.

'I'll get him out of your way then, dearie. I'm sure you've got better things to do with your day than chinwag with me.' And Mrs Wilson turned to leave the room. But Effie's thoughts were still with the baby, and what sad fate might lie before it.

'But what will you do, Mrs Wilson, if his mother doesn't return? What will become of the poor darling?'

Mrs Wilson paused on her way out, and turned back to Effie. 'Oh, don't you worry your pretty head about that, dearie,' she chirped, suddenly offhand. 'I'm sure that the lady will turn up soon.'

'But you said you thought she'd deserted him.'

'Did I?' Mrs Wilson said, now distinctly wary. 'Just a figure of speech, dear. Anyways, the authorities will be notified if the worst comes to the worst.'

'Oh,' Effie said, now seeing the sad prospect of a lonely orphanage and a lost childhood for little Alfie. 'What authorities do you mean?'

But Mrs Wilson was in no further mood for communication. 'The proper authorities,' she muttered, and made her exit, wheezing and shuffling her way in the direction of the kitchen, the baby still clasped to her breast.

Effie stood in thought for a while. She felt unsettled, as much by Mrs Wilson's manner as by the prospect of the baby being deserted. Her thoughts were interrupted by Mr Harris appearing in the doorway.

'I heard all that,' he said, leering down at her. 'Rum business, isn't it?'

'I just don't understand,' Effie murmured, almost to herself. 'How could his mother desert him like that?'

'That's not what I meant.' Mr Harris said, lowering his voice conspiratorially. 'It's disgraceful what that old bag is up to.' And he jerked his head in the direction of the kitchen.

'What do you mean?' Effie retorted, now fully focussed on Mr Harris. 'I don't understand.'

'She's done it before, you know. Baby shows up out of the blue, here for a while, and then it's gone. More than once, I can tell you. A lot more than once.'

Effie's eyes widened. 'What are you implying, Mr Harris? Are you saying there's something improper going on?'

'You tell me,' he responded darkly. 'But it wouldn't surprise me. That old cow would turn in her own mother for a shilling, not a doubt about it.'

No, thought Effie, this is just idle gossip, and I won't be a part of it. 'If you think there's something going on, you should go to the police, Mr Harris,' she said firmly, looking him directly in the eye.

'It's not my business to get involved,' he muttered. 'Anyway, there's no proof, I suppose.' And shrugging his shoulders, he turned and made for the door. But before leaving, he stopped and turned to her again, a sly grin appearing.

'But you never know, I could be right. She might be just like that woman they strung up a couple of years back. You know, the baby farmer that buried them all in the back garden.' And holding his hands out in front of him, he twisted them together in a gesture of mock strangling.

With a chuckle, he walked out, leaving Effie standing there, distraught and confused.

Effie sat in the Hopetoun Tea Rooms and tried to make conversation with Michael Standish. They had just passed what should have been a wonderful two hours in the National Gallery, admiring the latest exhibition from Mr Streeton. Michael, who had been enrolled at the Gallery School for some three years now, knew Mr Streeton personally, and was able to highlight all the features of the paintings and explain the philosophy behind the work.

Effie had marvelled at Michael's artistic knowledge, and was charmed by his enthusiasm. Yet, as they strolled from room to room, she had found herself continually becoming distracted and unable to focus on his conversation. Now as they sat in the fashionable surrounds of the Hopetoun, still she could not relax and give herself up to the simple pleasure of his company. Her thoughts kept returning to baby Alfie, and the uncertain future he faced. She could not get Mr Harris' snide insinuations out of her head, and the lingering dread that something awful could befall the little fellow.

Effie, like the rest of Melbourne, knew all about baby farming and the notorious Mrs Knorr, who had been hanged several years before. She had murdered a number of infants she had been paid to take from their desperate mothers, women who were either unmarried or too poor to care for them. Since then, the government had said it would clamp down on women taking in babies in return for payment. They had put in place licences, inspections, regulations: it was said that such a terrible event could never happen again. But Effie feared that where there was money involved there would always be people prepared to get around the law. And Mrs Wilson had obviously taken in babies before. Many of them, according to Mr Harris. And what had become of them? Mr Harris said some had just disappeared. Perhaps they too were buried at the bottom of the garden, like Mrs Knorr's victims.

These terrible thoughts kept going through Effie's mind, and she could not drive them away. She tried to focus on enjoying Michael's company. What had he just said? Something about Streeton's time at Eaglemont? She smiled politely at him, in the hope that he would assume she was following his words. He smiled back and kept on chatting. Effie drifted off again.

Perhaps she should talk to Michael about what had happened this morning. He was intelligent, a man of the world; she was sure she could rely on his judgement and sound opinion on the matter. But would he think her foolish and naive to pay any heed to Mr Harris's malicious gossip? The man obviously had it in for Mrs Wilson, and was clearly trying to malign her. In all probability, her landlady was exactly what she claimed to be, an honest widow keeping up a reputable establishment and generously helping out those in need when she could.

But then the image came again into her mind of dear Alfie, his tiny hands reaching out to her. She remembered his body cuddling against her breast. And the image came to her too of a pair of gnarled old hands tightening around his neck, squeezing and twisting. Effie gave an involuntary cry and tears sprang to her eyes.

Michael broke off his dissertation and looked at her with some alarm. 'Are you quite all right, Effie? You've gone quite pale.' He leaned over and took her hand in both of his. Effie saw kindness and concern in his eyes and knew he wouldn't judge her. Before she knew it, she had blurted out all her concerns about the morning's events. Michael sat listening to her attentively, his comforting hands still holding hers.

'You probably think me foolish and impressionable,' she said as she finished her story. 'But I just can't get out of my head what might happen to that poor, sweet baby. So alone in the world.'

'No, no, it's quite natural for you to feel concerned,' he reassured her. 'Especially after some of the terrible crimes we've seen in this city in recent years. Mrs Knorr, and others. Though one would hope that the authorities have now stamped out the practices that led to those murders.' He thought for a moment or two before continuing. 'What do you know about this Mr Harris? What does he do?'

'I don't know much about him really,' Effie admitted. ' I only met him when I came to Mrs Wilson's a few weeks ago. I get the impression he's been there quite a while. I think he told me once he's a salesman of some sort.' And she flushed, realising that in Michael's mind a person with such a shadowy background, spinning lurid yarns at the breakfast table, would have dubious credibility.

But Michael didn't raise his eyebrows in disbelief. Instead he continued to hold her hand and gaze at her sympathetically.

'Effie, I do believe you're right to feel concerned. But I'm not sure what credence we can put on that fellow's accusations. We just don't know if there are past quarrels or animosities between him and Mrs Wilson, and whether his comments are simply driven by personal malice. Or perhaps he's just a mischief-maker by nature. It's hard to tell.'

'I know I'm being foolish,' Effie cast her eyes down at the table. 'I know my fears aren't terribly rational.'

Michael smiled at her and leaned back, letting her hands go. She rather wished he hadn't and kept them on the table for the moment, hoping that he might be tempted to comfort her again.

'Your fears are entirely rational,' he reassured her. 'So let's plan a rational course of action. Here's what we'll do. It's my understanding, since those terrible events a few years ago, that the government now requires foster carers to be registered and properly regulated. With the Neglected Children's Department, I understand. And I'm pretty sure there's some other organisation set up to keep an eye on things. What say I make a few inquiries around the place and make sure Mrs Wilson is properly credentialed and all aboveboard?'

Effie smiled gratefully, a weight was being lifted off her shoulders. 'Would you? I'm sure Mrs Wilson is doing the right thing but it would be a great comfort to know she is properly set up, and that Alfie is not at risk. Thank you so much.'

'And in the meantime,' Michael said, leaning forward and to her delight, taking her hand again. 'In the meantime, I consider it my solemn duty to divert your thoughts from such troubling matters. Would next

Saturday evening, and *The Mikado* at the Theatre Royal, be sufficiently diverting? They say Mr Passmore is very amusing.'

'I think that might do the trick,' Effie said, now almost back to her usual self. 'In fact, I'm sure it would.' She felt at ease again. The dreadful visions that had been sown within her that morning had been dissipated by Michael's calm good sense and reassuring words. As they resumed their tea and pleasant chatter, she felt herself again basking in his charming presence. She was filled with gratitude that this delightful man was watching over her, and over baby Alfie.

Effie and Michael rose and joined in the standing ovation. The noise from down in the Theatre Royal pit in front of them was deafening – a thousand of the less cultured Gilbert and Sullivan devotees hooting and stamping their feet on the timber floor, until the din shook the very foundations of the grand building. Here in the stalls, the noise was less overwhelming but still wildly enthusiastic, while above and behind them in the two circle tiers, the more refined theatre goers managed to contain themselves to loud and sustained hand-clapping, and numerous cries of 'bravo' and 'encore'.

Up on the Theatre Royal stage, Nanki-Poo, Yum-Yum, Pooh-Bah, and all the rest of them bowed continuously and waved their fans at the audience. It was difficult to tell, beneath their white greasepaint, whether they were smiling or not. To Effie, some of the painted faces almost gave the impression of angry grimaces, rather than happy acknowledgement of the audience's appreciation.

On and on it went; the wild cheering, the thumping on the floor, the line of fantastic figures on stage, bowing and waving. Michael leaned over and shouted something in her ear. She couldn't make out his meaning, but when she glanced up at him, his rapturous expression signalled his emotion. She smiled brightly in return, and nodded her agreement with whatever it was he had just said. In truth she had found the performance entertaining, but dare she say it, just a touch silly and superficial. She couldn't quite see that it deserved all this fuss, but she went on clapping nevertheless, not wanting Michael to think she was half-hearted in her appreciation.

Eventually, almost as one and as if in response to some unseen signal, the gentry in the dress circle behind them abruptly stopped their applause and began a rapid sortie towards the exits. This was a signal for the rest of the audience below to follow suit, and soon the aisles were jam-packed with bodies, jostling their way to the exits and to the nearest bars. The din was almost as stupendous as inside the theatre, as post-mortems of the performance were carried on at shouting level by one and all.

Michael was obviously a practised hand at the required protocol for this part of the evening. One moment he had been standing there clapping and cheering, the next he had Effie by the arm and was guiding her towards the exit at a rapid pace. But despite his prompt action, they were nowhere near the front of the pack, and soon found themselves trapped, carried along by the weight of the crowd. Effie began to feel unwelcome waves of panic rising within her, and the memories of the recent crush outside Parliament House came flooding back. She looked about, ridiculously half-expecting to see the lanky frame of Harry Holloway reaching over to pull her to safety. She fought to get her growing alarm under control, glancing at the laughing faces all around her, and telling herself not to be so foolish. But she clung on more tightly to Michael's arm and, perhaps sensing her panic, he turned towards her, wrapped a strong arm around her shoulders, and shepherded her through the throng, parting the crowd ahead with his free arm. Seemingly within seconds they had forced their way from the theatre and into the opulent surrounds of the Crystal Bar. Here, though still in the midst of a noisy crowd, there was at least room to breathe. Effie surveyed their new surroundings while she tried to recover her composure.

She could not help but be overawed by what she saw. Above their heads, the ornately decorated domed ceiling rose at least thirty feet, with enormous chandeliers hanging from it, glittering brilliantly under the magical influence of myriad electric globes. Around them, the jewellery adorning the women in the crowd sparkled, reflecting the lights above and giving the whole scene a fairy-tale lustre. Effie took in the wonderful strangeness of it all.

Amidst the hubbub, she became aware of Michael talking to her. 'That was marvellous! Didn't you find that marvellous, Effie?' He was leaning in towards her as he spoke, to make himself heard.

'It's all just wonderful!' Effie exclaimed, and meant it. She was now as captured as he.

'I don't know about you, but all that cheering has given me quite a thirst. Champagne must be the order of the day. What do you say?'

'I say, yes please,' Effie replied. 'But I'm not sure how it's to be had.' And she pointed in the direction of the bar, which stretched along most of one side of the large room and was already packed at least four-deep over its entire length.

'Wait here,' he said, grinning, and left her to make his way towards the bar.

Standing at the back of the crush, he stood on tiptoe and began waving his arms above his head. Apparently catching someone's attention, he began an elaborate series of hand signals which ended with a thumbs up and a grin. Within a couple of minutes a handsome young waiter had pushed through the crowd, holding two brimming glasses of champagne on a tray above his head, and made his way to

Michael. The two shook hands warmly and exchanged greetings. The champagne was passed to Michael, and a coin was pressed into the waiter's hand. Michael leaned over and said something to the waiter, who laughed, patted Michael on the shoulder, and hurried back through the crowd to his post behind the bar.

'Well,' Effie said, as Michael returned, bearing his prize in triumph, 'I'm impressed! It's obviously not what you know around these parts, but who. You must be a regular here.'

Michael laughed. 'A fellow artist from the Gallery School. He makes ends meet behind the bar. I labour for much worse wages as a teacher, I'm afraid. You know what it's like.'

Effie couldn't resist a rejoinder. 'Actually, I wish I was on your wage. I can tell you I get a good deal less than you. What do you think we women teachers have been fighting for?'

Michael laughed again. 'Whoops! Put my foot in it there, didn't I? You're right as always, Miss Davis. I apologise unreservedly. Will you forgive me?' And he took her hand in a mock theatrical gesture.

Effie felt she should be piqued by his flippancy, but the general gaiety of the moment carried the day. She could not resist laughing as well.

Carrying on the charade, Michael executed an elaborate half-bow. He raised his glass of champagne.

'Miss Davis, may I propose a toast? What shall we drink to? To the wonderful world of Gilbert and Sullivan. And for that matter, to all the Arts.' And he clinked his glass against Effie's.

'I'm happy to drink to fine champagne,' Effie laughed. 'Especially when it's in such short supply.' Motioning to the frantic scenes at the bar.

'And of course, to friendship,' Michael added, and clinked glasses again.

'To friendship,' Effie responded, and wondered whether she should embellish the sentiment. She decided not to.

'Goodness me!' came a voice from behind Effie. 'What do we have here? Is this the next act of *The Mikado*?' Effie turned, and there was Lydia, as immaculate as ever, her petite, slim figure shown off to stunning effect in a tight-fitting red velvet gown. She was with a tall fellow, rather sallow and bookish, thinning hair grown long over his collar and with a distracted air about him. Lydia introduced him as her friend, Dr Ed Wright, apparently a well-known practitioner in the Melbourne medical profession.

'I've dragged Ed away from his work to experience some fun and frivolity,' Lydia explained. 'I've sworn to have him smiling before the evening's out. Though I haven't succeeded yet.' And she winked at Effie.

Something resembling an embarrassed smirk came over Ed Wright's pale features, and Lydia cried out in triumph. 'Ha, there we have it! I win! I saw it, definitely a smile. Wouldn't you agree, Effie?'

Effie laughed. 'Don't be such a tease, Lydia. Poor Dr Wright, he'll never want to come to the theatre again at this rate.'

Ed mumbled something about no harm done, but a pink glow betrayed his embarrassment. Effie introduced Michael, briefly wondering whether she should label him her friend or her colleague. She settled on colleague, glancing at Michael as she did so. He appeared not to notice her formality and shook hands enthusiastically with Lydia and Ed, before launching into lavish praise of *The Mikado*. Lydia interrupted him, pointing at their glasses of champagne.

'However did you manage to get hold of those?' she said. 'It's bedlam over there.'

'Oh, Michael seems to have undue influence over a handsome bartender,' Effie laughed. 'But I'm not sure whether his power extends to getting us more champagne.'

Michael smiled, 'Heavens, that might be stretching a friendship. But I'll see what can be done.' And again he approached the bar and attracted the bartender's attention. Again the drinks appeared, held high as the young man weaved his way adroitly through the crowd. Delivering the order, he went to hurry back behind the bar again, but not before Michael gripped his arm and, leading him over to them, introduced him as James Mathieson, one of Melbourne's most promising artists.

James shook hands cordially all round, then excused himself, joking that he would never get out of the garret if he was caught slacking and lost his job. Effie was struck by his unaffected, confident demeanour, and also by his looks. He really was most extraordinarily handsome, with wavy fair hair and the most piercing blue eyes. And regular, chiselled features that, though undoubtedly masculine, were also almost delicate in their beauty. Effie found herself following his progress back through the crowd, until he disappeared into the throng around the bar. She wondered, a tad guiltily, whether he had noticed her at all.

'Oh, this champagne is delicious!' Lydia enthused. 'Especially since no one else seems to have any yet.' Then, spying someone in the crowd, she exclaimed. 'Oh, look, there's Moira. And of course she's got that ghastly Sir Anthony with her. Should we invite her over? I suppose we must, mustn't we?'

'Of course we must,' Effie said in mock rebuke. 'Don't be so naughty, Lydia.'

'I actually know Sir Anthony,' Ed Wright said quietly, almost apologetically it seemed to Effie. 'I'm his family doctor. Have been for a good while.'

'I know him too, as it turns out,' Michael chimed in. 'Known him since I was a boy, actually. Friend of the family. His father and mine were in business together at one time.'

Lydia laughed gaily, completely unabashed by her faux pas. 'Oh gosh, how very undiplomatic of me! I shall have to be especially nice to him, and prove to you that I didn't really mean what I said.' And she began to wave vigorously, calling out to attract Moira's attention.

Effie marvelled how Lydia could manage to remain so graceful and charming, even as she jumped on the spot and waved her arms wildly about, as if engaging in an impromptu calisthenics performance. She glanced at Michael who was watching Lydia with an amused smile. Ed Wright had not taken his eyes off her since they had joined them. He was staring at her like a faithful puppy. Effie could see he was besotted with her. Most men were.

Lydia's antics soon attracted Moira's attention. A timid smile appeared as she recognised Lydia, and she turned to speak to her companion, pointing them out to him. Effie saw that Sir Anthony was, as she had suspected, much older than Lydia, thirty years or more, in Effie's estimation. He was a rotund fellow, rather short and quite bald, with a round, red face. Moira was not a tall woman, but she was at least Sir Anthony's height, Effie estimated. He did not seem to Effie to be the fearsome tyrant that Lydia had painted him; on the contrary, he had a rather comical appearance.

The couple made their way over, Sir Anthony in the lead, and Moira trailing deferentially behind. Sir Anthony had an odd way of leaning forward as he walked: it gave him the appearance of being in a hurry. Effie suspected he had spent most of his life hurrying, from one money-making scheme to the next.

Giving a peremptory nod of recognition to Ed Wright, Sir Anthony turned his beady gaze on Michael. He appeared not to notice the women; he certainly did not acknowledge them.

'You're young Standish, aren't you? Haven't seen you in a while.'

'Hello, Sir Anthony,' Michael replied, smiling pleasantly, and offering his hand. 'Good to see you again. May I introduce Miss Davis and Miss Smith.'

Effie smiled brightly and extended her hand as well. Sir Anthony stared at her briefly, nodded curtly, then redirected his attention to Michael. Effie felt herself reddening as she withdrew her hand.

'How's your father?' Sir Anthony boomed. 'Don't see him at the club much these days.'

'To tell the truth, I don't see a lot of him either,' Michael replied. 'I think he spends most of his time on the estate down on the peninsula.'

Effie glanced in surprise at Michael. This news was something of a shock to her. He had spoken of his family before, but only in the vaguest terms. There had certainly been no detail about estates on the peninsula. Now, in an instant, he metamorphosed from Michael the struggling artist into Michael the dilettante son of the landed aristocracy. Some things suddenly fell into place in Effie's mind. She had always wondered at his fine clothes and (to her at least) extravagant lifestyle. Off to the theatre every week, it seemed, and to expensive restaurants as well. She had always wondered how he managed this on a teacher's wage, which though markedly better than hers, was still meagre in the scheme of things. Now she understood.

'Are you following your father into business?' Sir Anthony inquired, still fixing Michael with what seemed to Effie a belligerent stare. 'I heard you were wasting your time fiddling around with drawing, or some such. That's all right when you're young, I suppose, but it's high time you were settling down and taking up a career.'

Michael smiled pleasantly again. 'Well, I think that is the career I will stick to. Drawing, I mean. I want to be an artist. In the meantime I am a teacher, at the same school as Miss Davis, as it turns out. A noble profession as well, I'm sure you would agree.'

Sir Anthony grunted, as if clearing his throat, and managing to express quite clearly with that single sound his firm view that teaching was far from a noble profession, certainly not one worthy of the son of a good family. He turned his attention away from Michael, and stared ahead in silence, wearing a morose expression. That stream of conversation was clearly at an end.

An embarrassed pause ensued – no one seemed inclined to offend Sir Anthony's lofty silence by indulging in small talk. Moira glanced anxiously at the great man, then sought to redirect the conversation to a more favourable topic.

'Sir Anthony's nephew is returning next week,' she said brightly. 'We'll have a little baby at Chittingly. I am so looking forward to it.'

Sir Anthony turned and glared at her. 'That's family business,' he growled. 'Can't see what it's got to do with you.'

Moira coloured bright red and bowed her head. Effie thought she saw her eyes moistening.

'That will be wonderful for you both,' Lydia said deliberately, looking directly at Moira and smiling. 'Has Sir Anthony's nephew been away?'

'They've been overseas for the past five years,' Moira murmured, glancing nervously at Sir Anthony. He had resumed his vacant stare into space, seemingly oblivious to her distress.

'Damn young fool has mended his ways, I hope,' said Sir Anthony to no one in particular. His tone did not display the kind of avuncular affection that might be expected for a long-departed nephew.

He turned to Michael and added, in a more approving tone. 'Done the right thing at last though, I suppose, keeping the family name going. Last of the Hartford line, you know.'

Seeking to jolly the old fellow along, Michael raised his glass in Sir Anthony's direction. 'That's well worth drinking to. What about a champagne, Sir Anthony? I can guarantee to have them in your hands within the minute, despite appearances to the contrary.' And he pointed in the direction of the crowded bar.

But Michael's invitation had the opposite result; Sir Anthony's expression transforming to one of florid anger. He stared at Michael as if he could not believe his ears.

'Never touch the stuff,' he exclaimed eventually. 'And she doesn't either,' he added, with a gesture towards Moira behind him. 'The curse of the devil, and the ruin of this country. Should be banned, in my opinion.'

Michael lapsed into silence, continuing to smile at Sir Anthony in a somewhat bemused way. Lydia drew Effie aside and took advantage of the chatter about them to whisper in her ear. 'The old fool's a famous temperance man, you know. Owns a couple of coffee palaces, I believe.'

Effie noticed Sir Anthony looking in their direction, and blushed involuntarily. She hoped he had not heard Lydia's words, and that his fierce stare was just his normal expression. She began to wish fervently that this old tyrant would leave them. She felt sorry for Moira, but Sir Anthony's rudeness had quite dissipated the pleasant gaiety of the evening. She tried to think of an excuse to take their farewells, but as usual Lydia beat her to the mark.

'Do excuse us, Sir Anthony. It's been delightful but I'm afraid we're late for supper with friends. Goodbye, Moira darling.' And she gave Moira a long and particularly affectionate hug, before seizing Ed Wright's hand and dragging him off into the crowd. Michael hastily bid farewell too, and he and Effie hurried off in pursuit of Lydia. They caught up with her and Ed in the crowded foyer. For the first time that Effie could remember, Lydia's breezy demeanour had deserted her. In fact she seemed angry, her pretty features creased with a stern frown.

'My goodness, what a nasty man,' she exclaimed. 'The way he treats poor Moira! Why does she put up with it?'

'Why indeed,' Michael said, raising his eyebrows. Effie glanced at him. Was Michael insinuating anything in that slightly quizzical look? That Moira was after Sir Anthony's money? But he smiled warmly at her and she was reassured. She really had to stop thinking the worst of people.

Lydia turned to Ed. 'It must be hard being his doctor. Putting up with that sort of behaviour all the time. Is he always that awful?'

Again Ed appeared ill-at-ease. 'I can't really say anything about Sir Anthony, you know,' he muttered. 'I have an obligation as his doctor. Confidentiality and all that.' But then, as if nervous about offending Lydia with this obfuscation, he added, 'I suppose Sir Anthony can be a bit difficult at times, but he is often under a good deal of pressure. And he has been quite generous to Miss Williamson, I can assure you.'

Effie thought this was a feeble excuse for such rude and bullying behaviour. And if generosity meant a few baubles given to Moira every now and then, it was a poor substitute for treating her with the respect she deserved. But she supposed that Ed was not really in a position to lambast his patient, so she said nothing.

Michael suggested they escape the crowd at the Crystal Bar and make their way down Bourke Street to the Melbourne Coffee Palace where, with a bit of luck, they might encounter the delightful Sir Anthony again. 'But seriously,' he added, 'it's less likely to be crowded at this time of the evening, and they say the reception room is quite charming. Apparently it's beautifully decorated, no expense spared.'

But for Effie the spell of the evening had been broken, and she suddenly felt tired. 'If you don't mind I would like to go home. I'm really rather done for.'

'Of course,' Michael said immediately. 'Let's call it a night then.'

Lydia, though still full of beans and no doubt ready for whatever adventure might be found, was happy to follow their lead. Bidding Effie and Michael a fond farewell, she seized Ed Wright's arm and headed for the exit, her exuberance now fully restored. Ed only had time for a cursory nod and a muttered goodnight, before he was dragged away.

'Well,' Effie said. 'Time to head home. I suppose we'd better hurry or we'll miss our tram. And you'll have to change trams once we get to Mrs Wilson's, so it will take you some time to get to your place. It's a long way.'

Michael smiled at her. 'Do you know, it's been such a delightful evening, we shouldn't spoil it by standing about waiting for trams. What do you say to a hansom cab ride?'

Effie glanced at him. Again she felt a tinge of something – was it envy, or perhaps resentment? That the cost of a hansom cab fare was obviously something Michael did not even need to consider. But another part of her was excited by the prospect of the two of them alone in a cab together for the ride home. She smiled gratefully, and accepted the invitation.

Soon they were trotting through the city streets, brightly lit at first, but darkening as they made their way down St Kilda Road towards Mrs Wilson's boarding house. It had not long since been a pastoralist's grand mansion, but had been sold for a song when its owner was ruined in the recent depression. It was now rather sadly neglected and, though still grand in a tatty kind of way, was distinctly fraying at the edges. Effie did not like living there very much, but it was all she could afford on a teacher's wage, and at least it was close to Merton Hall.

Within the cosy confines of the cab, sheltered from the gathering winter frost, and with a woollen rug thoughtfully provided for their comfort and wrapped over their legs, Effie gave herself up to the sheer pleasure of such close and prolonged proximity to Michael Standish. He was silent initially, staring out the window and deep in thought. Perhaps reflecting on the evening they had enjoyed together, perhaps thinking of something else entirely – she could not tell. She wondered if she placed her hand on the rug, as close as she dared to his leg, that he would perhaps feel inclined to take her hand in his.

Carefully she eased her right arm from under the rug and as casually as she could let her hand rest on top of it, almost against his knee. But he did not take up the invitation, did not even appear to notice the proximity of her hand. She glanced at him as he continued to stare out the window, and found herself admiring his handsome features, for the most part concealed in the gloom, but from time to time clearly illuminated as they passed the occasional streetlamp. Effie began to despair that he would be preoccupied for the entire journey, and decided that she had better take the initiative.

'Did you enjoy this evening,' she murmured, in what she hoped was her most sultry contralto timbre. 'I certainly did.'

Michael awoke from his reverie, and turned to her, smiling. 'It was wonderful, wasn't it? Only spoilt by Sir Anthony and his rather objectionable ways.'

Effie glanced across at him. 'I thought he was an old friend of yours?'

'He's an old family friend. But I don't have much time for him. Never have, really. Actually, I rather hope your friend Moira sees the error of her ways soon, and gets rid of the old goat.'

'Oh, I don't know Moira that well, I've only just met her. She's more Lydia's friend, really,' said Effie. 'But I do feel sorry for her. I don't think she has the courage to leave him, somehow.'

Michael said nothing. Effie suspected he was resisting the urge to be critical of Moira's timid acceptance of Sir Anthony's bombast. Then, after a short pause, he turned to her again. 'By the way, I made some enquiries in relation to Mrs Wilson and your young friend.'

Effie peered at him. There was something in his tone that did not reassure her. 'You sound rather hesitant. What have you found out?'

'Well, quite a bit actually,' Michael said. 'But, to be honest, it's all a bit confusing. Apparently, anyone fostering a child these days is required to be registered with the department. After all that terrible business with Mrs Knorr.'

'And did you find out whether Mrs Wilson is registered?'

'Well yes, she is, according to the police. Apparently they maintain the register and are meant to enforce it. But it seems that, in practice, it's more up to the Neglected Children's Department to deal with inspections and complaints and what not. And then there's the Society for the Prevention of Cruelty to Children. All volunteers, as I understand. Apparently they keep an eye on the department, and what it's up to. To keep them up to the mark, I suppose. But overall, I had the distinct impression that it's all a bit confused. I'm not certain that anybody is really doing very much at all. Certainly the police don't seem terribly keen to be involved.'

'That doesn't surprise me,' Effie said. 'Did you find out much about the society? I think it's called the VSPCC. Lydia mentioned them to me once, but I don't know much about them.'

'Not a lot, except that they're voluntary and a popular cause for the society women of Melbourne to support. And I did get a name. I was told to contact a Mrs Baxter if we suspect anything untoward. And actually I have heard of her, I think I met her once or twice when I was a boy. She's been a friend of my mother. Prominent in charitable circles, I think. I understand she has a house in Kew.'

Effie found all this information rather confusing, and not terribly reassuring. But she was moderately happier, and was beginning to be reassured that Alfie was, if not necessarily in safe hands, at least protected by the force of the law. She thought of the darling little fellow again, his sweet round face, his tiny fingers reaching out and locking around her long slender one, and a smile came to her.

'Is that Mrs Wilson's over there?' said Michael, pointing at an old Victorian mansion looming on their left-hand side, its facade obviously fading and worn, even in the dim light of the gas streetlamps.

'Yes, that's it.' Effie tried to keep the disappointment from her voice, that the cab ride home had not led to the romantic outcome she had hoped for. Not yet, at least.

Michael opened the trap door above their heads and called for the driver to pull over. The cab slowed and eased into the kerb, by the rusting iron fence and gate that fronted the boarding house. The cab door swung open as the cabbie plied his lever.

'Thank you so much, Michael,' Effie said, again lowering her voice to what she hoped was an alluring pitch. 'I had a wonderful time.' And she leaned ever so slightly towards him in the seat.

'My pleasure entirely, Miss Davis,' Michael said, again with that arch smile that Effie found so difficult to read. But she fancied that he began to lean in towards her, and her heart beat faster.

But then he stopped and straightened, turning and peering out the open door. 'What's going on?' he exclaimed.

From beyond the thick shrubs that lined Mrs Wilson's front path came the unmistakable sound of voices raised in violent argument. One was clearly a woman whose panic-stricken cries were becoming louder and louder, almost hysterical.

'I think she's being attacked!' Michael cried. He leapt out of the cab in an instant, and was through the gate and sprinting up the path. 'Stop, stop!' he shouted as he ran towards the commotion. Effie and the cab driver followed in close pursuit.

Effie was filled with trepidation as she followed the cabbie along the darkened path. She was terrified that she would come across Michael in the grip of some ruffian, or even worse, lying bleeding on the ground. 'Careful, Michael!' she managed to shout, but her voice sounded thin and feeble, as if fear had already driven the air from her lungs.

But when she emerged from the bushes at the old marble steps fronting the building, relief flooded over her as she saw, in the lantern light, Michael with the assailant firmly in his grip. He was holding the fellow off Mrs Wilson, who was cowering against the front door.

But then, confusion as Effie realised that the hysterical screams were coming from the attacker rather than Mrs Wilson. And the pitch of the cries revealed that the slight figure wrapped in a large brown coat, and held in Michael's firm grasp, was a woman. As she squirmed and turned fully into the lantern light, Effie saw that the woman was quite young, though gaunt and haggard. Tears were streaming down her cheeks and she stared about her wildly, all the while struggling to break free from Michael's hold.

'My baby!' she cried. 'Give me my baby! That woman's taken my baby!' And she lunged desperately at Mrs Wilson, who drew back in alarm. But Michael had the young woman securely in his grasp, his arms wrapped around her waist.

'For heavens sake, calm down, my girl!' he said, his voice low, but firm and insistent. 'You'll do yourself an injury. Just calm down and we'll sort this out.' But she was in no mind to be calm, thrashing about and now beginning to wail incoherently.

Effie suddenly reckoned on who this woman was. 'Is this Alfie's mother?' she said to Mrs Wilson. 'I thought you said she deserted him.'

Mrs Wilson put one hand on the front door knob as she drew back from the flailing figure, and for a moment Effie thought she was about to seek refuge inside the building. But then she thought better of it, and turned to face her accuser.

'She did desert him! She did!' Mrs Wilson's voice was tremulous and she too seemed close to tears, her face blotchy and her eyes reddened. 'Now she turns up out of the blue, at all hours of the night, and expects to get him back. Well, it's too late!'

'What do you mean 'too late'?' Effie couldn't understand what was going on. 'Can't you just give him back?'

Mrs Wilson stared at Effie, then turned away.

She spoke again, and now her jaw was set in stubborn defiance. 'No I can't. He's been handed in to the authorities.'

'What?' Effie cried. 'What do you mean? You were meant to be minding him for this lady!'

Mrs Wilson wheeled back to face Effie, and there was now anger in her voice, and in her eyes. 'Well, she didn't come back to get him. I thought she shot through. Happens all the time. I can't be expected to look after him forever. For nothing. Out of the goodness of me heart.'

The young woman turned to Effie too, and there was desperation in her voice. 'Oh, Miss, I couldn't help it, really I couldn't. I've been sick. I came back as soon as I could, but he's gone! She's given him away! My baby!' And again she began to cry hysterically.

Michael, who was supporting the young woman with an arm around her shoulder, was now forced to shift his grip back to her waist as she threatened to collapse beneath him. 'Come now, young lady.' His tone was sharp, almost stern. 'You must calm down. These tears will do you no good. If your baby has been mistakenly handed over to the authorities, then we will get him back from them. You will soon be reunited.'

Michael's sensible words seemed to have an immediate reassuring effect. The woman's cries died down to a soft whimper as she stared blankly at Michael. Effie could not quite tell whether her expression was one of renewed hope or just incomprehension. Michael appeared to assume the former, and pushed on encouragingly.

'That's better, my dear, much better. Now, Mrs Wilson, we'll just have to get the little fellow back to his mother, won't we? So tell me, who did you hand him in to?'

Now it was Mrs Wilson's turn to stare at Michael in apparent bewilderment. She said nothing, standing there open-mouthed.

'Come, come, Mrs Wilson, it's a simple question. Who did you hand him in to?'

Suddenly Mrs Wilson appeared to come to a decision. She faced Michael defiantly: 'I told you, it's too late. He's been given away.'

At this, the young woman cried out in distress and resumed her loud moaning. Effie reached out to comfort her, stroking her shoulder. It had no effect.

Michael's voice was raised; he was losing his patience. 'What do you mean, 'given away'? Who did you give him to?'

But Mrs Wilson was now adamant. 'None of your business!' she shouted at him. 'I've done everything right and proper and I don't have to answer to you! Now I'm going to bed, where I should have been hours ago. And you will too, Miss Davis, if you have any sense. And get this hussy off my premises! Or I'll call the police!'

With that she pushed open the front door and retreated inside, slamming it behind her. The small group remained at the front door, and Effie wondered what they should do now. Michael relaxed his hold on the young woman, who immediately burst free and flung herself at the door, attempting to follow Mrs Wilson inside, and crying out again for her baby. Michael quickly restrained her again.

'I'm sorry, Miss, but there's nothing to be done tonight. That woman will obviously not assist you, and the authorities won't be available until the morning. What you must do now is get some rest, or you'll become ill, and then you'll be of no use to your child.'

Effie thought this sound advice had probably come too late, the poor girl already was quite wretched, sallow and wild-haired, her eyes sunken and bloodshot. Effie lent her support to Michael, asking the girl if she had lodgings for the night.

'No, Miss, I have nowhere to stay. I came straight here, looking for my Alfie. I haven't had the chance to find a room. I was hoping that Mrs Wilson might have spare lodging for us.'

'Well, it's clear that option is no longer available,' Michael said. 'But I know for a fact that there is a spare apartment in my building. And I happen to be on very good terms with my landlord. So perhaps you will allow me to set you up there until we can sort out this mess.'

The girl eyed Michael doubtfully. Effie could see that she was reluctant to leave the premises, still perhaps clinging to the hope that Mrs Wilson was lying, and that her baby was inside.

'Come, my dear,' Effie said. 'I really don't think your Alfie is here, so the best thing is for you to come with Mr Standish, and into comfortable quarters where you can get some sleep. I will come too to make it right and proper, and I promise we'll start out bright and early tomorrow to track down your baby.'

'That we will,' Michael said. 'Miss Davis and I are creatures of leisure for the next three weeks, so we can devote our time to getting your little boy back. We should be able to clear it all up quickly. And see here, we have this very patient gentleman with his splendid cab all set to take us on our way. I'm sure all three of us can squeeze in without too much discomfort.'

The young woman had now composed herself to some degree, though she was still obviously distraught. But she agreed quietly enough to Michael's proposed course of action, and allowed herself to be seated in the hansom cab between Effie and Michael. Soon they were on their way to nearby Prahran, where it turned out Michael had his lodgings.

Despite the dramatic turn of events that had suddenly overtaken them, Effie still found herself wondering about Michael's home. Would it be of a standard befitting the son of landed gentry? Or perhaps he had decided to live more modestly, in keeping with his chosen path in life. Then she chastised herself for such mean-spirited thoughts at this time of crisis. She turned her attention back to the young woman.

As they made their way through the dark streets, and in between frequent bursts of sobbing and tears from their passenger, Effie slowly and patiently managed to coax the girl's story from her. Her name was Mary Guerin, an Irish girl of nineteen who had come from Ballarat to Melbourne to work as a seamstress in a clothing factory. She had fallen in love with a fellow who had taken advantage of her and got her with child. Of course the rogue had then deserted her immediately, and Mary was left all alone to her plight. She was too afraid to return to her strict Catholic parents, and had stayed in Melbourne to have the baby. Perhaps she was too naive to find a means to be rid of the pregnancy, or perhaps she was too religious to take such drastic action. In any event, with the help of her only friend, a lass from the factory where she worked, Mary had taken herself off to the Victorian Infant Asylum, where Alfie was delivered.

But her troubles were just starting. With no money coming in, and in fear of losing her employment, Mary had to return to work, but of course there was no one to care for Alfie while she was at the factory. Someone had told her that Mrs Wilson minded babies for a fee, and so Mary took to leaving Alfie with Mrs Wilson during her work hours. But she quickly realised that on her meagre wages she could not support herself and Alfie, as well as pay Mrs Wilson what seemed to her a very large sum for her fostering services. So, in desperation she had left Alfie with Mrs Wilson for two weeks while she went back to Ballarat to confess all to her parents, beg their forgiveness, and seek their assistance with her baby's care.

Far from forgiving her, her father had turned on her and told her that unless she did the right thing and entered into wedlock with Alfie's father, they would disown her completely and she could burn in hell for all he cared. This precipitated a terrible row between the parents, for it turned out Mary's mother was more sympathetic to her plight, and wanted her to bring Alfie to Ballarat where he could be properly cared for. While all this was going on, Mary fell ill with scarlet fever, and was laid up for many weeks, in a state of delirium. She was scarcely able to talk, let alone get word to Mrs Wilson to apprise her of the situation.

While Mary was convalescing, the argument continued to rage between her parents, and in the end her father had relented and allowed her to bring the baby back to them to be brought up. But his condition was that Mary could not live with them, and could only visit Alfie with their permission. Mary had no choice but to agree with this and so, as soon as she had sufficient strength, she had hastened back to Melbourne, only to be confronted with the calamitous circumstance she now found herself in.

By the time they had fully extracted this sad tale from Mary, the cab had reached Michael's residence. This turned out to be a double-storey Victorian terrace house, not large but very smart, with a triple arch ornamenting the ground floor. It was well sited, one street back from the busy Prahran central shopping precinct. And it turned out that the spare accommodation available for Mary was the apartment immediately next door, also owned by Michael's family, and which his parents used when they came to town.

Effie was secretly pleased as she took in Michael's lodgings. His family obviously had wealth, but the stylish, though relatively modest building before them showed that they did not believe in vulgar ostentation.

After reassuring Mary that she would be safe and secure in this accommodation, and after settling her in, Effie took her leave. Michael insisted that she be taken home in the cab, and arranged for the cabbie to pick her up again the following morning, first thing, at which time they would begin their efforts to find Alfie.

'I think this is really a matter for the police,' Michael confided, after they had left Mary in the spare apartment and were walking back to the cab together. 'I don't think it's going to be as simple as getting the little chap back from the relevant authorities. I don't trust Mrs Wilson for one moment. I didn't want to say anything in front of Mary, but the story that woman gave us sounded to me like it was all cock and bull. She could have done anything with the baby. She obviously had no further use for him.'

Effie's blood ran cold at the thought of all the possibilities. 'Don't say that,' she said to him in a low voice. 'We must not think such thoughts.'

'I am not suggesting that the worst has happened,' Michael said. 'Hopefully it won't come to that, but we must consider all possibilities."

On this gloomy note, Michael deposited her back in the cab, patting her hand encouragingly as he noticed the tears welling in her eyes.

'Don't worry, I'm sure it will all turn out for the best, and your little friend will be reunited with his mother. We'll make it our business to bring them back together. It will be our holiday adventure.'

But Effie was in no mood to be reassured. Her fears and anxieties did not abate, either on the trip home, or after she had slipped into the boarding house and retired to bed. She could not get the image of little Alfie – alone, motherless and facing unknown perils – out of her head.

CHAPTER THREE

→※←

EFFIE USUALLY LIKED to sleep in on a Sunday. It was the one day of the week that Mrs Wilson relaxed her strict eight o'clock breakfast curfew, and allowed her guests to luxuriate in the dining room over porridge, ham, eggs, toast and tea, right up to the decadent hour of nine o'clock. Effie always took full advantage of this surprising generosity of spirit, and every Sunday would rise late, eat a large and leisurely breakfast, lingering over a second cuppa until Mrs Wilson's help, Daisy, began to clear away the breakfast things.

But not on this Sunday morning. Effie had lain awake for much of the night, and sleep, when it fitfully came, brought with it vague and threatening dreams. Again and again she forced herself to wake from these nightmares, sitting up in bed, her nightgown damp with sweat, despite the chill in the night air. At half past six, waking yet again from a half-sleep, she gave up the fight and rose from her bed. At seven she was the first at table, much to the surprise of Daisy who was accustomed to having the dining room to herself for the first hour on a Sunday. But the porridge was ready on the stove, and so she bustled off to the kitchen to fetch it, and to get some bread toasting in the swivelling iron.

As she returned with a steaming bowl of porridge, she noticed Effie's appearance. 'My goodness, Miss, you look like something the cat's brought in. Are you all right?'

Effie smiled wanly. 'Didn't sleep well,' she replied. 'Not sure why.'

Daisy leaned towards her and whispered, 'Must be something going around. Mrs W aint herself this morning either. Put her head in the door, wandered about a bit, then said she was going back to bed. Her head was splitting, she said.'

'I don't wonder,' murmured Effie, almost to herself. She glanced again at Daisy, hesitated, then spoke.

'Did you know that Alfie has gone?' she asked, as casually as she could manage.

Daisy wrinkled her brow in puzzlement. Effie persevered. 'You know, the baby. The one that Mrs Wilson has been minding.'

'Oh, yes,' Daisy said. 'Now I know who you mean. Funny you should mention that. I saw Mrs W leaving with the little feller a couple of days ago. Must've been then that he went away, because she came back without him.'

'Was she with anyone?' Again Effie tried, not very successfully, to make her question seem like idle chat. But she could not fully conceal the urgency in her voice.

'She was, as a matter of fact. Tall bloke. They headed off in a cab together. Didn't get a good look at him though, I was watching from an upstairs window, and he was pretty well rugged up.'

'It's a bit odd, isn't it, just sending Alfie off like that? Out of the blue, really.'

Daisy's puzzled expression returned. 'I don't know, I wouldn't have thought so. Anyway, it's nothing new for Mrs W, she's always minding some little nipper or other.'

'Really?' Effie said, sensing the possibility of uncovering more of Mrs

Wilson's history. But Daisy did not have much to add.

'Oh, yes. I've been here about three years, and I reckon she's taken in half a dozen in that time. At least. Doesn't usually keep them for long though.'

'What happens to them?' Effie asked. 'Do they get adopted out?' But again Daisy was disappointingly vague.

'Don't know really. I expect their mums picked them up in the main. We never used to see them much, she kept them out of the way most of the time. In her rooms.'

Effie tried to keep the conversation going, but Daisy had her breakfast duties to attend to. 'Goodness me, Miss, I'd better get going. After all, I'm on my own this morning. And the octopus will be in soon, wanting his breakfast. Lord knows, I have to be on my toes to keep out of his way.' She winked knowingly at Effie, on whom the reference to Mr Harris was not lost. She raised her eyebrows in acknowledgement.

Daisy turned to make her way to the kitchen, then paused, peering out the front window. 'Well bless me, would you look at that,' she exclaimed. 'There's a fine looking gentleman just turned up outside, and he's heading our way. Isn't he a sight for sore eyes?'

Effie followed her gaze. Michael was striding up the front path in a most business-like manner. There was no sign of Mary. She was probably waiting in the cab.

Despite her low spirits, Effie still felt a thrill of excitement at the mere sight of Michael. She felt herself flushing, and her heart beginning to race.

'That's my friend, Mr Standish,' she said, as nonchalantly as she could, and pushed her chair back. 'I'd better not keep him waiting.'

'Oh, that's a shame, Miss, now you won't get your ham and eggs. Never mind, I reckon he looks tastier than ham and eggs any day.' And again she winked cheerily. Effie tried to maintain a casual demeanour, but to her annoyance she could feel her face reddening further. She gave Daisy what she feared was a foolish smirk in return, and hurried out to meet Michael.

>-<

Effie and Michael stood among the throng of Sunday morning customers at the Russell Street police headquarters. Mary was not with them. Despite Michael's reassurances, the poor girl had been stricken with anxiety that she would be in trouble with the law for abandoning her son. She was in terror of being arrested on the spot and thrown in jail, and so never having the chance to see Alfie again. Mrs Wilson's wild accusations had clearly taken hold.

Michael had tried to reason with her, but she would not be persuaded. Eventually he had decided that perhaps it might be best to leave her at his place and set out without her. In any case, in her current state she would hardly present a convincing image of the responsible parent seeking to reclaim her child. Their case might be better proselytised without her.

They had arrived at the drab, single story Russell Street premises and found their way to the reception area, a large, rather gloomily lit room with a counter at one end and benches arranged around the other three walls. Behind the counter, a few harassed police officers were engaged in attending to the large number of customers milling on the other side. Some, mostly thuggish coves in the company of stern-faced policemen, were clearly in strife with the law, no doubt after some Saturday night villainy gone wrong. A bedraggled young woman, in a considerable state of undress and inebriation, was loudly protesting that she was not a tart, and couldn't a girl have a drink and a good time without being persecuted by the law. Others were clearly there to pursue a grievance of one sort or another, theft and assault seemingly the main complaints on the agenda.

On first surveying this cacophony of Sunday morning discontent, Effie and Michael had despaired that they would find someone to listen to their concerns in anything like a reasonable timeframe. They had taken their place at the rear of the crowd, the prospect of hours of waiting ahead of them.

But they need not have worried. Michael's obviously gentlemanly dress and bearing quickly attracted the attention of one of the moustachioed officers behind the counter, who immediately broke off his dealings with a red-faced complainant, directed him rather sternly to be seated for the moment, then smiled obligingly to Michael and motioned him to the front of the queue.

Michael somewhat sheepishly approached, embarrassed to have been given such favoured treatment, but not sufficiently so as to turn the invitation down. He introduced himself and explained their business, that they were acting on behalf of a young mother whose baby had been taken from her in dubious circumstances, and there was a grave suspicion that the child had been abducted illegally. The officer, one PC Jackson according to his name badge, listened solemnly to their story, nodding knowingly from time to time to demonstrate his deep understanding of the case and all its implications. Michael finished his account by suggesting that this was surely a matter for urgent police investigation. PC Jackson did not immediately respond, but instead began to rub his chin and continued to fix Michael with a steady gaze. Michael wondered whether the fellow was ruminating on the case or was expecting him to continue. He decided to push on.

'I would think, Constable, that this case comes under the purview of the Infant Life Protection Act. And as such, is clearly a matter of police jurisdiction.'

PC Jackson nodded again, and this time did respond. 'Ah yes, of course, the Infant Life Protection Act. Just what I was thinking myself,

Sir.' Now apparently clear in his mind about the way forward, he smiled pleasantly and leaned forward, as if to take them into his confidence.

'This is one for the CIB, I reckon. They look after all the baby inquiries.'

'The CIB?' Michael was taken aback.

'The Criminal Investigation Branch. Haven't you heard of them? They're some of our finest. Top shelf. They'll sort out your problem in no time, Sir.' And he beamed, as if basking himself in the reflected glory of the CIB.

'Well, all right,' said Michael, uncertain as to whether this was a step forward or backward in progressing their cause. 'Could you direct us then to the right person in the CIB?'

'Certainly, Sir,' said PC Jackson brightly. His relief at offloading this obviously tricky case was palpable. 'If you take a seat in the interview room across the hall, I'll send in our CIB duty detective in a jiffy. Not sure if he's in the building at this precise moment, but if not, he's bound to be here shortly. You won't have long to wait.' And he gestured encouragingly to the door back into the entrance corridor, before returning his attention to his former customer, now advancing in an apoplectic state to resume his account of some stolen chickens.

So Effie and Michael returned from whence they came, back into the corridor and then into a small room on the other side. It bore the title of Interview Room, inscribed on a small brass plate attached to the door, and apparently acted as a waiting room for the better class of police clientele. 'Well, so far, so good,' said Michael as they took their seats. 'Shouldn't be too long now.'

And so they waited. And waited. The minutes rolled by, the hour on the clock above their heads ticked over, and still no one came. Effie began to feel as if perhaps they had been fobbed off by PC Jackson, and that there was in fact no CIB detective on, or anywhere near the premises to hear their concerns. She was about to suggest to Michael that they revisit the large room and try again, when the sound of heavy boots approaching down the main corridor rekindled their hopes. Next moment, the owner of the boots appeared in the doorway, his monolithic stature seeming to fill the entire door space.

Detective Constable Harry Holloway favoured them with a lopsided grin. 'Sorry to keep you waiting, folks. Bit of a late one last night. All in the line of duty, of course.'

His grin widened further as he recognised Effie. 'Miss Davis, if I'm not mistaken. A pleasure to see you again, and in less riotous circumstances than last time.'

Effie forced a polite smile, despite the prickle of annoyance rising within her. Again she felt herself flushing, and this annoyed her even more.

'Good morning, Sergeant Holloway,' she replied, in what she hoped was a coolly professional tone. 'I see you're still struggling to meet the dress standards of the police force.'

And it was true, his rough open shirt and jacket seemed hardly appropriate attire for a detective in the Criminal Investigation Branch. Harry Holloway took the jibe in excellent humour. 'Fair call, Miss Davis, you have a point, but actually this is my weekend uniform. We're allowed to dress down a bit. So as we don't stand out too much, you understand.'

'Well, anyway,' Effie said, unappeased. 'It's impolite to make us wait so long.'

Harry just grinned again and introduced himself to Michael, asking how could he help on this fine Sunday morning. Michael wasted no time retelling their experience of Mary's predicament, including his doubts about the veracity of Mrs Wilson's story. 'What can be done to get this poor lady's son back?' he concluded. 'Even if this Wilson woman is telling the truth, it seems that a tragic mistake has been made, and must be rectified.'

As Michael told his tale, Effie watched Harry's cheerful expression gradually disappear and an air of solemnity overtake him. He had taken a seat opposite them, across the table in the centre of the room, and when Michael had completed his narrative, he pushed his chair back, stood and wandered across to the small window, where he paused for some moments, hands in pockets, staring out through the grimy glass at the passing traffic. He slowly turned back towards them. His expression remained solemn.

'Folks, I'd like to help you and this poor girl, but I'm not sure I can. We know Rhonda Wilson, and to tell the truth, we've had some suspicions about her in the past. But she is registered and from what you say about this particular baby, she maintains that the paperwork has been signed off and everything's legal. I assume she's handed the boy into the VIA. That's the Victorian Infant Asylum, over in Berry Street, they look after most adoptions of this kind. Of course I'm happy to check that side of things for you, but if everything's in order, there's probably not much more that can be done.'

Effie's heart sank at this less than optimistic response. 'But Mrs Wilson had no right to hand Alfie anywhere! He doesn't belong to her, she was only minding him for Mary.'

Harry wandered back to his chair and resumed his seat. When he spoke, it was slowly and deliberately, a troubled expression now apparent on his angular features. 'Yes, I know, but that's not how the law may see it. After all, the mother did leave the child for an extended period without contacting anyone. Now, don't take this the wrong way, but are you completely sure that she wants the baby? I notice that she's not here to argue her own case.'

Effie bristled again. 'She's not here only because she's afraid of you lot. And no wonder, when you attack her and doubt her like that. Of course she wants Alfie! The poor girl's beside herself with worry!'

Harry raised his hands, palms out in defence. 'Whoa there, I'm not saying she's a bad mother, I was just asking the question. Believe me, it happens all the time. The woman can't support her child and gives it up, then changes her mind and wants it back, then realises that she can't manage it after all. I'm not blaming her, it's just a sad fact of life sometimes.'

'Well, it's not a fact of life in this case. So forget about that possibility.' Even as she spoke the words, a sliver of doubt was running through Effie. Could it be that Mary would give up Alfie again? Perhaps her absence today was not so much fear of the police but rather a reluctance to pursue getting Alfie back at any cost? She glared at Harry. She would so hate for this annoying man to be proved right.

'Fair enough, fair enough,' Harry said, raising his hands again in appeasement. 'I'm more than happy to check up on your behalf. If the adoption has been through the VIA it will be on the record, and will have been signed off by someone. Either the matron, or more likely one of the duty doctors. Let's see what that turns up. But don't get your hopes up too much, once a baby has been declared abandoned and then adopted out, it's very unusual for it to be given back. And again, don't take this the wrong way, but going to a good home where he is able to be well-cared for and supported may be the best thing for him in the long run.'

Effie thought of Mary and her panic-stricken despair and was again overwhelmed with anger and frustration at the unfairness of it all. She wanted to blame Harry Holloway and his pessimistic outlook, but a part of her realised that perhaps he was just being realistic. And reasonable. So she sat there, fuming inside, but said nothing. It was left to Michael to offer a civil response.

'Thank you, Detective Holloway, we appreciate you investigating the matter. Let's hope you're wrong, and the people he has been sent to understand that a mistake has been made.'

Harry shrugged and gave a sigh. 'Let's hope so.' But the tone of his voice told them that he did not expect such an outcome.

They rose to take their leave, and Harry escorted them to the door. 'By the way,' he said to Michael as they shook hands, 'no more of the Detective Holloway. It's Harry to anyone who's known me for more than five minutes.'

'Well, in that case, I'm Michael, and this is Effie.' Michael turned and smiled at Effie. 'I take it you're happy with that?' he asked her.

Michael was obviously comfortable, even glad, to be on such familiar terms with their investigator, but Effie was not so sure. She still harboured some resentment at the detective's recent behaviour, but decided she'd better swallow her pride.

'I suppose so,' she said, less than convivially, and extended her hand to Harry. He pumped it vigorously, grinning delightedly at her.

'Effie it is then. A great pleasure to finally be on first name terms.' And then, more seriously. 'And I promise to do my best to help you, if I possibly can.'

Effie felt herself moderately comforted by these words. As she and Michael left the building, she decided that, despite her initial poor impression of Harry Holloway, and despite his obviously gloomy view of their prospects, she would need to put her trust in him to help poor Mary get her little boy back. After all, it was clear that there was no one else who was prepared to take up her cause.

The rest of Sunday, and then Monday, dragged on interminably. Effie had holiday work to complete, preparing for next term's history syllabus, but she found it impossible to concentrate for any length of time. Mrs Wilson usually allowed her to use the table in the front parlour to prepare her lessons, and this always provided a quiet, productive environment to get her work done. But on this occasion her mind kept wandering to thoughts of Alfie and his mother, and she found herself constantly breaking off her work to stare out the window, trying to calm the welling anxiety within her.

She had not heard from Michael: she assumed he was keeping a close eye on Mary, comforting her and, like Effie, waiting for news from Harry Holloway.

She was not really expecting much from Harry's investigations. His pessimistic view of the case made her believe that his inquiries would be cursory at best. She also expected his progress would be slow. No doubt he had other priorities that were well in front of theirs in the queue. And she assumed that he would contact Michael once he had news.

So it was a considerable surprise when, shortly after lunch on Monday, during one of her sojourns at the window, she saw his lanky figure striding through the front gates and up the path. He was as dishevelled as ever, though she noticed he had deferred to weekday formalities by donning a tie. This had already come loose and was now doing a decidedly inadequate job of holding his shirt collar in place.

Seized with renewed hope that this early response might herald good news, Effie dashed to the front door and threw it open before he could even knock. She wanted to ask immediately what he had discovered, but instead found herself adopting a more combative greeting.

'Sergeant Holloway, this is a surprise! I didn't think I'd see you again so soon. Or anytime soon, for that matter.'

Harry smiled his infuriatingly cheerful smile. He seemed to be enjoying their sparring. 'Effie, I just couldn't help myself, I had to see you again. You're always so pleasant to me.' Then lowering his tone, 'And to tell the truth, I had another motive for popping in. I was hoping to catch up with Rhonda Wilson, just to see how she's feeling about life at the moment.' He touched his hand to his nose and raised an eyebrow. 'Has she been about?'

'I don't think so. She was here at breakfast, but only for ten minutes, and I haven't seen her since.'

'Oh well, never mind, let's have a chat first anyway.' And he pushed past Effie and headed straight into the front parlour, hanging his hat on the hallstand as he passed. He obviously knew his way around the premises. She followed close behind.

'Well,' he said, spreading himself onto the sofa, long legs extended into the centre of the room. 'I've got news for you, though I don't think you're going to like it much. Bottom line is, Alfie Guerin has been approved for adoption at the VIA. I've seen the register, everything seems in order. I'd say that's it, I'm afraid.'

Effie lowered herself unsteadily onto the settee opposite Harry. Her head spun and her legs suddenly seemed unable to support her. His words were so final. Surely that couldn't be the end of it.

'There must be more we can do,' she pleaded. 'Who are the people he has gone to? Can't we explain to them what has happened? If they're good people, they'll be bound to do the right thing and hand him back.'

Harry briefly rubbed his stubbly chin, contemplated his boots for a few seconds, then looked up at her and slowly shook his head. 'I'm afraid that's not going to be possible in this case.'

'Why ever not?' Effie had seized on this strategy as their last hope. Relying on the goodness of good people.

'Well, here's the thing. The new parents are not shown on the paperwork. It's marked as confidential. In fact, the whole file is confidential. Nothing to see.'

'What? How can that be? How do we know they're suitable? He could have gone anywhere.'

'Yes, it's a bit unusual, especially for a child so young. But it does happen sometimes, in particular cases. For example, if the parents are well-known, you know, in the public eye, they may wish to keep the adoption secret. But they would have been vetted, most certainly. And the whole business would have been approved by the honorary physician. It's just that the detail has been made confidential, so there really is nothing more we can do, I'm afraid. I know you think there's been a misunderstanding, but it's very unlikely we can show cause to overturn the process. Particularly given Mary's circumstances.'

Effie sat silently, at a loss as to what she could say. She was overwhelmed with a mixture of desolation and anger at the terrible injustice of it all, that poor Mary was being denied the one thing that made her life worthwhile. But Effie was also angry at herself, and at the small voice within her that told her this might be the best thing for both Mary and Alfie in the long run – letting Mary get back to making a living, and giving Alfie a decent future and a stable, loving family. She wanted to blame Harry Holloway for planting these thoughts within her, even as she suspected he was probably just being practical.

She was about to pour forth her invective at his heartlessness, but instead found herself suddenly bursting into tears. She sat there sobbing, trying to compose herself. For the first time, Harry's relaxed manner left him entirely. He looked about the room distractedly, anywhere but at her. But then, seeing that her distress was not abating, he leaned towards her and extracted a large handkerchief from his pocket.

Effie took the offering and dabbed her eyes. Then, noticing that the handkerchief had obviously been in use for some time, she quickly handed it back with a mumbled thank you. Harry stuffed it back into his pocket.

'I know it's tough,' he said quietly, 'but it's a sad fact of life, I'm afraid. And you must appreciate that I'm required to act according to the law.'

Effie tried to smile but could not, instead just nodding acknowledgement and acceptance of his words.

'I promise you,' he continued, earnestly now. 'If anything new crops up, particularly with regards to Rhonda Wilson, then I'll be onto it quick smart.'

Effie sighed. 'Thank you, but I suppose it's all quite hopeless. I was foolish to think anything else.'

'No no', he insisted. 'Not at all.' He opened his mouth as if to continue, but thought better of it. Instead he rose to take his leave.

Effie was now in control of her feelings. In fact, she was sufficiently recovered to realise that she must look a bit of a fright, and began making some futile efforts to wipe away any remaining tears with the sleeve of her shirt. Not that Harry was noticing her state, he now seemed intent on leaving as quickly as possible, heading towards the hall to retrieve his hat and coat. Effie stood too, and started to follow him. But Harry stopped abruptly and stood stock-still by the door, gesturing back over his shoulder at her to be silent. Then quickly he strode from the room and turned towards the stairs.

'Hello there, Rhonda, I thought that was you. Come on down for a chat.'

Effie emerged from the room to find Mrs Wilson making her way down the stairs, somewhat reluctantly, from the first floor landing. She had obviously been eavesdropping on their conversation.

'Good day to you, Sergeant,' she muttered sheepishly as she joined them in the hall.

'All very formal today, Rhonda,' Harry said cheerfully. 'It's Harry, usually.'

Mrs Wilson smiled nervously.

'I see you've been doing your bit for the poor and underprivileged again, Rhonda. All by the book, I hope?'

'Oh yes, Sir, that's right, I always do things right and proper. All by the book, like you say. You know me, Sir, I takes them in when I can, I like to do my bit to help the little tykes.'

'Rhonda, you're a shining example to all of us.' The irony in Harry's voice was clear to Effie, but appeared to be lost on Mrs Wilson. She beamed at this compliment.

Harry continued, 'But just make sure you stick to the straight and narrow, Rhonda. We don't want to see history repeat itself, do we?'

Mrs Wilson was obsequiousness itself. 'Of course not, Sir. Them was just honest mistakes, you know. It won't happen again, Sir, you can count on it.'

'I certainly will be counting on it,' Harry said casually. 'I'll say farewell then, ladies.' And taking his hat from the hall stand, he placed it on his head, tipped it in Mrs Wilson's direction, smiled crookedly at Effie, then bowled out the door.

Mrs Wilson gathered herself up importantly and turned on Effie. The obsequious smile had disappeared.

'That's that, then,' she said, a hard edge back in her voice. 'Now you'd better forget about making any more trouble, my girl. You can see I've got the law on my side. Any more nonsense from you, young lady, and you'll be out on your ear.'

But if Mrs Wilson thought Effie would be easily cowed, she was sadly mistaken. Anger and outrage surged again within her and she turned on the landlady.

'How dare you speak to me like that! I was simply trying to help a poor girl in trouble, and I can tell you I would do it again in the same circumstances. So don't you try to bully me.'

Mrs Wilson paused, startled by Effie's unexpected response. When she spoke again her tone had turned from aggressive to mocking. 'Well, your interfering certainly got you nowhere, didn't it? You and your fancy man. You picked the wrong side there, didn't you?'

Effie stared at her, furious, but at a loss for words. She couldn't let this woman get away with it. But there was nothing she could do. Harry had more or less said so.

Then it came to her. There was somewhere else they could go. She remembered Michael mentioning the lady from the children's cruelty society, or whatever it was called. And what was her name? That's right, Mrs Baxter. Mrs Baxter from Kew. That was the lady.

'We'll see about that,' she retorted firmly. 'We haven't quite finished yet.'

'Oh, really?' Mrs Wilson gloated. 'Can't you see the law's on my side? So that's the end of the business.'

'Not quite,' Effie said defiantly. 'We have an appointment tomorrow morning with Mrs Baxter. From the Children's Society. She's an old friend of Michael's. And she's told him to talk to her if we have any concerns at all about things like this.' Effie piled one lie on top of the other, but all in a good cause, she reassured herself. And anyway, she thought, by tomorrow morning, when Michael has arranged an appointment, it will be the truth.

Effie had hoped that mentioning Mrs Baxter would take the smug smile from Mrs Wilson's face. But she did not expect that it would be quite so effective in doing so. Mrs Wilson paled noticeably and stared at Effie in alarm. For a moment she seemed at a loss for words.

'Don't be foolish, girlie,' she said eventually. 'Sergeant Holloway has already said there's nothing more to be done. You'd be sensible to leave it at that, and forget all about it.'

But hope was flooding back into Effie. Mrs Wilson's reaction had encouraged her to believe that Mrs Baxter and her association might be prepared to support their cause.

'Well, we'll see what Mrs Baxter has to say,' she said. 'I think she might be interested to hear about the wrong that has been done to Mary.'

Mrs Wilson stared at her angrily, but behind the anger Effie thought she saw nervousness. And perhaps a trace of fear.

Mary and Alfie, we're still fighting for you, Effie thought, as she pushed past Mrs Wilson and climbed the stairs, leaving the landlady scowling back up at her.

She made her way to her room. There was no time to lose: she would need to catch the next tram to Michael's place, and trust that he would be home. Hopefully he would be there, keeping a close eye on Mary. At least she could now give the poor girl a sliver of hope, that something could be done after all.

CHAPTER FOUR

MICHAEL HAD RAISED HIS EYEBROWS when Effie turned up on his doorstep and confessed that she had unilaterally committed them to seeking Mrs Baxter's support. But Effie's embarrassment, and her now growing misgivings that such an approach had at best a forlorn chance of success, were dissipated by Michael's positive response.

'Great minds think alike, Effie. I was actually going to suggest the same thing. It's clear that the police are unwilling to do any more, and we must show poor Mary that we are doing everything possible.' He went on to explain that Mary was becoming more and more distraught and desperate, and he had real fears that she might do something foolish if they could not find Alfie soon.

Effie did not ask what he meant by this dire conjecture; she did not dare think on it. Instead she urged Michael to make sure Mary knew they were doing their best to explore every avenue, and that they would do their utmost to get Alfie back.

'Even better,' Michael said. 'Why don't you have a chat with her right now? I know she's taken a shine to you, she's more likely to be swayed by you than me, I think.'

So together they went next door where Mary was lodged. When she answered their knock, Effie was shocked by her appearance. She had become even more haggard and drawn, her eyes black circles, her hair lank and unkempt. And the panic had not left her; her eyes darted wildly about as she scanned their faces anxiously for any sign of hope. Impulsively Effie hugged her warmly. She felt the thin body press against her in return, but feebly, as if her strength had quite gone.

Effie had no idea what Michael had said to Mary about Harry's bleak prognosis, but she had to find a way to keep the poor girl's hopes alive without misleading her. She settled on honesty as the best way forward. The police had indicated that getting Alfie back would be difficult, she explained, but it was important to understand that by all accounts he was being well cared for. And they had an excellent contact, a woman with first-class credentials from the Society for the Prevention of Cruelty to Children, who might be able to help where the police could not. Effie hoped that this was not gilding the lily; she did not want to get Mary's hopes up if there was no chance of success. And she still suspected their chances were remote.

But Mary brightened visibly at this news, and Effie could see that a small germ of hope had lodged within her again. At least this might help quieten the helpless panic and fear that seemed to have possessed her. Effie took her hand again and squeezed it.

'Now dear, you must promise that you will stay here at these lodgings and be patient. I know it's hard, but there is really nothing to be gained by trying to find Alfie by yourself. And you must not despair; there is still hope for you. We have not exhausted all avenues, by any means.'

Mary nodded in timid assent and Effie felt reassured. But she also felt the weight of responsibility that now rested on her and Michael, and hoped that her own misgivings about their prospects, were not evident to Mary.

So she and Michael set off, trusting to luck that Mrs Baxter would be home and would not mind them turning up, uninvited, to seek her assistance, They walked the short distance from Wattle Street to Malvern Road, where they were able to quickly hail a cab to take them to Kew. Michael had Mrs Baxter's address, in Church Street at number thirty-seven. As they approached, they saw that it was not as grand as many of its neighbours, but was a sizeable brick villa nevertheless, ornately decorated and set in a large, leafy garden.

They walked together up the wide stone drive, where a couple of gardeners were busy pruning a row of rose bushes. One of these men paused in his labours as they approached, turning and straightening his tall frame as if to relieve the strain of hours of hunched work. He said nothing, just nodding briefly and pointing silently in the direction of a small portico at the front of the house, then turned back to resume his pruning.

'Friendly fellow!' Effie whispered to Michael as they followed his direction. Michael just smiled. 'Not paid to talk, I suppose,' he observed, as they approached the front door.

Michael's efforts on the bell pull were quickly rewarded by the sound of footsteps approaching on the other side of the door. A rather stiff old fellow, obviously a manservant, answered the door and Michael introduced himself, explaining that he hoped to see Mrs Baxter who was an old family friend. 'So sorry to turn up out of the blue like this,' he went on, 'but we have a rather urgent matter to discuss with her.'

The man-servant eyed them both up and down in what Effie felt was a rather condescending manner, then speaking with what seemed to Effie's unpractised ear to be a French accent, he invited them into an elegantly furnished drawing room while he went to inquire as to whether Madame Baxter was able to see them.

They waited while his footsteps receded down the long central corridor, then the faint sounds of conversation in the distance, before the sound of someone returning briskly. Effie expected to see the manservant appear to inform them that his mistress was not available. But it was a woman who swept into the room to greet them, and Effie knew immediately that it was Mrs Baxter.

What was it about Judith Baxter that so completely and so immediately captured Effie? Later, on the drive home, Effie asked herself that very question, but could not settle on a clear answer.

Perhaps it was a combination of influences. Her physical presence, certainly, was arresting –statuesque, with a figure that might have been considered in others perhaps too generous, but in her was enhanced by the easy grace and lightness of her bearing. Although she must be well into her forties, she was still an undeniable beauty, with high cheekbones, wide eyes and a clear, creamy complexion – features that seemed to defy the passage of time. Her deep auburn hair was now faintly flecked with grey but this only seemed to add to the overall impression of timeless beauty.

Immediately captivating too was Judith Baxter's aura of calm confidence, as she came forward to greet them. Effie had a distinct and powerful impression that here was a woman who was used to being in control of her life, and to commanding the allegiance of those within her orbit. Yet her manner was not at all overbearing or imperious. Indeed, as she shook Effie's hand, and as they engaged in the usual introductory pleasantries, Effie had an almost alarming sense of intimacy, as if this woman's direct gaze and welcoming smile were reserved for her alone, and were engaging with her at a deeply personal level.

The initial effect of Judith Baxter's fascinating presence was to render Effie flustered and awkward. She was eager to make a good impression, but was at a loss for words. Michael, though, appeared to have no such inhibitions. On the contrary, he and Judith quickly fell into animated conversation – firstly about family matters, then seamlessly onto artistic topics, for it transpired that Judith was as enthusiastic as he in that regard.

As Effie watched them chatting away, again she could not help but feel separate from Michael's world, as though their vastly different backgrounds had placed an impenetrable barrier between them. Then she chided herself for being so silly and self-pitying. It was she, not he, who was placing the barrier between them. She forced herself to smile brightly, telling herself to buck up and just enjoy the company of these two charming people.

Michael was now inquiring as to what had brought Judith back to Melbourne. He had heard she had been living on the continent for some time. Effie thought this rather audacious of Michael, but Judith seemed not to consider such questions into her private life impertinent, on the contrary appearing to welcome his interest. She smiled and said that she had loved her life in France, and had not really expected ever to return to Australia. Then her smile faded as she explained that the sudden death of her husband from a heart attack had changed everything. All the things that had previously enchanted her about life on the continent now only served to remind her of the life she had lost, and especially of the wonderful man who had meant everything to her.

Michael quickly apologised for raising these obviously painful memories, it was unthinking and stupid of him.

'No', Judith said, placing a sympathetic hand on his arm, 'you were not to know, and my fond memories of Charles are not something I seek to avoid. I love to talk with friends about those happy times.'

'And how do you find Melbourne?' Effie offered. 'It must seem terribly staid and boring after the life you were living abroad.'

Judith chuckled at this suggestion, but in a nice way, and the warmth in her gaze reassured Effie that she did not think it a silly question. 'Quite the contrary. Melbourne is every bit as marvellous as my friends had promised. Though I have not been out and about quite as much as I would have liked. I find that my charity work takes up much of my time.'

'I understand that you are heavily involved in protecting the interests of neglected and abandoned babies,' Michael said, 'The Victorian Society for something or other?'

Judith laughed, a pleasant tinkling sound that seemed to resonate through the room. 'It's the Victorian Society for the Prevention of Cruelty to Children, the VSPCC. Quite a mouthful, isn't it? It's more than just saving babies though. Our responsibility is also to provide support to those women who are struggling to care for their babies. Quite often through no fault of their own. Melbourne is not quite so marvellous for many young women, I can assure you.'

'We have personal and recent experience of that sad truth,' Michael said. 'In fact, that's why we have come to see you. Does your work involve you at all with the Victorian Infant Asylum? In Berry Street?'

'Of course,' Judith said. 'How could it not? The asylum plays a very important role in supporting women and babies in need. It's a wonderful institution. I am proud to say that I'm on its committee of management. And our society supports it in whatever ways we can. Mainly through promoting its good work to the government. Though it remains underfunded, I regret to say.'

'I understand the VIA also plays a role in facilitating adoptions,' Michael said.

'Yes, it does. But only as a last resort, you understand. When it's clear that abandoned babies have no other prospects. As I have explained, our resources are limited and there is a considerable demand for our services.'

'Of course,' Michael agreed. 'But we have come upon a circumstance where perhaps that course of action may have been followed too hastily. Let me explain.' And he went on to recount Mary's story and the terrible situation she now found herself in, as well as their interaction with the police and the dead-end they had encountered there. Judith listened silently to Michael's account, occasionally nodding sympathetically, as if in recognition of a familiar story.

'The real difficulty we now face is that we do not know where Alfie has been sent or who his adoptive parents are,' Michael concluded. 'I must say, it does seem to me rather peculiar that such information is kept secret. It's as though the little fellow has just vanished from the face of the Earth.'

'Sergeant Holloway was right,' Judith observed. 'Such confidentiality provisions, though quite rare, are sometimes put in place. It does seem less than ideal, I grant you, though there is a good reason. Regrettably there remains in our society a stigma attached to the children of unmarried mothers. I don't necessarily defend those who do not wish to publicly acknowledge the background of their adopted child, whether from shame, or fear that such information could be used against them. But I can assure you that in every other respect, such people invariably provide a nurturing and supportive home for the abandoned child.'

'But in this case the child has not been abandoned!' Effie blurted out, more loudly than she had intended. 'A terrible mistake has been made.'

'Yes, it would seem so.' Judith's concerned expression told Effie that rectifying the mistake would not be an easy task.

Judith walked to the window and gazed outside, at the expanse of green lawn and the gardeners, still at work on their roses. Then she turned to them again. 'You're right, it is a tragic circumstance, and one that we must hasten to correct, if at all possible. But I must be honest with you and confess that I agree with Sergeant Holloway. It will not be a simple matter to redress this mistake. I'm afraid the legal situation is not in our favour. The adoption papers have been signed.'

'Is there nothing that can be done?' Effie could not hide the frustration and despair in her voice.

'Don't worry,' Judith said, coming forward to take Effie's hand in hers, and giving it a comforting pat. 'There may be another path available to us. Although the confidentiality provisions for the adoptive parents are very strict, my position may allow me to get access to that information. I would not be permitted to reveal it to you, but if I can find out their identity, I would be prepared to approach Alfie's new parents and recount to them what has happened. And call on their good will to return Alfie to his mother.'

'Oh, would you?' Effie could not help but feel confident that, if anyone could, this strong, capable woman might be able to reunite Alfie and Mary.

'But I must remind you,' Judith added, and her tone was sober, 'I cannot compel them to return him. It would be entirely up to their good graces. Bear in mind that they'll be excited and happy about getting their new baby. And they will already have formed a strong bond with the little boy.'

'We understand that,' Michael reassured her. 'And we trust you to do your best.'

Judith gazed at them steadily, as if weighing something up in her mind. 'Now, please don't take this the wrong way, but are you sure that your friend Mary is capable of caring for her son? I am not questioning her character, but I need to know that if we take Alfie from what most certainly would be an excellent upbringing, we will not be delivering him into an uncertain future, and possible abandonment.'

Effie was about to exclaim her complete confidence in Mary's commitment, but was stopped by Michael's hand on hers. His response was more measured. 'Mrs Baxter, I cannot give you that guarantee. Mary is young, and her future is fraught and uncertain. But if I am any judge of character, I can guarantee you this. She truly loves Alfie, and she is desperate to get him back. Indeed I am worried that she is so desperate that she may do something foolish unless we can return Alfie to her soon. And if we can do that, I know she would do all she could to care for him and keep him safe. The rest is in God's hands.'

Judith Baxter smiled at them as she took Michael's proffered calling card. 'That is good enough for me. I will do what I can for you, and for Mary and her son. Leave it with me. I hope to bring you good news very soon.'

CHAPTER FIVE

✦✳✦

AS SHE WALKED PAST with the dinner plates, Daisy raised her eyebrows at Effie. The roll of her eyes and the glance back up the stairs told Effie that Mrs Wilson was in another of her moods. Effie smiled to herself, secretly heartened that their efforts were having an impact on Mrs Wilson's smugness. That could only mean that they were heading in the right direction, and the visit to Mrs Baxter had been a sensible move.

She had resolved not to gloat, or antagonise Mrs Wilson further, but instead maintain a dignified silence about their progress. But when her landlady did make an appearance in the dining room, her scowl confirming Daisy's warning, Effie could not help herself.

'I hope you've given up on that silly business with the young feller,' Mrs Wilson growled, intending to be sotto voce, but still loud enough for Mr Harris to glance up from his paper at the other table. 'I told you it was all fine and dandy. You should take notice of the law. If they're not interested, you shouldn't be either.'

Effie's hackles rose immediately. 'Well, we are interested, and we'll stay interested, thank you very much, as long as there's some hope of getting Alfie back with his rightful mother. And I'm happy to say we're making good progress.'

'What do you mean?' Mrs Wilson said quickly, and again there was a hint of alarm in her voice.

'I mean that Mrs Baxter is taking up the matter on our behalf, and we expect a successful result.' Effie could not help but embellish their prospects, anything to get under the skin of this woman.

It was clear her words had the desired effect, more than she could have hoped. Mrs Wilson stared hard at her, whether in alarm or disbelief it was difficult to tell.

'You stupid girl!' she spat out loudly, and with no attempt to conceal her anger. Her face was white with rage. She turned and stormed out of the room. At the next table, Mr Harris sniggered and winked in Effie's direction.

'Well done, lassie, that's got her going. I've never seen her so worked up. With a bit of luck she'll have a turn and keel over.'

Effie did not want to encourage this unlikely ally, and fixed him with what she hoped was a withering stare. Mr Harris laughed again. 'I told you she was up to no good,' he sneered. 'Gawd knows what she's done with that brat, but one thing's for sure, I'll bet it wasn't all aboveboard.' And he chuckled to himself again, and went back to his paper.

Effie felt anxiety envelop her again. What did he mean? What did he know? Were his words just malicious gossip, as Michael had suggested, or did he really know that Mrs Wilson was up to no good? Effie resisted the urge to question Mr Harris further, she knew it would do no good. Instead, now thoroughly rattled, she rose from the table and climbed the stairs to her room. She wished, more than anything, that Michael was here to reassure her. She realised that she was beginning to rely on his strength and calm confidence more and more.

Again Effie slept badly, tossing and turning through the night, and trying to get the awful possibilities of Alfie's fate out of her mind. She kept telling herself she was being irrational, but it did not seem to help.

Early in the morning, just as she had slipped back into a fitful sleep, she was awakened again by the unmistakable sound of the front door slamming.

Effie rose from her bed and peeped through the slit of her bedroom curtains. This was a rare sight. Seven in the morning, the sun barely up, and there was Mrs Wilson hovering at her front gate, clearly in a state of some agitation. One moment pacing up and down the path, the next hurrying out into the street and peering both ways along St Kilda Road. She was clearly expecting someone, and her anxiety seemed to be heightening with every passing minute. She was scarcely recognisable as her usual self. Her hair was awry and she had not yet dressed for the day. She was clad in what seemed to be a tatty old dressing gown.

My goodness, Effie thought. What is going on? Her previous satisfaction at getting under the skin of the old girl was now wholly replaced by apprehension. This was definitely not the behaviour of a woman who had done the right thing, and handed an abandoned baby in to the proper authorities for adoption. That scenario, while distressing in its own right, at least meant that Alfie was in safe hands, and was being cared for by a good family who wanted him. But if that was the case, why on earth was Mrs Wilson carrying on like this? Perhaps Alfie was not being cared for by a new loving family, perhaps something far more sinister had happened to him. Effie shuddered, the irrational thoughts she had struggled with all night surged again, and a clammy chill came over her as she imagined the possibilities.

Peering through the window, Effie noticed that Mrs Wilson's attention was now focused on somebody approaching – she was leaning out into the street waving vigorously. The next moment, a lad, a messenger boy, appeared at the front gate, leaping off his bicycle with a mock show of urgency, and doffing his cap to Mrs Wilson in an extravagant manner. Mrs Wilson wagged her finger at him, and even at this distance Effie could faintly hear her angry, raised voice. Thrusting some sort of envelope into his hands, she could be seen gesturing to him, probably instructions on where to deliver it, Effie thought. Next moment the lad was on his bike and off, expertly avoiding Mrs Wilson's clumsy swipe at his head, delivered no doubt in response to a departing witticism. Mrs Wilson turned and hurried back inside, and from her vantage point Effie could clearly see the worried expression on her face.

This time at breakfast, Effie was determined that she would not engage with Mrs Wilson in any way. She feared that her unwise words of the previous evening had somehow inflamed the situation. But the opportunity to test her resolve did not arise; Mrs Wilson did not appear at breakfast, and Daisy could shed no light on her whereabouts.

As the morning proceeded, Effie returned to her room and tried to tackle her school work, but could not settle to it. A part of her was also half expecting, or hoping, that Michael would visit, with news perhaps from Mrs Baxter. But that did not happen either.

The morning dragged on, and Effie sat in her room, having now abandoned any attempt to prepare for school, and resorting instead to Miss Austen's *Pride and Prejudice*. But again she was not able to engage with it. She found her thoughts continually wandering, and the words on the page somehow refused to enter her head.

At around half past eleven, a sudden rat-a-tat-tat sounded at the front door below, loud enough to attract the attention of the whole house. That must be Michael, Effie thought, dashing from her room towards the stairs, and almost colliding with Mrs Wilson hurrying from her rooms at the same time.

'That's for me,' Mrs Wilson muttered, as she barged past Effie and thumped down the stairs. Lingering on the landing, Effie suddenly realised that of course it must be the messenger boy; Michael would never knock like that.

She heard Mrs Wilson opening the door and then, distinctly, her urgent words: 'Well, what have you got for me? Come on, quickly, none of your cheek, give it to me.' And then the laughing reply of the boy.

'Hey, steady on, Missus, or I'll be thinking you've got a fancy man or sumpthink. What is that, a billy doo, is it?' And another cheeky laugh.

'Get out of here, you brat! And keep your trap shut. Here's your penny, and think yourself lucky you're getting anything, you little devil.'

'Pleased to be of service, Madam. Oh revoyer to you then.' And another laugh as he headed off.

Effie shrank back as she heard Mrs Wilson's heavy tread approaching the stairs again. On tiptoe she scurried as quickly as possible back to her room, closing the door quietly behind her, before Mrs Wilson appeared. She hoped she had not been seen snooping.

Effie sat on her bed and tried to think. Her heart was racing. She closed her eyes and forced herself to breathe steadily. What did all this mean? She was convinced that Mrs Wilson's odd behaviour this morning was a result of their conversation last night, and of the alarm that she had shown then. But why should Mrs Wilson be alarmed? Harry Holloway had said that the adoption was all done properly, so what did Mrs Wilson have to fear?

Effie could not understand it, but everything about Mrs Wilson's behaviour told her that something was wrong. Who was she exchanging notes with? Could it be with the new parents? The more she thought about it, the more it seemed the only possible explanation. Mrs Wilson was warning them that Alfie's mother had returned and was trying to get him back. And who knows what sort of lies she would peddle about Mary? No doubt she would be seeking to blacken her character as much as possible. But again, what would be her motive in doing so? Somehow or other, thought Effie, there is money involved in this. She suspected that profit was Mrs Wilson's primary consideration in all her child-fostering activities. Again she felt a surge of anxiety for Alfie, knowing that his fate was being decided by greed rather than love and compassion.

On the other side of her bedroom door came the sound of heavy footsteps again, unmistakably those of Mrs Wilson, and the rapid footfall indicated an uncharacteristic urgency to her movement as she clumped down the stairs. Effie sprang to her feet and hurried to the window. Sure enough, within seconds she heard the front door slam and Mrs Wilson appeared on the garden path, rugged up against the weather and striding purposefully towards the front gate. Effie did not hesitate. Pausing only to snatch her coat and hat, she hurried from her room, skipped down the stairs two at a time, dashed out the front door and was off in hot pursuit.

Effie stood on the footpath in Barkly Street and pondered her next move. She was breathing heavily; it had been a real struggle to keep Mrs Wilson in her sights. She couldn't believe that the old girl could keep up such a pace for so long. They must have hurried a mile or more along St Kilda Road, then down Carlisle Street, and finally along Barkly until they had reached the rather tatty brick facade of the Village Belle Hotel. Mrs Wilson had hurried inside without hesitation, but Effie did not immediately follow. She stood in the concealing shelter of a shop entrance and wondered what she should do next.

Of course she was anxious to find out who Mrs Wilson was meeting, but she was also feeling a growing reticence about entering the hotel. For a start, she was not in the habit of entering such premises unescorted, and she was uncertain about whether the Village Belle was the kind of place a young woman, even an independent young woman, could safely enter alone. She had heard that a number of pubs around St Kilda were rather disreputable, and a haven for criminals and other larrikin types. And she realised that her impulsive enthusiasm to discover the identity of Mrs Wilson's correspondent, and their possible connection to Alfie, had cooled considerably during the pursuit. She'd had time to realise the difficulty of the task ahead.

Her first plan had been that somehow she would burst in on Mrs Wilson meeting with Alfie's new parents, and confront them about the true situation. They would see reason, hand him back, and that would be that. All would be well. Now she realised that there were many other possible circumstances that could explain Mrs Wilson's visit to the Village Belle. Even if she was meeting with Alfie's adopted parents, they might not be at all amenable to being accosted by Effie, and told to hand back Alfie. And there was no guarantee that Mrs Wilson was in fact meeting with them, she could be seeing anyone, and perhaps not even about Alfie. Perhaps she was not meeting with anyone at all, perhaps she had simply felt the need to visit her local pub and take a drop to steady her nerves. Clearly, she was familiar with the place, and, if her usual body odour was any indication, she was familiar with a drop of liquor as well.

Effie began to feel rather foolish, and her resolve began to falter. Perhaps she should do the sensible thing and return home. Even perhaps do some shopping in Barkly Street, to justify the long walk. She would convince herself that she had not really been following Mrs Wilson, like some amateur detective, but was simply enjoying what any young woman on holidays would enjoy – a stroll down the high street on a sunny winter's day to do some carefree shopping. She turned and began to walk back down the street, towards the haberdashers she had noticed on her way past.

But then she stopped in her tracks, again seized by the image of Alfie, and his helplessness in the face of Mrs Wilson's uncaring machinations. Damn her, that woman was not going to get away with selling the poor little fellow off to the highest bidder. Because Effie was again convinced that was what was going on. She had to expose the truth, and she had to stand up for poor Mary, who had placed so much trust in them to get her baby back. She had no idea how she would achieve that, but she knew she must at least find out what was going on at the Village Belle.

Her resolve now firmly restored, Effie walked back to the pub. She strode determinedly up to the swinging, glass entrance doors that stood on the corner of the hotel, marking the exact division between Barkly and Acland Streets. She peered briefly through before pushing them open and entering the building.

Effie found herself in what she assumed was the entrance lobby, with a polished wooden desk on one side, deserted at this time of the day. Although the Belle was only a few years built, the furnishings were already displaying something of a decaying, tawdry air, perhaps as if taking on the nature of the hotel's regular clientele. The brass electric light fittings on the walls were already tarnished, and the carpet underfoot exhibited a variety of stains, where liquids of one sort or another had been spilt or deposited. The disagreeable odour of stale beer and tobacco filled the air.

On the left-hand side of the lobby, another large opaque glass door seemed to indicate a public area of some sort. A hubbub of voices indicated that a substantial clientele was already in residence there, even at this early hour of the day. Good, Effie thought, I should not be noticed if I mingle with the crowd. That is where she is likely to be, I suppose.

Effie thought she had made her entrance as surreptitiously as possible, as she slowly opened the glass door, took a step inside, and peered around the large bar in which she found herself. But the effect of her entrance could scarcely have been more dramatic. Within seconds the clamour of exclusively male voices had died almost completely, and all eyes in the bar seemed to be turned towards her. Then a couple of raucous whistles and several invitations to 'come and have a shandy'. And several other less welcoming suggestions, that she 'bugger off, girlie'.

Effie flushed bright red, but resisted the urge to flee before she had cast her eyes round the room. Thank heavens, Mrs Wilson was nowhere to be seen. She clearly knew better than Effie not to invade the male sanctuary of the front bar.

Retreating back through the glass door, Effie stood again in the lobby and tried to compose herself. Her nerve was on the wane, and she again contemplated returning home. But ahead of her, directly opposite the entrance doors, a long passageway seemed to promise entry to other parts of the hotel. It would do no harm to wander through and have a brief, careful exploration. If anyone challenged her, she could say she was looking for a friend, and was lost.

The first door she came to seemed to promise another public room. Again the sound of voices could be heard, but this time more subdued. Perhaps this was an area available for lady patrons. If so, it could be where Mrs Wilson was. This time, Effie proceeded even more cautiously, gently swinging the glass door back towards her a little way, then peering through the gap.

She could see there were only a smallish number of people in the room, though it was difficult to detect exactly how many through the thick haze of smoke that filled the air. Effie could distinguish a round table in the centre of a largish room, and around it fifteen or twenty figures. Such was their concentration on the cards in front of them, that no one at all noticed Effie standing just beyond the door. She could see that the players seated around the table were exclusively men – no sign of Mrs Wilson.

This is silly, Effie thought. I won't find her. She's probably already left the building with whoever it is she came to meet. She was about to let the door shut, and make her way home when she noticed a movement on the far side of the room. Two people were standing there, in an alcove off to the side of the room. And despite the dim light and the smoky air, she instantly recognised the squat frame and florid features of Mrs Wilson. She was standing close to her companion, talking animatedly and gesturing. Even in the dim light, her agitation was obvious.

Mrs Wilson's companion was less visible. He had his back to the room, and was listening to Mrs Wilson, nodding his head from time to time. All Effie could discern was his obvious height, and perhaps something familiar in the hunch of his shoulders as he towered over Mrs Wilson. He appeared not to be looking at her, but stared ahead, impervious to her agitated conversation. Effie swung the glass door back almost shut again, retaining the smallest of openings through which she could watch Mrs Wilson and her companion. Surely, he will turn around soon, Effie thought.

But the tall man did not turn. Instead it was Mrs Wilson who, suddenly and inexplicably, turned and stared full in Effie's direction. Effie's heart jumped and she instinctively recoiled, leaving the door to swing fully shut. She saw me! She saw me! was all that raced through her mind as she hurried back down the passageway, through the lobby and out into the street.

In a panic, she dashed back down Barkly Street, trying not to run and draw attention to herself, but unable to resist the urge to flee as fast as she could. She expected at any moment to hear the gruff shout of Mrs Wilson, angrily challenging her. But no such cry came, and when she reached the safe shelter of the nearest shop entrance and turned in dread to see who was following, there was no one. The street was empty.

She was safe, for now at least, but had she been seen? Had some movement betrayed her presence there, lurking in the crack of the door? Or had Mrs Wilson simply been looking around to ensure she and her companion were not disturbed, and had seen nothing except a door swinging shut?

And who was the tall man? Was he Alfie's new father? Or someone associated with the infant asylum? Was he the same tall man that Daisy had seen at the boarding house? Who could tell? And yet, there was certainly something faintly familiar about him. Effie had a vague feeling that she had seem him somewhere before.

Mrs Wilson had evidently interrupted his card game, but for what purpose? To warn him? To entreat him? To threaten him? Effie had no idea. But she knew, as she hastened home, that her discovery had not allayed in any way her anxiety about Alfie and his fate. There was something in the bearing of the tall man, in the hovering stillness of him, in the impassive way he stood there, listening to Mrs Wilson's agitated conversation, that somehow indicated a coldness, a certain disdain, and told Effie that Alfie's welfare would likely be of little interest to him. She found herself hoping, with all her heart, that he was not the man who now had Alfie's future in his hands.

CHAPTER SIX

FOR TWO DAYS EFFIE WAITED for Michael to call. She so desperately wanted to tell him her news, of her visit to the Village Belle, and of her anxiety that she had been caught spying. She had been filled with trepidation that Mrs Wilson would have it out with her on that score when they next met at the boarding house. But Mrs Wilson had made no accusation, nor had her features betrayed any hint of suspicion. She was surly and distracted, but no more so than she had been for the past few days.

Effie was also desperate for news from Judith Baxter, hoping against hope that her influence could quickly be brought to bear on Alfie's adoptive parents. But by Saturday morning, there was still no sign of Michael, and no news from Mrs Baxter. Effie told herself to be patient, it was foolish to think that Mrs Baxter could move mountains overnight, and surely Michael would call on her as soon as he had news. But a part of her could not help but feel disappointment, and worry, that Michael was perhaps now tiring of what might just have been a diverting holiday adventure.

She had made up her mind to give up on him, and pay a visit to Lydia. That would be guaranteed to lift her spirits. Then late on Saturday morning, just as she had finished dressing to go out, the doorbell rang. Racing to the window, Effie saw Michael below, pacing up and down the garden path. Dashing down the stairs two at a time, she managed to get to the door just as Daisy appeared from the kitchen.

'Goodness me, Miss, you're in a terrible hurry,' Daisy grinned. 'No need to guess who that is.'

Effie managed a brief smile in return as she dashed past. She flung open the door, and was about ask Michael if there was good news. But he spoke first, and the alarm in his voice evaporated her smile immediately.

'Have you seen Mary?' he asked. 'Has she visited you today?'

For a moment Effie was confused. 'Of course not. What is the matter? Has she gone missing?'

Michael stared at her grimly. 'It seems so. She wasn't at the apartment when I called on her this morning.'

Effie was still trying to make sense of his words. 'How can that be? When did she disappear? Perhaps she's just gone out for a walk this morning? When did you last see her?'

'Yesterday afternoon,' Michael said. 'So I don't really know when she left. But I fear the worst. That she may have gone off to try and find Alfie.'

'But where would she go? None of us knows where Alfie has been taken. She would not have the first idea where to search.'

'That is true,' Michael replied. 'But she's had it in her head for some while to go to the asylum, and to plead her case there to the authorities who have approved the adoption. She knows the address; Alfie was born there. I would imagine she could easily find her way to Berry Street.'

'Yes, yes, you're right!' Effie cried. 'That is where she has gone. But she must have left this morning, surely? She would have had nowhere to stay if she went last night.'

'I hope you're right,' Michael said. 'But she was in a bad state yesterday, and I wasn't at home last night. I was called away on business. So she may have taken matters into her own hands then. If she had called at the asylum, I'm sure they would have taken her in and put her up for the night, even if they could not reunite her with Alfie. They are very fine people there.'

'We must hurry,' Effie cried. 'She may still be there.'

Michael's hansom cab was still drawn up outside, and so he and Effie were quickly on their way, along St Kilda Road, then onto Punt Road heading towards Yarra Park. As they hurried along, Effie told Michael about everything that had happened since they last met. When she recounted her visit to the Village Belle, his expression became stern.

'Effie, that was not a sensible thing to do. Apart from the fact that the Village Belle has an unsavoury reputation, you may well have been putting yourself in danger by following Mrs Wilson like that. Particularly, if they had seen you.'

Effie felt like a child being scolded, but she was also gladdened by Michael's concern for her. 'I know, it was foolish, but it was a spur of the moment decision. I had no time to think. And anyway, I'm quite sure they did not see me.' Trying to sound more confident than she actually was.

Michael's tone softened. 'You were very brave. But we must be careful. Probably Harry Holloway is right and everything is aboveboard, but your landlady is acting rather strangely, and I have no doubt she has been on the wrong side of the law in the past, one way or another. So promise me you won't indulge in any more heroics. Without me there, at least.'

Effie smiled her assent, and changed the subject. 'You haven't heard from Mrs Baxter yet? I had hoped she might have made some progress by now.'

'No, nothing. But we must be patient, it's early days. I trust her to do the very best she can for us. And I know she carries a lot of weight with the authorities. If anyone can help, it will be her.'

They were now jogging along with the sweeping expanses of Yarra Park on their left, and soon their driver reefed in his horse and turned them into Vale Road. Then a short trot down the road and into Berry Street, and there, on their left, stood the asylum. Its key feature was a grand, white-stone, two-storey building, set back from the road in a pretty, well-tended garden. Then, next to the main building and closer to the road, were two smaller buildings, quite long and one behind the other. They appeared to be barracks of some sort.

All in all, the asylum presented a welcoming picture in the bright winter sunshine. But still, Effie thought, how difficult and frightening it must be for young women to come here in their time of distress. So far from family and friends, and all that was familiar to them. And she thought of Mary, perhaps standing in this very spot only hours earlier, working up the courage to go through the gates in search of her son. I hope it is just as congenial once we get inside, Effie thought, as she and Michael approached the front door of the main building.

And indeed it was. A woman in a nurse's uniform greeted them with a cheery smile, and showed them into a clean, brightly lit reception room, before hastening off to find the matron.

Shortly, a surprisingly young woman entered the room and introduced herself as Matron Denise Jackson. She was a plump, rosy-cheeked woman with auburn hair and freckles, all bustling efficiency as she greeted them cordially.

'What a very pleasant place you have here, Matron,' Michael said, being polite and not wanting to get to the point too abruptly. 'It's a great credit to you.'

The Matron laughed heartily, an uninhibited laugh that further enhanced Effie's initial good opinion of her. 'Well, Mr Standish, I am more than happy to take the credit if you wish to dispense it. But it would be under false pretences, I'm afraid. If we have achieved anything here, it is a credit to many people. But mainly the girls themselves, actually. They do all of the hard work, cooking, cleaning, doing the laundry. And in the main, they look after the older children too. As well as their own little ones, of course.'

'I'm sure you are too modest, Matron,' Effie said. 'You can accept at least some of the credit.'

'Well, we do as well as we can, I suppose. Given that we are always overcrowded and cannot keep up with the demand for our services. And we are not immune from tragedies. Too many, I'm afraid. Sickness always seems to be with us, it seems.' And her smile faded for the moment.

Then, just as quickly, her good cheer returned. 'But how am I able to help you? I'm sure you did not come here just to lavish compliments on me.'

Now it was Michael's turn to become serious, as he explained Mary's predicament and her disappearance. 'We think it is possible she has come here searching for her son,' he concluded. 'Either this morning, or even yesterday, perhaps. Have you seen her?'

As Michael related Mary's sad circumstances, Denise Jackson listened attentively. 'To answer your last question first, no, I have not seen her,' she replied. 'And I doubt if any of my staff have either. They would certainly have told me if they had.'

Michael continued his probing. 'I know that Alfie's adoption is marked confidential, but I take it you are privy to the full details?'

Denise Jackson's calm expression did not change. 'No, I am not privy. In fact, I was not even aware that we had organised that particular adoption.'

'Are you sure?' Michael pressed on, surprise in his voice. 'That seems rather odd.'

'Not really.' She returned his gaze steadily. 'It is possible that the adoption was organised through one of our doctors, and the baby was delivered straight to his new parents.'

'Really?' said Michael. 'That's a bit unusual, isn't it?'

'It doesn't happen often, but it does occur occasionally. If I showed you through our premises for five minutes, you would understand how desperately overcrowded and busy we are. If we can send the baby straight to his new home without putting him up here, even for just a day or so, then that is of real benefit.'

Effie decided to appeal to Matron Jackson's better nature. 'Miss Jackson, I know this case is marked confidential, but there really has been a dreadful mistake. Surely on this one occasion you can make an exception, and reveal the details of the new parents. We wouldn't harass them, just explain the unfortunate circumstances that have arisen, and see if they are prepared to redress the situation. And if they did not, we would leave them in peace.'

Matron Jackson's tone now took on a steelier edge. 'I'm afraid that is not possible. The file is sealed, and that's all there is to it. I don't know the details, and I don't wish to know the details. And even if I did, I could not tell you. Confidential means confidential.'

'But surely someone must know?' Effie said, exasperation in her voice. 'Sergeant Holloway told us that the adoption papers were approved by your honorary physician. Could you at least put us in touch with that person, so that we may speak with him?'

'And what would be the purpose of that? What further assistance could he add? He is bound to secrecy too, you know.' Matron Jackson was becoming a trifle short with them, as much as her good nature would allow.

'Well, at least he could reassure us he is satisfied Alfie has gone to a good home. That would be very important for Mary.' This was not quite the truth, Effie was hoping to get far more information than that from the doctor.

'I'm sorry, but I can't help you. We have three honorary physicians and any one of them could have signed off the adoption. And I do not know which one did because, as I said, the file is sealed. And I do not propose to ask them, to find out which one it was. That would be unprofessional.'

'Could you at least tell me their names?' Effie persisted.

Matron's transformation to steely bureaucrat was now complete. 'No, I could not. And I must warn you not to interfere any further. I can assure you the proper process has been followed.'

Effie was about to speak again, but Michael cut her short. 'We understand, Matron, though I must say, it seems more importance is placed on the rights of the adopters than those of the mother. But there is clearly nothing more that can we can do. Thank you for your time.' And he extended a conciliatory hand.

Matron Jackson shook his hand briefly and quickly showed them the door. 'Please excuse me, I am very busy. I think you can find your own way out.' And she hurried off, still looking mildly annoyed.

'I don't think we made a friend there,' Michael whispered as they walked down the corridor. 'Looks like it's a complete dead-end, I'm afraid. There really is nothing more we can do.'

'Not quite,' said Effie, noticing a young nurse approaching, and stepping into her path. 'Excuse me, Miss, could you help us, please?'

'Yes, Madam. Sir.' With a shy glance at Michael. 'Are you lost?'

Effie smiled her most winning smile. 'Actually we are looking for one of your doctors. We were referred to him to discuss the possibility of an adoption. For my husband and I.' And for dramatic effect, Effie took a surprised Michael's hand and smiled at him affectionately. 'But I'm afraid I've quite forgotten the doctor's name. Could you remind me of your honorary physicians.'

'Certainly, Miss. It would either be Dr Youl, Dr Shields or Dr Wright. But I'm afraid they are not here on a weekend. Dr Wright normally comes in on a Monday though.'

Effie smiled again, and took a stab in the dark. 'I think it was Dr Wright. Would that be Dr Ed Wright, I think that is the name I remember.' And when the girl nodded confirmation, 'Thank you, you have been very helpful. We will come back on Monday to see Dr Wright. Won't we, darling?' Effie was enjoying getting into the part.

As they left the building, Michael raised one eyebrow at her. 'My goodness, Effie Davis, I never realised what an accomplished schemer you are. Though your subterfuge probably won't help us. Chances are Ed Wright knows nothing, and if he does, it's unlikely he'd be able to tell us anyway.'

'Perhaps,' Effie conceded. 'But on the other hand, you are not counting on Lydia's persuasive powers. And I suspect those powers work very well on Ed Wright.'

Michael smiled wryly. 'Perhaps, perhaps not. We shall see. But first things first, we must find Mary.'

'Where to, Sir?' inquired the driver, as they clambered back into the hansom.

'Not sure, Tom,' Michael replied, helping Effie into the cab. 'Just wait here a moment, will you.' And he settled himself in beside Effie and swung the door shut. His expression, as he turned to her, was not encouraging.

'To tell the truth, I don't know where else we can look,' he said. 'I really don't think Mary had any other place she could go.'

'It's all quite hopeless, isn't it,' Effie said quietly.

'Let's not give up, we're not done yet,' Michael reassured her. 'We're only five minutes from Russell Street. I think we should alert Harry Holloway that Mary is missing. '

Effie thought he was just trying to be positive, but at least it was something. 'Yes, I suppose we could do that. Though he'll take some convincing there's not an innocent explanation. And you are sure there isn't one, aren't you? She couldn't have visited someone? Or just gone for a long walk?"

'I very much doubt it. I checked twice this morning, and no sign of her. No, I have a bad feeling about it. I think we should alert the police as quickly as possible.' And opening the trap door, he directed Tom to Russell Street, and as quick as he could.

And so they set off – a quick dash down Wellington Parade and Flinders Street, to the Russell Street Police Station.

'Do you think Ed Wright does know something about Alfie?' Effie asked, as they rattled along. 'We should ask him, I suppose.'

'Maybe,' Michael replied doubtfully. 'But even if he does know, it seems he's bound to secrecy. I'm not sure it's fair to ask him to break his word.'

'I suppose you're right,' Effie agreed. 'Anyway, from the sound of it, I don't think even Lydia could persuade him to tell us anything. So much for my clever idea.' And she lapsed into gloomy silence for the remainder of their short journey.

The Russell Street Police Station was again home to a motley assortment of complainants and miscreants milling around the reception area, but again, as luck would have it, their old friend, Constable Jackson, was on the desk. Spotting them in the crowd, he grinned in recognition and waved them forward, sternly motioning away his other customers, as if they were trespassing on the counter space.

'Make way there, Madam, please, just stand aside for a moment if you don't mind, we have an emergency here. Don't worry, I'll get to you soon, but I've got important business here first.' And he winked at Michael and Effie, who were hesitating at the back of the queue, again somewhat embarrassed at this preferential treatment. But the constable continued to motion them forward encouragingly, and so they approached the desk, as inconspicuously as possible.

'We're sorry to trouble you again, but is Sergeant Holloway available?' Michael asked. 'We wish to speak with him again about the matter we previously raised.'

Constable Jackson smiled delightedly at Michael's request. 'Sir, I must inform you that Detective Sergeant Holloway is otherwise engaged at the moment. On important police business.'

Michael frowned. 'Oh, that is unfortunate. We did rather want to see him urgently.'

Constable Jackson positively chuckled as he delivered his punchline. 'And I can also inform you, Sir, that Detective Sergeant Holloway has left instructions with me. Very specific instructions, Sir. That, in the event of your presence at these premises, you are to be escorted forthwith to his place of duty, where he would be pleased to meet with you.'

'Really?' Effie exclaimed, pleasantly surprised at this considerate treatment from Harry Holloway. 'Are you sure? Is he far away?'

Constable Jackson beamed at her. 'Not far at all, Madam, just a hop, skip and a jump away, as they say. He's on duty over at the cricket ground. There's a game of football in progress, I believe.'

'Well, well,' said Michael. 'That is a coincidence. That's where we have just come from. Or somewhere close by, at any rate. Is he likely to be able to meet with us?'

'He'll be busy, Sir, no doubt about that. They're a rowdy lot, that football crowd, and it's all hands on deck to keep them under control, I can tell you. Particularly today, I understand it's something of a grudge match. Carlton versus Collingwood, I believe. But he will make time to see you, Sir, I can assure you of that.'

'That is decent of him, I must say,' said Michael. 'And it is important business we have with him, I can assure you.'

'Well, we'd better not delay, Sir, in that case,' declared Constable Jackson, turning and waving imperiously in the direction of another young constable, lounging at a desk behind him. 'Constable Milton, could you run these folk around to the cricket ground, and find Harry Holloway for them. Most important.'

The constable smiled genially at them, or perhaps more particularly at Effie, and rose to his feet. 'See you out the front in a minute or two,' he offered, and wandered off out the back, showing far less urgency than his colleague.

Ten minutes later, a horse and trap appeared from the alley running down the side of the station, and their escort, perched up next to the driver, waved cheerily to them. 'Hop aboard folks, we'll have you there in a jiffy.'

Climbing up onto the passenger seat behind Constable Milton, Effie and Michael retraced their journey back down Flinders Street, but this time they did not proceed down Wellington Parade, turning instead into Jolimont Road. As they did so Effie noticed a sporting ground on their right, where men in brightly coloured clothing could be seen dashing about, with quite a few spectators on the sideline cheering enthusiastically. She leaned forward and tapped Constable Milton on the shoulder. 'Is that where we're going?' she asked.

The policeman snorted loudly. 'Not likely, Miss. That's the East Melbourne ground, and I reckon that's just the students having bit of a kick about. We're off to see Carlton and Collingwood, Miss. Believe me, there'll be a few more there than that.'

'Oh really,' Effie said brightly. 'I'm sorry, I know nothing about football. How many is a few more?'

'We're reckoning on twenty-five thousand today. It'll be on, for sure. You'll hear them soon. In fact, you can hear them now.'

Effie listened, and realised that what she had assumed to be the rumble of trams in the distance, was in fact the sound of voices, many, many voices. As they trotted down Jolimont Road, the rumble grew steadily louder. Suddenly, it swelled into a mighty roar, and Effie could not help but give a start. 'Goodness me, what happened then?'

'Someone's scored a goal, I suppose,' came back the answer from the front. 'Either that or someone's been king hit. We'll find out soon enough.'

Michael glanced at her, and raised his eyebrows. Clearly, football was not his entertainment of choice. 'Well, this will be an experience, of a sort,' he said with a half smile. Effie rolled her eyes in agreement.

As they approached the cricket ground, the roar of the crowd continued to swell, and then they were there, outside the huge grandstand and main entrance. Effie was amazed. The noise was now deafening, and on either side of the grandstand, where a view was afforded of the playing arena, Effie could see a vast sea of faces stretching around the perimeter of the ground, extending up the slope of the spectator area right to the rear fence. And beyond as well, for many of the trees surrounding the oval seemed to be filled with people, perched on strategic branches that enabled them to see over the heads of the paying spectators inside. Effie could also see a crowd of people even further away, gathered on a hill in the park, quite some distance from the ground, but from where they could obviously also observe the goings-on inside.

Constable Milton leapt from the trap, inviting them to follow him, and strode up to the main gate where a couple of old gentlemen in white coats were lounging about, guarding a row of a dozen or more turnstiles. 'G'day, Jack,' said the constable to one of the old fellows. 'Looks like a good crowd today.'

'Chock-a-block, son, chock-a-block,' came back the proud response. 'Twenty-five thousand, three hundred and twenty-two. And that's official.'

'And they seem pretty lively too?'

'Oh yes, pretty lively. There's quite a few been turfed out already, I can tell you. But that's what you get when you play Collingwood. They love to fight over that way, that's for sure.'

'We're after Harry, actually,' the constable said. 'Seen him about at all?'

'He's out here every five minutes or so, heaving another Collingwood bludger out of the ground,' the old bloke replied. 'Wait here, son, and you're bound to catch up with him soon.'

Sure enough, a couple of minutes later Harry appeared, with not one but two unruly spectators in tow, one in each hand, and both struggling futilely in Harry's massive grip. He deposited them in the roadside, with a warning to make their way home and sober up, before greeting them cheerfully.

'What brings you two here? I didn't know you were footy fans.'

'We're not,' Effie said. 'It's Mary. She's gone missing.'

'Oh.' Harry's cheerful grin disappeared. 'And you're obviously worried.'

'We're terribly afraid something awful has happened to her.' Effie could not hide the panic in her voice.

Harry eyed her sympathetically, and paused a moment or two, pensively rubbing his chin.

'I'll tell you what we'll do,' he ventured. 'I'm on duty here and I should really get back inside. It's a close game, and some of the Collingwood mob are getting a bit excited. But why don't you come back inside with me, we'll park you both in a safe spot, and you can tell me everything that's happened since we last met. There may be something important that will give me a clue as to the whereabouts of your friend. And you can get a taste of the world's greatest game at the same time.'

Michael seemed doubtful, but Effie was not about to let the opportunity pass. She was beginning to have an inkling that perhaps Harry Holloway might be on their side after all.

'Yes, yes, good idea,' she said gratefully. 'There is quite a lot to tell.' Thinking of Mrs Wilson and the visit to the Village Belle, and the meeting with the tall man.

'Are you sure it's safe in there for Miss Davis?' said Michael hesitantly. 'It seems rather violent.'

Harry laughed. 'Don't worry, as long as you're not wearing Carlton colours, you're probably quite safe. And anyway, we'll go to the members' area, you'll be fine there. It's in the outer that most of the fun happens.'

'Don't be such a stick-in-the-mud, Michael,' said Effie, though underneath her bravado there rippled a frisson of apprehension. 'I'm sure we'll be quite safe.'

Harry winked at her. 'That's the spirit. And after you've survived a rally at Parliament House, this will be child's play. You coming in too, Willy? The Blues were in front last time I looked. The boys are playing pretty well.'

Constable Milton expressed a keen interest in going in; apparently both he and Harry were committed Carlton supporters. So it was settled that they would go down to the fence in the members' enclosure, right next to the public area, and Constable Milton would help Harry keep an eye on the crowd, while Effie and Michael recounted the full detail of recent developments.

Bidding farewell to old Jack at the gate, they made their way through the turnstiles, finding themselves at first underneath the main grandstand. Above them resonated the thunderous stamping of feet and the roar of the crowd. Harry led the way through this dimly lit, cavernous space, then up a flight of steps towards the light.

As they made their way out into the daylight, the overwhelming noise of the crowd seem to physically strike them. As they stood in the sunshine, Effie stared about her, astonished and transfixed. Behind her towered the giant grandstand, completely filled with spectators. In front of her were rows and rows of tiered seating, also filled with people, right down to a picket fence adjoining the oval. A tall, wrought iron fence on both sides of this area separated the grandstand section from the rest of the oval perimeter. Effie could see that it was 'standing room only' in that part of the ground, and not much standing room available either, by the look of it. The spectators were packed in like sardines. She assumed this was the outer where Harry was dealing with most of the trouble.

Around the entire oval, wherever she looked, people were wearing what Effie assumed were their club colours, in either black and white, or blue and white motifs. Coloured scarves, hats, rosettes, some had even painted their faces in these club colours, and were dancing about like wild dervishes, at least as much as they could in the tightly confined spaces available to them.

As Harry guided them through the crowd, Effie's attention turned to the game being played on the oval. It was difficult to make out what was going on, with a large number of men seemingly milling around at random, then running in various directions, then milling around again. But after a while, Effie discerned that there were two distinct sets of uniforms being worn.

'Which team is which?' she shouted into Harry's ear. He grinned and shouted back at her. 'The ones in blue are the Blues. Carlton, that is. Best team in the world.'

Effie noticed a slight figure, dressed in a white shirt and wearing a small black cap set at a jaunty angle, running about on the field, and seeming to direct the proceedings. He seemed like a stripling, compared with the muscular giants surrounding him.

'And who is that?' she shouted again.

'The umpire. He's the one everyone hates.'

Harry led them along a narrow aisle, next to the barrier partitioning the members' area from the outer, right down to the front fence. He and Constable Milton leapt over the picket fence and positioned themselves inside the playing arena. Effie assumed they were back on duty, on the lookout for troublemakers, though their attention seemed to be focussed more on the players on the oval. After a minute or two, Harry turned and gestured to them to come forward and stand next to him on the other side of the fence.

'Righto,' he shouted. 'All's well. Now, tell me everything you can about Mary, and why you're worried about her.'

And so Michael recounted all that he knew about Mary's disappearance. Which, Effie now realised, wasn't terribly much. In fact, it seemed a rather insubstantial reason to be here at the football, bothering Harry Holloway. But Harry did not seem to mind.

'You were right to report her disappearance,' he said encouragingly. 'But it's probably still too early to start searching for her. There could be a number of reasons why she was not about this morning. For instance, she may have gone off to see one of her friends from work. Or even gone back up country, to her folks. Let's wait and see what the next couple of days bring. Michael, do you have any indication at all that she was gone last night? For example, did you happen to see whether there was a light in her room? That sort of thing?'

'I'm afraid not,' Michael replied. 'I was out last night. With friends. Until late.'

Harry shrugged. 'Never mind, can't be helped. As I said, let's see what tomorrow brings. Now, Effie, what about you? Anything to add?'

Effie had plenty to add, launching into an account of Mrs Wilson's peculiar behaviour, and her visit to the Village Belle. Harry continued to keep his attention focused on the football match, and Effie began to wonder whether he was paying her any attention. But when she came to Mrs Wilson's meeting with the tall man, he swivelled around and interrupted her.

'That's interesting. I know that pub pretty well, and most of the regulars. Might be worth a visit, if you think you can pick him out for me.'

'I'm afraid not,' Effie said, feeling rather deflated. 'He had his back to me, and I didn't see his face at all. But you know, there was something familiar about him. Though I'm not sure what it was.' Effie felt her story had come to a somewhat flat ending. Again she felt as though they had wasted Harry Holloway's time.

But Harry remained encouraging. 'That's okay, all good information, and it might come in handy in the future. If we need it. But let's not forget, there's not necessarily any problem here. I agree that Rhonda's behaviour was a bit odd, but that could be anything. Maybe nothing to do with Mary and her baby. And that would be a good thing, wouldn't it?'

'I suppose it would,' Effie said reluctantly, realising that Harry's view was probably quite reasonable. But still that uneasiness nagged at her, as she remembered Mrs Wilson's angry features. And as well as anger, alarm or perhaps fear in her eyes.

'But I still think there's a connection,' she added, fixing him with a slightly defiant glare.

Harry just shrugged and responded casually: 'Fair enough.'

Again, Effie wondered whether he was taking their concerns seriously enough.

'Oh, we forgot to mention,' Michael intervened, 'we have been to see Judith Baxter as well. Your people recommended her. The VSP... something or other.'

'The VSPCC,' Harry replied. 'They do good work. Very good work. I haven't come across Judith Baxter yet. Don't think she's been in the job long. Back from overseas somewhere, isn't she? But I hear she's very good, right on the ball.'

'Yes, she was very good,' Effie enthused, remembering Judith, her warmth and her calm confidence. 'Very helpful. She gave us hope that she would be able to help us find Alfie.'

Up until now their conversation had been conducted at almost shouting level to combat the constant pandemonium and clamour from the crowd around them. But now the roar of the crowd suddenly grew to a deafening level. Next to them Constable Milton was jumping up and down in excitement and pumping his fist in the air. 'Armstrong's got it!' he screamed. 'Go Blues, go!'

Effie looked out onto the oval, and saw that the pack of players had dispersed and everyone's attention was now focused on a Carlton player, who had seized the ball and was sprinting at an extraordinary speed along their side of the playing field. Slim and fair-haired, this Armstrong fellow had left the pursuing pack in his wake, and Effie could see that he was making for the end of the oval, and four white poles that stood there.

Around them, and all around the ground, the crowd was at a fever pitch of excitement. Effie could hear the baying of Collingwood supporters, shouting 'Kill him!' 'Knock his block off!' and similar exhortations, while the cheering Carlton mob urged him on. Next to them, Harry Holloway had quite forgotten their meeting and was jumping up and down excitedly and shouting his head off.

From the back of the field, near the white poles, Effie saw that a Collingwood player was running directly at young Armstrong, with obvious intent to stop his flight, and who knows, perhaps intending to knock his block off, as he was being encouraged to do from all sides. As the burly Collingwood man lunged at him, Armstrong stopped abruptly, sidestepped neatly, skipped over the diving body of his opponent, and punted the ball through the white posts ahead of him.

'Goal!' shouted the Carlton supporters around them, hugging each other in wild celebration. But almost instantly their joy turned to shocked despair. They stood staring, as the umpire in the white shirt and black cap sprinted to the goal area, blowing his whistle furiously as he ran, and waving his arms about in some strange gesture. He retrieved the ball from its resting place behind the goals, ran to a spot just before the goals, blew his whistle again, pointed to the ground, and threw the ball to a Collingwood player.

At this last action, another huge roar arose from the crowd, but Effie could see that this time it was the black and white supporters who were cheering delightedly, while a loud, braying booing arose from the Carlton crowd.

'What is going on?' Effie shouted to Harry, struggling to make herself heard.

'Damn!' Harry said, thumping his fist into his other palm. 'A free kick. I think he ran too far.'

As if supporting this verdict, the man in white began to run on the spot, throwing his arms out in a pantomime of a runner, while towering over him, the Carlton players remonstrated angrily.

'Does that mean the goal doesn't count?' Effie felt an unexpected surge of disappointment that the blond sprinter's efforts had gone unrewarded.

'Fraid so,' Harry said. 'But not to worry, we've got them on the run, I reckon.'

Next moment another mighty roar arose, and for a moment, Effie wondered what this signified. Harry too, it seemed, because he looked around in some puzzlement. But the cause was soon evident, because on their left, from the public area, there appeared onto the arena a very large woman, dressed in the most extraordinary blue and white costume, and with a large pointed hat embellished with blue and white streamers. Furiously waving a large pole, sporting a blue and white flag, she was making a surprisingly rapid beeline for the umpire, who, seeing her approaching, was taking up a strategic defensive position behind some of the burlier Collingwood players.

'Bloody hell,' said Harry. 'Doris is at it again!' And he dashed off onto the ground, approaching the umpire from the other direction and aiming to arrive there before his fellow Carlton supporter. He had little trouble achieving this, mainly because the umpire spotted him coming, recognised him, and dashed towards him to seek the protective arm of the law. Harry's presence did not seem to deter the lady in blue, her sense of outrage apparently over-reaching her respect for the law. But as she arrived, Harry quickly got a firm grip on her arm, dispossessed her of her pole, and led her back in their direction. Effie could see that he was chatting to her quietly as they approached.

'Excuse us folks,' he said cheerfully, as he opened a small gate in the picket fence near them, and led his now contrite prisoner off the arena. 'Doris and I are taking a short walk out the back to calm down. Willie will escort you two through as well.'

'I'm sorry, duck,' said the offender to Harry. Effie could see that she looked quite respectable beneath her strange garb. 'I'm sorry, but I couldn't help myself. That cheating little weasel has been on their side all day. He shouldn't be allowed to get away with it.'

'Never mind, Dorrie, I forgive you,' said Harry with a grin, 'but I'm afraid the entertainment is over for you today.' And he led her though the crowd, with Carlton supporters booing him and shouting 'shame', and the Collingwood crowd shouting just as vociferously for her to be locked up. Effie and Michael followed close behind, escorted by Constable Milton.

Outside the ground, Harry released his prisoner and bade Effie and Michael farewell.

'I know you're worried about Mary,' he said reassuringly. 'And I know I've said that there may well be a simple reason for her going missing. But don't think I'm not taking this seriously. If anything else crops up that concerns you, please contact me. Anytime.'

Effie felt her spirits lifted by his words. And her hopes too, that perhaps Mary might reappear, and that her disappearance would have a perfectly innocent explanation.

Michael had promised Effie that he would call on Sunday, whether or not he had news of Mary. True to his word, he appeared on the boarding house doorstep at nine in the morning, and was shown up by Daisy. Effie greeted him expectantly as he entered the parlour. But one glance at his expression dashed her hopes. He shook his head.

'No sign of her, I'm afraid. Nothing.'

'Oh no.' Effie felt her fears flooding back. 'I'm sure something has happened to her.'

'Perhaps Harry Holloway was right. Perhaps she has fled, for some reason.' But Michael did not sound convincing.

Effie felt like crying. 'But why would she do that? Why? There's no reason. We were her only hope.'

Michael shrugged. 'Who knows? Perhaps she wasn't thinking clearly. I only hope…' He paused.

'What?' Effie said, knowing, and fearing, what he was about to say. 'What do you hope?'

'Well, it must be said,' Michael answered quietly. 'I just hope she has not done herself harm, in her desperation.'

Effie shuddered. That terrible possibility had been lurking in the back of her mind, but now came into full focus. Michael thinking it too, and now putting it into words, made it even more dreadful.

'But I do have some other news,' he added. 'No new developments, I'm afraid, but some important new information.'

Effie urged him to go on. 'Well,' Michael said, 'I was talking to a friend last night who is a lawyer, and I was explaining the problem we and Mary face. About the adoption of Alfie, I mean. And Harry's advice that there is nothing we can do."

'Yes, yes,' Effie said impatiently. 'Go on, go on.'

'The upshot of what he told me was that technically there is no legal basis for adoption. It is a de facto arrangement.'

'I don't quite understand how that helps us.'

'Well, what it means is that whoever's signature is on the adoption papers, Ed Wright's or one of the others, it's not worth the paper it's written on. In a legal sense, that is. If Mary, as Alfie's birth mother, took the matter to court, she would have the legal right to claim him back.'

Now Effie understood. 'Really? Then why didn't Harry Holloway tell us that? And why can't she just go to the police and say she wants him back?'

'The very question I put to my friend. Apparently it's not that simple. Firstly, the authorities are loath to intervene once an adoption has been signed off. It's very difficult to get anyone prepared to do so. Hence Harry's reluctance, which I assume reflects what his superiors think. Secondly, to be successful, the poor mother is required to prove that she is a fit and proper person, which is bound to be difficult, given her decision to adopt out the baby in the first place.'

'But she didn't!' Effie cried. 'It was all a mistake.'

'I know, I know,' Michael hastily reassured her. 'But that's not how it would be painted in court. Which brings me to the third problem. The only way to succeed is by taking it to court, and that's an expensive business that would be well beyond the means of most single mothers.'

Effie looked at him, momentarily hesitating, before blurting out what had come into her mind, 'Is that the kind of financial support that would be within your means? If you wished to?'

Michael smiled. 'I'm not sure I'm as much the man of means that you think. But perhaps I could find the wherewithal to assist in that way. We must be realistic though. Given all the other difficulties Mary faces, it may simply be a waste of time and money. I'm not saying it is something I wouldn't do, but let's keep it up our sleeve as a last resort. First things first, we must find the poor girl.'

Effie was searching for the words to thank him, when the doorbell indicated the arrival of a visitor. Peering through the front window, Effie saw a smartly dressed lad with an envelope in his hand. Daisy appeared on the doorstep, and the messenger boy handed her the envelope, doffing his cap to her. Next moment, there was a knock on the parlour door.

'Beg pardon, Miss. Sorry to interrupt you and your friend, but the lad said this was urgent. He's waiting outside for your response.'

Effie took the envelope addressed to her and broke open the seal. She could smell the perfume wafting from it, quite exquisite. Inside was Judith Baxter's calling card, with a written message on the back. Effie read it out aloud.

My dear Effie,
I have some news to convey about your friend, Miss Guerin, and
her child. Would you and Mr Standish be able to meet me for tea

in the Moorish Hall at the Menzies, today at 3 pm? Sincerest regards,
Judith Baxter.

Effie glanced up at Michael. 'What do you think? Could this be good news? I don't know what to think anymore.'

'I can't imagine that Mrs Baxter has any news about Mary's whereabouts,' he replied soberly. 'But perhaps she has been able to locate Alfie, and talk to his new parents. And persuade them to hand him back. Let's hope for the best.'

Sunday high tea at the Menzies was becoming quite the rage for Melbourne society, according to Michael. Apparently, thirty thousand pounds had been spent on refurbishing the hotel, including its renowned Moorish Hall and the celebrated winter garden, with its glass-domed roof. The Menzies, and the Moorish Hall in particular, were very much the places to be seen.

And the hall was indeed spectacular. The sense of refined opulence that Effie felt, as they passed through the richly hung lobby and entered the hall itself, was overwhelming. Along each side of the long room, lustrously decorated tapestries hung the full height of the walls, right up to the huge domed ceiling. Between these tapestries, magnificent archways also stretched to the ceiling, and extended out into the room, their pillars stamped with burnished copper in a range of oriental motifs. The oriental theme was completed with the magnificent deep ruby carpets, running the entire length of the hall, complemented by matching embroidered cushions adorning the plush lounges scattered along the edges of the room. In the body of the hall, were large numbers of marble, circular dining tables. The hall was filled with customers, all elegantly and expensively dressed, the cream of Melbourne society.

The fortunate ones were seated at tables, while many others waited at the entrance to be seated.

'My goodness,' Effie whispered. 'This is magnificent. I don't dare go in. I feel so shabby compared with all this.'

Michael took her arm and led her in. 'Effie Davis, we'll have none of that talk. You're the measure of any of these women, and don't you dare think otherwise.' And he gave her an encouraging smile as he shepherded her towards the maître d'.

'Would you be so kind as to direct me to Mrs Baxter's table?' he said to the haughty gentleman, standing imperiously behind his rostrum. The maître d' nodded and bowed obsequiously, all in the one movement.

'Certainly, Mr Standish. A great pleasure to see you again, Sir. Mrs Baxter is at her usual table, and has asked me to escort you to her. This way, if you please, Sir. And Madam.'

It was obvious that the maître d's personal attention was reserved for only the most distinguished of guests. The crowded seas seemed to part as he strode down the room, Michael and Effie hurrying along in his wake. Mere waiters hastily removed themselves from his path, at the same time shepherding aside those customers ignorant of his eminence. They made their way to the end of the room and were guided to a table in the far corner, underneath one of the magnificent arches. Judith Baxter rose to greet them, kissing Effie warmly on the cheek before offering her hand to Michael. She looked wonderful, simply but elegantly dressed in deep blue silk, her hair up in a way that enhanced her classical features. The burnished copper in her hair seemed a reflection of the magnificent column by which she stood.

'I'm so glad you could both come,' Judith said, inviting them to sit, and offering them tea and petit fours. These looked delicious, but Effie was in no mood to sample them. She was too anxious for any news that Judith might have.

'Let me get straight to the point,' Judith said, after a hovering waiter had poured tea. 'I have quite a bit to tell.'

'We do too,' said Michael. 'Troubling news, I'm afraid.'

'Perhaps I'd better deal with my news first,' said Judith. 'Starting perhaps with the less welcome part. Sadly, I have been unable to locate the adoptive parents of Alfie Guerin. It has not been possible to surmount the confidentiality provisions.'

'That doesn't surprise us,' Effie said ruefully. 'The whole business seems very much shrouded in secrecy. Even getting the name of the doctor who approved the adoption was impossible.'

Judith glanced sympathetically at Effie. 'Yes, the rules are strict in that regard. Even though they are warranted. I do have other, shall we say, more informal sources of information. But regrettably, in this instance these sources were also in the dark. It's a well-held secret, and it seems that it will remain so. '

'Well, thank you for your efforts,' Michael said, and was about to continue when Judith leaned forward and touched his sleeve. 'I'm sorry to interrupt, but there is also some good news. There is hope. The Neglected Children's Department, which is the government body that manages all these matters, does have an appeals process for those aggrieved in any particular adoption matter. And I am pleased to say that I sit on that appeals committee as a representative of the society. I hope you don't mind, but I have set the wheels in motion for Mary to appear before the committee. Even at this late stage, it may be possible to have the adoption overturned. As long as she is willing to put her case, that is.'

'Perhaps this is where I should give you our news,' Michael said. 'Your good work may be to no avail because Mary has gone missing.' And he went on to recount the details of Mary's disappearance.

Judith was deeply affected by Michael's disturbing news. When she spoke, there was sadness in her voice.

'All too often this happens, I'm afraid. It is so very difficult for women in her position to continue to fight. There is so much that is weighing against her. Who can blame her if she has given up?'

'We are desperate to find her,' Effie said, 'and for her to know that we are still supporting her. She will be pleased to hear of your efforts too, I'm sure.'

'I hope so,' Judith said, and again there was sadness in her voice. 'And I do hope she has returned to her home in the country, or has sought the comfort of friends. Rather than taking any...more desperate action.'

Effie gave an involuntary shudder, and felt Michael's steady hand take her trembling one. 'We are refusing to think of that possibility,' he said firmly. 'We do not believe she would do such a thing.'

Judith looked at him gravely. 'I hope with all my heart you are right,' she said evenly. 'And I am sure you are. But sadly I have seen such tragic circumstances too many times. Forgive me for even mentioning the possibility.'

'Of course, of course,' Michael said quickly. 'There's nothing to forgive. Let us change the subject. There is another option for resolving this matter that I wanted to test with you. After we have tracked down Mary, of course.' And he went on to explain the advice from his friend about the legal status of adoption, and the possibility that action in the courts could be an avenue of last resort for Mary.

'You are well informed by your friend,' Judith said when he had finished. 'Everything he has told you is correct. But he has also quite rightly informed you of the difficulties of going down that path. If you think it's been difficult for Mary up to now, I can assure you that the pressure on her would be multiplied many times if you were to take that option. That is why we prefer to rely on the processes set up by the department, to allow appeals and mediation in these sorts of circumstances. And surprisingly enough, sometimes these approaches do in fact result in mothers being reunited with their babies.'

As she sat listening to Judith Baxter's reasoned yet compassionate words, Effie again felt herself being further drawn to this remarkable woman. She seemed to exude an aura of warm confidence that made you feel that in her world, and for everything touched by her world, all would eventually be well, could not help but be so under her strong, resolute influence.

She glanced across at Michael. He too seemed at ease and reassured in Judith Baxter's presence. As she watched him in easy conversation with Judith, Effie found herself briefly wondering how close Judith's past friendship had been with Michael's family. Had he known her well as a boy? She was very beautiful now, she must have been stunning as a younger woman. She imagined the boy Michael luxuriating in the presence of this charming visitor to his home, hanging on her every glance and smile, idolising her.

Again a pang of something like jealousy ran through Effie, and again she chastised herself for her pettiness. Why did she sometimes feel such an outsider in the presence of people like Michael and Judith Baxter? Why did she sometimes feel like she could never be part of their world? She gazed around the sumptuously furnished room, at the expensively dressed men and women, lounging and chatting idly. She suddenly felt that perhaps she did not know Michael at all, did not understand what he really stood for. And this time the feeling stayed with her, even after they had bid Judith Baxter good afternoon, and had left the opulent surrounds of the Menzies. The feeling of isolation, even loneliness, persisted well after she had arrived home and found herself sitting alone in her small, spare room in Mrs Wilson's boarding house.

CHAPTER SEVEN

→✳←

MONDAY MORNING, and a cold westerly change had blown in, bringing frequent squally showers to the city. The sun, when it did appear, was pallid and fleeting, quickly giving way to the next bank of grey clouds swelling up from the south-west.

Effie stared morosely at the wintry streetscape from her bedroom window and wondered why she felt so flat. She had tried to convince herself that yesterday had gone well, all things considered. She should have confidence that between them Michael and Judith Baxter, with their connections and their influence, had as good a chance as anyone of reuniting Mary and Alfie. And yet Effie remained fearful, anxiety gnawing away at her, still possessed of a foreboding that it would not end well.

Perhaps it was just tiredness. She had not slept well, wakened frequently by dreams in which vague betrayals threatened her and menacing figures closed in.

But she knew it was more than that. Of course I should be worried, she thought as she stood at her window. Mary is missing, and until we find her there remains the possibility that something terrible has happened.

Suddenly the thought of spending the day indoors, trying to do her work while dreadful possibilities kept nagging at her, was too much to bear. She must get out and visit someone, try to get her mind off these troubling thoughts. And who better to cheer her up than her friend Lydia? Just thinking about Lydia and her eternally sunny presence was enough to start dispersing Effie's gloom. With renewed purpose, she changed for the outdoors, wrapping herself in a warm hat and coat, before braving the chilly winds outside.

As Effie made her way into St Kilda Road, preparing to walk the hundred yards or so to the tram, she noticed a police trap heading her way from the direction of the city, and in it, hunched alongside the driver, the unmistakeable lanky form of Harry Holloway. At the same time he noticed her too, pointing her out to the driver who steered the trap to the kerbside next to her.

Harry touched his hat to her as they pulled up. Effie stared at him anxiously, searching for any sign that he was bringing good news rather than bad.

'Good morning, Effie, it's a miserable day to be out and about,' he ventured. But she fancied his greeting did not have its usual cheerful ring. In fact he was decidedly solemn.

'Do you have news of Mary?' she blurted out. 'Have you found her?'

'Do you mind if we get out of this weather first? Can we go inside?'

Effie knew immediately that the news was not good. She was desperate to hear what he had to say, and quickly made her way back inside, with Harry following. She took him into the empty parlour and turned on him.

'What is your news, Harry?' she exclaimed. 'Is it Mary?'

Harry seemed to be struggling for the right words. 'There's no easy way to say this, so I will come straight out with it,' he said eventually.

His voice was carefully unemotional, but there was sympathy in his eyes. He cleared his throat. 'The body of a young woman was retrieved from the Yarra this morning, and we need to establish whether or not it is that of Mary Guerin.'

Effie felt the blood drain from her face. She suddenly felt terribly cold. 'Is there something that makes you think it could be Mary?' Her voice sounded far-off, as if she was listening to herself in a dream.

'There's nothing definite,' Harry said. 'And I must stress that it may not be Mary. There is no identification on the body, but it does match the description you gave of her. And given the location of where it was found, near Yarra Park, it makes sense that we investigate that possibility first.'

Effie felt her legs grow weak, and the room begin to sway. She felt for the chair and half-fell into it. A wave of nausea overcame her, and she leant forward, head in hands. She felt Harry's big hand on her shoulder, his arm around her.

'Try to breathe steadily,' he said quietly, as he rubbed her shoulder.

Effie raised her head, and tried to gather her strength. 'I'm all right, Harry,' she said. 'What do you need me to do?'

'I'm sorry to have put you through this,' Harry said, his concern for her now openly visible. 'I went to see Michael, but he wasn't at home. And I did want to see Rhonda Wilson as well, so I came here.'

'There is no need to apologise.' Effie felt her strength returning. 'I'm glad you informed me as soon as possible. If it is Mary, I need to know.'

'We need you or Michael to come with me to the morgue,' Harry said gently. 'To identify her, if it is Mary. If you are not up to it, we can get Michael to do it. He may have returned home by now. If not, we can easily track him down.'

'No, no,' Effie said, quite resolute now. 'We must resolve this as quickly as possible. The morgue isn't far from here, is it? I'm ready to go when you are.'

Harry had an almost quizzical expression on his face. Perhaps he thought her now calm demeanour was a facade.

'Don't worry, Harry, I really am able to do what is needed. I'm not the feeble woman you perhaps think I am.'

Harry raised an eyebrow. 'That is certainly not what I think you are, Effie. Far from it.'

'Good. Then let us go, shall we?'

'Righto,' Harry said, suddenly brisk and business-like. 'But first I must speak to Rhonda Wilson. Is she about?'

'I've scarcely seen her the past few days,' Effie replied. 'But she must be about here somewhere.'

Calling Daisy into the room, Effie asked her to go to Mrs Wilson's quarters and instruct her that Sergeant Holloway wished to see her.

'Must see her,' Harry corrected, sterner than Effie had seen him before.

Daisy hurried off and soon returned with Mrs Wilson. Effie was shocked at her appearance. She was still in her dressing-gown, and looked dishevelled and ill, her normally florid features pudgy and ashen. She seemed exhausted, as if she had not slept in days, and a strong whiff of alcohol accompanied her into the room. She stared at Harry, almost timidly, far from her usual brash self.

Harry dispensed with any pleasantries. 'Mrs Wilson, I must ask you to be available to the police for the immediate future,' he said sternly. 'That is, we require you to be at these premises, and not to travel anywhere until we advise otherwise.'

Rhonda Wilson tried to adopt a defiant posture but failed. 'Why? What's happened?' she asked meekly.

'I'm not at liberty to say.' Harry's reply betrayed nothing. 'Just don't go anywhere. Good day to you. Let's go then, shall we, Miss Davis?'

And he and Effie made for the door, leaving Mrs Wilson standing there, open-mouthed, staring dully after the departing policeman.

The police trap turned off St Kilda Road, then rattled along the Yarra Bank Road as it followed the curve of the river. Willie Milton had the reins, with Effie and Harry Holloway alongside. At Harry's insistence, Effie had rugged up well with scarf, gloves and woolly bonnet, but still the biting wind and occasional sleeting rain stung her face and chilled her to the core.

Soon the city morgue came into view on their right, grey and sombre, a long, narrow stone building running alongside the river. On their left, the marshes that stretched all the way to Punt Road were already beginning to fill up. The autumn rains had been plentiful, and the river had already burst its banks several times.

Effie had heard horror stories of the morgue, of foul stenches, and marauding rats attacking corpses, and ghoulish spectators flocking to stare in morbid fascination at the laid-out bodies. She began to wish she had not been so stoic in offering to help.

'I suppose it will be quite horrible,' she murmured.

'It won't be pleasant, and I am sorry to put you through it,' he said, and then added, as if catching on to the full import of her words, 'But it's not like it used to be in the old morgue. It's clean and sanitary, and I have secured the post mortem room where the body is laid out. It will be quite private.'

As they drove up to the building's entrance, Effie steeled herself for the ordeal ahead. The first taller, more imposing building was not the morgue, according to Harry, but the coroner's court. The morgue was the long, low building at the rear of the courthouse, and connected to it by a passageway.

Harry led her down the side of the court and to the entrance of this second building, a plain arched doorway with 'City Morgue' inscribed above it. They entered a small vestibule, and immediately the sharp stinging odour of carbolic struck Effie. She gasped involuntarily, putting her hand to her mouth, before recovering her composure. Ahead of them, a doorway led into a large room. Effie could see tables and white sheets.

Harry's arm steered her away from this entrance and towards a smaller door on their left, where a constable stood on guard. He nodded to Harry, and swung the door open, gesturing for Effie to enter.

Mary Guerin lay on a metal table in the centre of a small room, her body concealed under a white sheet, her face exposed. Her hair was still damp, clinging here and there to her pallid, greying skin. Her eyes stared unseeing upward, her mouth slightly parted. She appeared so helpless, and so young. Effie felt the tears well up, and had to turn away. A wave of dizziness struck, and she staggered. She felt Harry's strong arm around her shoulders, and she briefly leaned against him while she regained her strength. Then, forcing herself to stand upright, she turned to face him.

'Yes, that is Mary,' she said in a low voice. 'There is no doubt.'

'Thank you,' Harry said. 'I know it's hard for you.'

Effie was suddenly and unexpectedly angry at Mary for ending her pain in this way. 'How could she? How could she do this?'

'How could she drown herself, you mean?'

'Yes, and leave Alfie without a mother. She should have kept fighting.'

Harry looked at her evenly, as if weighing up something in his mind. 'I don't think she did drown herself deliberately.'

Effie stared at him. 'Do you mean it was an accident? You think she fell in?'

Harry stepped forward and lifted one side of the sheet, then took one of Mary's thin white arms in his hand. He held it out so that it was fully exposed to the light and pointed to her wrist, where a faint blue mark traced its way across the skin. 'The other one's the same,' he said matter-of-factly. 'And her ankles. She's been bound, you see.'

Effie stared at him in disbelief. She struggled to get the words out. 'You mean she was killed? Murdered?'

'I believe so. There are no other marks on her, except for some small lacerations on the inside of her mouth. Consistent with a gag, I would think. I'd say someone has gone to considerable trouble to make it look like she has done herself in.'

'Are you sure?' Again Effie could not quite believe it.

'Fairly sure. Sure enough to recommend an investigation into her death, anyway. We'll wait and see what the autopsy says. I think it will confirm my suspicions.'

Effie looked at Mary, laid out on the cold steel table, and an intense sadness overwhelmed her. She thought of the terror that Mary would have felt as she lay bound and gagged, at the mercy of her attacker. Effie shivered and pulled her coat more tightly around her. Suddenly Mrs Wilson's strange behaviour and her visit to the Village Belle took on an entirely sinister complexion. Was she organising for Mary to be killed? But why? What could poor, powerless Mary do to harm Mrs Wilson? Or anyone else for that matter?

'I'm cold,' Effie murmured. 'Can we go?'

'Of course,' Harry said, steering her towards the door. 'Thank you for being so brave. Now let's get out of here.'

CHAPTER EIGHT

EFFIE COULD NOT BEAR to return home just yet. Harry had cautiously suggested they might like to call by Michael Standish's, perhaps he was home by now, and he seemed to be a good friend. In any event, Michael needed to be informed as soon as possible about Mary's death. But Effie said no, it would not be right to call on him unannounced, she would prefer it if Harry went to Michael's later, on his own. In truth, she could not face telling Michael the terrible news, of seeing his shock and sadness, of the responsibility she would feel to be strong and comfort him. She just wanted to be comforted herself. So she asked Harry if could he take her to Lydia's place instead.

Harry seemed pleased with this suggestion. 'A good idea,' he said. 'She'll cheer you up.'

So here was Effie, sitting on the couch in Lydia's smart Toorak terrace house, weeping unashamedly as she recounted to Lydia the events of that terrible morning.

'There, there, darling,' Lydia whispered as she held her friend tightly. 'It's been a terrible shock for you. It's all just so awful.'

'But why would anyone want to hurt poor Mary?' Effie cried. 'What has she done to deserve this? All she was trying to do was get her baby back.'

'Yes, darling,' Lydia soothed, stroking Effie's hair as she held her. 'It's the most horrible, evil thing. But who knows why such wicked things happen? Perhaps it had nothing to do with her search for the baby. Do you know if…if she was taken advantage of?'

'What do you mean?' Effie stared at her friend in confusion.

'Was she…attacked by a man?'

Effie sat up straight. 'Do you mean molested? I don't think so, Harry didn't say she was. But perhaps he wouldn't know until after they've examined her. Oh, I hadn't thought of that. Surely not!' She slumped against Lydia's shoulder and began to sob again.

'What an idiot I am! I'm sorry, darling, I shouldn't have mentioned that possibility, I'm sure it didn't happen.' After a pause she added, 'At least that nice policeman, Harry Holloway, is on the case. I'm sure he's very clever and will find out who did this terrible thing. He's not so infuriating after all, is he?'

Effie managed a small smile through her tears. 'I suppose not. Perhaps I judged him hastily. He seems to know what he's doing.'

'There, that's better,' Lydia said. 'It's good to see you smiling again. Now tell me, you said that you and Michael Standish were trying to find the baby and reunite him with Mary. What was that all about?'

Effie realised that Lydia was completely in the dark about the events of the past few days. She had been too preoccupied to visit her friend since the evening she and Michael had come across Mary on Mrs Wilson's doorstep. So she related to Lydia the whole sequence of events since then. As Effie began to recount their visit to the asylum, Lydia interrupted her. 'Oh, you should have spoken to me first. I might have been able to help. I'm a volunteer there, you know.'

'Really?'

'Yes, quite a few of my friends are involved too. It's a very worthy cause. And they rely on our help so much. To give some relief to the poor overworked nurses. And there has been a side benefit for me, it's where I met my darling Ed.'

'That's lovely,' Effie replied. 'About Ed, I mean. And you and your friends helping there. Their work is so important.'

'When did you and Michael visit?' asked Lydia. 'I could perhaps return there with you, if that would help.'

Effie shook her head. 'Thank you, dear, but I suppose there's really no point now. With Mary gone. Anyway, we went there on Saturday and Matron Jackson was very firm about Alfie. She wouldn't tell us anything about the adoption and who the new parents are. And she explained that Ed can't tell us anything either. Even if he knows about it.'

'Oh, that explains it,' Lydia said.

'Explains what?' Effie looked puzzled.

'Why I saw Michael there on Saturday morning. I was there myself, for my Saturday shift.'

'Where did you see Michael? I'm surprised you didn't see me as well.' Effie tried to recall their visit to the asylum. As far as she could remember she and Michael were together the whole time.

'I'm pretty sure it was Michael. A bit after nine, climbing into a cab in Berry Street.'

'No, no', Effie said. 'We weren't there until just before midday. Either you've got your times mixed up, or it wasn't Michael.'

'I haven't got my times mixed up,' Lydia said, 'because it was just before I began my shift. I waved, but he didn't see me, and then he was gone. Oh well, I suppose it couldn't have been him.' But Effie could see that Lydia's puzzled expression, and the tone of her voice, suggested otherwise.

Effie too was perplexed. How could Michael have been at Berry Street when he told her he was at home checking on Mary? And why would he not have mentioned a previous visit, when later that morning they went to the VIA? It was all very odd. No, Lydia must have been mistaken.

Her thoughts were interrupted by the sound of the doorbell. 'Oh bother!' Lydia exclaimed. 'That's Ed, I forgot he was coming around. Are you up to seeing him? I can easily send him away.'

'No, no,' Effie said hurriedly. 'It's perfectly all right. Besides, he needs to know about Mary's death because he'll probably be drawn into the police investigation anyway. On account of his position as a doctor at the asylum.'

'Of course,' Lydia said. 'Poor fellow, he'll hate that. He gets so anxious at the slightest thing.'

'It's only if he authorised the adoption,' Effie said. 'Then Harry… Sergeant Holloway will want to talk to him, I suppose. But I'm sure it would just be a formality.'

'Try telling him that,' Lydia muttered, raising her eyebrows. 'He really is such a dreadful, nervous nelly.'

The bell rang again, and Lydia got to her feet. 'I forgot it's Tillie's day off. I'd better go fetch him. All right, Ed, all right, I'm coming.'

Lydia returned a few minutes later with Ed in tow. He looked taller and thinner, and more stooped than ever in Lydia's cosy parlour. And decidedly uncomfortable in Effie's presence, murmuring a mumbled greeting, then standing there, shifting nervously from one foot to the other, at a loss as to what to say next.

'Oh, for goodness sake, Ed, sit down,' Lydia said, resuming her seat on the sofa next to Effie and pointing to the armchair opposite. 'Your bedside manner is awful.'

Ed did as he was told, perching himself on the edge of the seat, all gangling limbs and self-consciousness.

'Now dear,' Lydia began, 'Effie is here because she has received some terrible news today. And been forced to go through an awful experience.' And as gently as she could, she related the news about Mary's death. As she spoke, Effie watched Ed's reaction. He seemed genuinely shocked, his features becoming even more pallid than usual.

'Sorry to hear that,' he offered in Effie's general direction. 'Must have been a rum business.'

'You may have known Mary,' Effie said. 'Mary Guerin. She had a baby at the asylum, a little boy. And you adopted him out.'

Ed managed to be startled and defensive at the same time. 'I did? I don't think so. I can't recall doing that.'

'No, no,' Effie added hastily. 'I didn't mean you personally. I meant that the asylum authorised the adoption.'

'Oh,' Ed responded, not in the least settled by Effie's reassurance. 'I see. But that could have been authorised by anyone. Well, not anyone. But I'm not the only doctor there, you know.'

'We know, dear, we know,' Lydia said. 'Anyway, it's no crime if you did approve it, you were just doing your job.'

'As a matter of fact, I didn't approve it,' Ed said, a trifle crossly. 'I had nothing to do with it. And what has it got to do with the asylum anyway? This girl's death, I mean.'

'Well,' Effie replied, 'she was thrown into the Yarra quite close to the asylum. And we thought she might have gone there to try to get her baby back.'

'Oh,' Ed said, obviously taken aback, and shifting nervously in his chair. 'Oh, I see. Though I don't think that proves anything, really.'

'There's no need to get so defensive, Ed,' Lydia chided. 'Effie's not accusing you, or the asylum, of anything.' Then turning to Effie she said, 'Did you find out whether Mary actually visited the asylum on Friday?'

'It seems that she didn't. Matron Jackson was quite clear on that.'

'That's that then. You can rely on Denise Jackson's word. She's as straight as a die.'

'I suppose you're right.' Suddenly Effie felt very tired. And sad. The sight of Mary, lying pale and lifeless at the morgue, returned to her and despair enveloped her again.

'I think I would like to go home now,' she said to Lydia, and much to her chagrin, felt her lip tremble and tears begin to well again.

'Are you sure you will be all right, darling? You don't seem well still.' Lydia took her hand again and stroked it.

'I just feel rather tired, I'm afraid. It's all been rather a trial today. And I must hurry to catch my tram or it will be well and truly dark.'

'Nonsense, you're not up to going home by tram. I'll get Ed to give you a lift in a cab. He's just leaving now, aren't you, dear?'

'Am I?' Ed said, somewhat startled. Then, as he caught Lydia's sharp glance, he rose to his feet, looking about absently for his hat and coat. 'Yes, of course, must be off.'

In the cab on the way home, Effie could sense Ed's unease. Occasionally he made tentative attempts at small talk, but she was in no mood to encourage him. She couldn't stop thinking about Michael and Saturday morning. Why had he been at Berry Street twice in the one morning? And why had he not mentioned that first visit to her? Was he looking for Mary? Or trying to find out about Alfie? Or was he there for some completely different purpose? The more she thought about it, the more confusing it became.

She tried to drive the confusion from her mind by reassuring herself that Michael would have a perfectly reasonable explanation. But still, she could not fathom what it would be.

After another tentative attempt by Ed to strike up a conversation, Effie turned to him and said quietly, 'Do you mind if I shut my eyes and rest for the remainder of the journey? I really have rather a bad headache.'

'Of course, beg pardon,' Ed replied hastily. 'I understand completely.'

And they passed the rest of the journey to Mrs Wilson's in merciful silence.

Effie did not have to wait long to see Michael. At seven o'clock, just before dinner, he arrived at Mrs Wilson's doorstep, apologising for calling on her at this hour, but he had just read the note left by Harry about the body in the Yarra. Did she know anything? Had Harry spoken to her? Should they go immediately to see him? Clearly Harry had not had the chance to inform him of the day's events.

Effie had resolved to stay calm when she next saw Michael, but it was no use. She immediately burst into tears as she told him that the body was indeed Mary.

'Are you sure it was her?' he said in a low voice, ashen-faced and seemingly close to tears himself.

She nodded silently, and seeing his face crumple, she instinctively put her arms around him, holding him there on the front porch, feeling the silent sobs now wrack his body. Striving to recover his composure, Michael straightened himself.

'The poor girl. What despair she must have felt. To do that to herself.'

Effie took his hand and led him inside into the parlour. They took a seat on the sofa. Effie quietly explained to him what Harry had found, that in all probability Mary had been murdered. Michael stared at her silently, sitting upright and stiff on the sofa, his knuckles white where he tightly gripped the wooden sofa arm.

'Who would do that? And why?' He seemed at a complete loss.

'I don't know. But I do know that it must have something to do with Mrs Wilson. And the tall man.'

Michael nodded. 'Perhaps you're right. But I can't see how. I thought Harry Holloway checked all that, and she's in the clear. Have you told Mrs Wilson about Mary, by the way?'

'I haven't seen her since I got back, and Harry asked me not to reveal anything yet. I think he's going to interview her in the next day or so. He's busy with the autopsy report today, he told me. That may show how she was killed. You know, if she was killed before…before she was put in the river.' Effie's voice trailed off and failed her. The vision of Mary hurled into the river, alive but helpless, was too horrific to bear. Her eyes blurred again with tears and she hung her head.

Michael reached out and took her hand, stroking it while she recovered her composure. 'You have been very brave, Effie dear. It's a terrible time for you, I know.'

'And for you,' she said through her tears. 'Lydia was a great comfort to me,' she added. 'I called to see her after…after the morgue.'

'She would be. Such a cheerful person. Always.'

'By the way,' Effie said, trying to affect a casual tone. 'She thought she saw you at the asylum on Saturday morning. She wondered what you were doing there.' Effie watched Michael intently as she spoke, but there was no sign of hesitation.

'It must have been when we were there,' he said calmly.

'No,' Effie said firmly. 'It was at nine o'clock in the morning, before we were there. She waved, but you didn't see her.'

Now Michael did hesitate, she saw his eyes focus inward and she felt his hand slip from hers.

'Well, actually I was in the vicinity on Saturday morning,' he said slowly, 'but I wasn't at the asylum. I was visiting friends. In Berry Street.'

'That seems very early to be visiting friends,' Effie couldn't help it, and immediately regretted the implied accusation. But she continued anyway. 'And I wonder why you didn't tell me you had already been there.'

Michael glanced at her, then turned away. When he spoke, the strain in his voice was at odds with the casual tone he tried to convey. 'I suppose just because I didn't think to. It wasn't important.'

Something in his eyes was imploring Effie to stop her questions. It was becoming clear to her that he had a secret that he wanted to keep from her. She felt a surge of emotion — disappointment perhaps, or resentment, that he would not include her in his whole life.

Effie changed the subject, recounting Ed's appearance at Lydia's and his assertion that he had not been involved with the adoption. Michael visibly relaxed, listening attentively to her words. When she had finished, he sighed.

'Well, I suppose it now no longer matters who approved the adoption, or who the new parents are. I'm sure they are decent people and Alfie is best left with them. Now that he has no one else left in the world.'

'Perhaps so,' Effie said. 'But I'm not entirely convinced you're right. I still think that when Harry Holloway gets to the bottom of who killed poor Mary, it will somehow be connected with Alfie and what has happened to him.'

'Who knows, you may be right,' Michael said, but the tone of his voice implied some doubt. 'Let's just wait and see. I'm happy to leave all that to Harry Holloway.'

'I'm very tired,' Effie said, rising to her feet. 'It's been a terrible day. I think I'll have some dinner and retire early.'

'Of course,' Michael said, making for the door. With undue haste, almost as if he was escaping from her, Effie sensed, but she did not really care. All she wanted to do was to have her dinner and go to her bed, hopefully to find oblivion from the horrors that the day had brought.

Michael and Effie were back at Russell Street Police Headquarters. But this time, not on their own instigation. It had taken only a day for the police pathologist to confirm Harry's suspicions about Mary's death, and the case was now a murder investigation.

Harry's boss, Inspector Winston Marks, had wasted no time in identifying Michael and Effie as the key witnesses, and had summoned them to appear immediately for an interview.

Harry pulled them aside before they entered the inspector's office, and quietly suggested they keep their answers to his questions as brief and factual as possible. It might be wise, he advised, to avoid speculation as much as possible – for instance, Effie's pursuit of Mrs Wilson to the Belle, and her theories of what she was doing there, might not be terribly well received.

'Good advice,' Michael agreed, though Effie was not so sure. She considered her suspicions about Mrs Wilson entirely relevant to Mary's death.

Harry showed them into the inspector's office. Winston Marks did not bother to rise from where he sat behind his large desk in a leather chair. He eyed them both rather imperiously and Effie took an instant dislike. There was something repellent about him. For a start, his attire seemed rather inappropriate for a member of the police force. With his expensive suit, natty floral waistcoat and expensive silk tie, Effie considered him to be distinctly overdressed. And the rigidly upright set of his frame made him seem hawkish and ready to pounce on them. In contrast Harry was lounging casually in his chair next to her and Michael, as if he was just indulging in a pleasant chat with old friends.

At the inspector's insistence, Michael recounted what had happened since that evening, only a little more than a week ago, when they had first encountered Mary Guerin. Effie noted that he followed Harry's advice, and kept his story brief. There was no mention of the Village Belle, and only a cursory explanation of their efforts to reunite Mary with her son.

'Now, Mr Standish,' Inspector Marks said. 'I want to get very clear in my mind, the last time you saw Miss Guerin. I understand from your testimony that it was some time last Friday?'

'Yes,' Michael replied. 'About ten o'clock on Friday morning, I would think.'

'And you are certain about that? You didn't just assume she was at the premises in Wattle Street at that time?'

'No. That is, no, I did not assume. I entered the premises and checked that she was all right.'

Inspector Marks peered at him. 'You entered the premises? Invited or uninvited, may I ask.'

Effie heard a note of exasperation in Michael's voice as he replied, 'Invited of course. I knocked first, naturally. And, after all, it is my building.'

Inspector Marks nodded, eyeing Michael coldly. 'And would you say that the young lady was in good spirits on that morning?'

Michael looked at him in some surprise. 'As good a spirits as you could expect her to be in. Given her circumstances. I mean, she was upset and concerned, but I spoke to her for some little while, and I think I left her in a reasonably calm frame of mind.'

'And she showed no signs of preparing herself to leave the premises? Or to meet with any other person?'

'None whatsoever.' Michael sounded as if he could not have been more certain.

Inspector Marks pushed on. 'And you did not see her at all on Friday evening?'

'I told you,' Michael replied. 'I was out for the evening and did not have the chance to check on her.'

'And when you returned home, I suppose you assumed she had retired for the night?' suggested the inspector. 'And what time did you return home?'

Effie thought Michael looked somewhat taken aback. 'Really inspector,' he replied. 'Is that relevant? Does it really matter what time I got home?'

Inspector Marks began drumming his fingers on the desk. 'If you don't mind, Mr Standish, I'll decide what's relevant and what's not. Now, would you care to answer my question, please?' And he stared hard at Michael.

Effie fancied she saw Michael colour slightly, and he shuffled in his chair before replying. 'Well, in fact I did not return until the morning. I was out very late, and decided to stay with friends rather than return home in the small hours.'

'Ah,' said Inspector Marks, exhaling slowly as he spoke, and writing something in a notebook on his desk. 'So you would have no idea if Miss Guerin left the premises at any time on Friday night? Or if she left the premises with another person? Or indeed, if she was forced to leave the premises with another person?'

Michael looked at him, and again there was more than a hint of exasperation in his voice as he replied, 'Well, no, I couldn't know, but I thought I had already told you that.'

'Not quite, Mr Standish, not quite. I don't think you gave us the full detail, at any rate.'

As this apparently pointless grilling continued, Effie's immediate instinct was to spring to Michael's defence, to confront the inspector and suggest he focus on the real issues, like Mrs Wilson's obviously guilty behaviour. But just as strong was the anxiety that swept over her at this latest revelation from Michael – that he had been out all night on that fateful Friday evening. She remembered his nervousness yesterday, when she had confronted him about Lydia seeing him at Berry Street on the Saturday morning. This was worse, much worse. Now it was clear that Michael had been out all night in the vicinity of the asylum, on the same night that Mary had been murdered. And her body later found in the Yarra so close by. What was Michael doing there, and why was he so reluctant to tell her? Or anyone else, it would seem.

Just as quickly as these wild thoughts came to her, so did shame and regret, that she had even contemplated the possibility that there might be a connection between Michael and Mary's death. She must trust him, there would be an innocent reason for his behaviour that night, and there would be a good reason why he would not reveal any detail to her. He would tell her in due course, she must console herself with that.

Her focus shifted back to Inspector Marks and his inane questions, and just in time because the inspector now directed his attention to her. Again he seemed to delve into questions of marginal relevance, about her interactions with Mary on that first evening outside Mrs Wilson's, and later at Michael's place. And again the tenor of his questions to her was vaguely accusatory, as if somehow she and Michael had contributed to the tragedy of Mary's murder. Effie felt affronted, but tried to remain calm in her responses. She was doing her best to follow Harry's advice and stick to the facts, though at the same time she was itching to pour forth all her suspicions about Mrs Wilson and her shady dealings.

The inspector at last asked her a few questions about Mrs Wilson, but to Effie they did not seem terribly relevant, and did not go to the heart of the landlady's suspicious behaviour. Again she was sorely tempted to lead him down the right path, but again resisted.

Finally the inspector gave her an opening. 'Miss Davis, Mr Standish has indicated that you and he were engaged on some sort of enterprise on behalf of Miss Guerin. To overturn an adoption process, I understand.' There was a distinct tone of disapproval in his voice. 'Do you have anything to add in that regard?'

Effie had plenty to add. She immediately launched into a full account of their campaign, dwelling at some length on the injustice of it all.

The inspector's disapproving frown grew more pronounced, and it only lightened when she mentioned their visit to Judith Baxter.

'A very fine woman, very charming,' he offered. 'Her committee does very fine work, they are frequently a great help to us.'

Effie suspected that Winston Marks' approval had less to do with the fine work of Judith's committee and more to do with her captivating personal presence.

'She has been very helpful to us too,' Effie said.

'Yes, quite,' Inspector Marks said. 'I think that will do, Miss Davis. I've heard enough, I think.'

Almost as an afterthought he now turned to Harry: 'Anything you wish to add, Sergeant?' he asked curtly.

Harry shook his head. 'No boss, nothing to add. I reckon you've covered all that needs to be covered.'

Frowning, Inspector Marks rose to his feet and escorted them to the door, then bade them farewell with the most cursory of thanks. Harry showed them down the long corridor and out into the street. He offered them a ride home with Willie Milton, but Michael declined, saying it would be no trouble to catch a hansom. 'Fair enough', Harry said and bade them goodbye.

'Sorry about the grilling in there,' he added apologetically, a lopsided half-grin appearing at the same time. 'It's part of the process, I'm afraid.'

'Oh, well,' Effie replied. 'It wasn't too bad, I suppose. But I do hope that the police will soon be interviewing the real suspects.' And she raised an eyebrow at him to indicate that he should know who she was talking about.

Harry's grin disappeared, and his manner was very certain as he replied: 'Don't worry about that, Effie. We will, we most certainly will. In fact, I expect to be bringing in Rhonda Wilson for a chat tomorrow.'

CHAPTER NINE

✦✳✦

EFFIE SLEPT BADLY AGAIN that night and woke unrefreshed. She scarcely touched breakfast, managing only to nibble half-heartedly on a piece of toast. It tasted like cardboard and Effie pushed it away. Daisy glanced at her with concern as she cleared the table. 'Are you unwell, Miss Davis?' she inquired solicitously. 'You must eat, you know. Keep your strength up.'

Effie smiled wanly. 'Oh, it's just a headache. It will pass. I promise to eat a hearty dinner, Daisy.'

'I will make sure you do, Miss. We can't have you fading away. You're too thin already.'

Effie smiled, despite her tiredness and splitting head. Her slim figure was always the object of Daisy's concern, and the reason, Effie suspected, for the regularly huge plates of food that Daisy placed in front of her.

'Have you seen Mrs Wilson this morning?' Effie asked.

'As a matter of fact, I have,' Daisy replied, leaning over and whispering conspiratorially. 'She's gone out again. About half an hour ago, in a terrible hurry. Very strange, I must say, not like her at all. I've never seen her move so fast.'

'Did you see which way she was heading?'

'Well, she turned left out the gate, so I don't think she was heading for the tram or to town.'

'Towards the Village Belle perhaps?' Effie said, as offhandedly as she could.

'What's that? Oh, you mean the pub down the street. Yes, I suppose she was headed in that general direction.'

Effie hastily excused herself and went back to her room. She was seized with an impulse to run after Mrs Wilson. She was sure she was going to the Village Belle, and she was sure that she was intending to see the tall man again. They were bound to be behind Mary's murder, she told herself.

But this time her better judgement prevailed. There is nothing I can do, she reasoned, and after all, Harry will be here soon to fetch Mrs Wilson for the interview. He will want to know where she has gone, best wait until he arrives.

But she would be prepared for Harry's arrival, dressed and ready to go with him immediately. She put on her warm coat and scarf, and paced up and down her room, going to the window every minute or so to see if he was approaching. After what seemed an interminable period of time, she could stand it no longer and went outdoors to continue her vigil in Mrs Wilson's overgrown garden. At least it was a bright, cloudless day and the winter sun had a welcome warmth. She wandered about the garden, trying to calm herself and berating Harry for his tardiness.

It must have been close to eleven when she heard the sound of horse's hooves in the street outside. She dashed down the path and out into the street, just as Willy Milton was about to hitch the horse and trap to the old rail on the kerb. Harry almost bumped into her as she hurtled through the open gate.

'Steady there, Effie,' he exclaimed, catching her arm as she stumbled against him. 'What's the hurry?'

'She's gone,' gasped Effie, a little out of breath. 'Gone to see that man. The tall man.'

'What? Who do you mean? Rhonda Wilson?'

'Yes, yes, of course! Harry, we must hurry, we must catch them.'

'Hang on a moment,' Harry obviously had no intention of taking precipitous action, or any action for that matter, without due consideration. 'Now, just calm down a bit, and tell me what's happened this morning.'

Effie rattled off Daisy's news about Mrs Wilson and her early morning flight. 'So you see, there's no time to lose,' she urged. 'We must follow her.'

Harry scratched his head. 'And no one's seen her since she left?'

'No, no! I've been watching out for you since then, so I would have seen if she came back.'

'Fair enough. You know, I think you're right. And from what you say, she could well have gone to the Belle.'

'Yes, yes, can we get going?'

Harry eyed her doubtfully. 'Effie, I'm not sure you should be coming with us. The Belle can get a bit lively, and this is police business after all.'

Effie stared at him, a prickle of irritation rising. Her determination to avenge Mary was overwhelming and she was not going to be left out at this stage.

'But can't you see, you'll need me there, Harry. I'm the only one who can identify the tall man.'

'Do you think you could, if you saw him again.' Harry once more seemed doubtful.

'Yes, of course, I'm positive.' Though Effie was not positive, in fact she was very uncertain that her fleeting glimpse of the man's back would in any way assist to identify him. But it was their only chance, and besides, perhaps that fleeting familiarity she saw in his stance, in the way he hunched his shoulders, perhaps that would manifest itself more strongly if she got a better view of him.

Harry looked at her for a moment or two, then relented. 'Oh all right, I suppose you could be useful. Jump up there next to Willy and we'll get going.' And, with a surprisingly gentle hand on her waist, he assisted her up into the trap next to Constable Milton.

As they jogged off down St Kilda Road, Harry explained that he had been held up waiting for the pathologist's report. The examination had been complex, and the doctor had only been willing to give an opinion after undertaking a number of blood tests. He had worked right through the night, apparently.

As Effie listened, that other horrible possibility returned to her. 'Was she still alive when she was thrown in? I just couldn't bear to think of her being dragged down helpless into that freezing cold water.'

'Well, there are not many good ways to be murdered, I can tell you,' Harry said cautiously. 'But if it helps, the doctor is reasonably certain she was dead when she was thrown in. Or at least, if not dead, in some sort of coma. There was not a great deal of water in her lungs, you see.'

'Does he know how she was killed then?'

'That's the thing, he's not too sure. There were no marks on her at all, apart from those made by the ligatures and the gag, so he has ruled out strangulation or bashing. It seems that her stomach was quite empty, so she probably vomited. Which indicates poisoning, but who knows with what? He could find no trace of poison in her blood, so we just don't know, unfortunately.'

Effie steeled herself to ask the question. 'Was she, you know, molested?'

'No, no evidence of that,' Harry replied quickly, in a matter-of-fact tone. 'None whatsoever.'

Effie shivered and drew her coat more tightly around her. 'So what will happen now?'

'The Coroner will make his findings. I'd say it'll be murder, by person or persons unknown, by means unknown. Doesn't make our job any easier, of course. But one thing I am sure of – this wasn't a random killing. It was well thought out and well executed. And it had a purpose, to put an end to Mary Guerin and the trouble she was causing someone. And since the only thing she seems to have been occupied with here in Melbourne was getting her baby back, that would seem to be the reason for her murder. At least, that is the premise I'm working on for the moment.'

Effie glanced up at Harry. Her view of him was changing. She was beginning to see that behind the casual air and the cheerful, joking façade, a sharp intelligence was at work. Perhaps his offhand manner was deliberately affected, intended to convey a slackness of attitude, an obtuseness that would put criminals at their ease and off their guard.

'Thank you, Harry,' she said quietly.

'What for? Just doing my job.'

'But you're doing it very well. And I appreciate it.'

Effie led Harry to the back room of the Village Belle where she had previously seen Mrs Wilson. But this time it was empty, inhabited only by a lingering reek of beer and tobacco. So Harry suggested they try the front bar, normally out-of-bounds to the ladies, but that would be no impediment to Mrs Wilson.

Effie had been reluctant to enter, remembering the hostile reception she had met when she had ventured there last time. But Harry had reassured her, 'Don't worry, stick with me and you'll find no one will mind too much.'

It was not yet noon but the front bar was already packed. And Harry was proved right. When they entered, heads had swivelled, the hubbub had briefly waned, and she had felt again the threat of all those male eyes looking her up and down. But then Harry's towering presence had registered, the hostility had turned to casual interest, and then to indifference as the drinkers returned to their glasses and their discussions, and the din returned to its former level.

Effie peered anxiously about the room. 'She's not here,' she said, tugging on Harry's sleeve and leaning up towards his ear, to make herself heard above the bar chatter.

'Didn't really expect her to be,' Harry replied. 'But we might be able to get some information.'

He too was surveying the room from his vantage point above the heads of the crowd. Effie saw him recognise someone and give an almost imperceptible nod in the direction of the far corner of the room. Within seconds the object of Harry's interest had materialised from the crowd and sidled up to them. He was a sharp-featured little fellow, of indeterminate age, with a long, pointy nose and greasy, lank hair, slicked straight back and stuck to his scalp. His neck had disappeared into his ill-fitting coat collar, and as he approached his furtive eyes darted from side to side, as if he was ready to bolt at any sign of danger.

'G'day, Ferret, what's new?' Harry said cheerfully. 'Ferret, this is Effie, she's a mate of mine.'

The Ferret eyed Effie up and down, but, oddly enough, Effie did not feel affronted by his examination. His beady eyes seemed to be assessing her only as a potential threat, rather than as an object of desire. Apparently deciding that there was no danger in that quarter, he turned back to Harry.

'Number seven in the fourth at Caulfield, Saturday. A dead cert. Want to get something on?'

'Here's a quid,' Harry said, slipping a note into the Ferret's hand. 'Hope that's the good oil.'

The Ferret grinned and sniggered, a strange sound that had a certain menace to it, almost like the snarl of a dog protecting a bone. 'Geez, Harry, you know me, I save the best ones for you.'

'Of course you do, Ferret. And I reckon a tip like that's worth another quid. Call it commission.' And he waved another note in front of the Ferret, whose eyes darted back and forth, following the note greedily.

'But there's one small thing I need in return,' Harry continued, smiling pleasantly, then leaning forward and adding in a lower voice, 'I need to know if old Rhonda Wilson has been in here this morning. And if she's been talking to anyone. Is that worth a quid to you?'

'Too right,' the Ferret said enthusiastically. 'Leave it to me.' And just as furtively as he had appeared, he was gone, dissolving back into the crowd. Effie glanced at Harry.

'Goodness, he's a shifty fellow. Are you sure he's trustworthy?'

Harry grinned at her. 'Don't worry, the Ferret and I have a pretty good understanding. He knows that if he gives me the wrong mail, I'll find out eventually. I have a few things on him that I might be tempted to act on if he diddled me. And I know that he keeps a pretty sharp eye on everything that's happening around here. So it's a relationship of mutual respect, you could say, and generally quite fruitful, I find.'

Effie smiled. 'What about that racing tip? What was that all about?'

'Oh, the Ferret is generally a good turf analyst. He gathers excellent inside information, and no doubt he'll place the bet in due course, with Jack over there. He's our SP bookie.' And Harry pointed to a table not far from them, where a florid-faced, portly gentleman was sitting.

Effie watched Jack the bookie in whispered conversation with a fellow she assumed was one of his clients. She was wondering whether it was altogether prudent for Harry to be associating with an SP bookmaker. As far as she knew, such activity was not exactly legal. But then her eye drifted to the bar behind Jack, and her attention was caught by the vague familiarity of a tall figure sitting there, his back to them, hunched over a paper. Effie grabbed Harry's arm.

'That man! Over there at the bar. I think I recognise him.'

Harry followed her pointed finger. At that moment the hunched figure turned slightly towards a fellow drinker at the bar, and Harry smiled. 'I reckon you would know him. That's Ronnie Harris. Your fellow lodger, isn't he?'

Of course it was. Mr Harris's oily features were only too apparent, sniggering at some sleazy joke made by his companion, no doubt.

'Is he the one you saw here the other day?' Harry asked, still watching Mr Harris. 'You know, with Rhonda Wilson?'

Effie tried hard to remember. Was that the familiarity that had struck her when she saw the tall man talking to Mrs Wilson? Surely she would have recognised Mr Harris though, even at that distance and in that murky light? But on the other hand, she had only seen him from the back, and only for a short while.

'I don't know,' she said eventually. 'It might have been him, but I can't be sure. The room was very smoky and I only caught a glimpse. And I never saw his face.'

Harry shrugged. 'Never mind, we know Ronnie Harris well. He's always of interest to us. So let's have a chat with him anyway.'

Ronnie Harris's sneer expanded as he saw Harry approaching with Effie in tow. His leer, as he recognised Effie, managed to convey both contempt and lasciviousness at the same time.

'Got yourself a girlfriend I see, Sergeant,' he smirked. 'She tarts up pretty well, I must say. Not as good first thing in the morning though, I can tell you.' And he winked lewdly at Harry.

'G'day, Ronnie,' Harry said, completely ignoring the jibe. 'What are you doing here at this time of day? Thought you'd be at work.'

'A fella's not allowed to take a lunch break?' Ronnie Harris said, suddenly defensive.

'And a bit of refreshment too, I see,' Harry observed, glancing at the glass of whisky on the bar.

'Is that a crime? In that case, you'd better arrest everyone here.'

Harry continued on blithely. 'Been here long, Ronnie?'

'Not so long. A man's got to make a living, you know.'

'So you wouldn't have seen your charming landlady here this morning?'

Mr Harris stared at Harry. Was that alarm in his eyes, thought Effie, or just contempt for the law?

'No, I haven't seen the old hag. Why would I?'

'No reason. But if we asked around here, we wouldn't find anyone who could remember her with you this morning? Because perhaps you've got a very poor memory.'

Ronnie Harris rose from his stool, downed his whisky with one gulp, and stared angrily at Harry. 'You're bloody mad, copper, that's what you are. I'm getting out of here, and if you want me to stay, you'll bloody well have to arrest me.'

'Why would I want to do that, Ronnie? After such a pleasant chat? Good day to you, I'll let you get back to earning an honest crust.' And he touched his hat to Harris, who promptly turned on his heel and stormed from the room. Effie stared after him, still trying to connect him with her last visit to the hotel. But she just could not be certain.

'I detest that man!' she said to Harry. 'Do you think he's the one? The one that Mrs Wilson was meeting with? Do you think he murdered Mary?'

'I doubt it,' Harry said. 'Both he and Rhonda Wilson are dodgy, but they're both small time. A bit of fraud, stolen goods, that's Ronnie's sort of caper. I can't imagine him as a murderer. But you never know.'

Effie was suddenly aware that they had company again. The Ferret was standing alongside them, grinning up at Harry.

'Got the lowdown, boss,' he confided, looking at Harry expectantly.

Harry took the pound note from his pocket. 'Lowdown first, then the commission. You know how it is, Ferret.'

'She was here all right, Boss. For certain. Turned up nice and early and was giving the gin a good ole nudge. Early in the day, even for her.'

'And was she with anyone?'

'Yeh, but not sure who. Someone said they saw her leaving with some bloke, big feller he reckons, but couldn't remember who.'

'Not Ronnie Harris, by any chance?'

'Dunno. The feller who seen her wasn't taking a lot of notice. On account of he had a bit of a sore head, y'see.'

'I see. Thanks, Ferret, you've done well. Don't spend it all at once. And make sure you get that bet on for me.'

The Ferret seized the extra quid and departed triumphantly. Effie assumed that the note would be resting in the till of the Village Belle bar before long. Or perhaps in Jack's bag, invested on one of the Ferret's certainties.

'Well,' Harry said, taking her arm. 'Nothing more to be gained in here. Let's see what we can find outside.' And he shepherded her towards the exit.

CHAPTER TEN

OUT IN THE STREET the sunny morning had turned cold, a
southerly change blowing in from the ocean, bringing clouds scudding
across the sun and the threat of rain. But at least the air out here was
clear and Effie felt she could breathe again. She followed Harry to the
police trap where Willie Milton was waiting patiently.

Harry looked up and down the street, before helping Effie back into
the trap and leaping up next to her. He rubbed his chin and turned to
Willie. 'Well, she was here earlier in the day, but where she is now is
anyone's guess. Any ideas?'

Willie pointed back up Barkly Street, to the group of shops where
a rudimentary newspaper stand was set up on the street, its occupant
barely visible under a huge coat, his cap pulled down over his eyes. 'I
wouldn't know, Harry, but why don't we try the young bloke over there?
He might've seen something.'

Turning the trap around, they trotted back the forty or so yards to the
paperboy. 'G'day, son, been here long?' Harry ventured.

'Long enough,' he replied, peering out from under his cap. 'What's
it to you?'

Harry ignored the rudeness and persevered. 'I suppose you've seen a few people coming and going from the Belle this morning?'

'Course I have. I'm not blind.'

'Wonder if you saw a lady leaving earlier. Old girl, pretty large. She was with a bloke.'

'Might have. What's it worth?'

'Sixpence if you're telling the truth. The bloke she was with was a little feller. Would have been quite a bit smaller than her.'

The paperboy eyed him suspiciously, his sharp features pinched from the cold and screwed up in concentration. 'Nah, seen nothin like that. I did see an old tart leavin' with a bloke, but he was a big fella. Real big, I reckon. They was in a jinker.'

'Are you sure? You've got a good memory.' Harry eyed him steadily.

'Yeh, I'm sure. I remember cause they were bluein' on the way out of the pub, and after they got in the jinker. She was carryin' on fit to bust. Shouting at him, y'know, I could hear her from here. Then he gave her a good old what-for for her trouble. That shut her up.' And the young fellow gave a roundhouse swipe of his arm, to demonstrate the technique of the what-for.

'Didn't hear what the blue was about, by any chance?'

'Nah, not really. She was swearin' a lot, and I reckon she looked a bit scared. I did hear her say that she wouldn't tell. I heard her say that a couple of times.'

'Can't remember where they were headed, can you?"

The paperboy pointed back up the street past the Village Belle. 'Straight on up Barkly Street, and they headed off at a fair old split too, I can tell you.'

Harry took a coin from his pocket. 'Thanks son, it's good to see that there's an honest man left in this world. And just to show that honesty is the best policy, here's a shilling for your trouble.' And he flipped the coin in the grinning boy's direction.

'We'd better get going, Willie, we don't have much time,' Harry said. 'But first we'll need to return Effie to her lodgings.'

'No you won't,' Effie said firmly. 'You just said we don't have much time. I promise I won't get in the way.' And she looked at Harry beseechingly.

Harry frowned and glanced at Willy, who simply raised his eyebrows and looked the other way.

'Oh, all right,' Harry said, reluctantly. 'Against my better judgement. But you must promise to stay up here at all times. And don't try to do anything foolish.'

'Of course I won't. What do you take me for?' Effie retorted.

Willie sooled the horse into a brisk trot, and they were on their way. Effie glanced at Harry, and saw that he was frowning again. 'Where were they going?' she asked him. 'What's along this way?'

'Not much at all, that's what I'm worried about. Just the Elwood swamps and then the beach. Not really the ideal scenic drive, I wouldn't have thought.'

Sure enough, they had not gone more than half a mile down Barkly Street, when all signs of the city behind them petered out. The road turned into a pothole-strewn dirt track, and low-lying scrubby bush replaced the houses on each side of the road. Then the scrub disappeared too, and marshy swampland spread on both sides into the distance. On the horizon Effie could see sand dunes rising above the plain, marking the line of the coast. It was a dreary scene, made more depressing by the increasingly bitter wind that was now blowing strongly from the south.

Effie knew that Mrs Wilson would not take this trip voluntarily. She turned to Harry. 'He means her harm, doesn't he?' she said, speaking quite loudly to make herself heard above the howl of the wind.

'It would seem so,' Harry replied grimly.

'How do we know where he's taken her though?' Effie said, looking around. 'There's no one about, he could have gone anywhere.'

'Not really,' Harry said. 'If he's in a horse and cart, this is the only road he can take really. It's too wet to turn off it. Barkly Road stops at the abattoir, and the beach track beyond that is impassable at this time of year. So his options are limited.'

'How far to the abattoir?' Effie asked.

'It's not too far ahead. Maybe two or three miles. I'm hoping we can intercept him there, though he might have had time to get back to town by now. But if we do see him, Willie and I may be called on to make an arrest, and it could become quite dangerous. You must promise to stay up here out of harm's way.' And he gave Effie a stern look.

Effie nodded meekly. She was more than happy to leave the heroics to Harry and Willie. She looked at him with concern. 'Please take care, Harry, won't you.'

He didn't reply, just smiled reassuringly and patted her arm.

A further mile or so along the road, the ground began to rise and soon the swampland on either side gave way to a flat, treeless plain stretching to the line of low sandhills in the distance. The only feature discernible to Effie was what looked like a tall wooden tower of some sort, perhaps a mile or so away and directly ahead of them. There appeared to be a Union Jack flying from its top. 'What's that?' she asked, pointing.

'That is the celebrated Victorian Coal Mining Company,' Harry announced, with what Effie thought was something of a facetious flourish in his voice. He went on to explain that black coal was presently in great demand, and the company was hopeful of striking a rich seam in the Elwood region. What was rather interesting though, he added, was that the venture was operated solely by two women, Agnes Simmons and Geraldine Minet, who were apparently out to prove a point to the world.

'Fellow travellers of yours,' Harry said, grinning. 'And not just suffragettes, spiritualists too, it seems. They claim they were guided to this spot by a spirit with the name of Pat. They're very well known around town, and beyond. Famous really.'

Despite the tenseness of their situation, Effie found herself becoming intrigued. And combative. 'I hope you're not making fun of these women just because they have the gumption to tackle a difficult enterprise like that. It must take a lot of courage to set themselves up way out here. No doubt it's very hard work.'

'Don't get me wrong,' Harry replied hastily. 'I admire them greatly. You're right, it is damned hard work, quite dangerous too. I don't know about their chances of success, but good luck to them, I say.'

As they got closer to the mine pit head, Effie could see that further along, on the other side of the road, there was another settlement of some sort, a small cluster of two or three low buildings. This, Harry explained, was the abattoir, producing mutton and tallow for the Melbourne market. Next to the largest building in the group, Effie could make out two large tanks or vats, from which plumes of steam were rising. Even at this distance, the stench on the southerly wind was foul.

As they drove up to the mine, a figure appeared from a small wooden shed that stood beside the pithead. Tall and broad-shouldered, dressed in khaki overalls and check shirt, it was not until she removed her bushie's hat, revealing silver grey hair flowing down over her shoulders, that Effie realised it was a woman. As she strode up to the trap, Harry jumped down and she greeted him with a vigorous handshake.

'Harry, my boy, good to see you. How is Melbourne's finest today?'

'Can't complain, Agnes, no one would listen. How are you and Gerry? Struck it rich yet?'

'Early days, Harry, early days. Little bit of dirty brown so far, but no black. It'll be there though, nothing more certain. Pat's never been wrong yet.' And she chuckled and winked at Harry, turning to grin at Effie and Willie as well.

'Now, you're being very rude, Harry, you haven't introduced me to your lovely young friend.'

Harry introduced Effie, and pointed out that he had the pleasure of making her acquaintance at a suffragette rally.

'Bravo,' Agnes Simmons said. 'Good for you, Effie. Gerry and I don't get down to the rallies in town much these days – too busy trying to make a crust in this godforsaken place. But I hear that the show the other day went pretty well. We've got to keep up the pressure, you know. That's the only way we'll get anywhere with those politicians. You're with the Lady Teachers, are you?'

'Yes,' Effie said proudly. 'We think we're quite progressive.'

'You are, you are. You're doing great work. Just make sure you don't get into bed with those male teachers, politically or otherwise. Never trust a man with anything. They'll diddle you every time. Present company excepted, Harry.' And she let out a hearty burst of laughter.

Harry laughed too. 'Don't worry, Agnes, I don't think Effie needs any persuasion to stick with the cause. But I hope she doesn't take all your advice on board. About men, I mean.'

Effie found herself colouring at this exchange, and Agnes, noticing her discomfort, let out another belly laugh.

'Now we've embarrassed her, Harry, so we'd better change the subject. Anyway, I'm sure you didn't come all the way down here to have a pleasant chat. What's going on?'

'We're looking for a bloke in a buggy,' Harry said. 'I reckon he might have come down this way somewhere this morning. He may or may not have had a woman with him.'

'Hah!' Agnes shouted triumphantly. 'I knew it! I told Gerry that fellow was up to no good.'

'Tell me what you saw. Everything,' Harry said.

'Well, I didn't see a woman with him, but a fellow in a buggy came past here, maybe two hours ago. I thought it was odd at the time because we never get anyone here, except on business with the abattoir. And this fellow had no livestock with him. But he drove up there near the abattoir, and we kept watching him. On account of we thought it a bit strange, you see. Well, he pulled up at the abattoir, then he went around the side, behind them tanks. We couldn't see him for a little while, a few minutes I suppose. Then we saw him again, heading back this way, and in a fair old hurry, that's for sure.'

'Did you get a decent look at him?'

'Reasonable look. I reckon he knew we were around the place, so he kept himself pretty well covered on the way past. But then he turned around and gave us a squiz after he went past, and I got a bit of a look at him then. Big bloke, sort of hunched over.'

'Think you'd know him again?'

'Reckon I might. Or I might not. Hard to tell.'

'Thanks, Agnes, you've been a great help. We'd better push on. By the way, is there anyone at the abattoir today?'

'No, don't think they're killing today. Just boiling down. So it'll just be the caretaker. And his mad dogs, of course. Stay away from them.'

'We will.' And Harry swung himself back onto the seat next to Effie, as Willie Milton turned the trap towards the abattoir.

The stench became steadily more rancid and overpowering as they approached the abattoir. 'Wrap your scarf around your mouth,' Harry advised Effie. 'And whatever you do, don't get off the trap when we get there. There's three mad dogs around here somewhere, and they're not to be trusted.'

But there was no sign of life as they drove up to the long, low-slung stone building. Steam billowed from the two large vats standing by the side of the building, and it was from these that the foul stench arose.

'The boiling-down tanks,' Harry said by way of explanation, pointing to them. Then he pointed again, about fifty yards further up the track, to a small cottage with a plume of smoke rising from its chimney.

'Looks like Mr Lyons is having his lunch,' he said to Willie. 'Let's pay him a visit.'

As the trap approached the cottage, two huge, yellow-eyed dogs on the porch lurched at them, barking furiously, almost throwing themselves off their feet as they jerked their chains tight. A bare semi-circle of ground in front of the cottage marked the limits of their freedom. The cottage door swung open, and a wiry, bearded man, with unkempt greasy black hair, strode out. He had an angry look in his eye, and an old shotgun pointed straight at them. Effie froze with fear.

'Steady, Matty,' Harry said calmly. 'What's all this about?'

'Oh, it's you, Harry,' the fellow said, lowering the gun immediately, then roaring at the dogs to shut their blinky traps. The effect was instantaneous, both of the brutes slinking back onto the porch and slouching against the wall, from where they eyed the visitors suspiciously.

'You're lucky I didn't shoot you, Harry,' the caretaker said, still none too friendly. 'I thought it was that blanky basket comin' back. I was gonna give him both barrels.'

'The big bloke in the trap, you mean? What happened?'

Matty Lyons said nothing, just pointing to the old tank stand by the corner of the cottage. There lay another large, brindled dog, obviously dead. Dirt had stuck to its tongue as it lolled out on the ground, and a pool of blood was drying black on the ground around its smashed-in head.

'Did you see him do it?' Harry asked, staring at the dog.

'Nah, I was down feeding the pigs,' Matty said, with a backward jerk of his head. Effie spotted a group of pigs wandering about at some distance behind the cottage, feeding on some sort of straggly crop that had been planted there. 'Heard the dog barkin', then a yelp, then nothin'. By the time I got back up there he was well on his way, and the dog was lying there. Buggered.'

'Where?' Harry said urgently. Exactly where was the dog lying?'

'Up there, by the tanks,' Matty said.

'Show me exactly,' Harry said. 'Come with us. And bring a ladder. And a pitchfork.'

The caretaker set off at a brisk walk towards the abattoir building. Willie trotted the trap back down the track, and secured it to a sapling growing near the boiling-down vats. He and Harry leapt down and strode towards the tanks, looking around as they did. Harry pointed to the ground, and from her vantage point in the trap, Effie clearly saw the set of wheel tracks leading up to the side of a tank.

She saw Harry pointing again at a dark patch on the ground. Then, leaning the ladder brought by the caretaker against the side of the tank, he climbed up it and peered over the rim, trying to see through the steam.

'Fork!' he shouted abruptly, and she saw him take it from the caretaker, then stab it into the tank. He heaved down hard on the fork, using it as a lever on the edge of the vat. As he pushed down, a sodden, steaming bundle rose slowly above the level of the rim. Harry held it there for twenty seconds or so, allowing it to drain somewhat, then grasping it with one hand, he heaved again on the fork with the other, and the formless lump tumbled over the side of the tank.

Effie saw it hit the ground with a dull thud. She stared, stricken, at the sodden grey mess, as before her eyes it congealed into some semblance of human form. Two boots protruded at odd angles from twisted legs, and the semblance of a face, partly concealed by a wrapping of matted grey hair, became discernible within the shapeless heap. And as Effie stared, the grotesque features were transformed into the familiar, and it was Rhonda Wilson, hideously deformed but clearly recognisable, who stared sightlessly back at her.

Effie managed to turn away as the world grew dizzy around her. She fell forward, trying to steady herself on the rail of the trap, but retching convulsions suddenly racked her, and again she felt herself going down, unable to resist. The last thing she remembered, as the blackness enveloped her, were the strong arms of Harry Holloway, suddenly there to break her fall and lower her gently to the ground.

CHAPTER ELEVEN

EFFIE OPENED HER EYES and looked around the room. For a moment she was confused, failing to recognise the surrounds of her own bedroom, the familiar feel of the boarding house. Then she remembered; she was at Lydia's.

A sense of gratitude flooded over her as she took in the elegant surrounds of Lydia's guest bedroom. Gratitude that she did not have to face everything that the boarding house now threatened in her mind – the immediate horror of Mrs Wilson's terrible death, the lingering memory of poor Mary, wet and lifeless on the morgue table. And the real fear she now felt at the prospect of being alone in the presence of Mr Harris, with his sneering glances and sinister talk. Harry's revelations about the man's shady past had transformed her feelings towards him from mild disgust into a growing dread.

But here, in this bright room, with the fragrance of fresh gardenias wafting from the bouquet on the mantle, and the morning sun streaming through the first-floor window, it almost seemed that the world had returned to normal and that she could resume the usual happy tenor of her life.

Sitting up between the crisp sheets, she thought of Harry, who had insisted she could not stay at the boarding house, and that perhaps her friend Lydia might put her up for a day or two. And she thought too of Lydia, who had exclaimed, 'Nonsense! A day or two? You shall stay here for as long as you need. For ever, if necessary.' And had fussed about, making everything just right.

It had only been two nights, but they were two nights of relatively sound sleep. Already Effie felt refreshed and calmer. She rose, dressed and went downstairs. Lydia was sitting at the table in the dining room, lingering over a cup of tea. She was as immaculate as ever, dressed for the day, a cheery smile greeting Effie's entrance.

'Good morning, lazybones. I thought you were never going to wake up.'

'I'm sorry, dear, I felt like I could sleep forever. Have I ruined your day with my lateness?'

'Not at all, darling. I'm just happy to see you rested. Though you've slept through one visitor already this morning.'

'Was it Michael?' Effie's heart gave a bound.

'It was your other admirer, actually. Harry Holloway.'

'Oh, don't be silly,' Effie said offhandedly. But something inside her responded to the news of Harry's visit. 'What did Harry want?' she added, in the same casual tone.

'Just to see how you're getting along. I gave him a good report. That you're feeling better, and sleeping well.'

'I'm sorry I missed him,' Effie murmured, and again she felt a distinct thrill, comforted perhaps that Harry was looking out for her.

'Don't worry,' Lydia smiled. 'He's coming back later. For afternoon tea.'

'Goodness,' Effie exclaimed. 'He doesn't need to. I'm perfectly all right.' But her smile betrayed her.

Lydia smiled too. 'Well, it's not just the pleasure of your company that's bringing him back. He also wants to catch up with Ed, and Ed's always here for tea after Thursday surgery. So I thought, better he talks to Ed here rather than at the surgery. Or at the police station. And I'm sure it'll just be routine, Ed has nothing to hide. Anyway, Harry was happy with that. He said he doesn't want to put Ed out by making him go to Russell Street. He just wants to see what Ed knows about the Guerin baby and his adoption.'

'That's very thoughtful of him,' Effie said. 'I don't think Ed would be very comfortable at the station. Particularly if he was interviewed by that horrible inspector.'

'But that's not my only news,' Lydia said, smiling again, a mischievous twinkle in her eye. And she pushed a piece of paper across the dining room table. Effie glanced at it and recognised Michael's handwriting. 'He's popping in this morning,' Lydia added, retrieving the note before Effie had a chance to read it. 'Two men calling on you in the one morning! Effie Davis, you're turning into quite the seductress.'

Effie felt herself colouring, and her pulse starting to race. 'What does he say?' she asked, trying to appear only mildly interested. 'Has he heard about Mrs Wilson?'

Lydia glanced at the note. 'I'm not sure. The note's not very revealing. He went looking for you at the boarding house yesterday apparently, and Daisy directed him here. I suppose Harry must have let her know of your whereabouts.'

'Can I see?' Effie said, anxious to find some sign of Michael's state of mind. But it was exactly as Lydia had intimated, very matter-of-fact, no indication of any particular concern for her. But then, if he had not been told of Mrs Wilson's murder, why should he be concerned? And anyway, the note was directed to Lydia, quite properly, so naturally he would be more formal and less inclined to indicate his feelings.

Lydia noticed her apprehensive expression and smiled. 'Don't worry, darling, I'm sure he's keen to see you.'

Effie smiled back, but half-heartedly. 'I hope so. It's just that we had a little, I don't know, misunderstanding or something, the last time we met. About that Saturday morning. You know, when you saw him in Berry Street. He won't tell me about it, and now I feel there's a distance between us. Or at least there was when we last parted.'

Lydia gave her a quick hug, then took her gently by the shoulders. 'My darling, you need to stop thinking about such things. He obviously had a confidential meeting that morning, which for some reason, no doubt perfectly justified, he is not able to disclose to you. So trust him.'

Effie nodded. 'Yes, you're right, I know you're right. I must get it out of mind. I must trust him. And I do. Of course I do.'

Effie's anxiety about Michael's visit evaporated the moment he was shown into the drawing room by Lydia's maid, Tillie. He was the same old Michael, warm and affectionate to both of them. And for her he seemed especially concerned, giving her a warm hug.

'I've been to see Harry Holloway. What a terrible experience for you,' he said. 'You shouldn't have been exposed to that horrible sight.'

'It wasn't Harry's fault,' Effie replied quietly. 'I insisted on going with them. Harry wanted to take me home.'

'Yes, he told me all about it. I think he regrets he wasn't firmer with you. Anyway, it seems the whole thing is out of our hands, now that these murders have happened.'

'Yes,' Effie said. 'But I am still dreadfully worried for Alfie. Who knows what's happened to him?'

'What do you mean?' Michael seemed surprised. 'At least he has a home now, a decent one, I assume.'

'I'm not so sure about that,' Effie replied. 'And I think Harry has his doubts too. It seems that Mrs Wilson was up to no good. Harry seems to think that the tall man was her accomplice, and that they had a falling out. Who knows what they've done with Alfie?'

Michael looked puzzled. 'But Harry told us that the adoption papers were in order?'

'I know, but I think he's going to investigate that side of things more closely too. He seems to think there may be something irregular going on at the asylum.'

'Surely not!' Lydia exclaimed. 'The asylum does wonderful work. They're excellent people there, I would vouch for all of them.'

Effie shrugged. 'That's what I thought too, when Michael and I were there. But somebody has something to hide, that's obvious. Surely Mary and Mrs Wilson being murdered is just too much of a coincidence for it not to be connected to Alfie.'

Michael stared at her. 'Really? That's a little fanciful, isn't it? There could be any of a number of other explanations for what's happened.'

'Perhaps,' Effie said. 'But I'm convinced the tall man is behind it all, one way or another. Who is he, and what is his connection with Mrs Wilson? Once we find that out, perhaps we'll know what really happened.'

At that moment Tillie appeared at the door with the morning tea and Lydia motioned her in. As she poured the tea, Lydia fixed Effie and Michael with a stern expression. 'Now, you two. We'll have no more discussion about this terrible business. I absolutely forbid it. We are going to sit here and have a pleasant chat about all sorts of other things, nice things. The theatre, music, fashion. I'll even allow some talk about politics, as long as its from the perspective of the progressive woman.' And she smiled at Effie.

Effie smiled back, glad to abide by her instruction, and Michael too, it seemed. Soon they were chatting amiably, buoyed by Lydia's cheerfulness and good spirits. Effie was relieved to be rid of the memories of all the recent terrible events, if only for a little while. But she was the quietest of the three, content in the main to listen to the other two.

As she watched Michael talking easily to Lydia, a slight unease again niggled at her, a sense that he was in some way apart from her, that he had a life that somehow she could not share. And that perhaps it was connected to that Saturday morning when Lydia had seen him outside the asylum. Or perhaps it was just that she felt apart from his wealth, and the opportunities that such wealth provided him. She had to work for a living while he could afford to dabble at being a teacher and artist. He always had his wealth to fall back on if things went wrong, or if he got bored.

It was the same with Lydia, she thought, glancing around the room at the exquisite furnishings. With her independent means and her successful fashion boutique, she too could afford to dabble, to play at being a suffragette, while women like Mary, who were the real victims of male oppression, were the ones who suffered.

But as soon as these thoughts crossed her mind, Effie was seized with remorse. Why was she so unfair to these two dear people who had given her such good friendship? They couldn't help it if their families had bestowed wealth on them. She was just being jealous. For goodness sake, my girl, she said to herself, stop being so foolish.

And resolving never to think such nasty thoughts again, she made a renewed effort to join in the conversation. And so the morning continued, pleasantly enough, until Michael rose to make his farewells, promising to call in and see them again very soon.

'I know,' he said, as he kissed them both. 'Why don't we settle a day for us three to have dinner together? And Ed too, of course. I'm busy this weekend, but what about Friday of next week? At the Maison Dorée? It's very good.'

'Perfect,' Lydia exclaimed. 'Ed and I go there all the time. I agree, it's charming. And the food is quite exquisite.'

'That's settled, then,' Michael smiled. 'And you must all be my guests.'

Ed Wright seemed distinctly uncomfortable at the prospect of Sergeant Harry Holloway's visit. Lydia had told him not to be silly, it was just a formality and all he needed to do was tell Harry he had nothing to do with Alfie Guerin's adoption. But Ed could not be calmed, pacing around the drawing room like a caged beast, and wondering out loud why the dickens the police would want to talk to him. On more than one occasion Lydia was forced to reprimand him, 'Oh, do sit down, Ed, you're being quite silly about all this.'

When the doorbell rang and Tillie ushered in not just Harry Holloway but also Inspector Winston Marks, Ed Wright's already pallid features blanched even more, and his eyes darted nervously from one policeman to the other.

'Excuse us, Miss Smith, Miss Davis, Dr Wright,' said the inspector, taking control of the situation as soon as introductions had been completed. 'We are making some inquiries in relation to the Mary Guerin murder investigation. I understand that my colleague, Sergeant Holloway, has an appointment with Dr Wright at your premises today, so I have taken the liberty to accompany him. I trust you will not object, Doctor.'

'Not at all, Inspector, not at all. Happy to oblige,' Ed mumbled, his quavering voice and fidgeting hands indicating quite the contrary.

Behind the inspector, Harry stood silent and impassive, not his usual cheery self at all. This must be his 'I'm with the boss on police duty' manner, thought Effie, secretly rather approving of this more official side of Harry. She tried to break his formal veneer with a winning smile, but to no effect. Harry, it seemed, was determined to be serious today.

'Now, Doctor, I appreciate you may not wish to undertake our interview in the presence of these ladies,' Inspector Marks continued, offering a rather oily and deferential smirk in Lydia's direction. 'We are happy to escort you back to Russell Street Police Station, if you wish.'

'That is not necessary, Inspector,' Lydia said quickly. 'Ed has nothing to hide. He's quite happy to be interviewed here and now. It can all be quickly got out of the way, I'm sure.'

Inspector Marks seemed taken aback at Lydia's forthrightness, and Ed looked even more nervous. Beads of sweat were breaking out on his brow. But he cleared his throat and managed to respond. 'I can answer any questions you may have, Inspector. But I'm afraid there is nothing much I can help you with.'

'I'll be the judge of that,' the inspector said, and paused briefly before continuing. 'I want to ask you about Alfred Guerin's adoption papers. We considered it might be useful to have a better understanding of what transpired there, given the circumstances of his mother's death and the subsequent death of Rhonda Wilson, the woman who nursed him. But the file was sealed, so we applied to have it opened. Which we have now done, but we are none the wiser as to who the adoptive parents are. It is not revealed in the file.'

'That's not unusual' Ed replied without hesitation. 'It's common in fact. Quite often people wish their identity to remain secret. It is allowed under the guidelines. But whoever approved it would have signed off that the new parents are of good character.'

'You are right, Sir, that is exactly what the file does contain. An attestation as to the excellent credentials of the adoptive family. Signed by the approving doctor. And the signature on it is yours, Sir. You are the one who approved Alfred Guerin's adoption. Which is why we are now asking you for further information about the new parents.'

Ed stared open-mouthed at the inspector. He seemed at a complete loss for words.

'No, no!' he eventually managed to exclaim. 'It was not me! I know nothing about that adoption. Nothing!'

'I'm wondering then how you can explain your signature on the file, Sir,' Inspector Marks said, now fixing Ed with a direct and somewhat accusatory stare. Ed continued to stare back at him, open-mouthed and nonplussed.

'It's not possible,' he managed to exclaim eventually. 'I had nothing to do with that baby, I swear.' And he looked desperately at Lydia, as if to seek validation and support from that quarter.

'Are you sure, Ed?' Harry interposed. 'Perhaps it has slipped your mind. I know you're a very busy person. We would understand if you realise you've made a mistake.'

Ed turned to Harry, his arms outstretched in despairing appeal. 'I haven't made a mistake!' he exclaimed, becoming more and more strident. 'I haven't, I tell you! I take my duties very seriously in these matters, and I tell you, I would have remembered it. I didn't sign those papers!'

Lydia leaned over and grabbed Ed's sleeve. 'We believe you,' she said reassuringly, rubbing his arm. 'But darling, is it just possible that you have forgotten? After all, you know you can be quite absent-minded sometimes.'

'No, no!' Ed retorted, staring at her desperately. 'I would certainly have remembered. I always interview the applicants at great length. I would have remembered that.'

Lydia turned to Inspector Marks. 'You can see that he's telling the truth. There must be some mistake.'

'There is no mistake, Miss Smith,' Winston Marks said, and his manner could not have been more certain. Or less sympathetic. 'I have examined the file and there are only two explanations for that signature. Either Dr Wright has forgotten he signed it, which seems unlikely, given what he has just said. Or it is a forgery. Oh, and there is a possible third explanation, that Dr Wright is not telling the truth.'

'That is a terrible accusation!' Lydia cried, bristling. 'Ed is one of Melbourne's leading doctors, with an impeccable reputation. How dare you accuse him of lying!'

'I beg your pardon, Miss Smith,' the Inspector said haughtily, all trace of deference to Lydia now vanished. 'I'll remind you that this is a police interview into a very serious matter. I'll thank you to maintain your civility, if you don't mind.'

Behind Inspector Marks, Effie noticed that Harry now appeared concerned. 'We are not accusing Ed of anything, Lydia,' he broke in. 'We're simply pointing out all the possible explanations for this apparent discrepancy. And we're seeking Ed's assistance to get to the bottom of it. To find out whether there is any connection between that signature and Rhonda Wilson's death.'

Lydia glared at him without responding. Effie had never seen her friend in such a fierce mood, it was quite impressive. But at the same time rather unfair to Harry, Effie thought. After all he was only doing his duty, and very professionally too. She suddenly found herself speaking up on his behalf.

'Lydia dear, Harry is just doing his job. The police are obliged to investigate everything. I'm sure they will quickly establish that Ed is telling the truth.'

Effie's intervention did the trick. As quickly as it had flared up, Lydia's anger subsided. 'I suppose so,' she said quietly, turning towards Harry apologetically. 'I'm just upset that Ed does all this voluntary work for the asylum, and then he gets dragged into this dreadful business, when he has nothing to do with it. Because whoever is behind this has obviously sought to incriminate him. Of course he will cooperate with the police. Won't you, dear?'

Ed said nothing, just standing there wearing an expression of bewilderment. But he managed a nod.

'Good,' Inspector Marks said, 'your cooperation is noted, Dr Wright. We won't take up any more of your time now. We will require you to attend Russell Street at your earliest convenience, to make a statement in relation to this matter. Good afternoon to you, then.' And he rose and made to go, motioning to Harry that the interview was over. But Harry pulled him aside and whispered something to him. The inspector stared at him, somewhat suspiciously, Effie thought, but nevertheless curtly nodded his agreement.

'It seems that Sergeant Holloway has some further business with Miss Davis,' the inspector said to the room at large. 'So I will bid you all farewell. And you can find your own way back, Sergeant,' he added testily, as Tillie escorted him from the room.

With the inspector gone, Harry stood alone in front of them.

'I just wanted to make sure you're all right, Ed,' he said in a reassuring tone. 'I wanted to meet with you today just to reassure myself that the adoption you signed off on was all aboveboard. And that you were happy with the credentials of the parents. But your claim that you know nothing about your signature on the papers puts a whole new light on things. I'm sure you agree it's a puzzling development, and an important one. So we now need to explore all possibilities, as unlikely as some may be.'

Ed did not reply, and just sat there, still thoroughly miserable and downcast. But Lydia came forward and took Harry's arm. 'Thank you, Harry, we appreciate your concern. And I'm glad that you're the one investigating the case. We trust you to get to the bottom of it.'

Harry gave her a crooked smile and Effie could see that he was pleased to have calmed the waters.

'So, Sergeant Holloway,' Effie said, with mock formality. 'Do you really have any business with me, or was that just a ruse to stay behind and calm us all down?'

Harry started. 'No, no, I did want to see you about something,' he said hastily. 'Just something I need to clarify.'

Effie surveyed him quizzically, intrigued as to what the something could be. 'Certainly, Sergeant,' she replied, smiling. 'I'll show you out and we can talk on the way.'

CHAPTER TWELVE

EFFIE FOLLOWED HARRY into the street, shutting Lydia's front door behind her. 'Surely you don't think Ed has anything to do with this?' she said, turning toward him anxiously.

Harry took her arm and steered her a little way down the street before he replied. 'Of course not. If he were involved in some sort of racket with Rhonda Wilson, he'd either have to be very stupid or very arrogant to put his name to it like that. Even in a sealed file that was unlikely to be opened. And I don't think Ed Wright is either stupid or arrogant. But we can't make assumptions. We have to investigate all possibilities.'

'Did you have to bring that horrid inspector along? He certainly didn't help matters.'

Harry raised an eyebrow and grinned at her. 'Now, now, you mustn't say things like that about my boss.'

Effie found herself smiling too. 'I understand. I suppose there was nothing you could do to stop him coming.' Then she added, 'Poor Ed, I bet he'll worry dreadfully about all this.'

Harry shrugged. 'Nothing I can do about that. Anyway, I don't think we were too hard on him. Were we?'

'Well, you weren't, at least,' Effie reassured him, and gave his arm a pat. 'I thought you were very fair. But what are you saying about Mrs Wilson? What sort of racket could she be involved in? Do you mean baby farming?'

'Don't really know.' Again Harry shrugged. 'But she was involved in something, that's for sure. And knowing old Rhonda, it would have involved money, dodgy money, in one way or another.'

Effie did not want to ask the next question, but she had to. 'Do you think that Alfie is still alive?' she asked tentatively.

Harry frowned. 'This is not what you want to hear, I'm sure, Effie, but I have to be honest with you. It's impossible to say one way or the other. I suppose he could actually have been adopted out, but why keep it so secret? Why forge the approving doctor's signature? And why go to all this trouble, including murder, to hide it all, if it's all aboveboard? That doesn't make a lot of sense. So we do have to face the possibility that he's been, well, disposed of. Because he's no longer of use to somebody.'

'But I don't understand. It seems that one way or another he's been adopted out, so why would it make sense to kill him?'

Harry shrugged. 'Perhaps you're right. I just don't want to get your hopes up that he's alive, that's all. As I said, we have to consider all the possibilities. It seems to me that there are some vicious people involved in this business, and they're unlikely to be thinking too much about Alfie's welfare. Of course I do hope you're right and he is still alive, but it's just too soon to have any certainty about that.'

Effie shivered against the chilly wind gusting down the street. Again she imagined the possible horror of Alfie's fate. 'I'd best be getting back inside,' she murmured. Then she remembered, 'Oh, I'm sorry, Harry, you wanted to ask me something.'

'Oh yes,' Harry said, suddenly looking a little ill at ease. He examined his boots, then stared down the street before turning to her again.

'Actually it's not strictly business. In fact, it's not business at all, I suppose. It's just that I couldn't help noticing that you seemed quite interested in the football match you saw the other day.'

'It was rather intriguing,' Effie said, her sombre mood brightening. 'Not like I had imagined it would be at all.'

'Well, I'm planning to go on Saturday, to watch Carlton play. At the MCG again. Off duty, this time,' he added hurriedly. He paused again.

'That should be nice for you,' Effie said encouragingly. She had a good inkling of where the conversation was going, but she wasn't going to let Harry off the hook. 'Are you going with anyone?' she added innocently.

'Actually I was wondering if you would like to come with me,' Harry said hastily. 'So you can see a whole game.'

Effie looked at him impassively, giving nothing away. The prospect of watching the Carlton footballers again was surprisingly appealing. The prospect of Harry's company for a whole afternoon was even more appealing, but she wanted to keep him on tenterhooks for a while.

'I'm not sure that it would be proper for me to attend the football alone with you,' she said, trying not to smile. She was enjoying this.

Harry shuffled slightly, then noticed the smile playing at the corners of her mouth. 'Well, there would be twenty-five thousand chaperones there,' he said. 'And it will be a great match. We're playing Geelong, and it's always a fast, open affair between us. Which I think you'd like,' he added as an afterthought.

'I think I would,' Effie said, smiling. 'Particularly if Mr Armstrong is playing. I thought he was quite spectacular.'

'Bobby will certainly be playing,' Harry grinned in return. 'He is the hope of the side. That's settled then?'

Effie smiled and Harry's grin broadened. A time was agreed for him to call for her at Lydia's, and she returned inside, her spirits buoyed.

She smiled to herself, wondering how she would explain to Lydia her new-found fascination with Australian Rules Football.

Another Saturday afternoon at the MCG, another vast and noisy crowd in attendance. A crowd that included a recent convert to the church of Australian Rules. And after being exposed to the sacred rituals a second time, Effie was beginning to see them as less mysterious and arcane. She really felt she was starting to get the hang of what it was all about. She feared she must have been pestering Harry with her frequent questions about rules and tactics, but he seemed content enough to patiently explain what was going on, all the while with his eye on the playing field.

As the afternoon progressed, Effie felt she was gathering sufficient understanding of the game to appreciate skilful Carlton play when it occurred, and to cheer at the appropriate times. Ensconced in the back of the grandstand under a rug supplied by Harry, she felt warm and cosy. And by half-time, quite peckish too. She surprised herself by demolishing a rather large meat pie, procured from somewhere or other by Harry, who, for his part, had no difficulty in consuming two of the same pies, as well as a large glass of ale. Suitably fortified against the elements, they settled down to watch the second half.

As the game continued, the Geelong team, the Pivotonians as they were called, seemed to dominate proceedings, with the play mostly at their end of the ground. But Harry explained to her that the Carlton defence was holding up well, only one goal let through, and still a chance for the boys to make up the ground.

Right at the end, there was a piece of brilliant play from the Armstrong lad, who passed the ball to another Carlton player, all alone in the goal square, and an equalising goal was the result. Harry and

Effie leapt from their seats and cheered, as the Carlton crowd around them erupted into joyous frenzy.

The final siren blew and the match was over. The Carlton supporters seemed content with the drawn result, but not so the Pivotonian barrackers, who booed loudly, shouted abuse at the umpires as they came off the arena, and began throwing bottles and other articles onto the ground.

'Let's get out of here,' Harry said, shepherding Effie down the aisle of the grandstand towards the exit. 'Looks like there could be a bit of trouble, and I'm off duty. But I'll be forced to help out if they jump the fence.'

Harry steered her dexterously away from the milling Pivotonian supporters, and through the crowd spilling out of the ground. Before long, they were outside the main gate, and were about to set off for the tram terminus when Harry felt a tug on his sleeve. Looking around, he was confronted by the sly features of the Ferret, grinning up at him.

'Ferret! How the hell did you find me here?' Harry said, in some surprise.

The Ferret grinned again. 'Where else would I find a Blues man like yourself on the day of a big match?' he trumpeted, mightily pleased with himself.

Harry guided Effie away from the exiting crowd into a small alleyway. The Ferret followed close behind.

'I reckon you must have some important news, Ferret, to drag yourself out of the Belle on a Saturday afternoon. Have you got a winner for me?'

'Better than that, Boss,' said the Ferret, leaning in towards Harry confidentially. 'I've been asking around about the old girl, like you told me, and I've got something I reckon you'd like to know.'

'That's good, Ferret, that's good.'

'Worth a bit, I reckon.'

'I'll be the judge of that, Ferret. You know me, I'll pay you fairly if the information is good.'

The Ferret paused, eyeing Harry suspiciously for a moment, then glancing even more suspiciously at Effie.

'All right,' he continued. 'But it's worth a quid, any day of the week. You know, you wondered whether Rhonda was with Ronnie Harris that morning at the Belle.'

'If you could confirm that, it would certainly be worth a quid.'

'Well, she was,' the Ferret squealed. 'Someone seen them that morning.'

'And who might that be?' queried Harry patiently.

'That new barmaid. You know, the blonde one with the big...' And he gestured with his hands to demonstrate the size of the girl's bust, grinning lewdly at Effie while he did so.

'Ah, yes, Maggie, I know her well, she's one we haven't spoken to yet. Is she there today?' The Ferret nodded, and Harry continued. 'That's good. Well worth a quid, I'd say.' And he pulled a note from his pocket and handed it to the Ferret, who seized it and disappeared into the crowd, all in the same motion. Harry turned to Effie.

'Ha! A breakthrough. It's my lucky day. Carlton get off the hook and Ferret comes good with some useful information.'

'How did he find you here?' Effie asked, intrigued by the unlikely meeting with the Ferret. 'He didn't come all the way here on the off chance of seeing you, surely?'

'I doubt it. The Ferret is quite often at the footy, though I don't think he watches it much. More interested in seeing what items might accidentally come his way, I suspect.'

Effie raised her eyebrows and made a mental note to keep out of the Ferret's immediate proximity at all times. She imagined he would have quite nimble hands.

'I'm sorry, Effie,' Harry said. 'I was going to ask you if you'd like to join me for a drink, but I'll need to get down to the Belle now and talk to Maggie. I'll arrange for you to be taken back to Lydia's.'

Effie felt a surge of disappointment. Her spirits had lifted at the Ferret's news. It seemed that they were getting close to exposing the despicable Mr Harris as Mrs Wilson's killer. And probably Mary's too. She did not want to be left out now. She was curious about what the barmaid saw on that morning, and perhaps what she had heard too. And besides, she wanted to find out exactly how well Harry knew Maggie, of the blonde hair and the well-developed figure.

'No, Harry Holloway, you are taking me with you. We can have that drink you promised me at the Belle. They must have a lounge for the ladies.'

'They do actually,' Harry conceded. 'Not the most high class set-up you could wish for, but passable, I suppose. And I don't mind you hearing what Maggie has to say, so long as you promise to keep it to yourself and tell no one. Not even Lydia, I'm afraid.'

'Don't be silly, you know you can trust me.' And Effie felt a thrill of pleasure that Harry had taken her into his trust to such an extent. He offered her his arm, and they set off for the tram stop that would take them down St Kilda Road all the way to the Village Belle.

Maggie Jones was just a shade too pretty for Effie's taste, she decided. Golden blonde curls, cornflower blue eyes and a figure to die for. It was not hard to imagine that she would be one of the most popular features in the front bar of the Belle. Effie had imagined, or perhaps wished for, a blowsy, slightly coarse person, the archetypical worldly barmaid with a heart of gold, but Maggie was definitely not that. She seemed unspoiled by the grind of serving drinks to half-drunken men all day and, all in all, came across as sweet and unaffected. Effie imagined that she might be considered a perfect catch for a policeman like Harry.

And to make matters worse, she seemed very friendly towards Harry, unduly friendly, Effie thought.

'Hello, Harry dear,' she smiled at him, as she came into the ladies' lounge. 'I hear you want to speak to me. Better make it quick, the boss wants me back behind the bar in ten minutes.'

'I wouldn't mind wasting a bit of time in there myself, Maggie,' Harry said, grinning. 'But not today, business calls, I'm afraid.' And, after introducing Effie, he invited her to join them.

'Don't mind if I do,' Maggie said, taking the proffered seat. Effie could not help but note her impressive figure, amply displayed in the tight-fitting, revealing blouse she was wearing.

'I'd better not waste your time, since you're so keen to get away from me,' Harry said, winking at her. 'So I'll get straight to the point. We're interested in who was in here last Tuesday, probably around nine or ten in the morning. Our mutual friend, the Ferret, reckons you saw old Rhonda Wilson talking to Ronnie Harris sometime around then.'

'I sure did,' Maggie replied enthusiastically. 'Having a ding-dong old row they were, too.'

'Are you positive it was them? You didn't get either of them mixed up with anyone else?'

'No, I'm sure, Harry, absolutely sure. I know I haven't been here too long, but Rhonda and Ronnie are both regulars, I know them well. And I noticed it particularly, because there weren't too many people in at that time of the morning, and it was unusual to see Rhonda in the front bar. She's normally out in the lounge. And they was making a bit of a racket, swearing and carrying on. I was thinking about getting the boss to chuck them out. Rhonda in particular, she was really riled up.'

'Ah,' Harry said. 'That's interesting. How did Ronnie seem?'

'Oh, his usual slimy self. But not as worked up as Rhonda. Mind you, he was getting pretty fruity with the language too by the end of it.'

Harry raised his eyebrows and smiled encouragingly at Maggie. 'I can imagine. Did you see them leave? Were they together?'

'I don't think so,' Maggie said, her pretty features screwed up into a frown of concentration as she tried to remember. 'I was about to call the boss, but then I didn't need to because Rhonda stormed off into the lounge, and I remember Ronnie didn't follow her. But then I was serving someone, and by the time I'd finished he was gone. He could have gone into the lounge too, I suppose.'

Harry reached forward and patted Maggie's hand. 'Thank you, Mags, you've been very helpful. Very, very helpful. Now we'd better let you get back to work. Don't want to get you into trouble with the boss. Tell Ted that you were talking to me, he'll understand.'

'Glad I could help,' Maggie said, smiling sweetly. 'See you next Friday, as usual, I suppose.'

'Too right,' Harry said. 'Wouldn't miss it for quids.' And patting Maggie's hand again, Harry rose and bade her farewell.

'When are you going to arrest him?' Effie asked, as soon as they were in the street.

'Who?' Harry said.

'Mr Harris, of course. It's obvious he's killed Mrs Wilson. And probably Mary too.'

Harry shrugged. 'I'm not so sure. Not sure how he could have anything to do with those adoption papers at the asylum. Or even why he would go to that sort of trouble.'

'To hide his tracks, of course. To cover up whatever he and Mrs Wilson did to poor Alfie.' Effie stopped short, distraught at the thought of Alfie at the mercy of those two.

'Hmm, I suppose that's a possibility,' Harry said, without conviction. 'But we don't have enough evidence to make an arrest. He's certainly worth another chat though.'

Effie did not share his doubts. It seemed to her that they had all the evidence in the world. She wasn't sure that Harry was pursuing this as vigorously as he might.

'Really, Harry, I think it's perfectly obvious. What more evidence do you need, for goodness sake?'

But Harry just smiled, that infuriatingly casual grin, and taking her arm set off for the tram stop.

On the tram ride back to Lydia's, Harry sat silent and engrossed, scribbling in an old notebook he had produced from his inside pocket. Effie glanced at him from time to time, and eventually could resist no longer.

'Maggie is certainly a very pretty girl,' she ventured.

Harry glanced at her briefly and nodded, then went back to his scribbling.

'She seems fond of you?' Effie continued, putting an upward inflection in her voice to invite an answer.

Harry nodded again. 'She's fond of everyone,' he answered without looking up. 'She's paid to be friendly to the customers, it's part of her job.'

'And you seem very friendly with her,' continued Effie, undeterred. 'Is that part of your job too?'

Harry put down his notebook and turned to her, a smile playing on his lips. 'Well, I suppose I'm just a friendly sort of bloke. Part of my nature, really. Haven't you noticed?'

Effie pursed her lips, and stared back at him. There was a hint of belligerence in her voice when she spoke again. 'I think you were flirting with her. I thought you were rather unprofessional actually.'

'Heaven forbid!' Now Harry was grinning openly. 'Effie Davis, is it possible that you're just a tiny bit jealous?'

'Of course not,' Effie snapped. 'You've got rather a high opinion of yourself, Sergeant, if you think that.'

Harry chuckled and went back to his notebook, while Effie sat silent for the rest of the trip, grumpily imagining Harry relaxing at the Village Belle on Friday nights in Maggie's charming company.

CHAPTER THIRTEEN

LYDIA PLACED HER CUP OF TEA back on its saucer and, reaching across the breakfast table, took Effie's hand in hers.

'You can't go back there,' she said firmly. 'Given what's happened, it would be just too horrible.'

Effie diffidently returned Lydia's gaze. The thought of returning to the boarding house was indeed unpleasant, but she knew she would have to face it eventually. She couldn't keep imposing on Lydia forever, but perhaps a little longer would not be too rude.

'Would you mind terribly?' she murmured. 'It's just that I'm afraid to go back just now. With Mr Harris still there.'

'You're never going back there,' Lydia said decisively. 'You can stay here with me permanently. As you can see, I've got plenty of room.'

'Oh, I couldn't do that. It would be imposing. Financially, I mean.' But Effie didn't sound steely in her resolve.

Lydia laughed. 'Well, if that's the only problem, you can pay me some rent. But it's got to be half of what you paid that woman. I'm sure her rent was extortionate.'

'Well, it was rather more than I could really afford,' Effie admitted, more than glad to have been overruled.

'Good, it's settled then. And we'll head over there this morning to pick up all your things. Will they fit on a hansom?'

'I expect so. I don't really have much. But wouldn't it be better to leave it 'til this afternoon? When everyone is likely to be out.'

'Nonsense. No time like the present. If it's that nasty Mr Harris you're worried about, then don't. He won't give us any trouble in broad daylight, and anyway, we mustn't let him bully us.'

'I suppose so. If you're sure it will be alright.'

'I am. And besides, we've got an appointment this afternoon. We've been invited to the Federal Coffee Palace for afternoon tea. With Moira and Sir Anthony.'

'That'll be nice. And Ed will be coming too, I suppose?'

Lydia frowned. 'He was invited but the silly booby has refused to go. To tell the truth, I haven't seen much of him in the past few days, ever since that business with the forged signature. He seems to have gone into a big funk and refuses to see anyone.'

'Oh dear,' Effie exclaimed. 'I'm sure Harry doesn't think he's guilty of anything. He more or less told me so.'

Lydia glanced at her quickly, and her features brightened. 'That's a relief. Though I knew the poor dear had nothing to do with it. Don't worry, he's always like this, he's a real cowardy custard. He'll bury himself in his work for a week or so, and then come good. I'm used to his silliness. Anyway, enough of Ed, are we going to pick up your things, or aren't we?'

In the face of Lydia's cheerful insistence, Effie had no choice but to agree. So, in no time at all, they were pulling up outside Number 451, St Kilda Road. Their driver was a solid young fellow, with a physique that Effie estimated would be well-suited to a career in Australian football. Lydia smiled at him and he instantly became putty in her hands, insisting on accompanying them inside and carrying Effie's trunk down to the cab.

The door was flung open as they approached, and Daisy hurried out to greet them.

'Oh, Miss, it's lovely to see you!' she cried, impulsively seizing Effie by the hand. 'It's been so awful here, what with, you know, Mrs Wilson and everything.'

'How are you managing?' Effie asked, squeezing her hand in return. 'Who's looking after things?'

'That is all taken care of,' Daisy replied. 'They've put in a new landlady already. And she's an improvement, I suppose. Though I shouldn't speak ill of the, well, you know,' she added, her voice trailing off.

'Never mind,' Effie reassured her. 'We can't pretend that we liked Mrs Wilson. Even now that she's gone.' Then lowering her voice, 'But tell me, is Mr Harris still here? Have the police been at all?'

Daisy glanced around quickly, then whispered excitedly. 'Yes, that nice policeman, Sergeant Holloway, was here first thing to see Mr Harris. Spent a good half hour with him, I reckon. I heard them talking in the parlour. The language that man was using, terrible it was. Mr Harris, I mean, not Sergeant Holloway, of course.'

'So he's still here?' Effie said. 'I thought Harry might have, you know, taken him away.'

'Well,' Daisy said, 'I wasn't eavesdropping, I swear, but I did hear Sergeant Holloway say he's coming back for another chat very soon. And that Mr Harris better think long and hard about his position. His exact words, they was.'

'Is Mr Harris in at the moment?' Effie tried not to sound nervous.

'I'm not sure. I haven't seen him since then, he might be sulking in his room. But I shouldn't worry about him, Miss, I'm sure your young man here will protect you.' And she smiled winningly at the cabbie, who winked at her in return.

Effie had already packed most of her things into her trunk, and so the task was soon completed, the box heaved down the stairs and carted out to the waiting cab, while Effie and Lydia settled the rent. Daisy had alerted the new landlady, Mrs Pridmore, to Effie's arrival, and that lady soon appeared to see to the financial arrangements. Thin, with steel grey hair tightly constrained in a bun, Mrs Pridmore was prim and entirely business-like, a far cry from Mrs Wilson. She expressed sympathy for Effie and her decision to leave, but nevertheless remained strict in her adherence to Effie's rental conditions. 'Four weeks rent, they are the notice conditions as I'm sure you are aware, Miss Davis. You'll appreciate how difficult it is to rent out premises promptly these days, the market still being slow.'

Mrs Pridmore's insistence was unnecessary. Effie had no inclination to seek any leniency, being more than happy to pay what was owed and leave this place, with its bad memories, forever. She paid the amount, whereupon Mrs Pridmore's brisk business-like air turned immediately to cold indifference, and she retreated to her quarters with a barely audible good day.

'Just as well you're not staying,' Lydia whispered. 'Fancy coming down to that each morning.'

They made their way into the hall and towards the front door. And there, standing at the foot of the stairs and blocking their path, was Ron Harris, towering over them, anger contorting his florid features. Effie shrank back, but Lydia quickly seized her hand and went to push past him towards the front door. Harris moved with surprising speed to block their passage again. The smell of him, a mixture of tobacco and stale sweat, almost overwhelmed Effie.

'Well, look who's here. Miss Stuck-up and her fancy friend.'

Lydia drew herself up to her full height, and responded coolly. 'Excuse me, Sir, you are preventing us from leaving, please step aside.'

Mr Harris abandoned his supercilious tone and gave full vent to his anger. 'Shut up, you jumped up bitch!' he hissed. 'I'll let you go when I'm good and ready. Right after I've dealt with this little snitch.' And he glared at Effie with unbridled fury.

Lydia blanched, but held her nerve, unflinching and refusing to give way. Effie tried to speak, but the words wouldn't come. All she could do was cower back against the wall, her hand still in Lydia's.

'Not so high and mighty now, are you, Missie? Not without your copper mate. Think you can dob me in, do you? Well, let me give you a friendly warning, you better stick pretty close to him from now on, because you never know what might happen to you. You might just have a nasty accident.'

'Don't you dare threaten her!' Lydia spoke quietly, but the resolve in her voice did not waver. 'We're not afraid of you. It's none of your business what Miss Davis says or does, but if you must know, she did not 'dob you in' to anyone. You incriminated yourself, you big oaf. Now step out of our way, or I'll report you for assault.'

Harris did not respond or make any move to let them pass. He just stood staring at Lydia, his fists clenched at his sides. Then he thought better of it and moved to one side. 'Get out of here, you pair of sluts,' he spat out. 'And don't say I didn't warn you.'

Lydia pushed past him, her features pale and drawn, but still managing to convey an air of contemptuous disdain. Effie followed, still clinging to her friend's hand, and staring straight ahead as she hurried past and out the door. Whether from pent-up fear or sheer relief, she burst into tears as soon as the door shut behind them and they found themselves in the safety of the garden. Lydia held her tightly and stroked her head.

'There there, darling, it's all right.' And she steered her into the street, to where the cabbie was waiting, sitting up on the seat of his hansom.

'What happened, Miss?' he exclaimed to Lydia, seeing Effie distraught and weeping.

Lydia smiled, making light of it. 'Oh, nothing much, just a little disagreement with a very rude man.'

The cabbie jumped from his seat, assisting the two women into the cab, and offering to duck back into the boarding house to teach the fellow some manners. But Effie shook her head, suddenly feeling very tired. 'That's very good of you, but let's just leave. I want to get away from here and back home as soon as we can.'

They made their way back to Toorak, Effie gradually recovering her composure as they put the boarding house behind them. She reassured herself that she would not have to return to that place and face Mr Harris ever again. Lydia said nothing, looking out the window with her arm through Effie's, and occasionally giving it a comforting stroke. Once or twice, she glanced across.

'Feeling better?' she ventured.

Effie nodded, smiling gratefully. 'Thank you for…back there,' she murmured. 'You were very brave.'

Lydia grinned. 'Well, not quite that brave. I was putting on a bit of a show. I was rather scared underneath, I must admit.'

Effie laughed, and squeezed her friend's hand.

They sat in silence again, gazing out the window. As the cab turned into Toorak Road, Lydia patted her hand and spoke up, 'You said a very nice thing back there, you know.'

'Oh?' Effie replied, puzzled. 'What was that?'

'You said you wanted to go home. To our place. It's lovely that you think of it as home already.'

'Yes, I suppose I do,' Effie mused. 'But that's only because you have made me so welcome. You're such a good friend.'

And as she sat there, Effie thought too of her other friend, Michael, and the distance that seemed to have now grown between them. All because he had kept that visit to Berry Street secret from her. Was it her fault? Effie knew she needed to accept that it was entirely his business, but still the nagging doubt, the uncertainty, would not go away.

Tomorrow was the first day of the new term at school, and she and Michael would be thrust together again. She resolved to start out afresh, put all that behind her, and re-establish their friendship. It would be a new beginning.

As it turned out, Effie did not have to wait until the next day to make her peace with Michael. That afternoon, when they entered the plush surrounds of the Federal Coffee Palace dining room, they found Michael already ensconced with Sir Anthony and Moira. With them too was Judith Baxter, as elegantly dressed as ever.

Michael rose to greet them, kissing them both on the cheek, and affectionately taking Effie's hand as he expressed his hope that she was feeling better. He explained that he and Judith were dining at the Palace when they had noticed Sir Anthony and Moira across the room, and suggested they all take tea together.

Effie wanted to tell him everything that had happened, particularly about Mr Harris and his behaviour but, realising that such a conversation would best be conducted in private, she resisted the urge and instead thanked him for his concern.

Judith Baxter also rose and approached to greet her, taking her hand and leaned forward to kiss her softly on the cheek, murmuring her own sympathies for Effie's awful experience. Effie felt herself enveloped by the delicate presence of Lily of the Valley, and with the scent, an odd feeling of being uplifted, of being revitalised by Judith's mere presence.

'My dear, it must have been the worst thing for you, being dragged into such a sordid business with that woman. It seems as though the evils of baby farming have not yet ended. But what a terrible death for her, no matter how evil she was. Killed by her fellow conspirator. I take it that is what your policeman friend thinks happened?'

Effie was uncertain as to how she should respond. She realised she still had no clear idea of why Mrs Wilson had been killed. She wondered whether she should mention Harry's thoughts about the mystery of the adoption papers, and what that had to do with the murders. But then she reminded herself that, almost certainly, that had been told to her in confidence.

'I suppose that is what the authorities think,' was all she eventually said to Judith, rather lamely. 'Though of course, no one has told me anything. Is that what people are saying?'

'Oh, yes,' Moira exclaimed, breaking into the conversation. 'It's all people are talking about. How that woman was murdered by her accomplice after a falling out. Who knows how many poor little babies they disposed of between them? It could be another Mrs Knorr.' She seemed oddly animated, not her usual timid self at all.

Effie glanced at Lydia to see if she would offer an opinion. Lydia knew about the forged papers, and must know it was probably more complicated than just Mrs Wilson and Ronnie Harris committing terrible crimes. But Lydia made no comment, and Effie realised that she would hardly raise the fact that Ed's signature had been found on the adoption papers. It was natural that she should protect him from public rumour and gossip. And there was no reason that anyone else would know about that, except for the person who had done the forgery.

Resolving to try and put all these uncertainties to one side and simply enjoy the outing, Effie turned to greet Sir Anthony. Showing better manners than when they had last met, Sir Anthony nodded at her, half-rising in his seat and offering a reasonably civil, 'How do.' But as he did so, Effie realised that his usual ruddy complexion was a waxy grey, and he appeared to be having trouble breathing.

'Please sit down, Sir Anthony,' said Effie hastily. 'You don't seem well'.

Sir Anthony resumed his seat, gratefully. 'I feel damned awful. Have done for days. But it will pass, I suppose.'

Again Moira entered the conversation. 'I told him not to come today. He's too ill. But he insisted.'

'Nonsense,' Sir Anthony said, in a subdued tone, with only a hint of his usual gusto. 'I can't stay at home all day and let this damn illness get the better of me.'

'You silly thing,' Moira said, but with affection in her voice. 'You won't get better unless you do stay home.' Effie was struck by Moira's new-found confidence. It was almost as though she was flourishing in counterbalance to Sir Anthony's infirmity. She was seated next to Effie, and now confided quietly, 'Dr Wright is worried about him. He thinks it may be his heart.'

'What are you whispering about over there?' Sir Anthony exclaimed from the other side of the table. But there was no venom in his voice, he just sounded tired and worn out, as if he did not have the energy to get angry.

'Nothing, my dear, don't worry yourself,' Moira said, in the tone of a mother soothing her child. Changing the subject, she announced brightly to the table, 'Gregory and Joanna are going to join us today. They were held up with baby Anthony. He was putting on quite a tantrum.'

'Are they bringing him along?' Lydia asked. 'I'm dying to see him. I'm sure he's a darling little chap.'

'I don't think so. He's staying with his nanny. He's a real terror if he doesn't get his afternoon nap.'

'What a shame! I was so looking forward to a good cuddle.'

'Oh yes, he's such an affectionate little chap,' Moira said enthusiastically. 'And you can already see the family resemblance. Everyone says they can see Sir Anthony in him. Don't they, dear?'

At the mention of his namesake, Sir Anthony perked up considerably and some colour returned to his cheeks. He nodded proudly.

'No doubt about it. The spitting image of me as a baby. He's a real Hartford, that's for certain.'

At first Effie also felt rather sorry that she would not meet the baby Hartford that afternoon. Her experience with Alfie had awakened strong feelings of affection, and the prospect of cuddling another baby rekindled those same feelings. But being reminded of Alfie would also likely arouse other more painful feelings. It is better to put such memories and feelings out of my head, she thought. I have plenty of other things to think about – school tomorrow, my career, my women's causes.

Her reverie was broken by the appearance of Gregory and Joanna Hartford, making their way down the aisle towards their table. As the couple approached, Effie was instantly reminded of Sir Anthony. Gregory had the same short stature and bustling, bombastic bearing, and just like Sir Anthony with Moira, he was striding towards them well in advance of his wife. He was obviously accustomed to dominating proceedings in her presence.

Joanna Hartford followed discreetly behind, but she was certainly not overshadowed by her husband's presence. Though she could not be described as classically beautiful, Effie thought her strikingly attractive, slim with short cropped dark hair, an aquiline nose and large brown eyes. If she didn't know better, Effie would have assumed her to be of European background, perhaps Italian or French, though Lydia had previously told her that she was Australian-born and bred, her father a tailor from Parramatta in Sydney.

As they made their greetings, it was clear that Joanna was content to play the role of submissive wife, responding to each of Moira's introductions with a demure nod. Yet Effie did not get the impression that she was shy. She seemed to be wearing a mask of reserve, which perhaps concealed a different nature within.

It transpired from Moira's introductions that the Hartfords had never before met Michael or Lydia. Gregory Hartford shook Michael's hand vigorously, staring up at him defiantly and refusing to release his hand for what seemed an uncomfortable length of time. Finally letting go, he turned and took Lydia's hand, fixing her with a leer that managed to display both lust and scorn in equal measure.

'Do you know Judith Baxter?' Moira asked, taking his sleeve in her endeavours to extract Lydia from his unwelcome attention. Gregory turned to meet Judith, who rose from her seat and extended her elegant hand, like a queen welcoming a new courtier.

'Don't believe I have,' Gregory responded, with a sneer that Effie now realised was his standard manner with all women. 'How do, Mrs Baxter. A great pleasure.'

Effie was anticipating another leering examination from Gregory, and was surprised when he gave Judith only a cursory glance before taking his seat. His lust must be reserved for the younger beauties.

Gregory turned to his uncle. 'Feeling any better, old chap? I must say you have a bit more colour about you today.'

Sir Anthony momentarily bristled at his nephew's rather condescending familiarity, but did not appear to have the energy to take him to task. 'No I'm not,' he muttered, and left it at that.

Moira leaned over and touched his arm, stroking it sympathetically. Sir Anthony sighed, closing his eyes momentarily.

Lydia turned to Joanna and smiled brightly. 'We were saying before you arrived how lovely it would have been to meet baby

Anthony. But apparently he needs his beauty sleep in the afternoons.'

Joanna's lips curved into the semblance of a smile. 'Yes, like all babies, he sleeps often. And he is not used to crowds and loud noises.' With a slight gesture of her head, to indicate the throng of chattering diners around them.

'Of course, but we really must see him soon. Moira has told us what a delightful little chap he is.'

'I expect you will, as he gets bigger,' Joanna said, again with the faintest hint of a smile.

'Of course they will,' Gregory added loudly, glancing at Joanna with an expression Effie could not quite fathom. Annoyance perhaps, or impatience. Perhaps that was just his usual way with his wife.

'He's a first-rate little chap,' Gregory continued to the table at large. 'And we're as proud as punch of him. And why wouldn't we be when he's the spitting image of Uncle Anthony? Eh, old chap?' And he leaned over and nudged his uncle with his elbow.

Sir Anthony was again looking very ill, his already waxy features even greyer, but he endeavoured to be cheerful. 'Yes, a terrific little fellow, no doubt about it,' he managed to utter, then relapsed into stricken silence.

Moira leaned over and placed her hand on his. 'Are you sure you're up to this, my dear? We can go home if you like.'

'No, no, a cup of tea will do me good. Just hurry them along, can you?'

Before Moira could respond to Sir Anthony's plea, Gregory leapt to his feet and waved imperiously at the nearest waiter, demanding that tea be served without delay, and there would be hell to pay if Sir Anthony was kept waiting any longer. The waiter eyed him coolly.

'Very well, Sir,' he responded, his tone managing both politeness and disdain, and he strolled off unhurriedly in the direction of the kitchen.

There was an embarrassed silence at the table in the face of Gregory's unrestrained rudeness but, as always, Lydia came to the rescue, steering the conversation into safe waters, and before long they were chatting animatedly about the latest happenings on the Melbourne arts scene. It was obvious that Gregory was not an arts enthusiast, but his ignorance did not prevent him declaiming a loud opinion on every subject raised.

When the conversation turned to matters of Melbourne society gossip, Gregory was clearly better informed, and again intent on having his say on everything. But Effie noticed that his comments and observations had about them a malicious edge.

Effie had no inclination to impose herself into the conversation, happy to enjoy the wit and good humour of her friends while trying to ignore the gauche intrusions of Gregory Hartford. Again she found herself glancing at Joanna Hartford who was also sitting quietly, an expression of almost wry detachment on her face. At one point Joanna's gaze met Effie's and, for the briefest of moments, the mask dropped, and the brown eyes widened. In that second Effie saw a flash of – what was it? An acknowledgement of something? Perhaps a query? Effie could not be sure. Then the eyes averted, the mask returned, and the moment was gone.

Had Effie imagined it? She kept her gaze on Joanna for a while longer, trying to catch her eye again, but she would not be drawn. Effie turned her attention back to the table. The conversation meandered along, tea and petit fours were served and consumed, and all the while Sir Anthony grew paler and more withdrawn.

Moira glanced at him frequently, occasionally gently patting his arm. As soon as they had finished their tea, she suggested quietly to Sir Anthony that they should leave, and apologised to the rest of the table for their premature departure. Gregory, who up until now had seemed oblivious to his uncle's growing distress, suddenly became full of solicitous concern.

'Yes, we'd better get you home, old fellow. We'll come too. You're looking very poorly, I must say. You need to be careful, you know, with your heart the way it is.' And with a great show of dutiful attention, he rose and fussed about Sir Anthony, preparing to shepherd him through the still crowded room towards the entry foyer. Joanna rose and quietly bade them farewell, then followed behind, graceful and upright.

'Sir Anthony does not seem at all well,' Michael observed after they had gone. 'I hope it's not his heart. Has Ed said anything to you, Lydia?'

Lydia seemed surprised by Michael's question. 'Heavens no, he doesn't discuss his patients with me. He's very strict about confidentiality. But he must be concerned about Sir Anthony, I know he has been attending on him quite frequently.'

'I understand there is indeed a problem with Sir Anthony's heart,' Judith interposed, speaking quietly but with authority. 'I believe he is being treated for it.'

'That's a shame,' Michael said. 'He can be rather bombastic, I suppose, but underneath he's not a bad old stick. Must be a worry for Moira. And for his nephew too, I suppose.' The latter observation seemed an afterthought.

Effie could not help but notice that Michael made no mention of Joanna, and any concern she might have for Sir Anthony. It was almost as if Joanna was not part of the family, a stranger on the periphery of the Hartfords. Yet she was the mother of baby Anthony, the last of the Hartford line, and seemingly the apple of his great-uncle's eye. It was strange, thought Effie, that she seemed so emotionally detached from them all.

But Effie did not believe that Joanna was by nature cold and unfeeling. In that one brief look, Effie had caught a glimpse of another Joanna. Who is that other person, wondered Effie? And why does she feel the need to conceal her true self?

CHAPTER FOURTEEN

HOW STRANGE IT WAS to walk through the gates of Merton Hall on that Monday morning. It was almost as though she was seeing the facade of the grand stone building for the first time.

So much had happened in the two weeks since Effie was last here. So many dreadful shocks, and so much upheaval. It had almost driven the everyday familiarity of the school from her mind. And the girls milling about, chattering and laughing, smiling shyly in her direction, were at first like strangers, though two weeks ago they had been so much a part of her life, a part of her school family.

And when she entered her empty first-floor classroom to prepare for the day's lessons, she still did not feel at home. It all seemed so unfamiliar – the dozen or so desks crammed into the room, with her slightly larger desk facing them; the little blackboard set up on its easel to one side. A ripple of panic ran through her, as she wondered how she would cope with it all, the return to this now strangely alien environment.

But as she sat down and opened her mathematics text book, and remembered last term's work, her nervousness began to subside. And by the time she joined Michael and the Misses Hensley on the stage of the hall for school assembly, as she watched Miss Emily rise to welcome the students to another term, the old familiarity had returned and she was once again at ease.

With the normal school routine underway, the terrible events of the past days were driven from Effie's mind. And the further the morning went, the more distant those fearful memories became. Effie found herself embracing the comfort of the ordinary, and becoming absorbed again with her work and her girls.

Here at school, everything with Michael also seemed to return to how it had been before. He was the same old Michael, passionate about his work and warm towards her. Again she felt entirely at ease in his company as they sat chatting in the common room over lunch. Engaged again in the vocation they shared and loved, the incident that had driven uncertainty between them faded into insignificance. 'Whatever did I get so worked up over?' she wondered to herself. What does it matter if he didn't tell me everywhere he'd been? It must have been the stress she was under that had magnified its importance in her mind and feelings. She resolved to put it behind her.

But in the first period after lunch, her Roman History class, everything changed again. There was a brisk knock on the door and Miss Simpson, the school bursar, burst into the room before Effie had time to even move from her desk.

'Could I see you as a matter of urgency, Miss Davis,' she gasped, breathing heavily. She was a large woman and clearly had been hurrying. Her eyes were wide with the importance of her mission.

'There is a gentleman to see you,' she whispered none-too-quietly, as soon as Effie had closed the door and joined her in the corridor. 'In the library. He's from the Criminal Investigation Branch,' she added, staring wide-eyed at Effie, as if searching for some sign of shock or guilt in her face. 'He didn't give his name.'

'It's all right, Miss Simpson.' Effie smiled, affecting nonchalance, as if a visit from the CIB was almost an everyday occurrence. 'It's just a small matter that cropped up during vacation. Quite trivial, really.' But she knew it would be far from trivial for Harry to call at the school, and she feared the worst.

Leaving Miss Simpson in temporary charge of her girls, Effie hurried downstairs and into the small front room that served as the school library. As she entered, she searched Harry's face for some sign of the news he no doubt had for her. But he was impassive, and there was none of his usual cheerfulness.

'I wonder if we might talk in the garden, Effie?' he suggested. She looked questioningly at him, and he added, 'Some information for your ears only. Just need to make sure we're alone. Do you mind?'

Effie shrugged, and without speaking escorted him from the room and through the front door.

'This will do, I think,' he suggested after they had descended the stone steps, wandered across the lawn to a huge old Morton Bay fig tree, and found a garden seat under its canopy, well out of earshot of the building.

Effie could contain herself no longer. 'What is it, Harry? What's happened?'

Harry considered her gravely for a moment. 'There's been a development. It probably amounts to nothing, but it concerns you, so I need to ask you about it.'

'Yes, yes! What is it?' Effie stared at him impatiently.

'Well, Ronnie Harris has presented at Russell Street this morning, and has claimed that Mrs Wilson was a baby farmer. That he became suspicious when one of her fostered babies disappeared suddenly. And he claims he told you about his suspicions. Told you that Rhonda was up to no good.'

Effie continued to stare, but this time in alarm. The memory of that morning came flooding back, the memory of Mr Harris's sneering comments. For some reason, she felt a pang of guilt running through her. 'Well, yes, he did say something to me. That Mrs Wilson was like that lady, you know, the one that was hanged for killing babies.'

'Mrs Knopff.'

'That's right. But I thought he wasn't serious. I mean, he was serious, but I thought he was just being nasty. I didn't think he liked Mrs Wilson much.'

Harry stroked his chin and stared into the distance. 'That's interesting,' he said eventually. Then again, 'That is interesting.'

Effie couldn't quite see what he was getting at. 'But what's so new about that. We all know she was up to no good.'

Harry lowered his voice. 'The thing is, the boss thinks he was in it too. With Rhonda Wilson. That they've had a row, he's killed her, and now he's trying to make out she was in it alone. And that it's all too convenient, him coming forward now to dob her in. Now that she's not around to incriminate him too.'

'But you don't agree?'

'Well, for a start there's no direct evidence to incriminate him. Certainly not enough to make an arrest. And anyway, I don't think he did kill her.'

Effie was incredulous. 'Why ever not, Harry? Isn't it obvious?'

Harry returned her gaze impassively. 'Well, no, I don't think it is that obvious. I know it would be very convenient if Ronnie Harris was our man, but strangely enough, I believe him on this one. Not necessarily what he claims about Rhonda Wilson, but I don't think he murdered her. He's a rogue, no doubt about that, but why would he carry on about Rhonda to you if he was tied up with her in a racket of that sort. He'd be keeping dead quiet about it. Don't you think?'

'I suppose so,' Effie conceded, but there was doubt in her voice. She tried to think of Mr Harris and Mrs Wilson as partners in crime. It didn't seem likely. But perhaps that was what he was trying to do, raise suspicions about her in advance, so that people would not suspect him if anything went wrong. Just as it had now.

'But I can see the other side of it too,' she retorted. 'He's quite cunning.'

'I'm sure he's cunning. And I'm sure he's up to no good. But murder? I don't know. And I keep on coming back to Alfie, and Ed Wright's signature on his adoption papers. Apparently forged. What's that got to do with Ronnie? How could he have done that?'

'Perhaps he knows someone at the asylum. A nurse, or someone else who works there.'

'Perhaps, perhaps. I suppose that's an angle we could investigate.' Harry's tone clearly indicated his doubts that such an investigation would bear any fruit.

Harry lapsed into silence, staring absently at the garden. Effie was about to ask what was on his mind, but he spoke first.

'In the meantime, you shouldn't worry. About Ronnie Harris, I mean. We're keeping a close eye on him. He's still very much a person of interest.'

'Thank you, Harry, I appreciate that. I must say I'm still a bit afraid of him.' And Effie went on to describe their disturbing encounter with Ronnie Harris at the boarding house. As she did so, Harry's expression darkened.

'Make sure you don't put yourself in that position again. Harris is a bully, and like all bullies, happy to threaten defenceless women. But when push comes to shove, he's a coward at heart. I don't think he'd follow through on his threats. Anyway, as I said, we've got him in our sights, so you can take comfort in that.' And impulsively, he took her hand in his and gave it a squeeze.

'Thank you again, Harry.' Effie smiled warmly at him, her gratitude augmented by the agreeably pleasant touch of his hand on hers.

Harry smiled bashfully back at her, then rose to take his leave. 'I'd better go. I've taken up enough of your time.'

But Effie thought he still looked unsettled, not his normal unflappable self at all. Now it was her turn to reach out and take his hand in hers. 'I'm sure you'll get to the bottom of all this, Harry. No one's going to get the better of you, you're too clever for that.'

Harry gave her a lopsided grin. 'I suppose I will. Eventually. It's just that I hate these kinds of cases. You know, where babies are involved. I know it shouldn't, but it still upsets me. Not very professional, is it?'

'I'm glad,' Effie said. 'I'd be upset if you weren't upset. But I know you won't let it get in the way of your investigation. And I won't hold you up any longer. I'd better get back to my class.' She smiled and patted his hand again.

By the time Effie reached the main door into the building, Harry was already out the main gate and striding down the street. Even at this distance she thought she detected a renewed determination in his stride. She smiled to herself, quietly pleased that she had been able to have a positive effect on him. Pleased too that he needed her support and encouragement, and had been willing to seek it.

Despite Harry's disturbing news, Effie's mood remained positive throughout the school day. But as soon as she walked out of the gates and boarded the cable tram for the journey down Toorak Road to Lydia's apartment, she began again to feel the weight of all that had happened bearing down on her.

By the time she had completed the short walk down Williams Road and arrived at Lydia's fashionable terrace house, she found herself again dwelling on the dreadful business with Mrs Wilson, and on her fears about baby Alfie's welfare.

Even Lydia's bright presence and cheerful chatter about her day in the shop could not revive Effie's spirits. She tried to put on a happy face and return her friend's conversation, but Lydia quickly saw through the facade. She led her to the couch, sat her down and said firmly, 'Now, darling, you're too quiet, I can see that something is wrong. Was school very trying today?'

'Oh no,' Effie replied, eyes downcast. 'It was a great relief to be back there actually. It was wonderful to be with my girls again. It was all so, I don't know, normal, I suppose.'

'Was it Michael then?' Lydia ventured. 'Was he still distant?'

'No, no, Michael was just like his old self. Very friendly, very nice.'

'Well, what is it then? It always helps to get it off your chest.'

Effie sighed. 'It's just all this dreadful business with Mary and poor Alfie. And Mrs Wilson. And today Harry came to see me with more worrying news.' She had not meant to reveal this to anyone, was not sure she had Harry's permission, but she could not hold it in. She blurted out everything that Harry had told her, about Mr Harris's accusations, his suspicious behaviour, even about Harry's doubts. And she instantly felt her anxieties beginning to ebb, as if unburdening herself to Lydia somehow put it into a calmer perspective.

Lydia listened gravely and when Effie had finished, she said, 'It's all horrible, and I know it must be very upsetting for you. But you are free of it now. You're here with me, you're back at school, and gradually it will all fade away and become just a bad memory. And Harry Holloway is a good policeman, he will get to the bottom of it, and this man Harris, or whoever is behind it all, will be caught and punished.'

'I know, you're right. I was very wrong about Harry. He is a decent man. And he's been very nice to me.'

Lydia laughed and raised her eyebrows, and Effie felt herself reddening.

'Well, well, I think perhaps you are a touch sweet on the sergeant. I know he's certainly sweet on you.'

Effie reddened further. 'Don't be silly,' she retorted, rather too quickly. 'He's just being friendly.'

'Of course, darling,' Lydia said, still smiling. 'Anyway, I have a plan to get your mind off all these horrible memories. Two plans actually. Firstly, did you know that Miss Spence is speaking at the Storey Hall on Wednesday evening?'

'Really?' In all the turmoil of the past two weeks, Effie had completely lost touch with her women's interests. Catherine Spence stood alongside Henrietta Dugdale and Louisa Lawson in Effie's pantheon of suffragette heroines, and the opportunity to hear her speak sent a thrill of excitement through her.

'Yes, the Suffrage Society has organised a lecture. They say she is very knowledgeable, and quite entertaining too. So I hope you will come with me, I am counting on it.'

'Of course I will. I'm sure it will be very stimulating. And diverting.'

'Good, that's settled then.' And Lydia leaned back on the couch, looking pleased with herself.

'And what is your other plan?' Effie asked. 'I hope it's as interesting as the first.'

'Ah,' Lydia cried, springing to attention again. 'The second plan is even better, and more immediate. I guarantee it will make you forget all your cares.'

Effie managed a smile. 'Well then, you'd better tell me what it is.'

'We are going to Maison Dorée for dinner tonight. Just the two of us.'

'Oh, how delightful!' Effie said. But then she recalled Michael's descriptions of that exclusive establishment. 'But I've heard it's expensive. Rather more than I can afford, I'm afraid.'

'That's why it's my treat,' Lydia proclaimed. 'And before you object, I sold three French chiffoniers today, so we are celebrating. I insist.'

'Thank you, you're so good to me.' Effie felt herself close to tears, overwhelmed by her friend's kindness. She tried to think of the right words to express her gratitude, but Lydia was already on her feet and bustling about. 'Come on, we must hurry and get changed. The cab will be here soon and we can't have you appearing at Maison Dorée looking like you've come straight from the classroom. Off to your room now, and I shall see you in fifteen minutes, transformed into a Melbourne society beauty.'

From the street, the Maison Dorée appeared anything but the acme of sophisticated Melbourne dining. Squeezed between a tobacconist on one side and the Anglo American Tailors on the other, the restaurant's exterior was drab and uninviting. No light shone from the narrow front windows, which seemed to be hung on the inside with dark drapes. These curtained windows stood on either side of an unprepossessing wooden front door which opened directly onto the street, unprotected by awning or verandah. Were it not for the electric streetlight which cast its light onto the sign above the entrance, the place would have been easy to miss. Effie was beginning to have her doubts as she followed Lydia through the front door.

Once inside however, the contrast could not have been more stark. Soft lighting revealed rich red carpet, burnished brass lights on the walls, white linen and silver cutlery on the tables. There was an overwhelming aura of wealth and prestige. An elegantly dressed and very gallic maître d' materialised from nowhere, greeting Lydia formally, but with a familiarity that indicated she was a regular at his establishment.

'Good evening, Alphonse,' Lydia said brightly. 'We need some cheering up. We're looking forward to a selection of your finest dishes.'

'Of course, Miss Smith. Your regular table is waiting, madam,' he replied, taking their coats. A waiter discreetly appeared, ready to lead them to their table, but Alphonse waved him aside imperiously. No doubt to demonstrate Lydia's importance at the Maison Dorée, he insisted on leading them personally to a far corner of the room. Here their candle-lit table awaited, adorned with fresh roses. Effie took her seat somewhat self-consciously as waiters hovered with napkins at the ready.

'This is rather grand, isn't it?' she whispered to Lydia, as soon as the waiters had retreated sufficiently to be out of earshot. 'It makes me a little uncomfortable.'

Lydia raised her eyebrows and chuckled. 'Don't worry, darling, I don't think we're compromising our political principles by being pampered once in a while. Besides, I guarantee you will lose your misgivings once you taste the food.'

And she was right. First the devilled oysters, then sole meuniere, followed by delicate quails in a red wine sauce, and finished off with petite meringue cakes accompanied by fresh strawberries and clotted cream. With each delicious course, embellished with Lydia's always entertaining chatter, Effie felt the gloom begin to fade away and the brightness of life return. The flickering glow of the candlelight on their table seemed to reflect the mood of shared warmth between them, shrinking the world to this one corner, limiting it to the elegantly set table and Lydia's charming company.

'This has been good for me,' Effie found herself saying, after Lydia insisted on ordering a glass of the finest house Bordeaux to accompany their quail. 'It was a wonderful suggestion. Thank you.'

Lydia reached across and stroked her hand. 'I'm glad it helped. I thought it would. This place always has a wonderfully recuperative effect on me.'

'I can see why,' Effie said, sitting back, and glancing around the room. To her surprise, beyond the circle of candlelight that enclosed them, she could see that the room was now actually quite full. Cloistered with Lydia in their own little pool of light and their shared conversation, Effie had not noticed other diners arriving. Now she looked about her, wondering who all these privileged people were – these people who could afford to dine in such intimate luxury, and on a Monday evening too. Effie was again struck by a sense of the habitual world of the idle rich, a world that she would never really be a part of, did not even want to be a part of.

As Lydia chatted on, Effie continued to glance around the room, taking in the opulence of it all. Her attention was drawn to a table on the far side of the room where a couple were seated close together, their backs more or less to Effie, leaning towards each other in animated conversation. Nothing unusual in that, but it was the straight-backed familiarity of the man, the curl of his hair over his collar, the particular way he had of leaning confidentially towards his companion. Effie knew instantly who it was, and was in no way surprised when he turned his head and the unmistakeable profile of Michael Standish was revealed.

At the same time, the woman turned her face towards him, and it was the beautiful smiling features of Judith Baxter. Effie's heart missed a beat as she saw Judith move even closer to Michael. Her kiss seemed to linger for an eternity and, even at a distance and in the dim light, Effie thought she could sense the intimacy, the passion between them. She saw Michael take Judith's elegant hand in his, saw him looking into her eyes as they sat there, engaged in obviously ardent conversation. What words were passing between them? What had passed between them already? Effie did not dare think.

'My goodness, darling, are you all right? You look like you've seen a ghost.' The sound of Lydia's voice mercifully brought Effie's attention back from the scene across the room. She saw Lydia's alarmed expression and realised that the shock on her face must be obvious.

For a moment she was struck dumb, unable to convey what she had just seen. 'Oh, it's nothing,' was all she managed to stammer at first. Then realising that would not do: 'I think I saw someone: someone I know.'

'Oh, who?' Lydia said, instantly curious.

Immediately Effie regretted her words. She should have said nothing, should have pleaded feeling unwell and made her escape. Now it was too late, she would be forced to face them.

'Michael, I think,' she mumbled, trying to pretend his presence in the room was of only passing interest.

'Michael? What? Where? Oh yes, so it is, and Judith too. Let's go say hello.'

Effie could feel herself reddening, mortified at the prospect of interrupting what was obviously an intimate tete-a-tete.

'It's very late,' she said, rather lamely. 'Perhaps we should be going home. I have school tomorrow.'

'What are you talking about, darling? It would be very rude not to say hello.' And rising to her feet, she took Effie's arm and steered her in Michael's direction. 'Why are you being so coy?' she whispered affectionately, as they made their way across the room.

Judith saw them coming from some way off and smiled warmly, waving an elegant hand in their direction. She rose to her feet to embrace them both. Effie hardly dared look at Michael, but when she did sneak a glance she saw that he was far less at ease. He too rose, but his smile seemed forced, his manner tentative.

'How lovely to see you both,' Judith said, then turned to focus her full attention on Effie, taking her hand and squeezing it gently. 'How are you, my dear? I've been very worried for you over that baby farming business. What a dreadful thing to endure. I do hope you're bearing up.'

'We're doing our best to forget about it,' Lydia said, before Effie could think of a reply. 'We've had a lovely dinner in a superb restaurant and now we've encountered dear friends into the bargain. The pick-me-up is almost complete.'

'What a wonderful tonic,' Judith agreed. 'And I do hope you will join us for a coffee.'

Effie tried to think of a halfway convincing excuse, but it was too late. Lydia had already accepted enthusiastically, a waiter was summonsed to set up two more chairs, and then they were all together, making small talk around the table. To her mortification, Effie found herself seated opposite Michael, and spent her time trying to avoid his gaze. Which wasn't too difficult because he seemed to be trying to avoid hers as well.

'And what are you two doing here?' Lydia inquired brightly, seemingly oblivious to the possibility of a romantic tryst. Effie hoped the dim lighting was hiding the growing flush around her own neck. She studiously examined the cup of coffee that had just been placed in front of her.

But Judith remained as calm and at ease as ever. 'Michael and I have been having a wonderful dinner,' she explained. 'Nothing special, just two good friends enjoying a pleasant evening.' And she reached across and slowly stroked Michael's hand, placed rather formally on the table in front of him. She made it seem for all the world that it was the most natural of occasions, but Effie could patently sense, in the rigid set of Michael's posture, and in the almost proprietorial feeling that Judith emanated, that more than a casual chat had passed between them. And that kiss: was it just warm affection from an old family friend? Effie had an overwhelming impression that it conveyed something more intimate and, what's more, that Judith was not trying to hide the intimacy, was almost flaunting it, as she sat with her elegant hand casually placed on Michael's.

Lydia didn't seem to notice any of this, or if she did, was too polite, or too sophisticated, to react to it. She continued to chat animatedly about music, the theatre, and general Melbourne gossip. And of course about the suffragette meeting in two days, which, she was sure, they were all keenly anticipating.

Michael did his best to participate but Effie could see that his gaiety was forced, his laughter strained. Once he caught her eye and smiled tentatively. But behind the smile she could see ... what? Pain? Embarrassment? Regret? She could not tell. She smiled fleetingly back at him, then averted her eyes.

As soon as they had finished their coffee and a suitably polite interval had passed, Effie made her excuses and suggested they should make their way home. Michael agreed, rather too readily, and they all said their goodbyes. Effie had been dreading how she would say goodbye to Michael and was on the point of extending her hand to shake his, but he leaned in to kiss her cheek, then moved on to do the same with both Lydia and Judith. He would catch his own cab home, he explained to Judith, it was too far out of her way to go home via Prahran.

Effie felt some comfort at this, that at least they were now going their separate ways, but her relief was fleeting. Once she and Lydia were in the hansom cab for the journey home, all her doubts came flooding back. That show of parting in the restaurant was probably just for her benefit, she conjectured. Perhaps Michael and Judith's separate cabs had a common destination – Michael's cosy lodgings in Prahran, or the charming villa in Kew.

Don't be such a jealous fool, Effie castigated herself, why can't Michael have dinner with an old family friend? Surely that's all there was to it. And Judith's kiss, surely that too was simply a sign of affection between old friends. After all, in the dim light she couldn't be sure that Michael had responded to it, had actually kissed her back. But then, why was he so strange and unsettled when she and Lydia had interrupted them?

It was no use, the suspicions continued to swirl around inside her. The incident had quite destroyed her recovered equanimity, and she was again cast down into gloom. And with her despairing mood, all the other anxieties, the horrors of the past two weeks, returned as well.

Sitting in the hansom cab alongside Lydia, Effie shivered in the coldness of the Melbourne July night. She tried to think comforting thoughts, but none would come.

Effie found herself looking forward more and more to Wednesday evening's meeting. Not just for the chance to see and hear the famous Catherine Spence, a heroine to women teachers across the country, but also to take her mind off the painful thoughts that seemed to be continually engulfing her. School was no relief: she could not seem to focus her mind on her teaching, and found herself snapping unfairly at her girls when they answered incorrectly or did not understand their work.

And Michael, though he was polite and friendly enough, was not really his old self with her. In the teacher's common room, where he usually joined her to share lunch and chat about the morning's lessons, he now sat by himself, absorbed in his work. One part of Effie wanted to draw him aside, and ask him to confide in her, to offer her support for whatever was troubling him. But the opportunity did not seem to arise, there was always one of the Misses Hensley present, or within earshot. And besides, she knew another part of her did not want to hear what he might confess, that Judith Baxter was the focus of his affections, rather than herself.

Effie wondered if she had ever been the focus of Michael's affection. She had thought, had hoped, that there was a growing feeling and understanding between them. But what if, on his part, it was no more than a cheery friendship with a fellow teacher? What if, in his eyes, Judith Baxter was a fascinating, desirable woman of the world and she, Effie, was just a naive girl who he was taking under his wing out of the goodness of his heart?

Yet, as these thoughts ran around in her mind, there arose in her too a dawning awareness that perhaps she did not care that greatly if she was not the object of Michael's romantic affections. That what was really troubling her was his unwillingness to confide in her, to trust her to be his friend. And that he had obviously chosen Judith Baxter as his confidante instead. It was all so confusing and unsettling.

For the first time in her short teaching career, Effie found herself relieved and glad when the school day ended and she could retreat to the sanctuary of Lydia's apartment. Though she knew that she was not proving good company there either. She was silent and moody, and for the first time in their friendship she was beginning to resent Lydia's constant good cheer and chatter, annoyed that she was being forced to put on a happy face, when she was feeling not in the least inclined to do so.

So on the Wednesday evening, it was with some relief that she set off with Lydia for the Women's Temperance Assembly Hall in Flinders Street. There at least, she thought, I can sit and listen and not have to make the effort of conversation. And hopefully my thoughts will be diverted from all that has been going on.

When they entered the large, austere hall, a fair crowd of women had already gathered, well over one hundred in Effie's estimation. The attendees were seated in rows of chairs that had been set up near the front of the hall. Effie and Lydia hastened to take up two of the few remaining seats, in the back row but still with a decent view of the stage, where a row of chairs and a small dais had been set up. Here the more important women in the movement sat. Effie recognised Mrs Dugdale and some of the speakers at the recent rally.

'Which one is Miss Spence?' she whispered to Lydia.

'The lady on the end,' Lydia replied, pointing to an older woman with a round, kindly face. She had the dress and demeanour of a sweet old nanny rather than a radical firebrand, but Effie could see in the firm set of her jaw and the clear confidence of her gaze over the audience, that here was a woman of substance. Effie's sense of anticipation heightened.

A young woman with a prominent nose and rather aristocratic features rose and took her place at the dais. Effie recognised her from the Spring Street rally, it was Miss Vida Goldstein, who, together with her mother, was celebrated for bringing about the monster petition in support of universal suffrage. By Effie's reckoning, she must be of a similar age to herself, in her mid-twenties, but what a difference in what she had made of herself, what she had already achieved in her life. Effie resolved to herself that henceforward she must become more active in the movement, more committed to the cause.

Miss Goldstein gave a brief summary of Catherine Spence's long and distinguished career before announcing the topic of the night's presentation. Effie had been hoping for a lecture on education, and Miss Spence's experiences advocating for educational opportunities for girls. But instead Miss Goldstein announced that Miss Spence would talk about her work in the Boarding Out Society, and the important issue of improving the welfare and opportunities for destitute children.

Effie knew that this was another of Miss Spence's grand visions and lifelong passions. In normal circumstances she would have been intensely interested in what the great lady had to say, but as she spoke Effie began to feel uneasy. Miss Spence's examples of the great benefits accruing from fostering out children from institutions into the community now seemed flawed, in light of what had happened to Alfie. Fostering is all very well, Effie thought to herself, all good in theory, but there are always evil people prepared to prey on the weak and helpless.

When the speech had finished and everyone, to a woman, rose to their feet in rapturous applause, Effie was reluctant to follow suit. But she did so, offering only a half-hearted clap.

The formal part of the evening was now at an end, and Effie wanted to go straight home, she was in no mood for mingling, but Lydia would not hear of it. Supper and a cup of tea beckoned, and would it not be nice to catch up with the many friends who were here?

'Oh, very well,' Effie conceded reluctantly. 'But only for a short while. I'm rather tired, and I still have work to do for school tomorrow.'

'Oh, look!' Lydia exclaimed, pointing into the crowd. 'Isn't that Joanna Hartford? Over there, talking to Miss Goldstein!'

Effie was taken aback to see that it was indeed Joanna Hartford. She had not thought that the wife of Gregory Hartford would be interested in issues of women's rights. Then she remembered the brief glance that had been directed her way at afternoon tea, and the sense that behind those dark eyes dwelt a sensibility far removed from Gregory Hartford's crass boorishness. Perhaps she had misjudged the nature of this woman.

The two were engaged in earnest conversation. Apart from her close-cropped hair, Joanna bore a remarkable resemblance to the famous Miss Goldstein.

'I hope you don't mind if we interrupt you, but we just had to say hello,' Lydia exclaimed, breezing up to them.

Too bad if they do mind, thought Effie, trailing behind her friend, and hoping to convey the impression that barging in like this was certainly not her idea. But both Vida Goldstein and Joanna seemed unperturbed, breaking off their conversation and turning towards Lydia. Vida smiled warmly and offered her hand in greeting. Joanna simply nodded to both Lydia and Effie, fixing them with a steady gaze that was neither welcoming nor hostile. But guarded, thought Effie, definitely guarded.

Following the exchange of introductions, it was Lydia, as usual, who dominated the conversation. She hailed Miss Spence's stimulating address, enthused over the gratifying attendance at the meeting, speculated on the prospects for success on the suffrage issue, and hastened to remind Vida of the excellent work carried out by the infant asylum on behalf of destitute and deserted women and their babies. Vida listened attentively to Lydia's discourse, smiling politely, and from time to time adroitly punctuating Lydia's word stream with a well-considered comment or observation. Her intelligence was palpable, or at least so it seemed to Effie, and in a woman so young, even more impressive.

After a few minutes the women were joined by Judith Baxter, materialising out of the crowd with an almost regal presence. She was clearly well acquainted with Vida Goldstein, greeting her warmly, and embracing Lydia and Effie as well. Effie stiffened as she approached, trying to discern any crack in her perfect veneer. But she was as composed as ever, no sign of discomfort or embarrassment. She kissed Effie warmly and touched her arm, then immersed herself in conversation with Lydia and Vida.

Such was the animated discourse between the three, Effie would have found it difficult to intrude herself into the conversation, even if she had wanted to. But she was content to stand on the outside of the discussion, happy to play the role of the silent observer.

And so too, evidently, was Joanna, standing next to Effie and also content to simply listen to the others. After a short while, Effie could not resist a quick glance in her direction. To her surprise she found herself looking directly into Joanna's deep brown eyes.

Effie started slightly before recovering herself.

'How did you find Miss Spence's talk?' she ventured politely.

Joanna's steady gaze did not waver. 'It was instructive,' she replied, a quiet intensity in her voice. 'I'm sure her program is very worthy, but I wonder whether there is another side to the story. Sometimes the best-intentioned and most humane of actions can be thwarted by the power of evil.'

Effie was struck by the feeling apparent in Joanna's words, and by their resonance with her own thoughts. 'That is the very reservation that ran through my mind,' she replied. 'It's so interesting that we both had the same reaction.'

Something resembling a half-smile played on Joanna's lips. 'That is not so unusual,' she observed. 'When I first met you, I sensed we had much in common. I feel it more strongly now, even though we have only spoken briefly.'

Effie felt herself attracted to, and at the same time disquieted, by Joanna's quiet fervour. Again she sought to return the conversation to a more mundane level.

'Is that what you were discussing with Vida when we interrupted you? Your reservations, I mean.'

'I was asking her how she and Miss Spence could be certain that all fostered children were happy. That they were not abused or neglected in their new homes. That they had not simply exchanged one kind of misery for another.'

'And what did she say?'

'That she could not be certain about that. But that nothing in life is certain. And that they could only do their best to ensure the adopting parents were suitable. I thought it was an honest answer.'

Joanna lapsed into silence and Effie wondered what thoughts were running through her head. Thinking back too on her earlier words, she now felt emboldened to pose a question.

'You said earlier that you thought we were alike. I was wondering what gave you that impression? After all, we hardly know each other.'

Joanna smiled, and her words in response were spoken intensely but quietly, almost whispered, despite the hubbub around them and despite the fact that they had drifted away from the earshot of the others.

'I think we both come from a different world. Not like the world we now live in. Where people feel they are entitled to whatever they want, and have no concept of the suffering and deprivation that most of the world endures.' And with the faintest flicker of her eyes in the direction of Lydia and Judith, she made it clear who she was talking about.

Effie felt the urge to come to the defence of her friends, but at the same time Joanna's words struck a chord. It was the same unease that she had felt with Michael and Lydia and Judith, at their acceptance of the privileges they enjoyed, even as they busied themselves caring for the poor and underprivileged. But her unease was countered, as always, by the affection, the love she felt for her friends, and her gratitude for the love they had shown her.

'I understand your feelings,' she said carefully. 'But I'm sure you have a loving husband, and you're blessed with a sweet little baby. That must be a joy to you.'

Joanna looked at her again, very directly, and Effie fancied she saw moisture welling in the large brown eyes. But when she answered, her voice was steady.

'Yes, I should be grateful,' she said, slowly and deliberately. She paused again before speaking, and this time there was renewed urgency in her low tone. 'Do you sometimes feel that your life has been a great mistake? That you must change things before it is too late?' Not waiting for a response, Joanna took her arm and whispered in her ear. 'I do. That is what I feel. All the time now.'

Effie stood, shocked, taking in the confession she had just heard. She had thought that Gregory Hartford and Joanna were an unlikely couple, and in one way Joanna's words did not surprise her. But what shocked her was the frankness of her confession, and the bitterness evident in her words. And that she was prepared to draw a relative stranger into her innermost secret feelings. Why? Had she no intimate friend to confide in? Perhaps not, Effie thought. Perhaps she has seen me as a kindred spirit, and chosen me to share this secret with.

Effie was at a loss as to how she should respond to this entirely unexpected outpouring. But she was spared the need to find suitable words by the appearance of Judith at their side.

'I'm so sorry, we have been neglecting you both. We always get carried away at these meetings, I'm afraid. So many interesting issues, so many fascinating women.'

'Oh, that is perfectly understandable, Judith.' Effie hoped her voice did not reveal the confusion she was feeling. 'Joanna and I have been having an interesting discussion too,' she added, then immediately thought her words rather lame. She glanced across at Joanna for support, but the mask had come down again, as quickly as it had lifted, and Joanna simply gave an almost imperceptible nod of her head.

'I apologise again, Effie dear,' Judith said reaching out to touch her arm in sympathy. 'I should have asked you how you are feeling. You know, under the weight of that terrible business.'

'I am coping, thank you,' Effie responded, rather formally. She was determined not to show any emotion in front of Judith, to reveal any weakness that would further accentuate the difference between them. But at the same time, Effie felt the enticing warmth of her sympathy, and had to resist a brief and powerful urge to collapse into her arms, to be held and comforted by her. Perhaps this is what Michael felt, thought Effie. Perhaps this is what attracted him to her.

But of course Effie did not throw herself into Judith Baxter's arms. She just stood there, feeling awkward and wretched, but determined not to cry.

'I'm sure your Sergeant Holloway will get to the bottom of it,' Judith continued, smiling reassuringly. 'He seems very capable, and I'm sure he's a great comfort to you.'

He's not my Sergeant Holloway, Effie thought, annoyed at the assumption in Judith's comment. But she did not react, instead forcing a half-hearted smile and nodding vaguely.

'People are saying that he has a suspect. That an arrest is imminent.' Judith's raised eyebrow indicated that the second statement was really a question and a response was required.

'Oh, I don't know,' Effie responded, circumspect now and remembering her role as Harry's confidante. 'He doesn't tell me anything.'

Judith's half-smile somehow conveyed the impression that she did not believe this for a second, but she made no attempt to probe further, instead commenting on the recent pleasures of the Maison Dorée. Had Effie enjoyed her dinner? Did she try the lobster Newburg? It was absolutely exquisite. Judith's tone was chatty and friendly, but Effie could not help but think that there was a hint of triumph in her voice. That she was gloating at having been discovered dining intimately with Michael, at winning his affections away from her.

Effie felt herself wanting to challenge this woman, to tell her she did not believe her story about the dinner between friends, to demand to know what she was up to. But she was powerless to confront her, to challenge that immaculate, sophisticated veneer. And besides, how could she possibly claim that Judith was seeking to become romantically involved with Michael? It was ridiculous, she was almost old enough to be his mother. Just because a man and a woman were dining alone by candlelight did not of itself prove they were romantically involved. And yet, the air of intimacy between the two had been so obvious, she was sure there was something going on. And Michael's reaction? That embarrassed nervousness, what did that mean?

Mercifully they were now joined again by Lydia, bubbling over with excitement after talking to Vida Goldstein, and Effie could again take a back seat in the conversation. Joanna soon excused herself and drifted off, and then Judith too was called away to join a group of society matrons. They wanted her views on Miss Spence's speech and the adoption question. Judith smilingly excused herself, but not before embracing Effie, and kissing her softly on the cheek. Again Effie felt an alarming clash of emotions: anger and resentment fighting with a desire to be comforted. In the end she just felt miserable.

Now alone with Lydia, she took her friend's arm and implored: 'Can we go home now? I have such a dreadful headache coming on.'

'Of course, darling, of course! How shameful of me, I've been neglecting you terribly. We'll have you home in a jiffy.' And true to her word, Lydia bustled them out into the street and into a hansom, with instructions to the driver to hasten as much as was compatible with a comfortable ride home.

Effie leaned back against the leather upholstery, anticipating the pristine sheets and the cosy warmth of her bed at Lydia's. She must have dozed off, because she was half wakened by Lydia's exclamation.

'Hello, who's this? I do believe it's Harry Holloway. What does he want at this hour, I wonder?'

Fully awake now, Effie peered out the window, and saw a police trap drawn up outside Lydia's terrace house. Standing in the street next to it was the unmistakeable, towering form of Harry. As they drove alongside, Effie could see that he looked tired and drawn, his features jaundiced under the artificial yellow glow of the electric streetlights. Seeing them approach, he stepped forward, raising his arm, either in greeting, or perhaps simply as a signal to attract their attention.

A gamut of emotions ran through Effie in quick succession: a pleasant feeling at seeing him again, then concern at his obviously exhausted state, then dread at the news that was impending. At this hour of the night, she knew it would not be good.

CHAPTER FIFTEEN

→✳←

HARRY HOLLOWAY LOOKED DECIDEDLY SOLEMN. From his uncharacteristically worried frown, Effie knew something was up, seriously up. And he wasted no time in coming to the point.

'Sorry again for pestering you both at this time of the night, but it can't really wait for the morning,' he said, as he perched on Lydia's sofa.

'Why ever not?' Lydia asked, more intrigued than alarmed.

'Well, here's the thing.' Harry studied his boots for a moment before resuming. 'The thing is, Ronnie Harris has gone missing.'

Effie stared at him. 'What? What do you mean? I thought you were watching him? You told me not to worry!'

Harry's eyes were red-rimmed. 'We were watching him. Well, we were meant to be. But earlier today he slipped through our net somehow, and he's gone. No sign of him anywhere.'

'But how?' Effie could not believe it, her faith in Harry's competence beginning to falter again.

'It was at the Belle actually.' Harry's voice was low, as if he could hardly bring himself to recount the disastrous event. 'As you know, it's his regular pub, so we weren't too worried about him being there. And we had men watching both entrances, as well as one in the bar keeping an eye on him. But he just disappeared. Left the bar and disappeared. Never left the building, according to my blokes, and I trust them.'

'That's all very mysterious, and frustrating for you, I'm sure, Harry,' Lydia said, 'but I really can't see why the urgency to tell us about it.'

Harry frowned again. 'I don't know, perhaps I'm being too cautious about this, but I'd prefer to be on the safe side. Given what we now know about Ronnie, and given what he said the last time he saw Effie, I'd prefer to have one of our blokes keep an eye on her, starting from tonight. Until we track him down.'

Now it was Lydia's turn to be alarmed. 'Do you mean she's in danger?'

'I can see no reason why he would want to do anything to Effie,' Harry said quickly. 'It's just a precaution. Safety first.'

Effie sat in the armchair opposite Harry, trying to take in what he was saying. For some reason she didn't feel threatened by this latest development, felt instead a growing certainty that there was nothing to be afraid of. Perhaps it was because she trusted Harry to keep her from harm's way, had a strengthening awareness of his commitment to keeping her safe.

But there was also Mr Harris himself. She was beginning to agree with Harry, that there was no reason for Mr Harris to harm her. No, she thought, he is far more likely to be fleeing as fast as he can from the long arm of the Melbourne law, and chances are I will never see him again. For which she would be very thankful.

Instead of fearing for her own safety, Effie was feeling instead a mounting concern for Harry. She remembered that Winston Marks saw Ron Harris as the prime suspect. He would probably be displeased that their man had now disappeared. Perhaps Harry's current haggard expression was also on account of a dressing-down he had recently received from his boss.

'Will you get into trouble over this?' she asked quietly. 'It wasn't your fault that your men lost him.'

Harry forced a lopsided half-smile which did nothing to reassure her. 'Well, I can't say the boss is too happy about it, and he did give me a fair roasting. But we'll catch Ronnie Harris, and whoever else we need to catch, and life will go on.' But Effie could see that his confidence had been dented.

'Now, look here, Harry Holloway,' she said firmly, putting on her best schoolmarmish tone. 'You know you're a brilliant detective, twice as smart as that silly boss of yours, and don't you forget it. I don't want you getting all down in the mouth just because you've had a little setback.'

That did the trick. He perked up immediately, and she could see the old confidence returning. 'You're right, Miss Davis. As always.' And he winked at both of them, the old Harry grin reappearing in earnest. Effie smiled in return.

'Good, that's more like it. Now, get yourself home for a good night's sleep. I'm sure tomorrow will bring better news.'

Effie woke on Thursday morning, refreshed and determined to put on a positive face throughout the day. Particularly in her dealings at school with Michael. She would take Judith Baxter at her word, that her interest in Michael was as a family friend, and she would trust that Michael would be open and honest with her. And if he did not reveal his whole life to her, she would convince herself there were good reasons why that was necessary.

She was pleased too that Harry was as good as his word. When she opened Lydia's front door to make her way to the tram stop, there was Willie Milton, waiting for her in the street, dressed in civvies for his surveillance duties. He gave her a cheery good morning, and as they set off to the tram stop together, informed her that he had just replaced a colleague who had been watching the premises all night. Willie also advised that he would be in the vicinity of the school all day, keeping a sharp but inconspicuous eye out for any sign of Ronnie Harris. He could guarantee that if Ronnie did turn up he would snaffle him quick smart. And he would be waiting to take her home as well, so she need not worry on that score either.

Willie's cheerful company further boosted Effie's spirits. He spent the journey to school educating her about the finer points of Australian Rules football, and the glories of the Carlton football team. Effie listened with interest, happy to be diverted by this interesting new topic.

But when she arrived at school, there was no sign of Michael in his usual spot at the common room table. This was odd because he was usually so punctual. And when he had not turned up by assembly time at 8.30, Effie began to worry. Where could he possibly be?

After assembly, Miss Emily took her aside and asked, rather sheepishly, if she knew whether Mr Standish was indisposed. 'I wouldn't have asked, but I know you are rather friendly with Mr Standish, and I thought he might have got word to you somehow if he was ill.'

Effie shook her head, now thoroughly anxious about Michael's welfare. Her distraught expression must have alarmed Miss Emily. 'I do apologise, Miss Davis, I hope I didn't give the impression that I was implying anything improper. It's just that it's so unlike Mr Standish to be absent and not notify us. I am rather worried about him.'

'Oh no, Miss Hensley, no offence taken. But I've not heard from Mr Standish either. I haven't seen him since Sunday. I mean, away from school, that is.' Effie hoped she had not reinforced any impression Miss Emily might have of a special nature to her friendship with Michael. But Miss Emily just smiled absently at her, and hurried off to organise Miss Simpson to babysit Michael's now teacherless class.

All through her morning classes Effie continued to be distracted and anxious. Miss Emily was right, it was so unlike Michael to be absent without notice. Perhaps he had fallen ill overnight and was too poorly to get a message to the school. Perhaps even now he was lying in his sick bed with a raging fever and no way of getting assistance. More than once Effie contemplated approaching Miss Hensley and getting her permission to take a cab to Michael's house. Accompanied perhaps by Miss Simpson, for propriety's sake. Just to satisfy themselves that he was not in distress.

But each time Effie resisted the urge. And just as well, because when she came into the common room at lunch time there was Michael in his usual spot, hunched over his work.

'Where have you been?' she could not help but blurt out, more loudly that she should have, and sensed immediately the Misses Emily and Florence turning to look at her. 'We were wondering where you were.'

As Michael looked up and she took in his appearance, Effie instantly regretted her words. He looked absolutely wretched, tired and unshaven, his handsome features sunken and drawn.

'I'm sorry, Effie,' he said abjectly. 'I've conveyed my apologies to Miss Emily. But something came up. Something important. I was detained unavoidably.'

Effie felt herself close to tears. She was filled with anxiety about what could be troubling him so deeply. But she was also frustrated and deeply hurt, that he could not, or would not, confide in her about his troubles. She felt their friendship slipping inexorably away.

Despite the eyes that she knew were focussed on them, she approached the table and put her hand out to touch his shoulder. She spoke quietly: 'You know you can talk to me if there is something wrong. You know I'm your friend.'

Michael bowed his head and turned away briefly before composing himself. 'Thank you, I wish we could talk,' he whispered, and his voice was scarcely audible. 'But it is too hard at the moment.'

Effie sat in the chair next to him. 'Is it Mrs Baxter?' she found herself saying. 'I would understand.'

Michael turned his head to face her, and it seemed that, for a moment, he did not comprehend her words and their meaning. Then he seemed to focus, and slowly nodded his head, as if remembering something.

'No, it is not Judith. But she has been wonderful,' he said softly, and for a moment his features relaxed. 'She has been a good friend to me.'

Effie had never felt so alone, and so distant from him. There was nothing more she could say. She rose and returned to her seat while Michael returned to distractedly examining his preparations for the lesson ahead.

Then came the sound of Miss Emily ringing the bell to send them off to afternoon classes. Michael rose quickly to his feet and excused himself, but not before taking her hand impulsively.

'I am sorry for not confiding in you, Effie dear. One day perhaps I can. I hope I have not hurt you too much.'

Effie said nothing, not knowing how to respond. Oddly, she did not feel hurt by Michael's unwillingness to share his secret with her, at least not hurt in the way he seemed to be implying. Instead she was beginning to realise that what she thought she had felt for Michael, and what she had hoped he might feel for her, was perhaps just a fantasy, just a dream of her own making. And that her growing awareness of this was very much linked to Harry Holloway, and to the increasing prominence he was having in her thoughts and feelings.

✢

Effie's first-floor classroom faced towards Domain Road. In the autumn, the view from her windows had taken in the full glory of the front gardens – the spreading plane trees, the grand old Morton Bay fig, the curving rows of carefully tended flower beds that traced the outline of the green lawns. At that time of the year, Effie would often allow herself to pause at the window and take in this pleasant vista, perhaps indulging in a daydream or two as the girls behind her laboured quietly at their work.

In the winter though, with the plane trees now bare, her view was primarily of the busy street beyond the tall wrought-iron fence; not quite as soothing to the soul, but imbued with its own fascination nevertheless. Effie still occasionally enjoyed lingering there, watching the passing traffic, both human and vehicular, and wondering idly at the lives being lived out. Her view also took in the imposing school entrance gates, and the broad gravel drive that curved through the gardens, passed in front of their building, and then extended to the small asphalted quadrangle by the side of the building. This square was fringed with garden seats, where the girls sat to eat their lunch, and where school assemblies were held in the more pleasant months.

Today Effie had decided to set her girls an essay on the rise of the Roman Empire, a task that would consume the whole of the first afternoon lesson. And once she was satisfied that they were all fully occupied and engaged with their work, she soon found herself at her familiar position by the window. But today she gazed distractedly into the distance, taking in nothing. Her thoughts were entirely on Michael and the events of the morning. What did it mean? Why had he appeared so distraught? She knew there was not necessarily a connection with his visit to Berry Street the week before, but she could not get it out of her head that, somehow or other, whatever was troubling Michael was linked to that visit.

These troubling thoughts ran around Effie's mind, unresolved and unrelieved. But the sight of a familiar figure hurrying from the school building, down the gravel driveway towards the entrance gates, abruptly jolted her focus outwards towards the world beyond the classroom window.

As she watched, Michael strode, almost ran, through the gates, then stood in the street. As he did so, he was approached almost immediately by a female figure who, Effie realised, must have been waiting outside the gates, out of Effie's sight, hidden from her view by the tram shelter.

The young woman strode up to Michael, and Effie immediately recognised her brisk walk, her straight-backed confidence, even before she turned slightly and her nurse's uniform became apparent beneath her open coat, her auburn curls visible underneath the broad hat. It was unquestionably Denise Jackson, the matron they had met when she and Michael visited the asylum in search of Mary.

Even at this distance, Effie could detect the urgency in Michael's stride as he hastened towards her. The two met in the gateway, and Michael seized her hand as their heads inclined toward each other in conversation. Or had the matron seized his hand? Effie could not be sure, such was the mutual intensity of their greeting.

Effie watched, both fascinated and shocked, as the two stood on the footpath engaged in deep conversation. What could it mean? Less than two weeks ago, Michael had met this woman for the first time, or so he had professed, and here they were, locked in conversation that, whatever it was about, was not the polite chat between two strangers who had only met once previously. For the first time, Effie's bewilderment at Michael's recent actions became tinged with a dreadful shadow of suspicion, a creeping fear that his odd behaviour was not resulting from an illicit romance, but was somehow connected in some sinister way with the asylum and the terrible events of recent days.

As she stared transfixed, Michael stepped away from Denise Jackson and, clearly agitated, began to pace up and down in the street, gesticulating as he did so. The matron quickly strode after him, pulling him back towards her and seizing both his hands in hers. They stood in this manner for some time, still in animated discussion. Then, just as abruptly as they had come together, they parted, Michael hurrying back down the drive towards their building.

Denise Jackson stood still, watching him depart, then she slowly turned and walked away, towards the tram stop, Effie assumed.

Turning away from the window, Effie re-entered the world of her classroom. Her girls were labouring away as diligently as ever, all heads down and absorbed in their work. But Effie suspected that at least a few of those intent young heads had only just returned to the page in front of them, and had been staring at Miss Davis, and wondering at whatever it was outside the window that had so absorbed her attention.

CHAPTER SIXTEEN

FRIDAY CAME AND WENT, but nothing from Michael about his meeting with Matron Jackson. He was preoccupied and distant at school, and made no mention of visiting Effie and Lydia on the weekend. The proposed dinner at Maison Dorée also seemed to have slipped from his memory. For that at least, Effie was thankful; she was in no mood for false gaiety.

All in all, Michael scarcely even acknowledged her existence. There was no sign of Harry either; he seemed to have disappeared off the face of the earth. At least he has a reasonable excuse to avoid me, Effie thought, remembering Harry's harried manner when they had last met. She found herself wondering whether he was coping with the investigation, felt a knot of anxiety in the pit of her stomach, that Winston Marks's displeasure with him might be more profound than Harry had made out.

Effie knew that Harry coped with adversity by shrugging it off with a grin, dismissing setbacks as minor irritations in the inevitable push forward to achieving his goal. This indomitably cheerful optimism was one of the things she found herself liking in him. But the last time they had met, his air of nonchalance and confidence had been missing, replaced by an undisguised uncertainty. Effie found herself wanting to see him, to support him and to bolster his confidence again. She was tempted, but resisted the urge to quiz Willie Milton about Harry's whereabouts on their way home from school.

At least, Effie thought, I will have Lydia on the weekend to cheer me up. But that was not to be either. Over breakfast on Saturday morning, Lydia, looking far from her usual sunny self, announced that she would be gone for most of the day. Ed, she confided, was still in a terrible state about the forgery business, brooding endlessly on his conversation with Inspector Marks and Harry, and on the statement he had been forced to give at Russell Street. Apparently he was terribly afraid that it would all get out and his reputation would be in tatters. And Lydia could say nothing to convince him otherwise.

So Lydia had arranged a picnic in the country, just the two of them, hoping that the sunny winter's day, combined with the selection of delicacies she had arranged for their hamper, would lift his spirits, as much as could be expected with Ed at least.

'He is such a booby, he really is,' Lydia sighed, picking at her toast. 'Though I can't help but love him all the same.'

Despite herself, Effie smiled at this. She was beginning to understand the unlikely bond between her friend and Ed Wright. In some odd way they complemented each other.

Over a second cup of tea, Effie briefly contemplated confiding in Lydia about the strange meeting she had observed on Thursday from her school window. Lydia was a regular volunteer at the asylum. Perhaps she would have a simple explanation for the encounter between Michael and Matron Jackson. But somehow it seemed disloyal to Michael, as though she would be betraying him and whatever secret he was harbouring.

So she sat quietly, sipping her tea and smiling sympathetically as Lydia catalogued her various frustrations with Ed's current state of mind.

Effie had just finished her tea when Lydia's monologue was interrupted by the sound of the doorbell, rung three times in quick succession.

'I wonder who that is at this hour on a Saturday morning,' Lydia said, turning in her chair. 'Perhaps Ed's decided to come out of his funk and look on the bright side for a change. Let's hope so.'

They did not have to wait long for an answer to Lydia's question. Lydia's maid, Tillie, burst into the room, breathless and flustered. 'I'm sorry, Miss, but Miss Williamson is at the door,' she almost whispered. 'I think you'd better come.'

'Goodness, Tillie, show her up. Whatever is the matter with you?'

Tillie stood there, wide-eyed. 'Well, the thing is, Miss, she's in something of a state. An awful state. She didn't seem to know me. I think she may need help.'

Now Lydia was on her feet and through the door, Effie following as quickly as she could. By the time Effie was down the stairs and at the front lobby, Moira was already in Lydia's arms, clinging limply to her and sobbing uncontrollably.

'Whatever is the matter?' Effie cried, shocked to see Moira in such a state. But Moira did not respond, indeed did not seem to hear her.

The two friends managed to manoeuvre the stricken woman into the tiny downstairs sitting room and settle her into one of the two armchairs. Moira sat there, pale and crumpled, the colour quite drained from her face. Lydia perched on the armrest beside her, holding her hand tightly and stroking her hair. Moira was making an effort to calm herself, but to no avail. The sobs continued to wrack her body, though eventually the weeping subsided sufficiently for her to speak.

'He's gone,' was all she managed to say, in a voice that was scarcely audible.

Effie and Lydia glanced at each other, as the terrible possibilities in her words took hold.

'Do you mean Sir Anthony?' Lydia said, and then added, 'Has something happened to him?'

Moira's head sunk onto her chest, the life seemingly drained from her. 'He's gone,' she repeated. 'Taken from us. This morning.' And again she broke into distraught weeping.

'That's terrible,' Effie exclaimed. 'I knew he was ill, but I had no idea it was that bad.'

Effie's words seemed to help Moira compose herself, and she stopped weeping. 'It was his heart,' she said, now speaking dully, almost matter-of-factly, as if there was some kind of inevitability about Sir Anthony's death. 'Dr Wright said it was his heart. He's been with him all during the night.'

'I'm so sorry,' murmured Lydia. 'He didn't suffer, I hope?'

Moira looked at her blankly. She began to speak again, plaintively, almost as if to herself. 'What will happen to me now? He hates me, I know. What will happen to me? I will have nothing.'

'Who hates you, dear?' Lydia said softly. 'Who are you talking about?'

'Gregory,' Moira replied, staring about fearfully. Her eyes widened as she turned her gaze fully on Lydia. 'He threatened me, you know. Told me I was just after Anthony's fortune and he would make sure I never got a penny of it. What have I done to deserve that? I've always been nice to him.'

'Of course you have, dear,' Lydia said, stroking Moira's hair. 'Take no notice of what Gregory said. I'm sure that Sir Anthony would want you to be taken care of. And has made sure you will be.' But her glance across the room at Effie did not express the same confidence.

Moira began to sob again, quietly at first, then with increasing abandon. Despite the warm cosiness of the parlour, Lydia felt her begin to shiver violently. 'She needs a draught of something to calm her down,' she whispered across the room at Effie. 'I do wish Ed was here, I have nothing I can give her.'

To their surprise, these words prompted Moira to recover her composure momentarily. 'Dr Wright says he will come as soon as he can. He told me to tell you that. He said he will come after he has seen to everything.' And the thought of what Ed was seeing to precipitated a further burst of violent sobbing.

'You must lie down then, until he arrives,' Lydia said firmly, helping Moira onto the sofa and sending Tillie upstairs for blankets. 'I know it's hard, but you must try to calm yourself.'

'Thank you,' whispered Moira, closing her eyes. All of her recently found confidence had vanished as she lay there, a tiny, almost childlike figure, her features deathly pale, wisps of hair clinging damply across her face.

Ten minutes passed in silence – Effie sitting in the armchair and Lydia perched beside Moira on the sofa – as she lay there, eyes closed, her sobs gradually diminishing. Her breathing grew more rhythmic, and once or twice she twitched, as if caught in a bad dream. But she was not asleep, as Lydia discovered when she quietly tried to release her hand from Moira's apparently limp grasp. The fingers quickly tightened around Lydia's wrist with renewed intensity, and her eyes opened.

'Please don't leave me,' she implored, her voice an urgent whisper. 'I'm so afraid.'

Lydia smiled reassuringly. 'Shh, just try to be calm, dear. We'll take care of you.' And she sat patiently by her side as Moira again closed her eyes.

The sudden chiming of the doorbell broke the silence, and despite their expectation of Ed's arrival, both women could not help but be startled. Entering the room behind Tillie, Ed appeared tired and drawn, his eyes bloodshot, his features sallow. He looked completely done in. But he stepped forward quickly when he saw Moira on the sofa, opening his bag as he approached.

'I am sorry, my dear,' he murmured to Lydia, taking Moira's hand from her grasp and feeling the pulse. 'I came as quickly as I could, but there were requirements of me. Unavoidable.'

'Of course, of course,' Lydia replied quickly. 'Don't apologise. It's a terrible time. But I'm worried about you too, darling. You look awful, you need to get some rest.'

'I'm all right,' Ed replied wearily, as if he was just too exhausted to say more. 'I must see to this poor lady now.' But he held Lydia's glance briefly and Effie noticed the flicker of intimacy between them. The unspoken understanding that he would confide in her about the events of the past night when they were alone.

Moira glanced up at him as he sat himself beside her on the sofa, his usually ungainly form now surprisingly certain and sure in its movements. He produced a small bottle from his bag, and from it carefully poured a measure of clear liquid into a graduated glass tumbler.

'Sit up and drink this, Moira,' he instructed, his tone gentle but firm. 'It will calm you.'

Moira meekly obeyed his instruction, swallowing the measure with one gulp before sinking back onto the sofa. Ed rose and, catching Lydia's eye, pointed silently to the door. The two women joined him in the lobby. Effie glanced back over her shoulder as she left the room. Moira remained prone on the sofa with her eyes closed, waiting for the calming effects of the drug to take hold.

As soon as they were alone in the lobby, Ed spoke. 'She has been through a great shock and she needs to rest. That draft will soon take effect and she'll sleep.'

'But where can she stay now?' Lydia asked. 'She shouldn't be at her home alone, and I don't think she can stay at Chittingly. It would be too terrible for her, and besides, I think she's afraid of Gregory.'

'You're probably right.' Ed's usual worried air had returned. 'I'm not sure where she can go.'

'Well, that's settled then, she stays here. She can go into my bed and I'll take the sofa.'

'You will not,' Effie said firmly. 'If anyone is to take the sofa, it will be me. No argument now, we'll move her into my room.'

Lydia smiled briefly. 'Well, if you insist. I can see there's no point in starting an argument.' Then turning back to Ed, she asked in a low voice: 'Is it really as Moira says? About Sir Anthony? That his heart failed.'

'Yes', said Ed wearily. 'It appears so. Over the past two weeks he worsened rapidly, and there was nothing I could do, I'm afraid. But his end was peaceful, at least. There wasn't a great deal of pain.'

'But it was so sudden,' Lydia exclaimed. 'Only a few weeks ago he was so hale and hearty.'

Ed frowned slightly, as if he himself was not altogether comfortable with the rapid progression of Sir Anthony's illness. But his tone was quite certain when he spoke. 'Yes, it was a rapid decline. Unusually rapid, but in my experience not unprecedented. Sudden onset of heart failure can sometimes occur in men of bucolic disposition. And once the heart begins to weaken, sadly there is not much we can do.'

Ed stood there silently, his head drooping. Effie wondered whether he was pondering the events of the past day from a medical perspective, or whether he was simply too tired to speak or move.

Lydia took his hand and squeezed it. 'Get yourself off home and get some rest. We'll talk tomorrow.' Then impulsively she pulled his face down towards her and kissed him on the lips. 'You really are quite a wonderful man, you know.'

Ed, managing to look embarrassed and pleased at the same time, smiled wearily and said he would return in the morning. After he had departed, Effie and Lydia returned to the parlour. Their intention was to move Moira into Effie's bedroom, but she was already fast asleep: Ed's draft had done its work, and they decided to leave her there to sleep for the present. Lydia looked at the clock on the mantle.

'Goodness, it's two o'clock and we haven't had lunch,' she said. 'I'm not terribly hungry but we should eat something. I'll get Tillie to make us a sandwich.'

Effie nodded mutely, suddenly overwhelmed with weariness herself. But before they could make their way upstairs, the front door pealed again. 'Perhaps Ed has forgotten something,' Lydia exclaimed, and hurried to the door, calling out up the stairs to Tillie that she would take care of it.

But it was not Ed. 'Oh, hello, Michael,' Effie heard her exclaim to the visitor. 'Come in.'

Michael entered the parlour and, seeing Moira prostrate on the couch, whispered an apology and turned to leave again.

'Don't worry,' Lydia reassured him, taking his sleeve and guiding him back into the room. 'Ed has given her a draught. You won't disturb her.'

'I heard the dreadful news about Sir Anthony,' Michael said, still speaking in a low voice. 'I called around to Chittingly to pay my respects but things were in disarray, I'm afraid. No one was prepared to see me. But they said Moira and Ed had come around here, so I thought I'd see if I could be of any use.'

Effie tried to smile and behave normally but could not quite manage it. She felt a flush rising at her throat as she remembered watching Michael from her classroom window. She could not help but feel as if she had been spying.

'Michael dear, that is sweet of you,' Lydia said. 'But all is in hand. We've settled Moira and she is sleeping, thank heavens. The poor thing is distraught, as you can imagine.'

'Yes,' Michael said. 'He was a difficult fellow at times but she seemed genuinely fond of him. I assume she will be properly taken care of? In his will, I mean.'

'I hope so,' Lydia replied, 'but she is rather fearful that she will not be favoured. That the family will somehow cheat her out of any inheritance. They cannot, can they?'

'I'm no lawyer, but I can't see how they could if Sir Anthony has included her in his will. And I'm sure that, for all his faults, he did genuinely care for her.'

'I think he did.' But Lydia sounded less than convinced.

'Was it his heart?' Michael asked, changing the subject. 'That's what people are saying.'

'Ed thinks so,' Lydia said. 'He thinks it's a straightforward case. Nothing he could do for the poor man. A family weakness, perhaps.'

Michael nodded, slowly and absently. After another short silence, Lydia asked him if he would like to join them for a light lunch.

'Thank you, but no,' he replied. 'I'm sure you're both tired and would like to rest. I'll leave you be.'

'But I wonder if I might speak to you alone before I go, Effie,' he said, turning to her suddenly. Effie's heart jumped in her chest and she felt the flush growing warmer on her neck. She nodded her assent. Lydia smiled at Effie and her eyebrows ever so slightly arched upward. She bade Michael farewell and disappeared up the stairs. Michael stood in front of Effie, his hands clasped together.

'You look dog tired,' he began. 'Why don't you take tomorrow off from school. I can take your classes and explain to Miss Emily that you're unwell.'

Effie hoped that this was not what he had got her alone to discuss, and was impatient for him to get to his real purpose. But still, she was grateful for his offer. She felt as if she could sleep for a

week. So she accepted, thanking him for his kindness, then waited
for more.

'I also wanted to apologise to you,' he began after a further short
pause. 'I feel I have been neglecting you, and I know you've been under
great pressure. With the murders and everything. And that fellow Harris
still at large. I'm afraid I've not been a very good friend to you. But I
have been under some pressure myself.'

Effie stared at him evenly, her embarrassment gone. I'll just tell
him the truth, she thought, and spoke without hesitation. 'I know that
something is troubling you, Michael. I can see that. I said you could
confide in me but you seem not to trust me sufficiently, or value my
friendship sufficiently, to do so. That is what disappoints me.'

Effie was shocked to see Michael's eyes moistening. His hands
unclasped and reached out to hers. He looked into her eyes, speaking
very clearly, and she knew, without any subterfuge. 'It is because I
value your friendship so much that I cannot speak to you about what is
happening. But I hope to very soon.'

Effie's bitterness evaporated. Now she just wanted to help him, to
get her dear friend back. 'Is it something to do with the asylum?' she
ventured. Then dared to say, in a low voice, 'I saw you with Matron
Jackson at the school.'

Michael gave an involuntary start backward, as if struck, and his
features paled. He let go of her hands.

'No, it's not to do with the asylum,' he answered carefully. 'At least,
not directly. That is, my meeting with Denise was not about any
business of the asylum.'

'I'm puzzled,' Effie said, determined to push on. 'You refer to the
matron by name, and you were clearly familiar with her the other day.
Yet when we went to the asylum only two weeks ago, it seemed that we
both were meeting her for the first time.'

'It was the first time we had met,' Michael said hurriedly, and Effie found herself believing him. 'But since then, I've got to know her better. Through a mutual acquaintance.'

'Is that Judith Baxter?' Effie asked, and instantly regretted her words. He would think her foolishly jealous.

'No, not Judith,' Michael said, glancing at her with surprise now. 'Another friend, who is facing a difficult time. That's why I couldn't tell you.'

But the last part of the explanation seemed an afterthought, and Effie was not entirely convinced. Nevertheless she forced a smile and reached out to touch his arm.

'Well, I hope things improve for your friend, and soon,' she said.

'Thank you,' Michael said. 'That means a great deal to me. And I can tell you that my friend is very much on the mend. His future is much brighter.'

Suddenly everything seemed clear again to Effie. All the mystery of the last two weeks fell away. Michael, dear generous Michael, had simply been helping out an old friend who had fallen on hard times and had wished his difficult circumstances to be kept secret. Perhaps because he was from a well-to-do family. Yes, that must be it, how foolish she had been. And immature. What must Michael think of her?

'I'm sorry for being so inquisitive and nasty,' she said. 'You must think me an idiot.'

'Not at all,' he said with a smile. 'I can fully understand that you felt shut out. But we're still friends, aren't we?'

'Of course,' Effie said. 'Just no more secrets between us from now on. I want you to be able to confide in me.'

She saw a shadow pass across Michael's features, but he leant over and lightly kissed her cheek.

'Of course,' he said, 'I'll tell you everything.'

After he had gone, Effie remained by the door, thinking about what had just happened. She had almost felt the return of their former easy friendship. And yet she still knew that he was concealing something from her, there was something important in his life that he could not share with her.

But Effie decided, with a sense of gladness, that whatever his secret was, it would not distress her. He was her friend, and would remain so.

Despite the discomforts of Lydia's couch, Effie woke from a dreamless sleep the next morning and felt surprisingly reinvigorated. She found Lydia upstairs at the breakfast table, sipping on a second cup of tea.

'How's Moira this morning?' she asked. 'Did she sleep much?'

Lydia gave a wry smile. 'Whatever Ed gave her certainly did the trick. I think she slept all night, and she was very bleary this morning. I persuaded her to go back to bed and I think she's gone off again.'

Effie sat down to breakfast and listened while Lydia talked about Moira's future, and her fears that she would receive nothing from Sir Anthony's estate.

'Some people might say that she shouldn't expect anything,' Lydia mused. 'But she's given up her livelihood to be by his side and cater for his every whim. Surely she deserves to get something for all that sacrifice.'

'There may not be anything to worry about,' Effie reassured her. 'Hopefully his affairs are in order, and he has made sure she will get her fair share. I understand he was very wealthy.'

'Let's hope so,' Lydia said, still frowning. 'I actually think he was quite fond of her. But I just can't get it out of my head that perhaps she'll be neglected. Then what will she do?'

'Well, if that happens perhaps we could ask Michael for his advice. I understand he has friends who are lawyers, and I'm sure he would point us in the right direction.'

Lydia brightened at this suggestion. 'That's a good idea. I'd trust him to help out if needed.' She could not resist adding: 'By the way, you seemed happy when you returned from your tête-à-tête with Michael last night. I take it that all is well again on that front.'

Effie blushed, and said quickly, 'Hopefully so, hopefully we're friends again. I just want to get back to the nice friendship we had, before all these uncertainties cropped up. I want nothing more than that.'

Lydia broke into a smile, and said mischievously: 'I wonder how much your changed view towards Michael is caused by your interest in a certain detective sergeant?'

'What? Harry?' Effie contrived a scornful snort. 'Don't be silly. I must admit that my initial poor opinion of him has changed quite a bit, but that's all it is.'

'Right,' Lydia said, but her eyebrows remained arched and the smile still played about her lips. 'Are you sure about that? Because I think the good sergeant may feel differently.'

'He's not given me any indication of that,' Effie replied offhandedly, even as her heart skipped a beat.

'He's not the type. You may be a clever woman, Effie Davis, but you have a thing or two to learn about the male of the species.'

The downstairs peal of the doorbell prevented Effie from finding a suitable retort. Tillie appeared to announce that Sergeant Holloway was downstairs, and was wondering if he might speak to them.

'Certainly, Tillie, show him up. Effie is very keen to speak to him.' Lydia winked in her direction.

But Effie need not have worried that Harry had called with any romantic intention. He was at his most serious and business-like, stern even. She didn't know whether to be relieved or disappointed.

Harry apologised for intruding on them at what must be a difficult time, but he understood Miss Williamson was staying with them. He was anxious to interview her. Was she in a fit state to answer questions?

Lydia explained the previous day's events, and that Moira was still heavily sedated. But she would go and check whether she was able to meet with him. She left for the bedroom, and Effie was alone with Harry. She smiled in his direction, but his serious expression did not change. Instead he said in a low voice: 'There's something else I need to talk to you about. Alone preferably. Perhaps on the way out.'

'Of course. We can talk in the lobby.' Then, noticing the shadows around his eyes and his unshaven cheeks, she said: 'You look awfully tired. I hope you're getting some rest. Have you found Mr Harris yet?'

Harry allowed himself a brief, self-deprecating grin. 'I'm completely done in actually. I suppose I don't look too flash. But Ronnie Harris is what I wanted to talk to you about.' And again he looked serious, even worried.

'Are you making progress? With the investigation?'

'Things are starting to come together. I've had a bit of useful information actually. And this business with poor old Sir Anthony just might bring things to a head.'

'What do you mean?' Effie was puzzled, wondering if they were talking about the same thing. But before Harry could reply, Lydia entered the room with Moira behind her, an elegant blue dressing gown wrapped around her. Harry stepped towards her and offered his hand.

'My condolences for your loss, Miss Williamson. It must be a terrible shock.'

Moira smiled vaguely at him. She seemed dazed and confused.

'I won't keep you long,' Harry continued, motioning for her to take a seat at the table. 'But there are a couple of questions I'd like to ask you. About Sir Anthony.'

Moira slumped into the offered chair. Harry composed his large frame into the chair opposite her, and rested his arms on the table.

'I will be speaking to Dr Wright about the causes of Sir Anthony's death,' he began. 'But I would just like to get your thoughts on the progress of his illness.'

Moira stared at him confusedly. 'It just happened so quickly. So quickly. I can't believe it.' Her voice trailed off.

Harry asked gently, 'When did you first notice something was wrong with him?'

'I think it was about two weeks ago.' Moira looked like she was summoning up all her energy to recall what had happened. 'He began to complain of feeling ill.'

'What do you mean by ill?' Harry asked, his tone now more animated. 'Tired? Weak?'

'Mainly upset in the stomach. You know, ill in that way.'

Harry gave a short, sharp exhalation of breath.

'Tell me, Miss Williamson, was Sir Anthony taking any medicine that you were aware of?'

Moira paused for a moment, recalling. 'Only a tonic prescribed by Dr Wright. He had been feeling a bit tired, you see, and Ed had suggested a pick-me-up.'

'And how long had he been taking the tonic?'

'Oh, not very long. He didn't like it very much. The taste. He said it made his mouth feel peculiar.'

'In what way peculiar?' Harry asked. 'Was it burning? Did it make his mouth numb?'

'Yes, that's it,' Moira replied. 'He said it made his mouth burn. Like he was eating something spicy. And he hates … hated spicy foods.'

Harry ran his hand through his hair. 'Thank you, Miss Williamson, you have been very helpful.'

Moira looked at him, wide-eyed and pale. 'Do you think there was something wrong with the tonic? That it might have harmed him?'

Harry remained expressionless and his response was calm and quiet. 'I'm not suggesting anything, Miss Williamson. But it's something we'll follow up. With Dr Wright.' Then turning to Lydia: 'Can you tell me where I might find Ed today?'

Lydia looked at him absently. She too had paled, and still seemed to be taking in the import of what Moira had revealed. 'I'm not sure,' she replied eventually. 'Probably in his surgery, I suppose. Unless he's busy with whatever needs to be done for Sir Anthony.'

'Didn't he say he would come here this morning?' Effie said, without thinking.

Lydia gave a start, and Effie hoped she hadn't been indiscreet. 'Of course,' Lydia said, 'I'd forgotten. But I don't know when.'

'It doesn't matter,' Harry said pleasantly. 'I'll call by his rooms on the way home. But if I miss him and he turns up here, could you ask him to call around to Russell Street as soon as he can. It is quite urgent.'

Lydia nodded but said nothing. She looked distraught at the turn of events. Her usual cheery demeanour had deserted her.

Harry smiled reassuringly. 'Don't worry, I won't barge in on Ed at his rooms. It might be hard to believe, but I can be tactful when I need to be.'

Lydia tried to smile at his little joke, but her effort was not convincing. Harry rose to his feet, turning to Moira again.

'One last question, Miss Williamson, and I won't bother you again. Who is Sir Anthony's lawyer, his nephew doesn't seem to know.'

Moira again struggled to compose her thoughts, but after a moment replied: 'Sir Moses. Sir Moses Branson, I believe.'

'Are you sure?'

'Yes, I am. Because Anthony took me along to his office to sign some papers, only a few weeks ago.'

'Excellent,' Harry said, rising to his feet and shaking her hand solemnly. 'Good day to you, Miss Williamson, and to you, Lydia. And now if I could just have a few minutes of Effie's time, that would be appreciated.'

Effie sprang up. 'I'll come out with you. We can chat in the street.' And she went to follow him out the door, pausing to give Lydia a quick hug on the way. She had never seen her friend this way, so downcast and gloomy. The terrible turn of events seemed to be infecting them all.

'Don't worry, darling,' she consoled Lydia. 'I'm sure that Ed has nothing to worry about. He is a very good doctor and he would never have done anything to harm Sir Anthony.'

Effie joined Harry on the footpath, where he was already in conversation with Willie Milton. The pair spoke briefly, before Willie wandered off round the corner, no doubt to resume his surveillance.

'Sorry about that,' Harry said, turning to Effie. 'Just updating Willie on a few things. And he tells me he's seen nothing suspicious. No sign of Ronnie Harris.'

'Well, that's good, but what was all that about back there?' Effie said, motioning towards the apartment. 'Do you really think Sir Anthony's death is suspicious?'

Harry shrugged, glancing at her sideways. 'Well, when someone goes from pretty good health to dead in two weeks or so, it's probably worth looking into, wouldn't you say?'

'But didn't he already have a bad heart? He certainly seemed rather, well, florid.'

'Not sure that means much. Anyway, I'll know more after I've spoken to Ed.'

Effie looked at him anxiously. 'You surely don't think Ed had anything to do with his ill-health, do you?'

'Not for a moment,' Harry replied without hesitation.

'Thank heavens for that. I've never seen Lydia so worried.'

'The only reason I want to see Ed is to ask him about Sir Anthony's health. And I'm curious about this tonic he prescribed, and Sir Anthony's reaction to it. I'm pretty sure it shouldn't have that strange effect on the mouth.'

Effie stared at him. 'Poison?' she gasped.

'Possibly.' Harry's calm demeanour did not change. 'We'll find out if it was.'

'But why would anyone want to murder Sir Anthony? I know he wasn't the most pleasant of people, but still.'

Harry rubbed his chin, and gave her a wry smile. 'In my limited experience, Eff, greed is always a motive worth investigating. Particularly when the victim was as wealthy as Sir Anthony. That's why I'm off to see Sir Moses Branson. I'm keen to know who benefits in the will.'

'Oh. Of course' Effie felt slightly foolish.

'Not why I wanted to speak to you though,' Harry said, lowering his voice, and moving in a little closer to her. Something in his solemn tone alarmed Effie. Her heart sank.

'It's Alfie,' she said querulously. 'You've found him, haven't you? What did she do to him?'

'No, no,' said Harry hastily. 'We haven't found him. But we may have heard from Ronnie Harris.'

'What?' Effie said, and a tremor of fear ran through her. She had hoped somehow that Mr Harris had disappeared from the face of the earth. 'Have you seen him?'

'Well, no,' Harry said, and drew a piece of paper from his fob pocket. He thrust it into Effie's hands. 'This was pushed under the door at Russell Street overnight.'

Effie unfolded the dirty piece of paper. A few lines were scrawled on it, in large writing and in what seemed an unsteady hand.

I didn't do nothing. That old bitch was a baby murderer, just like I told the Davis woman. And if you look in the garden, back up in the corner by the stone wall, you'll find what she done. The note was signed *R Harris*, scrawled wildly across the bottom of the page.

Effie could feel her heart thumping in her chest as she formed the question she must ask. 'Find what?' she heard herself saying, in a voice that was tiny and distant.

Harry answered hesitantly, 'Well, I suppose the inference is that there might be a body buried there. A baby's body.' Then he quickly added, 'Of course we have no proof of such a thing. Nor do we know if this note is actually from Ronnie Harris.'

'But who else could it be from?'

Harry just shrugged. 'You don't recognise the writing by any chance?' he asked hopefully.

Effie examined the scrawl. 'No, I'm sorry, I don't think I ever saw his handwriting before.'

Harry shrugged again. 'That's okay. Didn't really expect you would have. And I suppose you never saw anything unusual in the garden during your time there?'

Again Effie was at a loss. 'What do you mean? Anything being buried there?'

'Yes. Or even just people coming and going at odd hours. Mrs Wilson? Ronnie? Anyone else?'

Effie thought briefly. 'I'm not sure I ever saw Mrs Wilson in the garden. It was quite overgrown. There was a gardener who came every now and then, but that's all I can remember.'

'Fair enough.' Harry stood silently with his hands in his pockets, as if contemplating his next question. Effie beat him to it.

'Are you going to dig up the garden?' she asked tentatively. 'It's quite large.'

Harry scratched his head. 'Well, I suppose we'd better have a go, starting near the old wall, like the note says. But I don't expect to find much. This whole note business might be designed to get us off the track.'

'Really?' Now Effie was intrigued.

'I'm getting close, I reckon,' Harry said, with what sounded to Effie like a touch of excitement. 'I might have it sorted in a couple of days.'

'Have what sorted?' Effie stared at him. It seemed to her that nothing at all was sorted. Alfie was gone, Mr Harris was still missing, and now there were dreadful suspicions about Sir Anthony's death. What was he talking about?

'Pretty much everything,' Harry ventured airily. 'As I said, I've had some recent good information. I think I know who's behind all this. Couple of loose ends to tidy up first though.'

'Do you mean you know where Alfie is? Is he still alive?'

Harry looked startled, as if suddenly realising he might have said too much. 'Steady now, I didn't say that. I can't say that. Let's just wait, I don't want to get your hopes up.'

But it was too late for that, something in his tone, in the optimistic edge to it, was telling Effie there was still hope. As much as she tried to manage her excitement, to tell herself not to assume anything, she couldn't help it. She was boosted by Harry's restored confidence. She suddenly realised she trusted him enormously.

'Harry Holloway, I hope you're not just blowing your bags about this.'

Harry smiled sheepishly. 'Just keep that news to yourself for the moment, Eff. There's certain people I don't want to alert. No one, you understand? Not even Lydia.'

'You can trust me, you know that.' And impulsively Effie reached across and tugged his sleeve. 'You'll let me know if you find anything at Mrs Wilson's?' And the anxiety crept back into her voice, as she realised the implication of what she was asking.

'Of course. I'll need to see you anyway if I do.' Harry's voice had resumed its solemn tone. 'Well, I'll see you later. Take care of yourself.' And there was no mistaking the warmth in his voice, or the surprisingly gentle touch of his hand on her shoulder as he bade her farewell.

CHAPTER SEVENTEEN

→✳←

EFFIE ROSE THE NEXT MORNING with the full intention of taking up Michael's offer to rest at home while he covered her classes. But she quickly realised she would not rest, could not do so while she was expecting further news from Harry. No, it would be preferable to maintain her normal routine – the classroom would take her mind off these latest awful developments.

Not that it did. She passed the day at school on tenterhooks, finding any excuse to cross to the window and stare down the path towards the gates, half-expecting, half-dreading to see Harry striding towards the school with news of a grisly find in Mrs Wilson's garden. She had wracked her brain, struggling to remember any untoward goings-on at the boarding house that might be related to that wild accusation by Mr Harris. But she could remember nothing, certainly nothing in the recent days after Alfie's disappearance.

As the day wore on and there was still no sign of Harry, Effie felt her anxiety growing, and with that anxiety a mounting uncertainty. She was no longer so sure about Harry's confidence of the previous day, his assertion that he was close to resolving the case. How could he be so certain? As far as Effie could see, nothing was resolved. But even as these doubts gnawed at her, she was reassured by her growing confidence in Harry, in her awareness of the sharp intelligence behind his casual demeanour. Surely he wouldn't have said what he did yesterday if he didn't have ample cause? And did his optimism mean that Alfie was safe? Effie could not help but hope for the best.

In this state of flux, alternating between hope and doubt, Effie passed the day, at the same time managing somehow to instruct her girls on the basic reasons for the decline of the Roman Empire. Or so she hoped. Then at five minutes to four, just as the school day was coming to a close, one final visit to the window revealed a familiar figure loping up the drive. Her heart sank and her stomach knotted: he had said he would only come if he had news of a find in the garden. She struggled to control herself as she dismissed her girls and hurried out of the building. She met him just as he was about to climb the steps onto the verandah. She hoped to see some sort of sign in his demeanour, but he was official Harry today, impassive and formal. Or was he just afraid to tell her his news?

'Did you find anything?' she blurted out, seizing his large hand in her two slender ones, uncaring about the surprised glances of two of her students walking past.

Harry led her along the gravel path, out of anyone's hearing. 'It was true,' he said in a low voice. 'We did find a body.' She gasped, and almost fell against him. He took her by the shoulders and hurriedly added, 'But it wasn't Alfie.'

'How do you know?' she wailed, still stricken. 'Who else could it be?'

Harry kept his hold on her, perhaps fearing she would collapse if he let go. 'It could not have been Alfie. The body was ... much older. I mean, it was a baby, but it had been there a long time. It was very decomposed, just a skeleton really.' He sounded distracted, and now that she studied him properly, quite distressed.

'It must have been there a good ten years,' he said eventually, to make things absolutely clear, and the relief flooded through her. It was not Alfie. Oh, thank heavens.

'Who was it then?' she asked, calmer now. 'What have you found out?'

'Quite a lot actually,' Harry said, and there was a certain weary satisfaction in his voice. 'But it'll take some telling. Would you like me to give you a lift home and we can talk in the cab?'

'I'll get my things.' Effie dashed back to her room, seized her satchel, stuffed it with the girls' work, and hurried back down the stairs. As she ran to the door she almost collided with Michael, coming from the other corridor.

'Steady!' he cried, laughing as he held her arm to support her. 'You'll do yourself an injury.'

Flustered and embarrassed, Effie paused to gather her breath, before exclaiming, 'Sorry, I'm in rather a hurry'. She was about to explain the reason for her haste, when she remembered Harry's insistence on secrecy. She realised she couldn't tell Michael anything about Harry's progress.

'Harry's offered me a lift home,' she said rather lamely, realising that this was no reason at all for her to be sprinting through the corridor.

'Oh,' Michael said, opening the door for her. 'Is he making progress on the case.'

'I'm not sure,' she murmured.

'A social visit then?' Michael said, still smiling encouragingly.

'Well, yes, I suppose so,' Effie said, feeling herself reddening. What must he think of her, blushing like a silly schoolgirl? But Michael's smile just broadened.

'Good for you,' he offered, almost cheerful in his tone. 'Harry is an excellent fellow, and obviously a very good policeman.' And leaning out the door he waved casually to Harry, standing, arms folded, on the gravel path. Harry waved back, doffing his cap as he did so.

'Yes he is,' Effie said, unaccountably filling with pride. 'Though he doesn't need telling that.' And she grinned at Michael as she went down the steps.

Michael smiled back, the open, unreserved smile of the old Michael. And she knew what else she saw in that smile. Relief, unmistakeable relief.

'So Mrs Wilson really was a baby farmer? Like that Mrs Knorr. I can't believe she could be so evil.'

Effie sat back in the corner of the police trap and surveyed Harry. She could not bear to mention Alfie, for fear of what news she might elicit.

But Harry just leaned back and sighed. 'Oh, I'm not sure she was that bad. We gave the place a pretty good going over and that one body was all we found. Not that it excuses what she did. But I don't think it was deliberate. My guess is that one of her babies sickened and she didn't do enough to help it. When the poor tyke died she probably panicked, took matters into her own hands, and disposed of the body. Must have been one of the abandoned ones, I suppose. No mother to claim it back. Neglectful of Rhonda, yes. Callous, yes. But murder, probably not.

Breathing deeply, Effie dared to broach the subject. 'Does that mean that ... she didn't kill Alfie?'

Harry eyed her steadily. 'I don't think so. No, actually I'm reasonably certain she didn't.' And it was all Effie could do not to throw her arms around him in her gratitude.

'So there's hope that he's still alive?' she continued tentatively, not yet daring to fully believe.

Harry nodded slowly. 'I think there is, yes. But I don't want to get your hopes up too much until we have absolute proof. And hopefully that is very close.'

'Oh, thank you, thank you, that is wonderful news.' And this time she could not resist seizing his hand again in hers. Harry looked embarrassed, but pleased too. She noticed he made no attempt to withdraw his hand, so she held onto it. It seemed the natural thing to do.

'There have been a couple of other developments you might like to know about,' he offered. 'First up, I've checked with Sir Anthony's lawyer, and managed to extract some information about his will. It took some doing, Sir Moses is a crusty old cove and didn't want to tell me anything. But he came good when I threatened him with a subpoena.'

Effie's thoughts flew to Moira, and Lydia's fears about her future. 'Is Moira in the will? Is she to benefit?'

'Very handsomely, actually. To the tune of one third of his estate. And believe me, that is quite an impressive amount.'

Effie gasped. 'Goodness me, that is far more than she expected. She'll be so relieved.'

'It seems the old fellow cared for her far more than many thought. You can tell her if you like. Sir Moses has agreed we can pass on the good news. But confidentially, if you don't mind. Tell her not to tell anyone else at this stage.'

'What about the rest of his estate? Am I allowed to know that?'

'I suppose I can tell you. Strictly speaking I shouldn't, but I know I can trust you to keep it quiet. One third goes to Gregory Hartford and one third to his grand-nephew, the baby Anthony Hartford, to be held in trust by Gregory Hartford, as the sole trustee, until the lad turns twenty-one.'

'He'll be a very wealthy little boy.'

'Yes, he will. It seems that Sir Anthony placed a great deal of importance on keeping the family line going. Seems as though Greg certainly did the right thing producing an heir.'

Effie smiled, remembering Sir Anthony's obvious pride in his namesake.

'It'll be a big responsibility for his parents, bringing him up with that kind of wealth ahead of him.'

Harry looked at her carefully, as if weighing up something. 'Well, there's been a bit of a development on that front too. Joanna Hartford has gone missing, it seems.'

'What?' Effie exclaimed. 'What's happened? Do you suspect foul play?'

Harry shook his head. 'I wouldn't think so. I called at Chitterling this morning to ask a few questions, and Gregory informed me that she's up and left. Packed a bag and gone.'

'Has she taken the baby with her? Little Anthony?'

'Well, that's the strange thing. The baby is still there.'

Effie stared at him, hardly comprehending. Joanna's strange conversation with her at the meeting came flooding back to her, the obvious intensity of her feelings about striking out on a new path. Effie could understand her feelings about leaving Gregory, she had always thought of them as an odd couple, and how could anyone keep on putting up with such contemptible arrogance? But to desert her baby too? How could she contemplate such a thing?

Lost in these thoughts, she became aware of Harry saying something. He was asking her whether she had any inkling of problems in the marriage. So she recounted the meeting with Joanna and her strange words.

'But I had no idea she would abandon her baby. She must be desperately unhappy.'

'So it would seem.'

Despite her dislike of Gregory Hartford, Effie felt a sliver of sympathy for him. On top of the death of his uncle, this latest blow must have hit hard.

'Poor Gregory,' she ventured. 'He must have been upset.'

Harry raised his eyebrows. 'More angry than upset actually. He was trying to put on a front, but my assessment is that he's stinking angry at his wife.'

Effie thought of Gregory and his bombastic ways. She imagined that his temper could be explosive. And reflecting on it further, she realised that a fleeing wife would more likely hurt his pride and dignity than fill him with grief.

But her thoughts dwelt more on baby Anthony, and how, just like Alfie, he had now lost his mother, the most important person in his life. Despite the enormous wealth he would come into, despite all the privilege that would come his way, he might never know his mother, never feel the joy and comfort of her love. Feelings welled up within her, anger at Joanna's selfishness, sadness at the baby's loss. She reached for her handkerchief to dry her eyes but Harry was already offering her his. Surprisingly, this time it was clean and well pressed.

'I know it's upsetting,' he said, 'but we must push on. I'm sure it will all turn out in the end.'

Effie could not see how it could, but nevertheless his words were comforting. His calmness always had a soothing effect on her. She dabbed her eyes and handed him back his handkerchief, smiling gratefully. Looking out the window she saw that they were turning into Lydia's street.

'Well, here we are,' she said. 'Thank you for bringing me home. And for your support. I do appreciate it.' And she touched his arm affectionately.

'You know you can count on me at any time,' he said, quietly, looking intently into her eyes. 'For anything.'

Effie averted her eyes but a part of her thrilled at his words. She turned her face up to him and smiled. As their eyes met again, Effie felt something pass between them. An understanding? A promise? Then the moment passed, and she found herself averting her eyes again. But her smile lingered.

'One more thing before you go,' Harry said, the businesslike tone back in his voice. 'Keep this Friday free. That's the day of the inquest into Sir Anthony's death and I'll probably want to call you as a witness. Don't be alarmed if you are called, it's only likely to be me questioning you, and it won't take long. So I'll send a trap round to pick up you, Lydia and Moira on Friday morning.'

Effie was shocked more than alarmed, and not just at the prospect of being a witness at the inquest.

'I didn't know there would be an inquest,' she managed to say. 'Its all very sudden, isn't it? I knew you had your suspicions, but I thought you had no proof.'

Harry shrugged and grinned his crooked grin. 'Well, the family, particularly Gregory Hartford, are up in arms about it, and my boss thinks it's completely unjustified. Waste of time and money, he said. But we've managed to convince the coroner it's necessary. Actually Ed Wright was very helpful in persuading Dr Youll to call the inquest. They know each other pretty well; they work together supporting the Berry Street asylum, it seems.'

'And you've obviously persuaded Ed that it's called for. He's changed his mind about Sir Anthony's death?'

Harry shrugged. 'Let's just say sufficient amounts of doubt and suspicion have entered his mind.'

'Do you have the proof you need, then?' Effie was marvelling at Harry's progress, but worried still that his actions could be premature if his boss was opposed to the inquest. He could not afford to fail again.

'Not quite,' Harry conceded, but there was no anxiety in his voice, just a calm confidence that satisfied Effie. 'I reckon I'll have everything I need by Friday though.'

'Good,' Effie said firmly, as they drew up outside Lydia's door. 'Make sure you do. And make sure you do well on Friday. I'll be barracking for you.' And suddenly it seemed the most natural thing in the world to lean over and kiss him lightly on the lips, before opening the door and stepping down from the trap. She turned to smile at him again, before heading up Lydia's front path. She thought she detected some additional colour in his already bronzed features. And the breadth of his Cheshire cat grin told her that her kiss had been very well received.

CHAPTER EIGHTEEN

AS THE WEEK WENT BY, Effie found herself thinking more and more about Friday's inquest.

According to Lydia, the news of the inquiry into Sir Anthony's death had created a sensation in Melbourne society. All manner of scuttlebutt gossip was flying around the town, as rumours of foul play and scandal took hold and flourished, each story more lurid and fanciful than the last.

At breakfast on Thursday morning, Lydia confided to Effie that of course, given the circumstances, many of these rumours centred on Moira and the various motives she might have for disposing of her 'fancy man'. With financial gain naturally being at the head of the list.

'We must ensure that she hears none of that vicious talk,' Lydia said, putting down her cup of tea and speaking in a confidential tone. 'Her health is steadily improving but she's still fragile, and I'm worried that hearing such gossip would set her back again. Could shatter her completely, actually.'

'I agree,' Effie mused. 'Though really, dear, there seems to be not much chance of her hearing anything, at least not in the immediate future. Isn't she spending all her time here resting?'

'She's certainly doing a lot of sleeping. She was in bed until ten thirty yesterday morning. She's been taking Ed's sleeping draught every night. It makes her quite befuddled in the mornings.'

'How are her spirits holding up?' Effie asked. 'She didn't seem too bad last night.'

'She was a lot better yesterday,' replied Lydia. 'She had a couple of letters from friends, condolence messages, she said. That seemed to buck her up no end. And I was able to assist her yesterday on the financial front. That should help put her mind at ease too.'

'What do you mean?' Effie said. 'Not from your own purse, surely?' She knew her friend was generous, and also had the means to give effect to that generosity, but surely such a gesture was not necessary, given Moira's newfound wealth.

'No, no,' Lydia replied, smiling. 'I took her to see Sir Moses yesterday, and he was able to provide her an advance on her legacy. A very decent amount. It will ensure she's not embarrassed for funds until the will is properly resolved.'

'Good,' Effie said, 'That must be a relief to her. Still, we must be watchful. She's not yet strong enough to cope with any further troubles.'

'Shhh,' Lydia whispered, as there came the sound of footsteps in the hall. She glanced at the clock: only eight o'clock and Moira was already up.

To their further surprise, Moira entered the dining room dressed for the outdoors, complete with hat, coat and gloves.

'Goodness, dear!' Lydia exclaimed. 'What's this? Where are you going?'

'Oh,' Moira said, hesitating. 'I think I'll take a walk. I feel a good deal better today.'

'Nonsense,' Lydia said firmly. 'We're delighted you're feeling better, but you need some breakfast first. I insist.' And she motioned for Moira to take a seat at table.

But Moira did not take the offered seat. 'No, no,' she replied, hesitating again. 'It is such a nice day outside, I feel like a stroll before breakfast. I shan't be long.'

One glance at the grey clouds through the dining room window put a lie to Moira's assertion, but Lydia simply shrugged. 'Very well, if you must, dear. But don't be long, I'll make sure breakfast is ready for you when you return.'

Moira smiled at them, then, with surprising alacrity, hurried from the room. Her footfall could be heard rapidly descending the stairs.

Lydia leaned back in her chair and shook her head. 'How very odd. The past two days I've been struggling to get her out of bed, and now look at her. It's certainly a surprising improvement.'

'I'm not so sure,' Effie said, getting out of her chair and striding to the window. 'I'm not sure what's got hold of her, but I'm worried she's not yet fully herself.'

She watched Moira through the window, making her way down Toorak Road at a brisk pace.

In an instant Effie's mind was made up. She turned abruptly to Lydia. 'Quick! We must follow her!'

'What?' exclaimed Lydia. 'Why on earth would we do that?'

'This behaviour is very strange. I'm worried she might do something foolish. And after all, she is our responsibility.'

Lydia needed no further encouragement. Leaping to her feet, she seized Effie's hand and headed for the door. 'Right then! No time to waste.'

'Shouldn't we rug up a bit,' Effie said, as she was guided down the stairs. 'It'll be cold outside.'

'No time for that,' Lydia cried. 'Come on, or we'll lose her. You should know that, you're used to this sort of business, aren't you? Following people down the street?'

'I suppose I am making a habit of it,' Effie said, as they dashed, hatless and coatless, out the door.

Effie need not have worried about getting cold following Moira, who was already well on her way, a couple of hundred yards or more in the distance. Though they scuttled along with unseemly haste, they could not seem to make up any ground on her. After ten minutes of the pursuit, they were both puffing appreciably and Effie felt herself beginning to sweat with the effort of the chase.

Fortunately they saw their quarry halt when she reached Fawkner Park. She paused there on the pavement for a few moments, facing the park. Then, as if making up her mind, or perhaps recognising someone, she began to make her way down one of the paths into the park proper, proceeding again at a lively pace.

Effie and Lydia quickened their pace again, fearing to lose sight of Moira in the recesses of the park, but as they approached the spot where she had turned off, they were forced to stop abruptly and dart behind the protection of a large oak tree on the edge of the footpath. Because there in front of them, sitting on a park bench not more than one hundred yards away, was Moira. And sitting beside Moira and holding her hand, was the unmistakeable, upright figure of Joanna Hartford. The two women were engaged in earnest conversation.

'My goodness!' Lydia whispered, leaning back against the trunk of the oak, and struggling to regain her breath. 'Whatever is going on?'

Effie's head was swimming, and not just from her recent exertion. This was a bewildering turn of events. What was Moira doing here with Joanna? Why was she meeting her alone here in the park? Try as she might, she could think of no sensible reason. Other than it must have some connection with the death of Sir Anthony, and such a reason could surely not be proper. But then she reassured herself there must be a perfectly sensible explanation. Perhaps Joanna was simply wanting to offer her condolences? Even though she had fled from Gregory Hartford, there was no reason why she should not want to comfort Moira. A completely understandable thing to do in the circumstances.

Effie began to feel foolish and embarrassed, lurking behind the tree with Lydia, like silly schoolgirls. She glanced at her friend.

'This is silly,' she whispered. 'We should speak to Joanna. She would appreciate that.'

But then they realised that it would seem very peculiar if they appeared, hatless and coatless and red in the face, in front of Joanna and Moira, and sought to pass it off as a chance meeting. Particularly since they had told Moira they would be at home, ensuring her breakfast would be ready when she returned.

'Perhaps we should wait a while, at least until we have recovered our breath,' Lydia whispered, and peeked out from behind the tree again to see what was going on.

'What's that?' she exclaimed suddenly, at the same time seizing Effie by the wrist. Effie peered around the tree too.

From their vantage point they could clearly see Moira handing an object to Joanna, who at first resisted, pushing it away and shaking her head. But after further animated discussion between the two, Joanna took the object and put it into her purse. And even at this distance they could see that the object was a small bundle of papers.

'It's the bank notes!' Lydia gasped. 'From Sir Moses.' And she leaned back against the oak tree again, as if summoning the strength to take in what was happening.

'Are you sure?' Effie whispered.

'Positive,' Lydia replied. 'Perhaps not all of them, but certainly most.'

Effie peeked out from behind the tree again, in time to see both women rise to their feet, embrace, then part from each other, Joanna heading further into the park, perhaps in the direction of Commercial Road, and Moira walking back towards Toorak Road, though fortunately, diagonally across the park and away from them.

The two friends stood there staring at each other for a few moments, each trying to make sense of this baffling development. For her part, Effie could think of no proper reason for Moira's actions.

'We'd better get back,' she said eventually. 'She'll be home soon for breakfast, I expect.'

'Yes, I suppose we should.' Lydia's words, like hers, sounded lame.

'But what do you think they were doing?' Effie exclaimed. 'What in heavens is going on?'

'I don't know,' Lydia said. 'It's very odd. But there must be a logical explanation.'

'I'm sure there is,' Effie said quietly. 'But I don't like to think what that explanation might be.' Suddenly Effie was sure of what they must do, and before Lydia could say anything, she added: 'I think we must tell Harry about this. I'm terribly afraid it might have something to do with Sir Anthony's death. And if it is connected, we can't conceal it from Harry.'

'Are you sure?' Lydia said, and the uncertainty in her voice showed that she shared Effie's suspicion.

'Quite sure. Don't worry, dear, it may not be anything untoward, but whatever it is, Harry will get to the bottom of it. You can count on that.'

><

Harry Holloway breezed into the anteroom at the Russell Street Police Headquarters, full of apology for having kept them waiting so long.

'Just getting ready for tomorrow, and there's a million things to do. But I came as quick as I could when I heard it was urgent.'

Effie looked him up and down, and liked what she saw. It was the old Harry, cheery, relaxed, emanating confidence. Her spirits were momentarily boosted by his presence. 'Sorry for interrupting your preparations, but something perplexing has happened. We thought we should tell you immediately.' And she launched into an account of what they had witnessed.

As she talked, Harry lounged in his chair, legs outstretched and hands clasped behind his neck. And as he listened to her story, Effie noticed that his relaxed demeanour didn't change, indeed if anything he became even more relaxed, smiling at her as she talked. When she got to the part about the money changing hands, he nodded and grinned again. Effie felt a prickle of annoyance, that perhaps he was not taking this dramatic development seriously. She paused.

'Are you listening to me, Harry? Do you understand what we are saying?'

'I think so,' Harry said pleasantly. 'Moira met Joanna Hartford in a park and gave her some money.'

'Don't you find that rather odd, in the circumstances?'

Harry smiled pleasantly again. 'Not particularly. As far as I know, there's no law against being generous to your friends. Let's hope she's just as generous to her other friends.' And he winked at Lydia, who smiled back at him.

Effie's annoyance increased. 'Well, we found it rather strange. We're terribly worried that it might have something to do with Sir Anthony's death.'

Harry hauled himself upright on his chair. His expression became serious. 'Eff, I can think of quite a few reasonable explanations for Moira's behaviour, none of them suspicious. And I can assure you that her actions have nothing to do with Sir Anthony's death. Nothing.'

Effie looked at him doubtfully. 'Can you be sure of that?'

Harry's response was certain. 'Absolutely sure.'

'That's wonderful, Harry,' Lydia said. 'A great relief. I must say we were a little concerned. But you have put our minds at ease. Hasn't he, Effie?' she added, noticing Effie's still doubtful expression.

'I suppose so,' Effie said slowly, a flicker of annoyance lingering. 'Does that mean you know what happened to Sir Anthony? And to the others?'

Harry's face was expressionless, but his response was immediate and confident. 'Sorry Eff, I'd like to tell you more, but I can't. You'll just have to wait til tomorrow. And besides, I've got a few things on my plate, so I'm going to have to scoot.'

He rose and bade them a hasty farewell, reminding them that he had organised a police trap to pick them up and take them to the inquest in the morning.

Harry offered his hand to her, and as she took it, Effie felt relief replace her irritation. Relief, not just that Harry had no concerns about Moira, but also that he was so confident about the impending inquest. And as his hand lingered over hers, and as she looked into his smiling eyes, she felt something else too, something that gladdened her heart and lifted her spirits immeasurably.

CHAPTER NINETEEN

→※←

TRUE TO HARRY'S WORD, a young constable arrived at half past ten to take Effie, Lydia and Moira to the inquest. It was a beautiful Melbourne July day, the sun shining and a hint of unseasonal warmth in the air.

Both Lydia and Effie had resolved to ignore yesterday's events, and to put their trust in Harry's advice that Moira was in no way implicated in Sir Anthony's death. And so they had bustled around her as usual, solicitous for her welfare, and concerned to help her get through the difficult day ahead.

But they need not have worried. Moira seemed to have found a renewed strength, reassuring them that she would manage, though she knew the inquest would be something of an ordeal.

As they trotted along in the trap by the side of the Yarra, Moira turned to them and quietly thanked them for caring for her. They had both been wonderful, and true friends. She could not have managed today alone, she confided, with all those people staring at her, and wondering if she was involved in some way in Sir Anthony's death.

Effie squeezed her hand, and tried to ignore the guilty pang she felt as she recalled the suspicions she and Lydia had shared only a day before.

The Coroner's Court was located at the city morgue, one of two grim, grey buildings on the edge of the Yarra, joined by a narrow, arched passageway. As they jogged along in the police trap, Effie's thoughts returned to her last visit to the morgue, and the memory of poor Mary, pale and lifeless on the stone slab. She shivered and wrapped her shawl more tightly around herself.

But when they arrived at the building, the atmosphere was very different from that previous time. An enormous crowd had gathered, conveyances of all kinds drawn up next to the courtroom, and well-dressed folk pushing and shoving to get into the building. The feeling was almost carnival-like, as if this occasion was not a solemn legal enquiry, but rather the latest festive attraction for Melbourne society.

And it was just as well they had a police escort, else they would never have got through the milling throng bustling around the courtroom door. But their constable adroitly steered them through the crowd and into the court, showing a surprising amount of authority for one so young. Effie suspected he had been hand-picked by Harry for the task of assisting them.

The courtroom itself was not particularly large, and was already crammed with officials and observers, leaving standing room only for most of the interested onlookers. Their escort shepherded them purposefully to the front of the room, spotting three well-dressed older men engaged in conversation at the end of the third row. He tapped one of them on the shoulder.

'Are you gentlemen here in an official capacity?' he demanded, in a rather loud voice.

The gentlemen in question shook their heads and turned away to resume their conversation.

'In that case I'll request that you vacate these seats. These ladies are official witnesses and need to be seated here.'

The gentlemen began to protest their outrage, but were quickly ejected from their seats under threat of forcible removal. The three women took the vacated seats, a little embarrassed at the attention their entrance had attracted. Moira was seated between Lydia and Effie, her head held high. Behind them the whole of Melbourne society seemed to have gathered. Effie was not well connected to that society, but was still able to recognise a number of celebrated faces in the crowd.

In the front two rows along from them were seated those who might be required to take part in the proceedings. There was Harry in the front row, long legs stretched out in front of him, rummaging through a sheaf of papers, a frown creasing his brow. Next to him sat Inspector Marks, as immaculately dressed as ever. Everything about his demeanour spoke of his distaste at being dragged into the day's proceedings.

On Harry's other side sat a small dapper man, perhaps in his thirties, elegantly dressed in a morning suit, with a round, smooth face, neatly trimmed dark hair plastered to his scalp and a tanned complexion. Unlike Inspector Marks, this fellow seemed perfectly at ease, smiling pleasantly and nodding to various acquaintances in the room. Effie nudged Lydia in the ribs and pointed.

'Who is that little man next to Harry?' she whispered.

'Oh, that's Molly,' Lydia whispered back immediately. 'Crawford Mollison. Harry's done well, he's the best pathologist in Melbourne.'

Effie also noticed Ed Wright in the front row, nervous as ever, and starting to sweat rather profusely in the stifling atmosphere of the crowded courtroom. In the second row along from them, she noticed Gregory Hartford, sitting next to an austere, greying fellow who Effie guessed was his lawyer. Of Joanna Hartford, there was no sign.

With a slight start, Effie noticed Michael, also seated in the second row, and alongside him a man she recognised as his friend James, the artist she had met at the theatre. And then Matron Jackson from the asylum, seated next to Judith Baxter, the latter as cool and elegant as ever. Then a number of other older gentlemen, well-dressed and sombre, who Effie took to be either friends or business associates of Sir Anthony.

Effie wondered whether any of these people would be called as witnesses: she couldn't imagine what possible connection most of them could have with Sir Anthony's death. Perhaps they were just interested spectators, granted seats at the front on account of their various close associations with the Hartford family. After all, it seemed that the inquest was the place to be in Melbourne on this fine winter's morning.

Effie's gaze wandered to a row of benches along one wall, at which sat a dozen or so people, all men and all well-dressed fellows of some standing, by the look of them. Effie assumed these to be the jury, not that they seemed to be taking their solemn duty too seriously. They were chatting casually among themselves, apparently caught up in the carnival atmosphere of the proceedings.

At the front of the room, at a more imposing desk facing the crowd, sat an elderly, red-faced gentleman who Effie took to be the coroner, Dr Richard Youl. He was engaged in impatient discussion with a clerk, glancing up from time to time to survey the growing crowd with obvious displeasure. Whether it was the stuffy atmosphere, or perhaps a prevailing illness, but Dr Youl appeared decidedly unwell, occasionally grimacing in pain, his face pockmarked and swollen. He frequently reached for a large glass of water placed in front of him.

As Effie watched, he consulted a fob watch, nodded to his clerk, then raised a large gavel and rapped loudly on the desk. But such was the hubbub in the room, that those near the back did not hear his call to order, and there was only a minor lessening of the din. Dr Youl rapped again, more loudly, and at the same time the clerk sprang to his feet, shouting at the top of his voice, 'Order! Order in the court!'

'Thank you,' Dr Youl said, as the chattering died away. 'Ladies and gentlemen, I know most of you probably think you are at the circus, but this is a sitting of a court of law and I'll thank you for some respect.' Silence descended on the room and Dr Youl resumed.

'It's damned hot in here and I've something of a mind to throw all the hangers-on out of the court so that we can conduct this hearing with a modicum of comfort. But I know I would probably be drummed out of the Melbourne Club if I tried that, so we shall just have to put up with things, I'm afraid.' At this witticism, a rumble of guffaws and a few titters echoed around the room, quickly fading as Dr Youl raised his hand, like a conductor directing his orchestra.

'Now, we are here to enquire into the tragic death of Sir Anthony Hartford, one of the leaders of industry in our state and a distinguished member of our community.'

Immediately, the grey gentleman sitting with Gregory Hartford leapt to his feet. 'Your honour, on behalf of the Hartford family, I wish to object to your decision to conduct an inquest into Sir Anthony's death. His demise was entirely due to natural causes, as certified by his consulting physician, and to have his affairs, and his family, subject to this kind of public spectacle is scandalous, and an affront to common decency.' He waved his arms theatrically to indicate the extent of the public prurience to which Sir Anthony's good name would be subject.

Effie glanced in Ed Wright's direction. He was looking more uncomfortable than ever, sweat trickling down his brow, his head downcast. She felt Lydia squirming by her side.

Meanwhile Dr Youl motioned for the lawyer to sit down. 'Resume your seat, Mr Stanford, if you don't mind,' he said sharply. 'You will have your turn. I am aware that Dr Wright made an initial diagnosis of death by natural causes, but he saw fit to review that judgement, and as a result an autopsy has been performed on the body.'

At this news a chorus of mutterings arose.

'Quiet!' Dr Youl barked, and the hubbub died away. 'I understand that Dr Mollison has performed the autopsy, so I will call him in due course.' At this Crawford Mollison half rose from his seat, and bowed in the crowd's direction, much like the star performer of a theatrical performance acknowledging his enthusiastic audience. A hum went round the room, and Effie almost expected to hear applause breaking out. Dr Youl scowled at this display of ostentation, and smacked his gavel on the desk again.

'Quiet, please. Let us all try to control ourselves, can we?' With a sharp glance in the direction of Crawford Mollison, Dr Youl resumed, 'The first witness I call is Dr Edward Wright, Sir Anthony's physician.'

Ed rose and took his place in the witness box, set up at the front of the room and to one side, so that he faced both Dr Youl and the crowded courtroom. He took the oath from the clerk in a passably steady voice, mopping his brow before he faced Dr Youl.

'Dr Wright, you were Sir Anthony's physician, and had been for some considerable time?'

'Five years or more, I suppose.'

'And how would you describe Sir Anthony's state of health in the period immediately preceding his illness and death.'

Ed paused, searching for the right words. 'Reasonable, Sir, I would say.'

Dr Youl pressed the point. 'A little more detail , Dr Wright, if you will. Take your time.'

It was clear that Dr Youl was prepared to go gently with Ed. Lydia had said they were colleagues and good friends. Effie thought he might not be so gentle with Harry.

'Well, he had a number of ailments quite common to a man of his years. A touch of gout, digestive difficulties from time to time, that sort of thing.'

'And his heart? Would you say his heart was sound?'

Ed paused for some little while, considering the question. Silent expectation filled the room. Ed finally looked up at the coroner and spoke, slowly and carefully.

'That is a difficult question, Sir, but I would answer it like this. Although until just before his death I had never seen any medical evidence of heart disease in Sir Anthony, nevertheless I would say he was the kind of patient in whom it would not be surprising to see the development of such disease. Perhaps the rapid development of heart failure. I say that, Sir, because he had a somewhat heightened blood pressure and a generally rather apoplectic nature. I suspect that there would have been a considerable strain on his heart on occasion, and I frequently counselled him that he must take greater care of himself in that respect.'

Dr Youl sat back in his chair and scratched his ear. 'And what symptoms did you observe in Sir Anthony during his final sudden illness?'

Ed again seemed uncertain how to answer, and hesitated before speaking. 'A rapid onset of weakness and debilitation, consistent with the onset of heart disease,' he ventured.

'And other symptoms? Stomach upset? Nausea?'

'To some extent, Sir. But again, not inconsistent with a rapidly weakening heart.'

'Not inconsistent with the effects of certain kinds of poison either?' And Dr Youl fixed Ed with a less benevolent stare.

'Yes, Sir, I suppose so,' Ed conceded, after another painful pause. Beads of sweat continued to gather on his brow.

'Well, we shall find out, I suppose. We shall find out. That will be all, Dr Wright. You may step down. I now call Dr Crawford Mollison.'

Ed scuttled from the dock with unseemly haste, looking decidedly relieved.

'That wasn't too bad,' Effie whispered in Lydia's ear.

'Good old Dickie,' she whispered back. 'I knew he wouldn't go too hard on him.'

Ed's hasty retreat only accentuated the extreme confidence with which Dr Mollison strode to the dock. With his dapper attire and immaculate grooming, he appeared for all the world like a famous actor about to give a virtuoso performance. Grasping the lectern firmly with both hands, he took the oath, then flashed a quick smile at his audience before turning to Dr Youl expectantly.

'Dr Mollison, you have conducted an autopsy on the body of Sir Anthony Hartford?' began the coroner.

'I have, Sir, on Wednesday of this week.' Dr Mollison spoke in a mellifluous baritone.

Everything about the man is perfect, Effie thought. Too perfect by half.

'And have you established the cause of death?' Dr Youl continued.

'I have,' Dr Mollison said firmly, waiting for the coroner to continue. Effie got the impression that he was drawing out the conversation for maximum dramatic effect.

'Well?' Dr Youl asked, a touch of impatience rising in his voice.

Dr Mollison paused briefly, glancing around the room before declaring in stern, ringing tones, 'Death by poisoning.'

A collective gasp went up around the room, followed by a chorus of exclamations. Dr Youl took to his gavel again.

'Quiet! Ladies and gentlemen, I would remind you again that this is not the circus or a pantomime. Dr Mollison, have you identified the poisoning agent?'

'I have, Sir, the agent was the cardiac glucoside, oleandrin.'

'From the oleander plant, I take it,' Dr Youl added, for the benefit of the crowded room.

'Of course,' Dr Mollison agreed, smiling benignly at his audience.

'Are you able to identify how the poison entered Sir Anthony's system?'

'Undoubtedly it was ingested. I identified some corrosion of the mucous membranes in the mouth, and there were traces of blood in the bowel. Both consistent with the ingestion of this particular poison. Then I was able to isolate the oleandrin digitalin in a sample of the stomach contents. Through the application of bismuth iodide, and then by straining through pure alcohol and ether in turn. A method which you may note, Sir, has only been developed in recent times. I believe it is at the cutting edge of pharmacological practice.' And Dr Mollison smiled serenely at the crowded courtroom. Again, he almost seemed to Effie like he was waiting for them to applaud his brilliance.

Dr Youl seemed determined not to be cast too far into the shadow of the younger man. 'It seems strange that the digestive symptoms were not as severe as the effect on Sir Anthony's heart,' he observed. 'Not the usual pattern of oleandrin poisoning, I would have thought.'

'Indeed not.' Dr Mollison nodded approvingly at this observation, much like a teacher noting a clever answer from one of his pupils. 'In my view, Sir, the poison was deliberately applied in small doses, to prevent an immediate violent reaction, and in order to weaken the heart over a period of time, albeit a relatively short period. You see, the amount of oleandrin in the stomach contents was very small. Traces only. But not minute enough to escape detection, I am pleased to say.' And again he smiled happily, at this triumph of modern science.

Dr Youl looked slightly peeved at Mollison's theatrical display, but continued his questioning.

'And are you able to state how the poison was given to Sir Anthony? In his food perhaps?'

'Not with absolute certainty, Sir, but as Sergeant Holloway will later attest, the most likely vehicle would have been the tonic prescribed by Dr Wright.'

At this, another collective outburst from the body of the court. This time it was Dr Mollison who held up his hand, commanding silence. The noise died away quickly and he resumed.

'I understand that Miss Williamson, Sir Anthony's friend, observed that Sir Anthony complained of a strange sensation in his mouth after taking his tonic. Consistent with the effect of oleandrin when ingested. So I think we can assume that was the method applied. Though I also understand from Sergeant Holloway that the bottle of tonic has now disappeared and cannot be found.'

After more scientific parrying back and forth between the coroner and his witness, Dr Mollison was thanked and invited to resume his seat. Would he be prepared to answer any further questions that might arise in the course of the hearing? 'Of course, Sir,' he reassured the coroner, and, still smiling, resumed his seat in the front row.

Next it was Harry's turn, and as he strode to the witness box Effie glanced across at Gregory Hartford. He was engaged in deep conversation with his lawyer. Effie saw that he had gone quite pale. She was aware that many other pairs of eyes were directed on him as well.

Dr Youl saw Harry sworn in, then stated, 'Sergeant Holloway, you are Officer in Charge for the purposes of this inquest. I understand that it was at your instigation that the autopsy and this inquiry were ordered?'

Harry nodded. 'Yes Sir, there were a number of irregular aspects to Sir Anthony's death that warranted further investigation.'

'Well done, Sergeant, very commendable, fully justified as it turns out. Excellent police work, if I may say so.'

Harry simply nodded impassively. Effie noticed Inspector Marks looking pained and shifting in his seat.

Dr Youl began with a few questions about Harry's observations of Sir Anthony's death, including his conversation with Moira about the tonic. Harry answered these questions succinctly and in a matter-of-fact tone.

He showed no sign of nerves and seemed entirely in his element. Effie felt her own nerves on his behalf subside, and began to feel herself glowing with pride in his performance.

'Well,' Dr Youl continued, 'it seems that all the medical and scientific questions I have to ask have been answered by the expert medical witnesses. It seems equally clear that we are moving towards a finding of death by unlawful killing. I assume that you would conclude, at this early stage, that the finding should also be killing by a person or persons unknown, and that you would like me to recommend to the jury a full police investigation into this matter.'

Harry looked steadily back at Dr Youl. His voice was unwavering as he replied, 'I agree with your first proposed finding, Sir. That the death of Sir Anthony was by unlawful killing. But not with your second.'

'You mean you don't want to investigate?' queried Dr Youl, a puzzled expression appearing.

'No, no, I mean your finding of killing by persons unknown. You see, I think we're in a position to name a number of persons of interest.'

A buzz went around the room, as the crowd fully appreciated the import of Harry's words. Again resorting to the gavel, Dr Youl cut in. 'Hang on a moment there, Sergeant, don't be too hasty. How can you be in a position to name anyone at this early stage. We've already heard that there's no definitive proof of how the poison was given to the victim and, as far as I've heard, we have no witnesses to any foul play, so I can't imagine how you could possibly name anyone who might have been involved.'

Clearly the crowded courtroom shared Dr Youl's doubts. People were staring at Harry as though he were either a conjurer, or mad, or both. Effie's glowing confidence in him had evaporated, and she was beginning to fear that he was about to make a complete fool of himself. Or worse. But Harry continued to speak in measured tones.

'The thing is, Sir, for the past few weeks I have been investigating another matter, and made very good progress towards an arrest. I have every reason to believe that Sir Anthony Hartford's death is directly connected to that matter, and that the guilty parties are the same in both cases.'

Effie knew immediately what Harry was talking about, but not so Dr Youl. Amid the rising clamour, he rapped again with his gavel, and demanded: 'Elaborate please, Sergeant Holloway. What case are you referring to?'

Harry stood up straight and said in a loud, clear voice: 'Sir, the murders of Miss Mary Guerin and Mrs Rhonda Wilson, and the illegal abduction of the baby Alfred Guerin.'

'What do you mean 'illegal abduction'?' Dr Youl queried, almost shouting now to make himself heard above the courtroom clamour. He had given up on his gavel. 'My limited understanding of that case is that the baby Guerin was adopted out through the infant asylum.'

Effie remembered that Dr Youl was one of the volunteer physicians at the asylum.

Harry continued, 'No, Sir, it is my contention that the baby was illegally taken through fraudulent means, and that the murders were the direct consequence of that action. As indeed was the murder of Sir Anthony Hartford.'

Dr Youl still looked incredulous but pursued his questioning. 'And just who, Sergeant Holloway, are you contending is responsible for all of this?' At this question, the hubbub died to an expectant murmur, then dead silence as all eyes focused on Harry.

Harry answered immediately, his voice clear and firm. 'It is my contention that Mr Gregory Hartford is a person of interest in these three deaths, and in the abduction of Alfred Guerin.'

At this, a roar swelled and reverberated throughout the courtroom.

Before Dr Youl could respond, another voice rang out above the din, and Effie saw Gregory Hartford's lawyer on his feet. 'This is an outrage, Sir! A baseless, false, outrageous accusation! My client demands an immediate retraction!'

'Sit down, Mr Stanford, sit down!' shouted Dr Youl, resorting again to the gavel. 'You will have ample opportunity to question Sergeant Holloway at a later time today. If you still wish to.' Then turning to Harry, 'Now Sergeant, that is a serious allegation against a very prominent member of our community. I trust you have an adequate basis for your claim. And a credible motive.'

'I believe I do, Sir,' Harry replied, steadily. 'I am alleging that Mr Gregory Hartford arranged the illegal abduction of Alfred Guerin for fraudulent purposes, and then conspired with other parties to murder three persons, namely Mary Guerin, Rhonda Wilson and Sir Anthony Hartford, in order to conceal the crime and to perpetuate the fraud.'

'What are you saying, Sir?' Dr Youl still looked mystified and was losing patience. 'Why on earth would Mr Hartford wish to abduct a baby?'

Harry returned his gaze unwaveringly. 'In order to pass off the baby as his own. So that he could gain access to Sir Anthony Hartford's fortune.'

The shocked crowd let out another collective gasp. 'Perhaps if I might elaborate, Sir,' Harry continued quickly. 'I have obtained information from Sir Anthony Hartford's lawyer, Sir Moses Branson, that his will was changed some months ago to include Mr Gregory Hartford and the baby Anthony Hartford, each as a third share beneficiary of his will, the baby's share to be held in trust by Gregory Hartford. Before that, Mr Hartford and his family were not beneficiaries in any way under Sir Anthony's will.'

'So?' Dr Youl said. 'That is no basis in itself to make the allegations you have put to us.'

'Indeed not,' Harry agreed. 'But I have established a number of facts, Sir. Firstly, that there is no record of Mr and Mrs Hartford and their baby in any of the ship's logs of passenger vessels arriving on our shores at the time when they say they arrived in Australia, two months ago.'

Dr Youl raised his eyebrows. 'So? Where is this taking us?'

'But after extensive searching, we have discovered that a Mr and Mrs Hartigan were passengers aboard a merchant vessel bound from Calais to Sydney in March this year, some four months ago. After interviewing the captain of that vessel, I have established that Mr and Mrs Hartigan match the description of Gregory and Joanna Hartford, and I am confident that they will be identified as such by Captain Blake in due course.' Harry paused and glanced around the room. 'Captain Blake has also confirmed that Mr and Mrs Hartigan were not accompanied by a baby on their trip.'

Effie glanced across and saw Gregory Hartford, now gone dead pale, leaning forward with his head in his hands. His lawyer was looking straight ahead.

Dr Youl pushed on and now his tone was different, any hint of incredulity gone. 'Sergeant Holloway, you indicated that there is another guilty party, or parties, associated with this matter. I assume you are referring to Mrs Joanna Hartford, who I understand has disappeared, presumably fled. Are the police seeking Mrs Hartford?'

'We are, Sir, though I do not expect any immediate success in that regard. But in any case, Sir, my interest in finding Mrs Hartford is purely to corroborate the case against her husband and his accomplices. She is not a person of interest in this matter.'

'Really?' Dr Youl again looked puzzled. 'How can you be sure of that? Surely you must suspect she was involved in the conspiracy?'

'I do not believe so,' Harry replied firmly. 'My view is that Joanna Hartford's only crime was to be persuaded by her husband not to reveal to Sir Anthony and the world that their baby was adopted. I am confident that she believed that the adoption was legitimate. And I believe she had nothing to do with any of the murders.'

'Then why did she flee?'

'Most likely because she began to realise the purpose of the subterfuge she had agreed to about their baby. And as time went on I'm sure her suspicions began to grow about other matters as well. And she wanted no part of it.'

Amid the confusion of thoughts and emotions running around her head, Effie felt a profound sense of relief at this judgement from Harry. She felt a strong sympathy for Joanna Hartford, and for her situation. She remembered the intensity and the depth of feeling she had sensed in their brief conversation.

'Are you able to justify these assumptions about Mrs Hartford?' Dr Youl was again sounding doubtful. 'If not his wife, who are you saying Mr Hartford conspired with? Do you have any suspects?'

'Oh, yes,' Harry replied clearly. 'I am quite certain of who he was in league with. And it was not his wife.' He paused for a moment and cleared his throat. 'Perhaps I had better go on, Sir. I have been making some enquiries with our colleagues in France, the gendarmerie. Australia's telegraph link with Europe is a wonderful thing, and has enabled ready access to information from the police over there. Though it has been a challenging and time-consuming task to track down the relevant criminal records and the relevant French officers dealing with the matters of interest to us. But I have now established the following, Sir.'

'Yes, yes, Sir. Go on, go on.'

Harry glanced around the room, then continued. 'Firstly, that Sir Charles Baxter did not die of a heart attack, as is commonly understood.

Instead he died at his own hand after losing his family's fortune at the gambling tables in Nice. And his widow, Mrs Judith Baxter, was left virtually penniless.'

A shocked and expectant hush came over the room.

'Secondly, that Mrs Baxter came to the attention of law enforcement authorities in France on a number of occasions, in relation to allegations of fraud and deception. Mostly by wealthy older men, and none of which ever resulted in prosecution.'

Effie looked across at Judith Baxter, who was sitting stock still, as unruffled and elegant as ever, looking directly at Harry. Effie did not dare guess at her thoughts.

'Thirdly,' Harry continued, 'that Mrs Baxter and Mr Gregory Hartford were known to each other in France. More than that, while I cannot prove it, I am confident that she and Gregory Hartford were on intimate terms.'

The court remained strangely quiet, as if these shocking revelations were too much to take in.

Dr Youl pressed on. 'Even if what you say is true, isn't it all still circumstantial? Is there anything to connect Mrs Baxter directly to the matters before this court? Or to the matter of the baby Guerin? This woman is, after all, a distinguished lady in Melbourne society, highly regarded for her good works.'

Harry raised his eyebrows. 'Including as a committee member of the Victorian Infant Asylum, which I note she became involved with almost immediately on her return from France eight months ago. But in answer to your question, Sir, no, I have nothing to directly connect Mrs Baxter to these deaths and to Gregory Hartford's scheme to inherit his uncle's fortune. Mrs Baxter is an intelligent and resourceful woman, she has covered her tracks very cleverly and very thoroughly. In the past, when she worked alone in France, the authorities were not able to prove anything about her various schemes. But in this case, she has been required to collude with, and therefore put her trust in, two others. Mr Gregory Hartford, obviously, and Monsieur Robert Guillot.'

'Who the dickens is he?' Dr Youl had dispensed with the courtroom formalities.

'He is Mrs Baxter's gardener and, I should say, many other things besides. He is a person of very great interest to the French gendarmerie in relation to a number of unsolved crimes – violent crimes in a number of cases. He is the person we will allege murdered both Mary Guerin and Rhonda Wilson. And unfortunately for Mrs Baxter, he is not quite as clever or as circumspect as his employer. We have evidence from a Mr Joseph Smedley, a regular patron of the Village Belle in St Kilda, identifying Mr Guillot as a fellow participant in illegal gaming activities at that establishment. More importantly, Mr Smedley can attest to a meeting between Mr Guillot and Mrs Wilson on the morning of Thursday 11 June at the Village Belle, and to subsequent threats made by Mr Guillot against the life of Mrs Wilson. My men have arrested Mr Guillot this morning, and I am confident his identity will be confirmed by Mr Smedley. I am also confident that he will be identified by Miss Agnes Simmons, proprietor of the Victorian Coal Mining Company, as the person who was seen in the vicinity of the St Kilda abattoir on Tuesday 16 June, the day that Mrs Wilson's body was discovered at that location.'

Dr Youl sat silently, absorbing the full import of Harry's words. Judith Baxter did not move either, sitting straight and still, her handsome features impassive.

At length Dr Youl resumed, speaking slowly, and with heightened respect in his voice. 'Now, let me see, Sergeant Holloway, perhaps I can try to sum up what you are saying. That Gregory Hartford and Mrs Baxter, and this French fellow, conspired to deceive Sir Anthony

Hartford into believing he had an heir to whom he could leave his fortune, or a substantial portion of it. I take it Sir Anthony had previously held a rather dim view of his nephew?'

Harry nodded his agreement. 'Extremely dim, we understand, Sir.'

'And that they organised a secret arrangement with Rhonda Wilson to get access to a baby boy, Alfred Guerin, who Mrs Baxter organised to be adopted though the infant asylum. How am I going so far, Sergeant?'

'Absolutely correct, Sir.'

'And that Mrs Baxter, or Gregory Hartford, or both of them, plotted for Mary Guerin and Rhonda Wilson to be murdered by the French fellow – why exactly, Sergeant?'

'Undoubtedly because, in Mary's case, she was becoming a nuisance to them, appearing out of the blue, agitating to get her baby back, and threatening the whole scheme. So she had to be disposed of. And was. I suspect she was lured to the vicinity of the VIA under the pretence of being reunited with her son, and then, as we know, was murdered and thrown into the Yarra.'

'Exactly how was she killed, Sergeant? I understand the autopsy was inconclusive as to the cause of Miss Guerin's death.'

'Indeed it was, Sir. But in recent days we have had the body exhumed and re-examined. By Dr Mollison, who we consider to be the pre-eminent expert available to us in the science of toxicology. He did not do the original autopsy.'

Dr Mollison beamed expansively at this testament to his prowess.

'And did you find anything new?' Dr Youl leaned forward in his chair, now fully engrossed in these latest developments.

'We did, Sir. Traces of aconitine, a plant poison contained in the common monkshood plant, in sufficient quantities to at least stupefy Miss Guerin, if not to kill her. It is a substance notoriously difficult to identify post-mortem. But not when the latest techniques are applied, and by a leading expert in the field.'

Dr Mollison bowed his head in mute acknowledgement of the truth of Harry's words.

Harry continued. 'I believe the plan was to stupefy her so that her death would appear to be suicide by drowning. But it did not go quite to plan. She must have struggled and Judith Baxter's henchman was forced to tie her up before the poison took full effect. Hence the ligature marks I noted on the body.'

Dr Youl nodded slowly. 'Good work, Sergeant. Excellent work, in fact. And Mrs Wilson, what was the motive there?'

'She was becoming frightened and panicky. Afraid that she would be accused of baby farming. And she was being blackmailed by Mr Ronald Harris, over a fostered child she had neglected in the past and who had died on her premises.'

'And I assume they poisoned Sir Anthony to get access to his fortune, before he could change his mind again.'

Harry nodded. 'And before anything else could go wrong.'

Dr Youl sat back in his chair, reflecting on Harry's testimony, taking it all in. But before he could resume, Greg Hartford's lawyer sprang to his feet again.

'My client denies all this absolutely. Sergeant Holloway has woven a colourful story, but everything he has claimed is entirely circumstantial. What concrete evidence does he have for this ridiculous fantasy that Mr Hartford's son is really some foundling from the Victorian Infant Asylum?'

Dr Youl raised his hand, motioning for the lawyer to resume his seat. 'You will cease your interjections, Mr Stanford!' Then, turning to Harry: 'But it is a fair point, Sergeant. What you have said makes coherent sense, but it is an extraordinary claim, you must agree. And the evidence is rather circumstantial, as Mr Stanford has indicated.'

'We do not agree with that,' Harry replied calmly. 'Once we have identified Mr Guillot to be responsible for Mrs Wilson's death, once we have found Joanna Hartford and heard her story, on top of what we already have, I think we will be able to mount a compelling case. But in any case, Sir, I can prove conclusively that the baby, Anthony Hartford, is in fact Alfred Guerin. Could the clerk ask Miss Whitford to enter the court?'

Again a commotion rippled through the court, as the clerk walked down the aisle and out the door into the anteroom. All eyes were turned to that door as he reappeared with a young woman in a nurse's uniform, carrying a baby. It appeared to be sleeping peacefully in her arms.

Now Gregory Hartford sprang to his feet. 'How dare you?' he shouted, his face contorted with fury. 'How dare you steal my son from my house? You will pay for this, damn you!'

'Sit down, Mr Hartford!' Dr Youl shouted, anger rising in his voice as well. 'The baby is perfectly safe and well. Given what we have just heard, I think it entirely appropriate that it be brought into the court.'

'Thank you, Sir,' Harry said. 'I call Miss Evangeline Davis to the stand.'

Effie's heart gave a mighty thump as she realised what Harry was doing in calling her name. She rose unsteadily to her feet and walked tentatively towards the lectern, now vacated by Harry. He advanced towards her, taking her by the arm and leading her to the witness stand. He smiled encouragingly at her, and returned to the floor, standing off to one side so that she remained in direct view of Dr Youl.

The clerk came forward and Effie was sworn in. Her voice, as she took the oath, was soft and tremulous, despite her best endeavours to control her nerves.

'You will need to speak up, Miss Davis,' Dr Youl instructed, in a kindly tone and with an encouraging smile. Effie gave a faint smile in return.

'Sir, may I act on your behalf to question the witness?' Harry asked.

'Certainly, please do.'

Harry turned to Effie and smiled again. Suddenly it was just him and her in the crowded courtroom, and her confidence returned. He began. 'Miss Davis, have you ever seen the baby Anthony Hartford before?'

'No, Sir,' she replied, and was surprised at how loud and confident her voice now sounded.

'And have you ever seen the baby Alfred Guerin before?'

'Yes, Sir.'

'Where and when, Miss Davis?'

'At Mrs Wilson's residence, Sir. I cared for him there once.'

'And are there any characteristics of Alfred Guerin that you are aware of, and that would enable you to recognise him?'

Effie recalled her first meeting with baby Alfie, a meeting she had reported in great detail to Harry. She now knew exactly what Harry was looking for, and what she would say.

'Yes, Sir, he has a birthmark on his arm. On his right arm. It is in the shape of a small heart.'

Harry turned to the nurse, who was now sitting in the front row with the baby still asleep in her arms. 'Miss Whitford, could I trouble you to bring the baby forward?'

The nurse did so, and as she walked towards the witness box the baby awoke, yawning and stretching in its swaddling cloth. Effie stepped down from the witness box as the nurse handed her the baby. She took him in her arms and he looked up at her, still drowsy with sleep. He gurgled quietly and reached out to her. She let him take her offered finger in his tiny hand. With her other hand, she carefully peeled away the blanket covering his arm. 'Hello there, Alfie,' she said quietly.

Taking great care, she walked over to Dr Youl and showed him the tiny birthmark, standing out rose-coloured on his white skin. Dr Youl nodded, and she turned to hand Alfie back to the nurse. As she did so, she saw Judith Baxter rise from her seat. Judith looked directly at her, smiled the slightest of smiles, then turned and walked calmly down the aisle and from the room.

When she reached the crowd standing jam-packed at the rear of the Court, she did not hesitate and kept walking, the crowd parting silently to allow her to continue on her way. No one made a move to impede her. As she reached the door, she turned and nodded at the constable, standing guard there. He obediently followed her from the room, walking almost deferentially in her wake, but then hastening forward and assisting her into the police trap waiting outside.

CHAPTER TWENTY

'IT WAS ALWAYS THE PAPERS. The forged adoption papers. That's what I couldn't work out. Solve that and I solve the case, that's what I always thought.'

Harry paused and sipped on his tea, his large frame dwarfing Lydia's dainty settee. Next to him sat Ed Wright, as relaxed as Effie had ever seen him.

'Did you think all along that Alfie might be safe and well?' she asked Harry. 'Why didn't you say something?' And she fixed him with a faintly accusatory look.

Harry raised his hands in the air in mock surrender. 'Perhaps I should have been a bit more positive. Once we'd established that Ed hadn't signed those papers, I thought it was the most likely option. That someone had taken Alfie in secret as their child, for some purpose or other. But I wasn't quite sure, and I didn't want to get your hopes up. There was always the possibility that he had been ... disposed of. I mean, I knew we were dealing with ruthless people, after what happened to his mother and to Rhonda Wilson.'

'I can understand how you might have been suspicious of Gregory Hartford, particularly after the death of Sir Anthony,' Effie mused. 'But

Judith Baxter, what on earth led you to her.'

Harry took a long slurp of tea, as if deliberately prolonging the suspense. 'Well,' he resumed, 'Process of elimination, really. The more I thought about Mary's murder, the more it seemed as if it must be connected with baby Alfie in some way. In other words, it wasn't just a random killing. And the more I thought about that, the more I thought the murderer must have been stalking Mary. And in that case, must have known where she was living.'

'Oh, right.'

'And really, Effie, there were very few people who knew she was at Michael's place. Mrs Wilson might have guessed, Ronnie Harris probably not, not unless he was in league with Mrs Wilson. But Judith Baxter knew, she knew everything. So I thought about that for a while and, unlikely as it seemed, I thought it was worth following up. Once the information came through from the French police, it all started to fall into place.'

'And Mrs Wilson, what did she know of all this? Was she an accomplice?' Effie asked, thinking back to that lady's strange behaviour.

'Not really,' Harry said. 'I don't think she knew much at all. She was reassured that it was a proper adoption, otherwise I don't think she would have gone into it. But she was sworn to the utmost secrecy, obviously more so than was necessary. And being well acquainted with the wrong side of the law in the past, I'm sure she began to have a sniff that something was going on. Of course, when Mary was killed she knew that she was caught up in something pretty serious, and that she was in big trouble. From both sides, Judith Baxter and the law. From three sides, if you include Ronnie Harris and the screws he was putting on her.'

'It was certainly a cunning scheme,' Effie reflected. 'But risky, surely? I mean, as soon as Ed saw the papers and identified the forgery, the game would be up.'

Ed cut in, shaking his head. 'Not so, actually, it was as safe as houses. You see, you need to understand how the system works. Where there is a confidential adoption the file is sealed, with the approving doctor's signature in it. Then the file is locked away. In the normal course of events no one would ever see it again, unless there was a problem. And, of course, there would not have been a problem if Mary Guerin had not returned and made things difficult.'

'As we told you, we opened the file after the second murder,' Harry added, 'and, of course, there was nothing in it. Well, not quite nothing, but no names of the adopting parents, just a lot of hogwash about how they had been vetted and what upstanding pillars of society they were. But for reasons of confidentiality their names had been withheld. So, even if the file was examined, it wouldn't lead anyone to Greg Hartford. And of course Judith Baxter knew these systems very well. She knew she could carry out the deception with very little risk.'

Effie shook her head in bewilderment. 'I don't know why the Hartfords didn't just tell the truth. Tell Sir Anthony that they would adopt a child. Surely he would have accepted a beautiful baby as one of the family?'

Harry looked at Effie fondly and sighed. 'I wish everyone was as good-hearted as you, Effie Davis. But sadly they're not. I'm afraid Sir Anthony held many of the prejudices against adopted children that are only too common. Particularly among the so-called upper classes. I understand that he had made those prejudices abundantly clear, to the world generally and to his nephew in particular, on more than one occasion before that gentleman travelled to France. Gregory Hartford was very aware that adopting a 'foundling bastard' was no way to Sir Anthony's heart, and to delivering him an heir to his fortune. He knew only too well that only a legitimate male heir would do the trick. And when he was unable to produce such an heir, he had to find a way of convincing Sir Anthony that he had.'

'And what of Joanna?' Effie said. 'You said in court you didn't think she was involved.'

'She wasn't. Greg Hartford himself has confirmed that. Exonerating her is about the only decent thing he's done through this whole business. He told us he played the fairness card with her to get her involved in the deception about Alfie's adoption. You know, 'Sir Anthony is a nice old stick, but he has this thing about adopted babies. We need to make out he's really ours or else baby Anthony will not get what should be his.' Which in a strange way was pretty close to the truth, I suppose. Oh, and Joanna was under the impression that the adoption had all been carried out aboveboard and properly.'

'But then she found out?' Effie suggested.

'I don't know whether she found out exactly. But she began to have suspicions. For example, about the extraordinary level of secrecy he was going to. And I think she may have found out about Gregory and Judith Baxter. Because I strongly suspect they were continuing to carry on their affair here in Melbourne. I think Joanna Hartford began to realise not just that Gregory's adoption line was bogus, but that her whole marriage was a sham.'

Effie wondered where Joanna was now, and what she would make of her life. 'Are you going to find her and charge her?' she said quietly to Harry.

'Charge her with what?' Harry replied. 'Of being taken in like the rest of us? I don't think so. No, we were never seriously looking for Joanna Hartford, and what inquiries we did put out have now ended. We no longer need her as a witness to prove our case.'

'And what of Moira and Joanna? You know, that meeting?' Effie still felt lingering shame for the suspicions she and Lydia had held.

And for their actions in spying on Moira. But it had to be raised.

Harry smiled at her affectionately, he was clearly not judging her over the incident. 'Well, as I said, there's no law against generosity of spirit. It seems that Joanna did have one friend at Chittingly. A good friend, apparently. Not that surprising when you think about it. After all, they were really both outsiders in that circle.'

Effie nodded, recalling her own sense of alienation from the privileged life she had been introduced to. But it was a distance that she no longer felt. She now felt nothing but warmth for Lydia, and for Michael. Entirely comfortable in their presence. Why was that?

Effie realised that it was because she now felt at ease with herself, sure of where she belonged in the world. And that sense of belonging seemed to have a lot to do with the man sitting opposite her, his smiling eyes fixed on her. She understood just how dear to her Harry Holloway had become.

Lydia, who had been sitting quietly, now spoke up, 'One thing I don't quite understand is how Judith expected to profit from all this. I mean, Greg Hartford would get access to his one-third of his uncle's fortune, and probably to most of baby Anthony's share too. Judith might expect to benefit from that for a while, but surely she would have been beholden to Greg for any financial gain from his new fortune.'

Harry shrugged and smiled quietly. 'You're too innocent in the ways of the world too, I'm afraid, Lydia. You need to understand the way Judith operated. Her approach was to gain power over men. She would have bled Greg Hartford dry, slowly but surely. At first through the emotional and sexual hold she had over him, but don't worry, she would've had no qualms about resorting to blackmail if those other ties wore off.'

'And are you still searching for Mr Harris?' Effie asked. For her it was the last piece of the puzzle. She knew that Ronnie was not the murderer, but she still held a lingering fear of him and the threats he had made against her. It would be nice to know he was no longer out there and able to hurt her.

Harry shrugged again. 'We're certainly still on the lookout for Ronnie, but I'm not sure we'll ever find him. My best guess is that he was knocked off by the Frenchman in the Belle, and his body secreted out somehow. My boys reported a delivery cart leaving late on the day he disappeared, but they thought nothing of it when they saw the driver was not Ronnie Harris.

I reckon Ronnie might have found out too much, nosing around Rhonda Wilson and her dealings, and got too greedy. He was already blackmailing her over the baby she had disposed of, and he was looking for more. But it's one thing to blackmail an old biddy like Rhonda, it's an entirely different thing to take on Judith Baxter. He made a big mistake, I suspect.'

'And that note from him to the police? A forgery?'

'I reckon so,' Harry replied. 'Again designed to lead us down the wrong path.'

'But how did they know about all those details? About the dead baby, I mean. Where it was buried.'

Harry shrugged. 'Friendly persuasion, I suppose. On Ronnie, or Rhonda Wilson. They would have had no qualms in doing whatever was required to get that information. They are not very nice people.'

Effie shuddered. She had despised Mr Harris, but she was still shocked at what was most likely his violent end.

'Don't worry, Eff,' Harry said gently, 'it's all in the past now. Time to get on with the future. Lots to look forward to. For example, Carlton happens to be playing at the G this Saturday. Interested?'

Effie grinned. 'I could be persuaded.'

'Good,' Harry said. 'On that happier note I'd better be going. Still lots of paperwork to wrap up. Bane of a policeman's life, I'm afraid.'

Shaking Ed's hand warmly, and giving Lydia an affectionate kiss on the cheek, Harry turned to go.

'I'll see you out,' Effie said, taking his arm. She had one last question and she wanted to be alone with him to ask it.

Once they were outside in the winter sunshine, she began. 'Sorry to bail you up on your own like this but ...'

'Any chance to be alone with you is fine by me,' he interrupted. 'But I suspect the pleasure of my company is not the only reason we're here.'

Effie took his hand and found herself impulsively leaning in to him. Kissing him again seemed a natural thing to do, and she knew he felt it too. 'I do like your company,' she whispered. 'Very much.' Then she stood back from him. 'But I do have another question to ask you.'

Harry smiled and extended his arms towards her. 'Ask away.'

'It's about Michael and his relationship with Judith Baxter,' she said, then hastened to add. 'It's only because he's a good friend. And that's all.' She looked at him to see if he understood her meaning. His calm smile told her he did.

'You said in there that Judith got men under her power,' she began slowly. 'You know, sexually.' And to her annoyance, she found she could not quite hold his gaze as she said this. But she persevered. 'I always thought Judith had Michael under her spell in some way. I wonder if that was the cause of his anxiety and unhappiness.'

'She had no intimate relationship with him,' Harry replied quickly. 'You can be certain of that. But remember I said she gained information about people and held that over them, even if not immediately. I think that was the kind of relationship she was cultivating with Michael.'

'What information did she possess that could gain power over him?' she asked. 'I don't understand.'

In reply Harry just smiled, then leant over and kissed her softly. 'That, my dear, is something that I can't answer. It's up to you to ask Michael that directly, and for him to tell you if he wishes.'

Effie smiled at him in return, and her voice was now certain. 'As always, you're right. And do you know, I will ask him. I think it's a conversation that is long overdue.'

Michael and Effie strolled through the school grounds, taking the gravel path between the carefully cultivated rows of English boxes. 'Shall we sit here?' Effie said, as they reached the garden seat at the base of the huge old Moreton Bay fig.

They settled themselves on the bench. Michael had been somewhat perplexed at her suggestion they take a short walk during the lunch hour, even though her assertion that it was a beautiful day could not be denied.

'Effie Davis, what is this all about?' he inquired, as they sat in the sunshine. 'We've been teaching at this school together for half a year, and this is the first time you have asked me to take a turn in the garden. I suspect an ulterior motive.'

'Well, there's a first time for everything,' Effie responded, a hint of banter in her voice. 'But you're right, there's something I want to ask you. Or rather, something that I think we need to clear up between us.'

'Is there?' he replied, and she saw the veil of reserve come over him again. So she pressed on, taking his hand in hers. He looked a little startled, and she felt him draw back slightly. But she did not let his hand go.

'Michael Standish, we are good friends, are we not?'

'Yes, I hope so.' But again there was the suggestion of defensiveness in his manner.

'But I want you to know that, from my side at least, there is nothing else. No other expectation. You're simply my good friend and I greatly value your friendship.' She looked him in the eye and saw the shadow of reserve drop away.

'Thank you. You don't know how much that means to me,' he said gently.

'Good,' she said softly. 'And you know you can trust me?'

He nodded in response but said nothing.

Effie gathered her resolve, then took the plunge. 'Michael, I know you've been keeping something from me. Something about your life. I want you to know that you can confide in me, if it helps. That is what friends are for.'

She saw his eyes moistening. His voice was breaking as he spoke. 'Thank you, dear Effie. I would like to confide in you, but I don't know where to start. It is rather difficult.'

'Just try,' Effie said, quietly but with a surprising firmness and insistence.

'Very well,' he said, then sat silently, working up his courage. Effie waited patiently. 'The thing is,' Michael resumed, 'I thought perhaps you might have feelings for me and I could not reciprocate. I had ... have feelings for another.'

Effie smiled at him. 'I know that now,' she said. 'I should have known it then, too, but I was, well, not seeing properly. Anyway it is now all clear on that front, so we can get on with our friendship.'

Again Michael paused, before resuming. 'There is a difficulty though. You see, the person for whom I have feelings is ... is ...'

'Yes?'

'Well, our friendship is ... frowned upon by some. By many, I suppose.'

Effie remembered Michael sitting at the inquest with the fair young man. She remembered the gaiety between them that evening at the Theatre Royal bar. Suddenly all became clear to her.

'Your friend is James, isn't it?' she said quietly.

He looked at her cautiously, hope in his eyes. He nodded silently.

'And it must have been very difficult for you. For you both.' She squeezed his hand sympathetically.

'It was difficult,' Michael sighed. 'Particularly for James. His parents are very religious and strict, you see. He was torn.'

'What happened?' Effie persevered.

'He went away,' Michael said. 'I don't know where, he didn't say. But we were worried about him. Denise and I, that is.'

'Denise? You mean Matron Jackson?'

'She's his sister.'

'His sister? But she has a different name?'

'That's her married name. She has a young family.'

Effie felt embarrassed. 'How foolish of me. I had assumed she was unmarried. Because she was working. What a conventional assumption. So much for my progressive views.'

Michael continued. 'As I told you, I didn't know Denise when we visited the asylum. I only found out that she was James's sister when she called on me shortly after he disappeared. Apparently he had mentioned me to her as the cause of his distress and she realised who I was.'

'Oh,' Effie said. 'Oh, I see. And what is his state of mind now? Is he still troubled?'

'He returned because he realised he could not live apart from me. And I feel the same. So we're determined to make the best of it. No matter what might happen to us.'

At that moment, Effie felt a deep sympathy and warmth towards him. She could not resist reaching over and hugging him closely. 'You can always count on my support,' she whispered to him.

'Thank you, dear Effie, thank you,' he murmured, holding her tightly in return. Effie fancied she heard him choke with emotion again, but when she stood back she saw that he was dry-eyed and smiling.

'You know, for the first time in a long time I feel I have the strength to continue. I feel I have a future to look forward to. Thank you so much.'

Effie gave a little laugh. 'That's the spirit, I'm pleased to see it. But what I want to know is, when am I going to meet your James? Really meet him, I mean.'

For a moment Michael looked reticent, then he smiled. 'Well, I suppose there's no time like the present. Would you like to come around for dinner tomorrow night? We would be delighted to have you as our guest.'

Effie laughed happily and took his hand again. 'I'd love to come to dinner with you. But there is one condition I must insist on.'

'What's that?' he replied, looking quizzically at her.

'That I be allowed to bring a friend too.' And she smiled at him winningly. Michael hesitated, then a broad grin crossed his face as he understood her meaning.

'Of course,' he said happily. 'Permission granted.'

Effie and Harry caught the red cable tram from Lydia's for the short journey to Michael's place in Prahran. Like Effie, Harry liked to ride at the front of the dummy car, out in the open, come rain, hail or shine. Tonight they were both rugged up against the chill of the encroaching July evening. Effie felt cosy as she snuggled up against Harry and watched the road disappearing underneath them.

Harry too sat quietly, but as they rounded the bend from Toorak Road into Chapel Street he said casually: 'You know, a decision needs to be made about Alfie. What's going to become of him, I mean.'

It was an issue that had crossed Effie's mind on more than one occasion in recent days, but she had put serious thinking about it aside for later. Somehow, vaguely, she had assumed that Alfie's grandparents would want to take charge of him, even though the thought of that possibility distressed her.

She sighed, and put into words her concerns. 'I thought perhaps his grandparents might adopt him.'

'I'm afraid not,' Harry replied evenly. 'They're of the Anthony Hartford school of thought. Very religious and full of Christian charity, until the time comes to actually demonstrate some. Despite what they previously told Mary, they now want to have nothing to do with him. His grandfather is most adamant, and he rules the roost in that household.'

Effie stared at him. 'So what's his future?' she asked, though she knew the answer.

'It's the orphanage, I'm afraid,' Harry said sombrely. 'Unless, of course, we can find a home for him. You know, adoption. Got any ideas?' He raised an eyebrow in her direction, and the beginnings of his crooked grin appeared.

Effie immediately understood the gist of the idea he was planting. 'You mean me?' she said. 'I could adopt him?'

'I thought you might be interested. And I reckon I could make it happen. I can guarantee you'd get very good references.'

Effie looked at him incredulously. 'Harry,' she cried, 'you know I would like nothing better. But how could I adopt Alfie? I have a career to think of. I wouldn't have the time. Nor could I afford it.'

Harry nodded slowly, and continued. 'I see your point,' he agreed. 'It would be rather difficult. And I know your career is important to you. But I've been doing some thinking about the issue. I reckon a teacher and a policeman between them could just about afford to put on a nanny during school hours. And a policeman could call on his dear old mum to help out as well, even if his wife's folks lived up country, and weren't around to help. And you know, a policeman could even find time in the evenings to care for a baby himself while his wife prepared for school. Or marked the homework, or whatever it is that teachers do.'

Effie laid her head on his shoulder as a wonderful future opened up before her. 'Harry Holloway, are you saying what I think you're saying?'

'And after all, the Carlton Football Club does offer family membership, at a considerable discount.'

Effie pulled his face towards her and kissed him. Then she snuggled up against him again. 'The answer to your proposition is yes, by the way. Yes and yes.'

'Good,' Harry said matter-of-factly. 'That's settled then. I'll organise the paperwork. For Alfie and for us.'

And so they rode on in silence, Effie watching the road disappearing under their feet. She felt like they were floating over its surface, like swans gliding on a pond. It was a sensation that never failed to make her happy.

AUTHOR'S NOTE

Although this novel is peopled in part by historical figures, and deals with historically important issues, it is solely a work of fiction. The roles played by the historical characters in *Taken In* are entirely my creation, as are the descriptions of their personalities and characteristics.

I wish to acknowledge the assistance of Melbourne Girls' Grammar for information on the history of Merton Hall, and also the assistance of Janice Roberts for information on the history of the Victorian Infant Asylum at Berry Street.

In particular I would like to thank my editor, Irma Gold, for her brilliant and insightful assistance and advice. And many thanks, too, to Sandy Cull for her wonderful cover and book design.

www.ingramcontent.com/pod-product-compliance
Lightning Source LLC
Chambersburg PA
CBHW021410110726
47901CB00008B/2133